David A. Gemmell's first novel *Legend*, a powerful heroic fantasy, was first published in 1984. It is still in print twelve years on. Gemmell's bestsellers include the *Jerusalem Man*, *Wolf in Shadow*, *The Last Guardian* and *Bloodstone*, the continuing *Drenai* series, and the epic *Lion of Macedon*. His most recent bestseller, *The Legend of Deathwalker*, was published by Bantam Press.

A full-time novelist since 1986 he lives in East Sussex.

DAVID A. GEMMELL

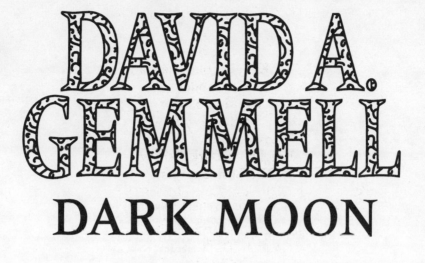

DARK MOON

BANTAM PRESS

LONDON · NEW YORK · TORONTO · SYDNEY · AUCKLAND

TRANSWORLD PUBLISHERS LTD
61–63 Uxbridge Road, London W5 5SA

TRANSWORLD PUBLISHERS (AUSTRALIA) PTY LTD
15–25 Helles Avenue, Moorebank, NSW 2170

TRANSWORLD PUBLISHERS (NZ) LTD
3 William Pickering Drive, Albany, Auckland

Published 1996 by Bantam Press
a division of Transworld Publishers Ltd
Copyright © by David Gemmell 1996

The right of David Gemmell to be identified
as the author of this work has been asserted in accordance
with sections 77 and 78 of the Copyright Designs and Patents
Act 1988.

A catalogue record for this book is available
from the British Library.

ISBN 0593 03709X (cased)
ISBN 0593 040651 (tpb)

Typeset in 11/13pt Sabon by
Hewer Text Composition Services, Edinburgh.
Printed in Great Britain by
Clays Ltd, Bungay, Suffolk.

Dark Moon is dedicated, with much love, to the memory of Olive 'Lady' Woodford, who taught me that style is everything. A former dancer, she lost her left leg to cancer. The day after the operation she ordered a bottle of champagne to 'toast the leg on its way' and six months later, with an over-size NHS artificial limb strapped to her knee, stepped out onto a dance floor to waltz.

My thanks as always to my editor Liza Reeves, copy editor Jean Maund, and test readers Val Gemmell and Stella Graham. Thanks also to Big Oz for the inspiration, and Mary Sanderson for the fingers of bone.

Special thanks to Alan Fisher for his many valuable insights into the mysteries of the craft.

CHAPTER ONE

TARANTIO WAS A WARRIOR. BEFORE THAT HE HAD BEEN A SAILOR, a miner, a breaker of horses, and an apprentice cleric to an elderly writer. Before that a child: quiet and solitary, living with a widowed father who drank in the mornings and wept in the afternoons.

His mother was an acrobat in a travelling group of gypsies, who entertained at banquets and public gatherings. It was from her he inherited his nimbleness of foot, his speed of hand and his dark, swarthy good looks. She had died of the plague when Tarantio was six years old. He could hardly remember her now, save for one memory of a laughing girl-woman who threw him high in the air. From his father he had – he believed – inherited nothing. Save, perhaps, for the demon within that was Dace.

Now Tarantio was a young man and had lived with Dace for most of his life.

A cold wind whispered into the cave. Tarantio's dark, curly hair had been shaved close to the scalp to prevent lice, and the draught chilled his neck. He lifted the collar of his heavy grey coat and, drawing one of his short swords, he laid it close to hand. Outside

9

the rain was heavy, and he could hear water cascading down the cliff walls. The pursuers would surely have taken shelter somewhere.

'*They may be just outside*,' whispered the voice of Dace in his mind. '*Creeping up on us. Ready to cut our throats*.'

'*You'd like that, Dace. More men to kill*.'

'*Each to his own*,' said Dace amiably. Tarantio was too tired to argue further, but Dace's intrusion made him sombre. Seven years ago war had descended upon the Duchies like a sentient hurricane, sucking men into his angry heart. And in the whirling maelstrom of his fury he fed them hatred and filled them with a love of destruction. The War Demon had many faces, none of them kind. Eyes of death, cloak of plague, mouth of famine and hands of dark despair.

War and Dace were made for each other. Within the beast's hungry heart Dace was in ecstasy. Men admired him for his lethal skills, for his deadly talents. They sought him out as if he were a talisman.

Dace was a killer of men. There was a time when Tarantio had known how many had died under his blades. Before that, there was a time when he had remembered every face. Now only two remained firmly in his mind: the first, his eyes bulging, his jaw hanging slack, blood seeping over the satin sheets. And the second, a slim bearded thief and killer whose swords Tarantio now wore.

Tarantio added two logs to the fire, watching the flame shadows dancing on the walls of the cave. His two companions were stretched out on the floor, one sleeping, the other dying. '*Why do you still think of the slaughter on the beach*?' asked Dace. Tarantio shivered as the memories flared again.

Seven years ago the old ship had been beached against a storm, the mast dismantled, the sail wrapped and laid against the cliff wall. The crew were sitting around fires talking and laughing, playing dice. Against all odds they had survived the storm. They were alive, and their relieved laughter echoed around the cliffs, the sound drifting into the shadow-haunted woods beyond.

The killers had attacked silently from those woods – appearing like demons, the firelight gleaming from raised swords and axes. The unarmed sailors had no chance and were hacked down without mercy, their blood staining the sand.

Tarantio, as always, had been sitting away from the others, lying on his back in the rocks, staring up at the distant stars. At the first screams he had rolled to his knees, and watched the slaughter in the moonlight. Unarmed and unskilled, the young sailor had been powerless to help his comrades. Crouching down he hid, trembling, on the cold stones, the incoming tide lapping at his legs. He could hear the thieves plundering the ship, tearing open the hatches and unloading the booty. Spices and liquor from the islands, silks from the southern continent, and a shipment of silver ingots bound for the mint at Loretheli.

Towards dawn one of the attackers had walked into the rocks to relieve himself. Terror filled Tarantio with panic and Dace rose within him, flaring like a light within the skull. Dace reared up before the astonished reaver, crashing a fist-sized rock against the man's head. The thief pitched forward without a sound. Dragging him out of sight of his comrades, Dace drew a knife from the man's belt and stabbed him to death.

The dead man wore two short swords, their black hilts tightly bound with leather. Dace had unbuckled the sword-belt and swung it around his own waist. Relieving the man of his bulging purse, Dace had stolen away through the rocks, leaving the scene of the massacre far behind.

Once clear, the panic gone, Tarantio dragged Dace back and resumed control. Dace had not objected; without the prospect of violence, and the need to kill, he was easily bored.

Alone and friendless, Tarantio had walked the thirty miles west to the Corsair city of Loretheli, looking for a berth on a new ship. Instead he had met Sigellus the Swordsman. Tarantio thought of him often, and of the perils they had faced together. But the thoughts were always tinged with sadness and the velvet claw of regret at his death. Sigellus had understood about Dace. During one of their training sessions Dace had broken loose, and had tried to kill Sigellus. The Swordsman had been too skilled for him then, but Dace managed to cut him before Sigellus blocked a thrust and hammered his iron fist into Dace's chin, spinning him from his feet.

'What the Hell is wrong with you, boy?' he had asked, when Tarantio regained consciousness. For the second time in his young life, he talked about Dace. Sigellus had listened, his grey eyes expressionless, blood dripping from a shallow cut to his right cheek just below the eye. When at last he had told it all, including the murders, Sigellus sat back and let out a deep sigh. 'All men

11

carry demons, Chio,' he said. 'At least you have made an effort to control yours. May I speak with Dace?'

'You don't think I am insane?'

'I do not know what you are, my boy. But let me speak with Dace.'

'He can hear you, sir,' said Tarantio. 'I do not wish to let him free.'

'Very well. Hear me, Dace, you fight with great passion, and you are uncannily fast. But it will take you time to learn to be half as good as I am. So understand this. If you try to kill me again, I will spear your belly and gut you like a fish.' He looked into Chio's dark blue eyes. 'Did he understand that?'

'Yes, sir. He understood.'

'That is good.' Sigellus had smiled then, and, with a silk handkerchief he had mopped the trickle of blood from his face. 'Now I think that is enough practice for today. I can hear a jug of wine calling my name.'

'*I hate him,*' said Dace. '*One day I will kill him.*'

'*That is a lie,*' Tarantio told him. '*You don't hate him at all.*'

For a time Dace was silent. When at last his voice whispered into Tarantio's mind it was softer than at any time before. '*He is the first person, apart from you, to ever speak to me. To speak to Dace.*'

In that instant Tarantio felt a surge of jealousy. '*He threatened to kill you,*' he pointed out.

'*He said I was good. Uncannily fast.*'

'*He is my friend.*'

'*You want me to kill him?*'

'*No!*'

'*Then you must let him be my friend too.*'

Tarantio shivered and pushed the painful memories from his mind.

The War of the Pearl had begun, and the Four Duchies were recruiting fighting men. Few had even seen the artefact they were willing to kill – or die – for. Fewer still understood the importance of the Pearl. Rumours were rife: it was a weapon of enormous power; it was a healing stone which could grant immortality; it was a prophetic jewel which could read the future. No-one really knew.

After his time with Sigellus, he and Dace had wandered through the warring Duchies, taking employment with various mercenary

12

units and twice holding commissions in regular forces, taking part in sieges, cavalry attacks, minor skirmishes and several pitched battles. Mostly they had the good fortune to be with the victorious side, but four times they had – as now – been among the refugees of a ruined army.

The camp-fire burned low in the shallow cave and Tarantio sat before it, the heat barely reaching his cold hands. By the far wall lay Kiriel, his life fading. Belly wounds were always the worst, and this one was particularly bad, having severed the intestines. The boy moaned and cried out. Tarantio moved to him, laying his fingers over the boy's mouth. 'Be strong, Kiriel. Be silent. The enemy are close.' Kiriel's fever-bright eyes opened. They were cornflower blue, the eyes of a child, frightened and longing for reassurance.

'I am hurting, Tarantio,' he whispered. 'Am I dying?'

'Dying? From a little scratch like that? You just rest. By dawn you'll feel like wrestling a bear.'

'Truly?'

'Truly,' lied Tarantio, knowing that by dawn the boy would be dead. Kiriel closed his eyes. Tarantio stroked his blond hair until he slept, then returned to the fire. A huge figure stirred by the far wall, then rose and sat opposite the warrior.

'To lie is a kindness sometimes,' said the big man softly, firelight reflecting in his twin-forked red beard, his green eyes shining like cold jewels. 'I think the thrust must have burst his spleen. The wound stinks.'

Tarantio nodded, then added the last of the fuel to the fire as the other man chuckled. 'Thought we were finished back there – until you attacked them. I have to be honest, Tarantio, I had heard of your skills but never believed the stories. Shem's tits, but I do now! Never seen the like. I'm just glad I was close enough to make the break with you. You think any of the others survived?'

Tarantio considered the question. 'Maybe one or two. Like us. But it is unlikely. That was a killing party; they weren't seeking prisoners.'

'You think they're still following us?'

Tarantio shrugged. 'They are or they aren't. We'll know tomorrow.'

'Which way should we head?'

13

'Any way you choose, Forin. But we'll not be travelling together. I'm heading over the mountains. Alone.'

'Something about my company you don't like?' asked the big man, anger flaring.

Tarantio looked up into the man's glittering eyes. Forin was a killer – a man on the edge. During the summer he had killed two mercenaries with his bare hands after a fight over an unpaid wager. To anger him would not be wise. Tarantio was seeking some conciliatory comment when he felt Dace flare up inside him. Normally he would have fought back, held the demon in check by force of will. But he was bone-weary, and Dace flashed through his defences. Dace grinned at Forin. 'What is there to like? You're a brute. You have no conscience. You'd cut your mother's throat for a silver penny.'

Forin tensed, his hand closing around his sword-hilt. Dace laughed at him. 'But bear in mind, you ugly son of a bitch, that I could cut you in half without breaking sweat. I could swallow you whole if someone buttered your head and pinned your ears back.'

For a heartbeat the giant sat stock-still, then his laughter boomed out. 'By Heaven, you think a lot of yourself, little man! I think I would prove a mouthful even for the legendary Tarantio. However, such talk is foolishness. We are being hunted and it makes no sense to fight amongst ourselves. Now tell me why we should not move on together.'

Within the halls of his own subconscious, Tarantio felt Dace's disappointment. In that moment Tarantio surged back into control; he blinked, and took a deep breath. 'They will have seen our tracks,' he told Forin, 'and know that one of us is wounded. They are unlikely therefore to follow us in strength. I would think eight to ten men may be on our trail. When we part company, and they find the tracks, they will be forced to either split their numbers or choose just one of us to follow. Either way the odds will be better for all of us.'

'All of us? The boy will be dead by morning.'

'I meant both you and I,' said Tarantio swiftly.

Forin nodded. 'Why did you not give that reason in the first place? Why the insults?'

Tarantio shrugged. 'Gypsy blood. Don't be too offended, Forin. I don't like anybody much.'

Forin relaxed. 'I'm not offended. There was a time when I would have paid considerably more than a silver penny for the privilege of cutting my mother's throat. I was a child then. All I knew was that she had broken my father's heart. And she'd abandoned me. So you were not too far wrong.' He gave an embarrassed grin, and idly tugged at the braids of his beard. 'He was a good man, my father. A great story-teller. All the village children would gather at our home to listen to him. He knew history too. All the stories of the ancient kingdoms, the Eldarin, the Daroth and the old Empire. He used to mix them with myth. Wonderful nights! We would sit with our eyes wide open in terror, our jaws hanging. He had a great voice, deep and sepulchral.'

'*I frightened him,*' said Dace. '*Now he wants to be our friend.*'

'*Perhaps,*' agreed Tarantio. '*But then you frighten everyone – including me.*'

'What happened to your father?' asked Tarantio aloud.

'He caught the lung sickness and faded away.' Forin lapsed into silence and began to brush the mud from his brown leather leggings. Tarantio saw that the big man was struggling with his emotions. Forin cleared his throat, then drew his hunting-knife. From a deep pocket he produced a whetstone and began to sharpen the blade with long, smooth strokes. At last satisfied with the edge, he took a small oval, silver-edged mirror from the same pocket and began to shave the stubble above the line of his red beard. When he had finished he sheathed the blade and returned the mirror to his pocket. He glanced at the silent Tarantio. 'My father was a good man. He deserved better. He weighed no more than a child when he died.'

'A bad way to go,' agreed Tarantio.

'No-one's yet told me of a good way,' Forin pointed out. 'You know, I saw an Eldarin once. He came to see my father. I was about seven years old then. Frightened the life out of me. But he sat quietly by the hearth and I peeked at him from behind my father's chair. It wasn't the fur on his face and arms that was so disturbing; it was the eyes. They were so large. But he spoke softly and my father insisted I step forward and shake hands. He was right. Once I was close, I lost my fear.'

Tarantio nodded. 'I was apprenticed to an old man who wrote histories. He described the Eldarin. Said they had faces that resembled wolves.'

'That's not exactly right,' said Forin. 'Wolves gives the wrong impression. It suggests savagery, and there was nothing savage about this one. But then I'm seeing him through the eyes of a trusting seven-year-old. He let me touch the white fur on his face and brow. It was soft, like rabbit pelt. I fell asleep by the fire as he and my father talked. In the morning he was gone.'

'What did they talk about?'

'I don't remember much of it. Poetry. Stories. The Daroth massacres fascinated my father, but the Eldarin would not speak of them.' Forin's green eyes caught Tarantio's steady gaze. 'If you don't like people, why did you carry the boy here? You hardly knew him. He only joined us a few days ago.'

'Who knows? Let's get some sleep.' Using his heavy woollen coat as a blanket, Tarantio lay down by the dying fire.

The dream was sharp and clear. Once again he and the other mercenaries were surrounded, the enemy rushing in out of the darkness with sharp swords in their hands. Caught in a trap, scores died within the opening moments of the charge. Tarantio had frozen momentarily, but Dace had not. Drawing both his swords, Dace scanned the advancing line, and then charged. He did not know that Forin and Kiriel had followed him. Nor did he care. His deadly swords slashing left and right, he cut a path through the attackers, then sprinted for the darkness of the trees. Forin and Kiriel got through, though the boy took a terrible stab to the stomach. There was little moonlight, but Dace's night vision was good and, eyes narrowed, he led them deep into the heart of the forest. Kiriel collapsed against a tree, blood soaking his shirt and leggings. Safe now, Tarantio resumed control of his body and had half-carried the boy on. Then, when Kiriel finally collapsed, Forin had lifted him into his arms and brought him to the cave.

In the dream Tarantio became the boy, fear of death filling him with terror. And the faces of the men Dace had killed to break free became old friends and comrades of past skirmishes.

An old man's face floated before him. 'The truth burns, Chio,' it said. 'The truth is a bright light, and it hurts so much.'

*

Tarantio awoke in the faint light of the pre-dawn. As always he came fully awake immediately, senses alert and mind sharp. It was the only period of the day when Dace was absent, and Tarantio felt at one with himself and the world. He took a slow deep breath, revelling in the emotional privacy.

The sound of cloth scraping on stone came from his left and Tarantio sat up. The huge form of the red-bearded warrior Forin was kneeling over the body of Kiriel, furtively searching through the dead boy's pockets.

'He has no coin,' said Tarantio softly.

Forin sat back. 'None of us have coin,' he grunted. 'Three months' back pay, and you think we'll get it now – even if we make it back to the border?'

Tarantio rolled to his feet and stepped outside the cave. The sun was clearing the eastern mountains, bathing the forest with golden light. The harsh cold stone of the cliff, corpse-grey in the twilight of the night before, now shone like coral. Tarantio emptied his bladder, then returned to the cave.

'It was that damned woman . . . Karis,' said Forin. 'I'll bet she's a witch.'

'She needs no sorcery,' said Tarantio, swinging his sword-belt around his waist.

'You know her?'

'Rode with her for two campaigns. Cold she is, and hard, and she can out-think and out-plan any general I ever served.'

'Why did you quit her service?' asked the giant.

'I didn't. I was with her when she fought for the Duke of Corduin. At the end of the season she resigned and joined the army of Romark. He was said to have offered her six thousand in gold. I don't doubt it is an exaggeration – but not by much, I'd wager.'

'Six thousand!' whispered Forin, awed by the sum.

Tarantio moved to Kiriel's body. The boy looked peaceful, his face relaxed. He could have been sleeping, save for the statue stillness of his features. 'He was a good lad,' said Tarantio, 'but too young and too slow.'

'It was his first campaign,' said Forin. 'He ran away from the farm to enlist. Thought it would be safer to be surrounded by soldiers.' The big man looked up at Tarantio. 'He was just a farm boy. Not a killer, like you – or me.'

'And now he's a dead farm boy,' said Tarantio. Forin nodded, then rose and faced the swordsman.

'What drives you, man?' he asked suddenly. 'Last night I

17

saw the light of madness in your eyes. You wanted to kill me. Why?'

'It is what we do,' whispered Tarantio. He walked to the mouth of the cave and scanned the tree-line. There was no sign of the pursuers. Swinging back, he met Forin's gaze. 'Good luck to you,' he said. Dipping into his pouch, he produced a small golden coin which he tossed to the surprised warrior.

'What is this for?' asked Forin.

'I was wrong about you, big man. You're a man to match the mountains.'

Forin looked embarrassed. 'How do you know?'

Tarantio smiled. 'Instinct. Try to stay alive.' With that he headed off towards the west.

If he could avoid his pursuers for another full day, they would give up and return to the main force. Two days was generally all that could be allowed for hunting down stragglers. The main purpose of such hunting-parties was not merely for the sport, but to prevent small groups of mercenaries re-forming behind the advancing line. Once the following group realized their quarry had separated, they would likely turn back, Tarantio reasoned.

As he walked on through stands of birch and alder and oak, Tarantio's mood lightened. He had always liked trees. They were restful on the eye, from the slender silver birch to the great oaks, gnarled giants impervious to the passing of man's years. As a child – in the days before Dace – he had often climbed high trees and sat, perched like an eagle, way above the ground. Tarantio shivered. It was growing cold here in the high country, and Fall flowers were in bloom upon the hillsides. It would be good to rest in Corduin. The war had not touched it yet, save for shortages of food and supplies. Tarantio had ventured some of his wages there with the merchant, Lunder. With luck his investments would pay for a winter of leisure.

The ground below his feet was muddy from recent heavy rain, and his left boot leaked badly, soaking through the thick woollen sock which squelched as he walked. For an hour he moved on, leaving a trail a blind man could follow, heading always west. Then, as he passed beneath a spreading oak he leapt up and drew himself into the branches. Traversing the tree, he jumped down on

18

to a wide rocky ledge. Mud from his boots stained the stone, and he wiped it clear with the hem of his heavy grey coat before moving on more carefully over firmer ground. Leaving no tracks, he headed north-west.

For another hour he travelled, moving with care, always keeping a wary eye on his back-trail, and rarely emerging on to open ground without first scanning the tree-line. Now, high above the point at which he had switched direction, he climbed into the branches of a tall beech and settled down to watch the trail. From a pouch on his sword-belt he drew the last of his dried meat, tore off a chunk and began to chew.

Before he had finished his meagre meal the pursuers came into sight. There were eight of them, armed with bows and spears. At this distance they looked insect-sized as they inched their way down the hillside, pausing below the oak. For a while they stood still, and Tarantio could imagine the argument among them. From the point where they now gathered, the distance to any one of four different towns or cities was around the same. To the west, beyond the mountains, was the lake city of Hlobane. North-east lay Morgallis, capital of the Duke of Romark. To the south was Loretheli, a neutral port, governed by the Corsairs. And to the north-west – Tarantio's destination – the oldest and finest city in the Duchies, Corduin.

For a little while the men searched the area for sign of Tarantio's trail. Finding nothing, they held a hurried meeting, then turned back the way they had come.

Tarantio leaned back against the bole of the beech and allowed himself to relax. He had left his helm back at the cave, along with the crimson sash that signalled his service with the new Duke of The Marches. Now there was nothing that linked him to any of the four combatants. Once again he was a free man, ready to offer Dace's services to the highest bidder. Dropping down from the tree, he continued on his way throughout the afternoon, crossing valleys and heading for a distant lake that sparkled in the afternoon sunshine. It was long and narrow, widening at the centre and flaring at the tip, like the tail of a great fish. There was a small island at the centre, on which a stand of pine reared against the backdrop of the mountains. The sun was warmer now and Tarantio shrugged off his heavy jacket, laying it on a flat rock.

19

'*When will we eat?*' asked Dace. Tarantio had been aware of his presence from the moment he sighted the pursuers.

'Perhaps you would like to catch the fish this time?' he said, aloud.

'*Too boring. And you do it so well!*'

Tarantio removed his shirt, leggings and boots and waded slowly out into the cold, clear waters of the lake. Here he stood, staring down at the gravel around his feet.

It was spawning time for the speckled trout and after a while he saw a female with red lateral spots upon her body. She swam in close to the motionless man and began to make sweeping motions with her tail against the loose gravel, scraping out a hole in which to lay her eggs. Several males were swimming close by, identified by the reddish bands upon their flanks. With his hands below the surface Tarantio waited patiently, trying to ignore the fish with his conscious mind. The cold water was seeping into his bones, and he felt a rise of irritation that the males kept circling away from him. Be calm, he told himself. The good hunter is never anxious or hasty.

A good-sized male, weighing around three pounds, swam by him, brushing his leg. Tarantio did not move. The fish glided over his hands. With an explosive surge Tarantio reared upright, his right hand catching the trout and flicking it out to the bank, where it flapped upon the soft earth. The other fish disappeared instantly. Tarantio waded from the lake, killed the fish, then gutted it expertly.

'*Neatly done,*' said Dace.

Preparing a small fire in the rocks Tarantio sat down, naked, and cooked his dinner. The flavour of the trout was bland; some would call it delicate. Tarantio wished he had kept just a pinch of his salt.

As the sun sank into the west, the temperature fell. Tarantio dressed and settled down by the fire.

He should have quit last season when Karis joined Romark. The Duke of The Marches was a poor general, and a miser to boot. With Karis leading the opposition cavalry, the prospects had been none too good for the mercenary units patrolling the border. He wondered about the 6,000 gold pieces. What would she do with such a sum? He grinned in the fading light. Karis was no farmer. Nor did she seem to enjoy what men termed the good life. Her clothes were always ill-fitting; only her armour showed the glint of great expense. Oh, and her horses, he remembered. Three geldings, each over sixteen hands. Fine animals, strong, proud and fearless in battle. Not one of them cost less than 600 silver pieces. But as for Karis herself, she wore no jewellery, sported no brooches or bracelets, nor did she yearn to own property. What will you do with all that gold, he wondered?

'*You just don't understand her,*' said Dace.

'*And you do?*'

'*Of course.*'

'*Then explain it to me.*'

'*She is driven by something in her past – that's what Gatien would have said. A traumatic event, or a tragedy. Because of this she is not comfortable being a woman, and seeks to hide her femininity in a man's armour.*'

'*I don't believe Gatien would have made it sound so simple.*'

'*Yes,*' agreed Dace, '*he was an old windbag.*'

'*And a fine foster-father. No one else offered to take us in.*'

'*He got a cleric he didn't have to pay for, and someone to listen to his interminable stories.*'

'*I don't know why you pretend you did not like him. He was good to us.*'

'*He was good to you. He would not acknowledge my existence, save as an imaginary playmate you had somehow conjured.*'

'*Maybe that is all you are, Dace. Have you ever thought of that?*'

'*You would be surprised by what I think of,*' Dace told him.

Adding fuel to the fire, Tarantio leaned back, using his coat for a pillow. The stars were out now, and he gazed at the constellation of the Fire Dancer twinkling high above the crescent moon.

'It is all mathematically perfect, Chio,' Gatien had told him. 'The stars move in their preordained paths, rising and falling to a cosmic heartbeat.' Tarantio had listened, awe-struck, to the wisdom of the white-bearded old man.

'My father told me they were the candles of the gods,' he said.

Gatien ruffled his hair. 'You still miss him, I expect.'

'No, he was weak and stupid,' said Tarantio. 'He hanged himself.'

' He was a good man, Chio. Life dealt with him unkindly.'

21

'He quit. Gave up!' stormed the boy. 'He did not love me at all. And we do not care that he is gone.'

'Yes, we do,' said Gatien, misunderstanding. 'But we will not argue about that. Life can be harsh, and many souls are ill-equipped to face it. Your father fell to three curses. Love, which can be the greatest gift the Heavens can offer, or worse than black poison. Drink, which, like a travelling apothecary, offers much and supplies nothing. And a little wealth, without which he would not have been able to afford the dubious delights of the bottle.' Gatien sighed. 'I liked him, Chio. He was a gentle man, with a love of poetry and a fine singing voice. However, that is enough maudlin talk. We have work to do.'

'Why do you write your books, Master Gatien? No one buys them.'

Gatien gave an eloquent shrug. 'They are my monument to the future. And they are dangerous, Chio, more powerful than spells. Do not tell people – any people – what you have read in my home.'

'What can be more dangerous than spells, Master Gatien?'

'The truth. Men will blind themselves with hot irons, rather than face it.'

Tarantio looked down into the flickering flames of the camp-fire now, and remembered the great, roaring blaze which had engulfed the house of Master Gatien. He saw again the soldiers of the Duke of The Marches, holding their torches high, and with immense sadness he recalled the old man running back into the burning building, desperate to save his life's work. His last sight of Master Gatien was of a screeching human torch, his beard and clothes aflame, staggering past the windows of the upper corridor.

Up until then Dace had merely been a disembodied voice in his mind. He had first heard him when he looked up at his father's body, hanging by the neck from the balcony rail, his features bloated and purple, his trews stained with urine.

'*We don't care,*' said the voice. '*He was weak, and he didn't love us.*'

But when Gatien burned, Dace found a pathway to the world of flesh. '*We will avenge him,*' he said.

'*We can't!*' objected Tarantio. '*He lives in a castle surrounded by guards. We ... I ... am only fifteen. I'm not a soldier, not a killer.*'

'*Then let me do it,*' said Dace. '*Or are you a coward?*'

Two nights later Dace had crept to the walls of the Duke's castle and scaled them, slipping past the sleeping sentries. Then he had made his way down the long circular stairwell to the main corridor of the castle keep. There were no guards. The Duke's bedroom was lit by a single lantern, the Duke himself asleep in his wide four-poster bed. Dace gently pulled back the satin sheet, exposing the Duke's fat chest. Without a moment of hesitation he rammed the small knife deep into the man's heart. The Duke surged upright, his mouth hanging open; then he sagged back.

'Gatien was our friend,' said Dace. 'Rot in hell, you miserable bastard!'

The old Duke had died without another sound, but his bowels had opened and the stench filled the room. Dace had sat quietly, staring down at the corpse. He had drawn Tarantio forward to share the scene. Tarantio remembered his father's face, bloated and swollen, his tongue protruding from his mouth, the rope tight around his neck. Death was always ugly, but this time it had a sweetness Tarantio could taste.

'Never again,' whispered Tarantio. 'I'll never kill again.'

'*You won't have to,*' Dace told him. '*I'll do it for you. I enjoyed it.*'

With a surge of willpower Tarantio dragged control from Dace. Then he fled the castle, confused and uncertain. He had been raised on stories of heroes, of knights and chivalry. No hero would have felt as he did now. The soaring, ecstatic burst of joy Dace had experienced filled the fifteen-year-old with disgust. And yet he had also tasted that joy.

Now by the lake, with such sombre thoughts in his mind, Tarantio found sleep difficult, and when at last he did succumb, he dreamt again of the old man. 'The truth burns, Chio,' he said. 'The truth is a bright light, and it hurts so much.'

*

It rained in the night, putting out his fire, and he awoke cold and shivering. Rolling to his knees he pushed himself upright, slipped, and fell face first into the mud. The sound of Dace's laughter drifted into his mind. '*Ah, life at one with nature,*' mocked Dace. Tarantio swore. '*Now, now,*' said Dace. '*Always try to keep a sense of humour.*'

23

'*You like humour?*' said Tarantio. '*Laugh at this, then*!' Closing his eyes, he opened the inner pathways and fell back into himself. Dace tried to stop him, but the move was so sudden and unexpected that before he could summon any defences Dace found himself hurtled forward into control of the wet shivering body.

'*You whoreson!*' spluttered Dace, water pouring down his face.

'*You try being at one with nature,*' said Tarantio happily, safe and warm within the borders of the mind. Dace tried the same manoeuvre, struggling to drag Tarantio from his sanctuary, but it did not work. Furious now, Dace looked around, then took shelter within the bole of a spreading oak. The huge tree had at one time been struck by lightning, splitting the trunk, but amazingly it had survived. Dace climbed inside. There was not much room for a full-grown man, but he removed his sword-belt and wedged his back against the dry bark and watched the downpour outside.

'*You've made your point, Chio,*' said Dace. '*Now let me back. I'm cold and I'm bored.*'

'*I like it here.*'

Out on the lake the rain sheeted down, and a distant rumble of thunder drummed out. Dace swore. If lightning were to strike the tree again, he would be fried alive.

He swore again. Then grinned. All life is chance, he decided. And at least, for the moment, he was out of the rain and wind.

'*All right, you can come back,*' said Tarantio, failing to keep the fear from showing.

'*No, no. I'm just getting used to it,*' responded Dace.

Lightning flashed nearby, illuminating the lake and the island at its centre. Dace bared his teeth in a wolf's-head grin. 'Come!' he yelled. 'Strike me if you dare!'

'*Do you want us to die?* asked Tarantio.

'*I don't much care,*' replied Dace. '*Perhaps that is what makes me the best.*'

The storm passed as suddenly as it had come, and the moon shone bright in a clear sky. '*Come then, brother,*' said Dace. '*Come out into the world of mud and mediocrity. I have had my fun.*'

Tarantio took control and eased himself from the tree, then turned back to gather dry bark and dead wood from the hole. With this he started a new fire.

'*We could have been in a palace,*' Dace reminded him. '*In that

24

large soft bed with satin sheets, within the room of silvered mirrors.'

'You would have killed her, Dace. Don't deny it. I could feel the desire in you.'

The Duke of Corduin had sent a famous courtesan to him: the Lady Miriac. Miriac of the golden hair. Her skills had been intoxicating. Even without the mirrors the night would have been the most memorable of his young life, but with them Tarantio had seen himself make love, and be made love to, from every angle, giving him memories he would carry for as long as the breath of life clung to him. He sighed.

But at the height of his passion he had felt Dace's anger and jealousy. The raw power of the emotions had frightened him.

And Tarantio had fled the arms of Miriac, and turned his back on the promise of riches.

'I would have been a great Champion,' said Dace. 'We could have been rich.'

'Why did you want to kill her?'

'She was bad for us. You were falling in love with her, and she with you. The courtesan could not resist the young virgin boy with the deadly sword. She stroked your face when you wept. How touching! How sickening! Is that why we are going to Corduin? To see the bitch?'

Tarantio sighed. 'You don't really exist, Dace. I am insane. One day someone will recognize it. Then I'll be locked away, or hanged.'

'I exist,' said Dace. 'I am here. I will always be here. Sigellus knew that. He spoke to me often. He liked me.'

*

With the dawn came fresh pangs of hunger. Tarantio spent an hour trying to catch another trout, but luck was not with him. He scooped a two-pound female, but she wriggled in his grasp, turned a graceful somersault in the air and returned to the depths. Drying himself, he dressed and strode off towards the higher country.

The air was thinner here, the wind cold against his face. Autumn was closing fast, and within a few short weeks the snow would come. Slowly and carefully Tarantio climbed a steep slope, moving warily among huge boulders which littered the mountainside. He wondered

25

idly how the boulders had come to be here, since they were not of the same stone as the surrounding cliffs. Many of them had deep grooves along the base, as if haphazardly chiselled by a stonemason.

'*Volcanic eruptions,*' said Dace, '*way back in the past. Gatien used to talk of them, but then you had little interest in geology.*'

'*I remember that you liked stories of earthquakes and volcanoes. Death and destruction have always fascinated you, Dace.*'

'*Death is the only absolute, the only certainty.*'

Finally, with the sun beginning its long, slow fall to the west, Tarantio reached level ground and stopped to rest. Several rabbits emerged from a grassy knoll and he killed one with a throwing knife. Finding a flat rock he skinned the beast, then removed the entrails, separating the heart and kidneys. There was a small stream nearby, and close to it he found a bed of nettles, and beyond it some chives. Further searching brought him the added treasure of wild onions. Returning to his camp-site, he prepared a fire. Once it had caught well, he drew his knife and cut two large square sections of bark from a silver birch. Using a forked stick he held one section of bark over the fire, warming it, making it easier to fold. Then he scored the bark and expertly folded it into a small bowl. Repeating the process with the second square, he grew impatient and the bark split. Tarantio swore at himself. Painstakingly he selected and cut another section.

Filling the first bowl with water from the stream, he returned to the fire, built a second blaze and fed it steadily with dry wood. When the coals were ready, he placed the bowl on the fire and added a handful of nettles, chopped chives and several onions. On the first fire he skewered and cooked the rabbit. The meat was greasy and tender, and he ate half of it immediately, tearing the remainder and adding it to his simmering bowl.

At this high altitude the water boiled away swiftly and three times Tarantio was forced to fetch more water from the stream to add to his stew. Bark bowls would not burn – unless the flames of the fire rose above the water line.

Back at the mercenaries' camp he had left several fine copper cooking pots and various utensils gathered over the years. But when Karis's lancers had struck there had been no time to think of possessions.

Tarantio lay back, staring up at the sky. It was difficult now to focus on a time when there had been no wars. Almost a third of his life had been spent marching from one battle site to another, while Dace and others fought to hold a town, or take it – charging an enemy line, or resisting a charge.

Up here in the mountains such petty squabbles seemed far away. But then so did the charms of beautiful women like the Lady Miriac. Dace was right. He had fallen in love with her and he thought of her often, remembering the satin softness of her skin and the sweetness of her breath. It mattered nothing that she was a courtesan, a whore for the nobility. He felt he had seen something beyond that, something deeper and more enduring.

'*Such a romantic, you are, brother. At the first glint of gold she would hurl herself on her back and open her legs. Your gold or someone else's. It would mean nothing to her.*'

'*You said she was falling in love with me,*' he reminded Dace.

'*In love with the virgin, I said. That's what touched her. After a while she would have tired of you.*'

'*We'll never know, will we?*'

At dusk Tarantio ate the stew. It was bitter and good, but the memory of his last meal with added salt back among the mercenaries eroded the pleasure. Dace had fallen silent, for which Tarantio was grateful. He could still sense his presence, but the lack of conversation was welcome.

The following morning he continued on his way, across narrow valleys full of alder and birch and pine. The weather had cleared and the sun shone now in a clear sky, the snow on the distant peaks glowing like white flame.

As he walked, his mind was far from battles and war, recalling gentle days with Gatien, researching ancient texts, trying to make sense of the tortured history of this fertile continent. If ever these wars end, I will become a scholar, Tarantio decided.

Even as the thought came to him he could hear Dace's mocking laughter.

CHAPTER TWO

THREE HUNDRED MILES TO THE NORTH-EAST, AT THE CENTRE OF a new desert of barren rocks, a slender, blond-haired man climbed to the top of what had once been Capritas Hill. His green cloak was torn and threadbare, the soles of his shoes worn thin as paper. Duvodas the Harp Carrier stood at the summit and fought to hold down a rising tide of desolation and despair. His gentle face and soft grey-green eyes reflected the sorrow he felt. There was no magic left in the land. Black and grey mountains bare of earth reared up from the plains like rotting teeth, and Duvodas felt as if he was sitting in the jaws of death. Where once had been sculpted beauty, amid forests and streams and verdant valleys, now nothing remained. The flesh of the land had been stripped to the bone, clawed away by a hand larger than eternity. The four cities of the Eldarin had vanished, and even the whispering wind flowing over the dry rocks could find no memory of their existence. Not a trace. Not a broken cup, not a tombstone, not a child's toy.

His grey-green eyes scanned the jagged peaks, pausing at the Twins, two pinnacles of rock that for centuries had been an elegant backdrop to the city of Eldarisa. Upon reaching the age of majority the children of the Eldarin would climb Bizha, the left-hand peak, then leap the eight feet to the rugged platform atop the neighbouring Puzhac. The pinnacles had graced the Enchanted Park, and many and glorious were the flowers that grew there. Now all was dead stone. Not a single blade of grass grew here now, and even his memories could not flower in this barren place. Duvodas rose and unwrapped his small harp.

It seemed almost blasphemous to consider music in such a cold and empty landscape, but music was all he had, and his slender fingers danced upon the strings, sending out a stream of melancholy notes to echo among the rocks. Closing his eyes he sang the Song of Elyda, and her love of the Forest King, his voice almost breaking as he reached the chorus of farewell, where Elyda stood by the dark river watching as her lover's body was borne away to eternity on the black barge of the night.

The music faded away and Duvodas covered the harp and swung it to his shoulders.

Leaving the hillside, he took what once had been the forest road and walked swiftly towards the distant plains. Eight years before he had travelled this way, striding under the overhanging branches, watching sunlight dapple the trail, listening to the ceaseless music of stream and river. Bird-song had filled the air then, sweet and piping, and the scent of the forest had intoxicated him. Now dry dust billowed around his feet, and not a sound disturbed the graveyard silence.

For most of the day he walked, angling his journey to the north-east. By dusk he could see the long black line of earth, like a ten-foot dike thrown up against a threatening sea. It stretched for miles across his path. He reached it as night was falling and scrambled up its loose banks, pausing at the crest. This was once the northernmost border of Eldarin land. Shrouded in mist, protected by magic, it was here that Duvodas had crossed during that long-ago autumn night. There were still oaks growing here, but it was no longer a wood. Many trees had died through lack of water.

He had expected to feel more comfortable with earth once more beneath his feet, but it was not so. The smell of grass, wet from the recent rain, made a bitter contrast to the desolation he had left behind.

29

Duvodas trudged on through the trees. Eight years ago he had come to a village, a thriving farm community on the banks of the River Cruin. Unlike the furry-skinned Eldarin who raised him, Duvodas, being human, could walk among the races of Man without fear. Even so, without coin he had not been welcomed, nor offered a place for the night. Not even a bowl of soup. The villagers had viewed him with suspicion, and when he offered to sing for his supper had told him they had no need of music.

Tired and hungry, Duvodas had moved on.

Now he stood at the edge of the village once more. The houses were deserted, the forty-foot-wide river bed dry and cracked.

Whatever dread force had ripped away the soil of the mountains had sucked the river dry. Without water the farmland had been robbed of its sustenance. In the moonlight Duvodas could see that the villagers had vainly tried to sink wells to feed their crops.

He sheltered for the night in a deserted barn, then moved on at first light to higher country, remembering the kindness of the hunter and his family whose long cabin had been built in a fold of land bordering the tree-line of the hills. Eight years ago he had arrived there wet and miserable, a victim of hunger and desperate weariness. When a huge dog had rushed at him, baring its teeth, Duvodas had no time to react. One moment he was on his feet, the next the dog had leapt, crashing into his chest and hurling him to the ground. All air was punched from his lungs and he lay gasping under the weight of the mastiff, listening to its low, rumbling growl. A man's voice had sounded. The dog reluctantly backed away.

'You must be a stranger to these parts, my friend,' said the voice. A powerful hand gripped his arm, hauling him upright. In the moonlight the hunter's hair seemed to glint with flecks of steel, and his pale grey eyes shone like silver.

'I am indeed,' Duvodas told him. 'I am a . . . minstrel. I would be pleased to sing you a song, or tell a story in return . . .'

'You don't need to sing,' said the man. 'Come, we have food and a warm cabin.'

The memory lifted his spirits and he walked on, coming to the cabin just after noon. It was as he remembered it, long and low beneath a roof of turf, though the second section built for the children had now weathered in, losing its newness and blending with the old. The door was open.

Duvodas strode through the vegetable patch and entered the cabin. It was dark inside, but he heard a groan and saw the hunter lying naked on the floor by the hearth. Moving to him, Duvodas knelt. The man's skin was hot and dry, and black plague boils had erupted on his neck, armpits and groin; one had split, and the skin was stained with pus and blood. Leaving him, Duvodas moved to the first of the back rooms. The hunter's wife was unconscious in the bed; her face was fleshless, and she too had the plague. Duvodas opened the door to the new section. When last he had been here the couple had only one child, a boy of nine. There were three youngsters in the room, two young girls and an infant boy all in one bed. The boy was dead, the two girls fading fast. Duvodas pulled back the blanket covering them.

Duvodas unwrapped his harp and returned to the main room. His mouth was dry, his heart beating fast. Pulling up a chair he sat in the centre of the room, closed his eyes, and sought the inner peace from which all magic flowed. His breathing deepened. He had learned much in his time among the Eldarin but, being human, healing magic had never come easily to him. The power was born of tranquillity and harmony, twin skills that Man could never master fully.

'Your veins are full of stimulants to violent activity,' Ranaloth had told him, as they sat beneath the shadow of the Great Library. 'Humans are essentially hunter-killers. They glory in physical strength and heroism. This is not in itself evil, you understand, but it prepares the soul for potential evil. The human is ejected from the mother, and its first instinct is to rage against the violation of its resting place in the womb.'

'We can learn, though, Master Ranaloth. I have learned.'

'You have learned,' agreed the old man. 'As an individual, and a fine one. I do not see great hope for your race, however.'

'The Eldarin were once hunter-killers,' argued Duvodas.

'That is not strictly true, Duvo. We had – and we retain – a capacity for violence in defence of our lives. But we have no lust for it. At the dawn of our time, so our scientists tell us, we hunted in packs. We killed our prey and ate it. At no time, however, did we take part in random slaughter as the humans do.'

'If you hold the humans in such low regard, sir, why is it that the Eldarin invest the rivers with magic, keeping the humans free of disease and plague?'

'We do it because we love life, Duvo.'

'And why not tell the humans about the enchantment in the water? Would they not then lose their hatred of you?'

'No, they would not. They would disbelieve us and hate us the more. Now, once more, try to reach the purity of Air Magic.'

Duvodas dragged his mind from the warmth of his memories now and gazed down at the hunter. Without the healing waters, plague and disease had ripped across the land. Lifting the harp, his fingers touched the strings, sending out a series of light, rippling notes. The scent of roses in bloom filled the cabin, rich and heady. Duvodas continued to play, the music swelling. A golden light radiated from his harp, bathing the walls, flowing through doorways, sending dancing shadows on the low ceiling. Dust motes gleamed in the air like tiny diamonds, and the atmosphere in the cabin – moments before pungent with the smell of disease – became fresh, clean and sharp as the breeze of spring.

There was a pitcher of curdled milk on the table beside him. Moment by moment it changed. First the fur of mildew on the pitcher rim receded, then the texture of the semi-liquid contents altered, re-emulsifying, the lumps fading, melting back into the creamy richness of fresh milk.

The music continued, the mood changing from lilting and light to the powerful rhythms and the rippling chords of the dance.

The hunter groaned softly. The black boils were receding now. Sweat bathed the face of the singer as he rose from his chair. Still playing his harp he opened his grey-green eyes and slowly made his way into the back bedroom. The music flowed over the dying woman, holding to her, soaking into her soul. Duvodas felt a terrible weariness weighing down on him like a boulder, but his fingers danced upon the strings, never faltering. Moving, on he came to the second bedroom. The golden light of his harp shone upon the bed and the faces of the two girls, the oldest of them not more than five.

Almost at the end of his strength, Duvodas changed the rhythm and style once more, the notes less complicated and complex, becoming a simple lullaby, soft and soothing. He played on for several more minutes, then his right hand cramped. The music died, the golden light fading.

Duvodas opened the window wide and took a deep breath. Then

moving to the bedside, he sat down. The two older children were sleeping peacefully. Laying his hand upon the head of the dead toddler, he brushed back a wisp of golden hair from the cold brow.

'I wish I had been here sooner, little one,' he said.

He found an old blanket and wrapped the body, tying it with two lengths of cord.

Carrying the corpse outside, he laid it gently on the ground beside two freshly-dug graves a little way from the cabin. There was a shovel leaning against a tree. Duvodas dug a shallow grave and placed the body inside.

As he was completing his work, he heard a movement behind him.

'How is it that we are alive?' asked the hunter.

'The fever must have passed, my friend,' Duvodas told him. 'I am sorry about your son. I should have dug deeper, but I did not have the strength.'

The man's strong face trembled, and tears flowed, but he blinked them back. 'The Eldarin did this to us,' he said, the words choking him. 'They sent the plague. May they all rot in Hell! I curse them all! I wish they had but one neck, and I would crush it in my hands.'

*

The fist struck the old man full in the face, sending him sprawling to the dirt. Bright lights shone before his eyes and, disoriented, Browyn tried to rise. Dizziness swamped him and he fell back to the soft earth. Through a great buzzing in his ears he heard the sound of smashing crockery coming from his cabin, and then an iron hand gripped his throat. 'You tell, you old bastard, or I swear I'll cut your eyes out!'

'Maybe it was all just lies,' said another voice. 'Maybe there never was any gold.'

'There was gold,' grunted the first man. 'I *know* it. He paid Simian with it. Small nuggets. Simian wouldn't lie to me. He knows better.'

Browyn was dragged to his knees. 'Can you hear me, old fool? Can you?'

The old man fought to focus on the flat, brutal face that was now inches from his own. In all his life he had enjoyed one great talent:

33

he could see the souls of men. In this moment of terror his gift was like a curse, for he looked into the face of his tormentor and saw only darkness and spite. The image of the man's soul was scaled and pitted, the eyes red as blood, the mouth thin, a pointed blue tongue licking at grey lips. Browyn knew in that moment that his life was over. Nothing would prevent this man from killing him. He could see the enjoyment of the torture in the blood-red eyes of the naked soul.

'I can hear you,' he said, tasting blood on his lips.

'So where is it?'

He had already told them about the single nugget he had found in the stream beyond the cabin. It was with this he had paid Simian for last winter's supplies. But he had never found more, despite long days of searching. The nugget must have been washed down from higher in the mountains, and wedged itself in the bend of the stream.

The third man emerged from the cabin. 'There's nothing there, Brys,' he said. 'He's almost out of food. Maybe he's telling the truth.'

'We'll find out,' said Brys, drawing a dagger and pricking it under the skin of Browyn's eye. The point was needle-sharp and the old man felt a trickle of blood on his cheek. 'Which eye would you like to lose first, scum-bucket?' he hissed.

'Brys!' the third man called out. 'There's someone coming!'

The mercenary let go of Browyn's throat and the old man fell gratefully from his grasp. Blinking, he strained to focus on the newcomer. He was a slim young man, with dark, close-cropped hair; over his shoulder he carried a heavy woollen coat of storm-cloud grey, and around his waist was a sword-belt from which hung two short swords. Browyn could also see the hilt of a throwing-knife in the man's knee-length boot. As the warrior came closer Browyn rubbed sweat from his eyes . . . the blows he had taken must have blurred his senses. The newcomer had not one soul – but two. The first was almost a mirror image of the man himself, darkly handsome, but golden light radiated from the face. But the second . . . Browyn's heart sank. The second had a face of corpse-grey, and a shock of white hair like a lion's mane. The eyes were yellow, and slitted like those of a hunting cat.

'Good morning,' said the newcomer, laying his coat over a tree-stump. Moving past the three mercenaries, he helped Browyn to

34

his feet. 'Is this your cabin, sir?' Browyn nodded dumbly. 'Would you object to me resting here for a while? It is a long walk from the lowlands, and I would be grateful for your hospitality.'

'Who do you think you are?' shouted Brys, storming forward. The newcomer leaned to the left, his right foot slamming into the mercenary's stomach, hurling him from his feet. Brys slumped to the ground, howling in pain. Dropping his dagger, he gasped for breath and continued to groan.

'You two will need to carry your friend back to his horse,' said the young man amiably.

'Kill him!' grunted Brys. 'Kill the bastard.' The other two men did not move or speak.

The newcomer knelt beside Brys. 'I think your friends are brighter than you,' he said, picking up the man's dagger and slipping it back into the mercenary's sheath. Rising, he turned back to the old man. 'Do you have any salt?' he asked.

Browyn nodded and the newcomer smiled. 'You have no idea what a relief that is.'

'What the hell's the matter with you two?' shouted Brys, struggling to his knees.

'He's Tarantio,' replied one of them. 'I saw him fight that duel in Corduin. I'm right, aren't I?' he said, looking at the newcomer.

'Indeed you are.'

'There's no gold here,' said the mercenary. 'We would have found it.'

Tarantio shrugged. 'Whatever you say.'

'Are you going to kill us?'

'No. I am not in a killing mood.'

'Well, I am, you scum-sucking bastard!' shouted Brys, drawing his sword.

'Brys! Don't!' shouted his comrades. But he ignored them.

'*You'd better let me take him*,' said Dace.

'No,' answered Tarantio. '*Sigellus trained us both, and I am not afraid.*'

'*Don't try to disarm him*,' warned Dace. '*Just kill the whoreson.*'

The mercenary attacked, his sword slashing towards Tarantio's head. The two short swords flashed up to block the stroke, but Brys was ready for the move and spun to his left, his elbow slamming against Tarantio's cheek. Tarantio staggered back, vision blurring. Brys aimed a wild cut at Tarantio's head. The blade slashed high, as Tarantio dropped to one knee and then surged upright, the left-hand blade snaking out. Brys made a desperate block, but the weapon pricked his shoulder, tearing the skin of his chest. Brys fell back. He grinned. 'You're good, Tarantio,' he said. 'But you are not that good. I am better.'

'*He is right, you know,*' said Dace. '*He'll wear you down and kill you. Let me have him.*'

Brys launched a sudden attack, sword raised high. As Tarantio made to block, the voice of Dace hissed at him: '*He's got a knife in his left hand!*' Tarantio leapt back – then launched himself forward. The move caught Brys by surprise and before he could react Tarantio's right-hand sword had slashed down on his hand. Three fingers were chopped away, the dagger falling clear.

'You bastard!' screamed Brys, charging forward. Terrible pain exploded in the mercenary's body . . . his sword fell from his hand and he stared down at the blade embedded in his belly. An agonized groan burst from his lips as acid fire filled him. His knees buckled, but the jutting sword held him upright, the blade driving deeper.

'*Let me feel the joy!*' shouted Dace.

'*There is no joy,*' said Tarantio, dragging the sword clear. Brys toppled to his right. 'Take the body with you,' ordered Tarantio, turning to the other mercenaries. 'And leave his horse behind.'

'We don't want to die,' said the first man.

'No-one wants to die,' Tarantio told him.

Together the man and his companion lifted the dead man, and heaved him over the saddle of a brown mare. Then they mounted.

As they rode away, Tarantio swung to the old man. 'How badly are you hurt?' he asked him.

'Not half as badly as I would have been. I am grateful to you. What they said is true. There is no gold.'

'No. But there is salt,' said Tarantio wearily.

'*You were lucky,*' whispered Dace. '*Where would you have been had I not seen the knife?*'

'*Dead,*' answered Tarantio, moving across the open ground to the dead man's horse. Just over sixteen hands tall, the gelding stood quietly as Tarantio ran his hand over the beast's flanks. The coat was flat with a healthy sheen, and the skin below was supple and strong. Its front conformation was good, the point of the shoulders in line with knee and hoof. At the rear it tended towards a slight cow-hocked stance, which in humans was called knock-kneed. This was probably why a mercenary could afford such a potentially expensive mount. Cow-hocked horses often strain ligaments on the inside of the limb. Speaking to it gently Tarantio moved around the horse, stroking its long nose and looking into its bright, brown eyes. Lastly he checked the legs. They were powerful, with no sign of heat or swelling, and the gelding had been recently re-shod. Moving to the rear of the horse, Tarantio watched the swelling of its rib-cage; its breathing was even and slow. 'Well, well,' said Tarantio softly, patting the gelding's flank, 'he may have been a vile man, but he certainly looked after you. I'll try to do the same.'

Browyn moved alongside him, checking the gelding's nose and mouth. 'I'd say around nine years old,' said the old man, 'with plenty of speed and strength.'

Tarantio stood back from the gelding, casting his eye along the line of its back, the length of the neck and the shape of the head. 'Without the cow-hocked stance, he would bring around four hundred in silver. As he is, he would fetch less than fifty.'

'There's no sense in it,' agreed Browyn. 'He is a fine animal.'

Browyn relaxed. In that moment a great weariness descended upon him. The aftershock of the attack caused him to tremble and Tarantio took his arm. 'You need to sit down,' said the warrior. 'Come, I'll help you inside.'

The cabin was a mess, papers strewn about the floor among shards of smashed pottery and two broken shelves. There was a beautifully carved bench seat by a large open hearth and Tarantio half carried the old man to it. Browyn sank down gratefully, and Tarantio fetched him a cup of water. Browyn began to shiver. The fire had died down, and Tarantio added logs from a stack in the hearth.

'Age makes fools of all of us,' said Browyn miserably. 'There was a time when I would have fancied my chances of taking all three.'

'Is that true?' Tarantio asked him.

'Of course it isn't true,' said Browyn, with a smile. 'But it is the sort of thing old people are expected to say. The real truth – if such a spectacular beast exists – is that I was a bridge-builder with no taste for violence whatever. And I have to admit that it is not a skill I ever wished to acquire.' His keen blue eyes stared hard at the younger man. 'I hope you don't consider that an offensive remark.'

'Why would I? I agree with the sentiments. You sit there for a while. I'll clear up the mess.'

Browyn eased his bruised frame back on to the bench seat and stared into the fire. Sleep came easily, and he dreamt of youth and the race he had run against the three great champions. Five long miles. He had finished ninth, but the memory of running alongside such athletes remained with him, like a warming fire in the room of memories.

When he awoke, the shutters of the small windows on either side of the main door were closed. His two lanterns, hanging in their iron brackets on the west wall, were lit, and the cabin was filled with the aroma of cooking meat and spicy herbs. Browyn stretched and sat up, but he groaned as the pain from his bruises flared.

'How are you feeling?' asked the young man. Browyn blinked and looked around. The cabin was now neat and tidy, only the broken shelves giving evidence of the day's savagery. Nervously he opened the path to his talent and sought out the image of the young man's soul. With relief he saw that there was only one. The beating he had taken at the hands of the raiders must have confused him, he thought. Tarantio's soul was bright, and as untainted by evil as any human spirit could be. Which, Browyn realized sadly, merely meant that the darkness was considerably smaller than the light.

'My name is Browyn. And I am feeling a little better. Welcome to my home, Tarantio.'

'It is good to be here,' the young man told him. 'I took the liberty of raiding your food store. I also found some onions growing nearby and I have made a thick soup.'

'Did you see to the horse?'

'I did,' said Tarantio. 'I fed him some oats, and he is tethered close by.'

They ate in silence, then Browyn slept again for an hour. He was embarrassed when he woke. 'Old men do this, you know,' he said. 'We cat-nap.'

'How old are you?'

'Eighty-two. Doesn't seem possible, does it? In a world gone mad, one bridge-builder can reach eighty-two, while young men in the fullness of their strength rush around with sharp swords and cut themselves to pieces. How old are you, Tarantio?'

'Twenty-one. But sometimes I feel eighty-two.'

'You are a strange young man – if you don't mind me pointing it out?' Tarantio smiled and shook his head. 'You killed that swine very expertly, which shows that you are a man accustomed to violence. And yet you have cleaned my cabin in a manner which would have brought words of praise from my dear wife – a rare thing, I can tell you. And you cook better than she did – which sadly is no rare thing. Those men were afraid of you. Are you famous?'

'They were the kind of men to be afraid,' Tarantio said softly, 'and reputations have a habit of growing on their own. The deed itself can be an acorn, but once men hear of it the tale soon becomes a mighty oak.'

'Even so, I would like to hear of the acorn.'

'I would like to hear about bridge-building. And since I am the guest, and you the host, my wishes should be paramount.'

'You have been well trained, boy,' said Browyn admiringly. 'I think I like you. And I do know something of the acorn. You were the student of Sigellus the Swordsman. I knew him, you know.'

'No-one knew him,' said Tarantio sadly.

The old man nodded. 'Yes, he was a very enigmatic man. You were friends?'

'I think that we were – for a while. You should rest now, Browyn. Give those bruises a chance to heal.'

'Will you be here when I wake?'

'I will.'

*

In the darkest hour of the night Tarantio sat on the floor by the fire, his back against the bench seat. It was wonderfully quiet, and so easy to believe that the world he knew, of war and death, was merely the memory of another age. He gazed around the room, lit now only by the flickering flames of the log fire. With Dace asleep there was nothing here that spoke of violence – save for his own swords lying on the carved pine table.

The old man had asked him about the acorn of his legend, but it was not a tale Tarantio relished telling. Nor, save for the first hours of pleasure with the Lady Miriac, did he like recalling the events of the last day.

'Never give in to hate,' Sigellus had told him. 'Hate blurs the mind. Stay cool in combat, no matter what your opponent does. Understand this, boy, if he seeks to make you angry he does not do it for your benefit. Are you listening, Dace?'

'He is listening,' Tarantio told him.

'That's good.'

Tarantio remembered the bright sunshine in the open courtyard, the light glinting from the steel practice blades. Pulling clear his face-mask, he asked Sigellus, 'Why is Dace so much stronger and faster than me? We use the same muscles.'

'I have given much thought to that, Chio. It is a complex matter. Years ago I studied to be a surgeon – before I realized my skills with the blade were better suited to the work I do now. Muscles are made up of thousands of bands of fibre. The energy they expend is used up in a heartbeat. Therefore they work economically – several hundred, perhaps, at a time.' Sigellus lifted his sword into the air. 'As I do this,' he said, 'the muscles are taking it in turn to expend energy. That is where the economy comes in. Now Dace, perhaps through a greater surge of adrenalin, can make his muscles work harder, more bands operating at a single command. That is why you always feel so weary after Dace fights. Put simply, he expends more energy than you.'

Tarantio smiled as he remembered the grey-garbed swordsman. As the fire slowly died, he recalled their first meeting. After the massacre of his shipmates, Tarantio had made his way along the coast to the Corsair city of Loretheli, hoping to find employment with a merchant ship. There were no berths, and he had worked for a month as a labourer on a farm just outside Loretheli, earning the few coins he now had in his purse. With the harvest over he was back at the docks moving from ship to ship, seeking a crewman's wage. But the war fleets of the Duchies were now at sea and the port of Loretheli was effectively sealed. No-one was hiring sailors. He was heading towards the last ship berthed at the dock when he saw Sigellus. The man was obviously drunk. He was swaying as if on a ship's deck, and he was using the sabre in his hand as a support, the point against the cobbled stones. Facing him were two corsairs, gaudily dressed in leggings and shirts of bright yellow silk. Both held curved cutlasses. Sigellus was a tall man and slender, clean-shaven and thin-faced. His head was shaved above both ears in sweeping crescents, yet worn long from the crown like the plume of an officer's helm. He was wearing a doublet of grey silk embroidered with silver thread, and leggings of a darker grey that matched his calf-length boots. Tarantio paused and watched the scene. The corsairs were about to attack, and surely the drunken man would be cut down. Yet there was something about the man that caught Tarantio's attention. The swaying stopped and he stood, statue-still.

'This is not wise,' he told the corsairs, his voice slurred.

The first of his attackers leapt forward, the cutlass slashing from right to left, aiming for the swordsman's neck. As Sigellus dropped to one knee, the corsair's blade sliced air above him and his own sabre licked out to nick the man's bicep. A flash of crimson bloomed on the yellow silk shirt. Off balance, the corsair stumbled and fell. Sigellus rose smoothly as the second man lunged. He parried the thrust, spun on his heel and hammered his elbow against the man's ear. The corsair tumbled to the cobbled stone.

Both men rose and advanced again. 'You have already shown a lack of wisdom, lads,' said Sigellus, his voice now cold and steady. 'There is no need for you to die.'

'We don't intend to die, you old whoreson,' said the first man, blood dripping from the wound in his upper arm.

As Tarantio watched he saw a movement behind the swordsman. Another corsair stepped silently from the shadows, a curved dagger in his hand.

'Behind you!' yelled Tarantio and Sigellus spun instantly, the sabre hissing out, the blade slicing through the corsair's throat, half decapitating him. Blood sprayed out as the man fell. The other two attackers rushed in. Tarantio watched them both die. The speed of the swordsman's movements was dazzling. Wiping his blade on the shirt of one of the corpses, Sigellus stepped across to where Tarantio stood open-mouthed.

'My thanks to you, friend,' he said, returning the sabre to its scabbard. 'Come, I will repay your kindness with a meal and a jug of wine. You look as if you could use one.'

A jug of wine was always close to Sigellus, recalled Tarantio with a touch of sadness. It was wine which killed him, for he had been the worse for drink when he had fought the Marches Champion, Carlyn.

41

He had been humilated, and cut several times, before the death stroke was administered. Dace had instantly challenged Carlyn, and they had fought in the High Hall of Corduin palace the following night. As Carlyn fell dead not one cheer was raised, for Dace had cruelly and mercilessly toyed with the swordsman, cutting off both his ears and slicing open his nose during the duel . . .

A log fell from the hearth and rolled on to the rug at his feet, jerking Tarantio from his memories. Using a set of iron tongs, he lifted it back to the fire and then stretched out on the floor. 'When you draw your sword, Chio,' Sigellus had warned him, 'always fight to kill. There is no other way. A wounded man can still deal a death stroke.'

'You didn't fight to kill against those corsairs. Not at first.'

'Ah, that's true. But then I'm special. I am – and I say this humbly, dear boy – the best there ever was. And, drunk or sober, the best there ever will be.'

He was wrong. For now there was Dace.

*

The dream was the same. A child was crying and Tarantio was trying to find him. Deep below the earth, down darkened tunnels of stone, Tarantio searched. He knew the tunnels well. He had worked them for four months as a miner in the mountains near Prentuis, digging out the coal, shovelling it to the low-backed wagons. But now the tunnels were empty, and a gaping fissure had opened in the face. Through this came the thin, piping cries of terror.

'The demons are coming! The demons are coming!' he heard the child cry.

'I am with you,' he answered. 'Stay where you are!'

Easing himself through the fissure, he moved on. It should have been pitch-dark in here, for there were no torches, and yet the walls themselves glowed with a pale green light strong enough to throw shadows. As always in his dream he emerged into a wide hall, the high ceiling supported by three rows of columns. Ragged men moved into sight, grey-skinned, opal-eyed. At first he thought they were blind, but they came towards him steadily. In their hands were the tools of mining - sharp pickaxes and heavy hammers.

'Where is the boy?' he demanded.

'Dead. As you are,' came a new voice in his mind. It was not

42

*Dace. In that moment Tarantio realized he was truly alone. Dace
had vanished.*

'I am not dead.'

*'You are dead, Tarantio,' argued the voice. 'Where is your passion?
Where is your lust for life? Where are your dreams? What is life
without these things? It is nothing.'*

'I have dreams!' shouted Tarantio.

'Name one!'

*His mouth opened, but he could think of nothing to say. 'Where
is the boy?' he screamed.*

'The boy weeps,' said the voice.

*

Tarantio awoke with a start, his heart beating fast. 'I do have
dreams,' he said, aloud.

'Indeed you do,' said Browyn, 'and that one must have been
powerful indeed. You were talking in your sleep.' The old man
was sitting at the table. Tarantio rose from the floor. The fire was
almost dead. Adding thin pieces of kindling he blew the flames to
life and Browyn hung a kettle over the blaze. 'You are very pale,'
he said, leaning forward and squinting into Tarantio's face. 'I think
it was more of a nightmare.'

'It was,' agreed Tarantio. 'I have it often.' Rubbing his eyes, he
moved to the window. The sun was high over the mountains. 'I do
not usually sleep this late. It must be the mountain air.'

'Aye,' said Browyn. 'Would you like some rose-hip tea? It is made
to my own recipe.'

'Thank you.'

'Why do you think this nightmare haunts you?'

Tarantio shrugged. 'I don't know. A long time ago I worked as
a miner. I hated it. They lowered us into the centre of the earth – or
so it seemed. The days were black with coal dust, and twice there
were roof falls that crushed men to pulp.'

'And you dream of digging coal?'

'No. But I am back in the mine. I can hear a child calling. He
needs help but I cannot find him.'

'It must mean something,' said Browyn, moving to the hearth.
Wrapping a cloth around his hand he lifted the kettle from its
bracket and returned to the table, filling two large cups with boiling

water. To each he added a small muslin bag. A sweet aroma filled the room. 'Dreams always have meaning,' continued the old man.

'I think it is telling me to avoid working in mines,' said Tarantio as, rising, he moved to the table. Browyn stirred the contents of the cups, then hooked out the bags. Tarantio tasted the brew. 'It is good,' he said. 'There is a hint of apple here.'

'How will the war end?' asked Browyn suddenly.

Tarantio shrugged. 'When men are tired of fighting.'

'You know why it began?' Browyn asked.

'Of course. The Eldarin were planning to enslave us all.'

Browyn laughed. 'Ah yes, the evil Eldarin. The Demon People. With their terrible magic and their arcane weapons. Bloody nonsense! Stop and think, Tarantio. The Eldarin were an ancient people. They had dwelt in these mountains for millennia. When had they ever caused a war? Look to history. They were a scholarly people who kept to themselves. Their crime was to appear rich. Greed, envy and fear began this war. It will take a hero to end it. Why are you a warrior, my boy? Why do you play their game?'

'What other games are there, Browyn? A man must eat.'

'And you can see no end to the madness?'

'I don't think about it. It is hard enough trying to stay alive.'

Browyn's face showed his disappointment. Refilling the cups and adding two more muslin bags, he remained silent for a while. 'I was there, you know, seven years ago when the Holy Army marched to the Eldarin borders. We had three sorcerers who claimed they knew a spell to breach the magical barrier. We were full of righteous anger against the Eldarin, and we believed all the lies about their preparations for war. We were also in a rage because of the village that had been massacred: women and children torn to pieces by Eldarin talons. Three years later I spoke to a scout who had been the first on the scene. He said there were no talon marks. The villagers had been killed by swords and arrows, and they had been robbed of all copper and silver coin. But we did not know that then. Our leaders fed us with stories of Eldarin brutality.

'However, I am losing the thread of the story . . . From where I stood on that day I could see, above the mist, the green mountains of Eldarin, the forests and the woods, the fields and the distant spires of a beautiful city. Then an old man came out of the mist and stood before our battle-lines. His back was bent, and the fur of his face was cloud-white. Like a ghostly wolf. "Why are you doing this?" he asked.

'No one answered him. A young man with a sling moved forward and let fly. The stone struck the old man high on the head, he staggered, then stepped back into the mist. Soldiers charged forward, but they struck the invisible wall that separated the mountains of the Eldarin from the valleys of men. The sorcerers stepped forward then, and began to chant. Behind them ten thousand soldiers waited. Suddenly there was a blinding flash of light, and the mist that shielded the barrier disappeared. It was an astonishing moment, Tarantio. The sun shone brightly upon a barren landscape. Grey rock as far as the eye could see. No grass, no forests and woods. No city. To our right there was a river that, moments before, had flowed down through the mists to water the valleys. Eighty feet wide, and very deep. Now there was no flowing water, and we watched the last of the moisture soaking into the clay at the river bed. The Eldarin had gone. In an instant. Gone! Ahead of us the earth was scored away, and we stood on the edge of an earth wall maybe ten feet high.

'We moved into the mountains, searching for them. There was nothing to find. Then a search party came back with the body of a single Eldarin. It was the old man. They had caught him hiding in a cave. He had with him the Pearl.' Browyn's eyes shone with the memory. 'It was so beautiful, the size of a man's fist, and swimming with colour – opal grey, dawn pink, holy white . . . You could sense its power. But I digress . . . The Demon War was over before it had begun, and our army of ten thousand had killed one old man. Within weeks the new war had begun, the War of the Pearl. How many thousands have died since that day? Plagues, starvation, drought and famine. And we are no closer to a conclusion. Does it not make you long to change the world?'

'I cannot change it,' said Tarantio.

They finished their drinks in silence, then Browyn led Tarantio out of the cabin and into the sunlight. 'There's something I'd like to show you,' said the old man. 'Follow me.' Together they walked up the hillside, along an old deer trail flanked by tall pines. At the top was a clearing, and at the centre, on a raised scaffold, stood a fishing boat, its sides sleek and beautifully crafted. There was a central cabin, and a tall mast from which hung no sail. The craft was fully forty feet long. Tarantio stood amazed for a moment, then he walked to where a ladder rested against the scaffold. Swiftly he climbed to the boat's deck, Browyn following. 'What do you think?' asked Browyn.

'She is beautiful,' said Tarantio. 'But we are a mile above the lake. How will you float her?'

'I don't intend to float her. I just wanted to build her.'

Tarantio laughed. 'I don't believe this,' he said. 'I am standing on a boat on a mountain. There is no sense in it.'

Browyn's smile faded. 'Sense? Why does it have to make sense? I always dreamed of building a boat. Now I have achieved it. Can you not understand that?'

'But a boat must have water,' argued Tarantio. 'Only then can it fulfil its purpose.'

Browyn shook his head angrily. 'First we speak of sense, now of purpose. You are a warrior, Tarantio. Where is the sense in war? What is the purpose of it? This boat is my dream. Mine. Therefore it is for me to say what purpose it serves.' Stepping forward, Browyn put his hands on the young man's shoulders. 'You know,' he said, sadly, 'you do not think like a young man. You are old before your time. A young man would understand my boat. Come, let us get back to the cabin. I have work to do. And you have a journey to make.'

CHAPTER THREE

Browyn gave Tarantio an old cooking pot, two plates and a cup cast from pewter, a worn-out rucksack and a leather-bound water canteen. Tarantio strapped his swords to his waist. 'I thank you,' he told the older man. Striding out from the cabin, he approached the bay gelding owned by the dead Brys.

Tarantio saddled him and hooked his rucksack over the pommel. 'I'll be on my way. But before I go, tell me why my reaction irritated you? What did you expect of me, Browyn?'

'You know what I like about the young?' countered the old man. 'Their passion for life, and their ability to see beyond the mundane. They don't look at the world and see what can't be done. They try to do it. Often they are arrogant, and their ideas fall from the sky like weary birds. But they try, Tarantio.'

'And you judge me unworthy because I fail to see the point to a ship on a mountain?'

'No, no, no! I do not judge you unworthy,' insisted Browyn. 'You are a good man, and you risked yourself to save me. And it is not your reaction to the boat that depresses me; it is your reaction to

47

life itself. God's teeth, man, if the young can't change the world, who can?'

Tarantio felt his anger rise as he looked into the man's earnest grey eyes. 'You have known me for a few hours, Browyn. You do not know me. You have no idea of who I am, and what I am capable of.'

In that moment Dace awoke and Browyn stepped back, the colour draining from his face. Tarantio's soul shimmered and changed, separating. To the left now was the face of corpse grey, with the shock of white spiky hair. Browyn looked into the yellow slitted eyes and blinked nervously.

'I do not want to die,' he heard himself say, fear making his voice tremble.

'What are you talking about? I wouldn't kill you.'

'*He sees me,*' said Dace. '*Is that not true, old man?*'

'I see you,' admitted Browyn.

Tarantio stood for a moment, stunned. 'You . . . can see Dace? Truly?'

'Yes. It is a talent I have, for seeing souls. It has helped me in my life . . . knowing who to trust. Don't kill me, Tarantio. I will tell no-one.'

'*What do I look like, old man? Am I handsome?*'

'Yes. Very handsome.'

'I can hardly believe it . . . he does exist then,' said Tarantio. 'I am not insane.' He walked to a carved bench of oak built around the bole of a beech tree and sat down. Browyn stood where he was. Tarantio beckoned him over. 'Have you ever seen a man with two souls before?' he asked.

'Once only. He was standing on a scaffold with a rope around his neck.'

'Do you have any idea how this happened to me . . . to us?'

'None. Will you spare me, Tarantio? I am near death anyway.'

'Sweet Heaven, Browyn! Will you stop this? I have no intention of harming you in any way. Why would I?'

'Not you . . . but him. Dace wants me dead. Ask him.'

'*He knows, Chio. He must die. I will make it quick and painless.*'

'No. *There is no need. No danger. And would you really know joy by killing a harmless old man?*'

'Yes.'

'Why?'

'He lied to me. Said I was handsome. I am ugly, Chio. I could see my reflection in his eyes.'

Tarantio felt Dace swelling inside his mind, trying to force a path to the world, but Tarantio fought back. '*Curse you!*' screamed Dace. '*Let me out!*'

'No,' said Tarantio, aloud.

'*One day, Chio. One day I will find a way to set myself free.*'

'*But not today, brother.*' He glanced at Browyn and gave a weary smile. 'You are safe, old man. However, I had best be on my way.'

'It is a shame the Eldarin are gone,' said Browyn, as Tarantio stepped into the saddle. 'I think their magic could have helped you both.'

'We need no help. We are – if not happy – then mostly content. Dace is not all bad, Browyn. I sense the good in him sometimes.'

Browyn said nothing. Nor did he wave as Tarantio heeled the gelding and rode from the clearing.

*

Tarantio rode down into the valley, and once on flat, open ground, gave the gelding his head. The horse thundered across the valley floor, and Tarantio felt the sheer joy in the animal as it sped across the grassland in a mile-eating gallop. After some minutes he allowed the horse to slow to a walk. Then he dismounted and examined the beast again. Satisfied, he stepped into the saddle and continued on his way.

'*I have the face of a demon,*' said Dace suddenly.

'*I cannot tell,*' put in Tarantio. '*I have never seen you.*'

'*I have white hair, and a grey face. My eyes are yellow, and slitted like a cat. Why should I look like this?*'

'*I do not know how souls are supposed to look.*'

'*Am I a demon, Chio? Are you a man possessed?*'

Tarantio thought about it for a while. '*I do not know what we are, brother. Perhaps it is I who possesses you.*'

'*Would you be happier if I were gone?*'

Tarantio laughed. '*Sometimes I think I would. But not often. We are brothers, Dace. It is just that we share the same form. And the*

49

*truth is, I am fond of you. And I meant what I said to the old man
. . . I do see good in you.'*

'*Pah! You see what you want to see. As for me, I wish I could
be rid of you.*'

Tarantio shook his head and smiled. Dace fell silent and Tarantio
rode on, passing the burned-out remains of two farming villages.
There were no corpses, but a hastily built cairn showed where the
bodies had been buried. The fields close by had not been harvested,
the corn rotting on the stalk.

On the far side of the meadow he saw some women moving
through the fields, carrying large wicker baskets. They stood
silently as he rode by. Further on he came to a wide military
road and passed a ruined postal station. Ten years ago, so he
had been informed, there was an efficient postal service that
connected all four Duchies. A letter written in Corduin, Gatien
had told him, could be carried the 300 miles south-west to
Hlobane in just four days. From Hlobane to the Duke of The
Marches' capital of Prentuis – 570 miles east over rough country
– in ten days.

No letters were carried now. In fact, any private citizen who
considered sending one to another Duchy would be arrested and
probably hanged. The Duchies were engaged in a terrible war,
composed of pitched battles, guerrilla raids, changing allegiances,
betrayal and confusion. Mercenaries plied their trade from the
southern sea at Loretheli to the northern mountains of Morgallis,
from Hlobane in the west to Prentuis in the east. Few common
warriors knew who was allied to whom. At the start of this summer
campaign the Duke of The Marches had been allied with Duke Sirano
of Romark against Belliese, the Corsair Duke, and Duke Albreck
of Corduin. Belliese had switched sides early in June, and then the
Duke of The Marches had quarrelled with Sirano and formed a new
alliance with Albreck.

Few could follow the twists and tantrums of the warring nobility.
Most soldiers did not try. Tarantio had been part of a mercenary
regiment holding a fort against the besieging troops of Romark and
The Marches. A herald brought news of his change of allegiance. It
was laughable. After three weeks of intense fighting the men within
the walls – some, like Tarantio, serving Belliese, others Corduin –
found themselves in the ludicrous situation of sharing the inner walls

with a new enemy, while men who had been trying to kill them for weeks were now friends who waited outside with their siege engines. The captains arranged a hasty council to debate the question of who was now attacking what. Some of the troops besieging the fort now wished to defend it, while one group of the defenders – who should now be attacking it – were already inside it. The council meeting went on for five days.

Since no agreement could be reached, the three captains came up with a new solution. All four groups of mercenaries set about undermining the walls of the fort, bringing the old stones crashing down. Hence there was no longer a fort to defend, and they could all march away with honour satisfied.

Three hundred and twenty-nine men had died during the siege. Their bodies were buried in a communal grave.

Two weeks later, Tarantio and a thousand men were back at the fort, rebuilding the walls.

The awesome follies of war, for which Tarantio received twenty silver pieces a month.

Four miles along the road, with dusk deepening, Tarantio saw the glimmer of a camp-fire in the trees to the west. Angling his horse, he rode towards the wood. '*Try to be careful*,' warned Dace. '*We don't have too many friends in this area.*'

'*Would you like to ride in?*'

'*Thank you, brother*,' said Dace. He drew in a deep breath, and felt the cool breeze upon his skin. The gelding became suddenly skittish, his ears flattening.

'*He senses you*,' said Tarantio. '*Best to soothe him, or he'll throw you.*' Dace stroked the gelding's long neck and, keeping his voice low and soothing, said, aloud, 'Throw me, you ugly son of a bitch, and I'll cut your eyes out.' Still nervous, the gelding moved forward as Dace touched his heels to the beast's flanks. Right hand raised, Dace rode slowly towards the wood. 'Hello the fire!' he called.

'Are you alone?' came a voice.

'Indeed I am friend. Do I smell beef cooking?'

'You have a good nose. Ride in.'

Warily Dace did so. As soon as he came close enough to recognize the men he grinned. '*Ride out! Now*!' urged Tarantio.

'*Before the fun has started, brother? Surely not.*' Before Tarantio could wrest back control, Dace leapt from the saddle and led his horse towards the fire.

There were three men seated around a fire-pit above which a leg of beef was being turned on a spit by a fourth – the red-bearded warrior Forin. Two of the others were the comrades of the dead mercenary Brys. Dace tethered his horse to a bush.

'There's too much for just the four of us,' said the first man, a tall and slender swordsman in forester's garb of fringed buckskin. He was thin-faced, with an easy smile not echoed in his close-set pale eyes.

'The bowman in the bushes is not eating?' asked Dace, stepping in close.

'You've a sharp eye as well as a sharp nose,' said the other, with a wide grin. Turning his head he called. 'Come in, Brune! There's no danger here. Now, Tarantio, let me introduce you to my Knights of the Cess Pit. The clumsy bowman is Brune. I told him to lie low, but he bobs like a rabbit.' A tall, gangly, sandy-haired young man stepped from the bushes and shifted uneasily from foot to foot. 'Useless, he is. I only keep him with me out of pity. The big man by the fire is a newcomer to our band. He calls himself Forin.'

Forin rose, the firelight glinting on his red-forked beard. 'Good to meet you,' he said, his face devoid of expression.

'And I am Latais,' said the leader. 'Welcome to my camp, Tarantio. You put the fear of Hell into my last two Knights. Step up, you dung beetles!' The two mercenaries rose and edged forward. 'These two, who understand when to put wisdom before valour, are Styart and Tobin. When the gods sketched out their personalities, they failed to place courage high on the list.'

'Perhaps wisdom is preferable,' said Dace.

'*It is a trap*,' said Tarantio.

'*Of course it is*,' agreed Dace. '*The question is, which side is Forin on? I should have killed him back at the cave. I wonder if he's still got our gold coin?*'

'Find yourself a place to sit,' said Latais amiably, 'and I'll bring you some food.'

Dace moved around the fire and sat on a tree-stump. Forin took up a wooden plate and cut himself some beef; then he sat away from the others. Latais brought Tarantio some meat and flat bread and the two men ate in silence. When he had finished, Dace cleaned the plate on the grass and returned it to the mercenary leader.

'So where are you heading?' asked Latais.

'Corduin. I think I'll winter there.'

'You have enough funds to sit out the cold season?'

'No, but I'll survive. What about you?'

Latais drew his dagger and picked a piece of beef from between his teeth. 'There's an army gathering near Hlobane, and Duke Albreck is offering thirty pieces of silver for veterans.'

'I'd hardly call your group veterans – save for the big man.'

'Yes, he has the look of eagles, as they say.' Styart and Tobin lifted the spit from the fire, while the bowman, Brune, added fuel to the fire pit, flames flaring up and illuminating the clearing. Dace's gaze did not flicker. He sat calmly watching Latais, aware that the man still held his dagger. 'You are younger than I expected,' said the leader. 'If all your exploits are to be believed you should have been at least fifty.'

'They should all be believed,' Dace told him.

'Does this mean you really are swifter than a lightning bolt?'

Dace said nothing for a moment. 'You know,' he said finally, 'the resemblance is clear.'

'Resemblance?'

'Was Brys not your brother?'

Latais smiled. The dagger flashed for Dace's chest.

His left hand shot out, his fingers closing around Latais' wrist. The blade stopped inches short. 'Faster than lightning,' said Dace, eyes glittering. Latais struggled to pull back from the iron grip. Dace's right hand came up, and firelight gleamed on the silver blade of his throwing-knife. 'And twice as deadly.'

His arm snapped forward, the knife slamming into the unprotected neck of the mercenary leader. Blood gouted from the severed jugular, drenching Dace's hand. Latais's struggles grew weaker, and he slumped against the tree. Bright images flashed across Dace's mind: his mother lying dead in her bed, the plague boils still weeping pus, the child crying for her and calling her name; his father hanging from the long branch, his face bloated and black, and old Gatien running through the burning house with his hair and beard ablaze. The sharpness of his sorrow faded away in the pulsing red light that flowed in his brain, eased by the warm red blood that bubbled over his knife hand.

Dace sighed and pulled clear the blade, letting the body of Latais fall. Wiping the knife, he returned it to his boot and rose to his feet drawing his swords. The flames were six feet high now, and Dace could not see who stood beyond the fire. But he guessed that Latais had ordered his men to be ready.

'Come on then, you gutter scum!' he yelled, leaping through the flames and across the fire-pit. As he landed, ready for battle, he saw the bowman, Brune, lying on the ground, Forin standing above him with a wooden club in his hand. 'Where are the other two?' demanded Dace.

'You've never seen men run so fast. Didn't even stop to saddle their horses. You want to kill this one?'

The answer was yes, but Dace felt his irritation rise. What right had this man to offer him a death? 'Why should I?' he heard himself say.

Forin shrugged. 'I thought you enjoyed killing.'

'What I enjoy is none of your damned business. Why did you help me?'

'A whim. They saw you coming. Latais thought Brune could bring you down as you entered the camp. But you put the horse between you as you dismounted. Smooth move, my friend. You're a canny man.'

Brune groaned and sat up. 'He hit me with a lump of wood,' he complained.

'You were about to shoot through the fire and kill me,' said Dace, wishing he had killed the man as he lay unconscious. There was still time.

'That's what I were told to do,' said Brune sullenly.

Dace looked into the man's face. 'Your leader is dead. You want to fight me?'

'I didn't want to kill you in the first place. He told me to.' Dace could feel the longing for blood growing in him, but he looked into the hulking young man's plain, open face and saw the absence of malice there. A farm boy lost in a world at war. Dace could see him lovingly working the fields, caring for stock, raising a family as dull and as solid as himself.

'Gather your gear and move out,' he said.

54

'Why do you want me to go? Aren't you the leader now?' Brune reached up and rubbed his sandy hair. His fingers came away bloody. 'Anyway, my head hurts.'

Forin chuckled. 'Tell me,' he said to the injured man, 'is there a lot of in-breeding in your village? You're not the sharpest arrow in the quiver, are you?'

'No, I'm not,' admitted Brune. 'That's why I do what I'm told.'

'*Come back to the world, brother,*' said Dace. '*This numbskull is too stupid to kill, and if I stay here any longer I'll rip his throat out.*'

Tarantio found it hard to keep the smile from his face as he resumed control. 'Let me see that head,' he told Brune. 'Move closer to the fire.' Brune obeyed and Tarantio's fingers probed the bowman's scalp. 'You've a lump the size of a goose egg, but it doesn't need stitching. Go and get some sleep.'

'You're not sending me away then?'

'No. Tell me, are you skilled with that bow?'

'Not really. But I'm worse with a sword.'

Forin's laughter boomed out. 'Is there anything you're good at?' asked the red-bearded warrior.

'I don't like you,' said Brune. 'And I am good at . . . things. I know livestock. Pigs and cattle.'

'A handy talent for a soldier,' said Forin. 'If we're ever attacked by a rampaging herd of wild pigs, you'll be the man to plan our strategy.'

'Go and rest,' Tarantio ordered the young man. Obediently Brune stood up, but he swayed and almost fell. Forin caught him and half carried him to where his blankets lay. The young man slumped down and was asleep within moments. Forin returned to the fire.

'You mind if I travel with you and your dog to Corduin?'

'Why would you want to?' countered Tarantio.

Forin chuckled. 'No one ever gave me a gold piece before. Is that good enough?'

*

Tarantio awoke at dawn. He yawned and stretched, enjoying the sense of emotional solitude that came when Dace slept. Forin lay wrapped in his blankets, snoring quietly, but of Brune there was no sign. And the body of Latais was gone. Tarantio rose and followed

55

Brune's tracks, finding him some fifty feet from the camp-site. The body of the dead leader was wrapped in its cloak, and Brune was humming a monotonous tune as he dug a shallow grave in the soft earth. Tarantio sat down on a fallen tree and watched in silence. With the grave some four feet deep Brune scrambled out, his face and upper body streaked with sweat and mud. Carefully, he pulled the body to the edge of the hole, climbed in himself, then lowered the dead man to his resting place. The act was tender and gentle, as if Brune feared bruising the corpse. Slowly, reverently, Brune scooped earth over the grave.

'You must have cared for him,' said Tarantio softly.

'He looked after me,' said Brune. 'And my dad always said dead men should go back to the earth. That's how plagues start, he said – when bodies are left to rot in the air.'

'I suppose there is some good in all men,' said Tarantio.

'He looked after me,' repeated Brune. 'I didn't have nowhere to go. He let me ride with him.' He continued to fill the grave, pressing the earth down with his hands. When he had finished he stood and slapped his hands together, trying to dislodge the mud clinging to his fingers.

'You should hate me then, for killing him,' suggested Tarantio.

'I don't hate nobody,' said Brune. 'Never have. Never will, I 'spect,' For a moment he stood staring down at the grave. 'When people in the village died, there was someone to speak for them. Lots of pretty things were said. I don't remember them. Does it matter, do you think?'

'To whom?' asked Tarantio, mystified. 'You think Latais will hear them?'

'I don't know,' admitted Brune. 'I just wish I knew some of the pretty words. Do you know any?'

'None that would suit *this* occasion. Why not just say what's in your heart?'

Brune nodded. Clasping his hands together, he closed his eyes. 'Thanks, Lat, for all you done for me,' he said. 'I'm sorry I couldn't do what you asked, but they hit me with a lump of wood.'

'*Touching and poetic,*' said Dace. '*It certainly brought a lump to my throat.*'

Despite the jeering tone, Tarantio sensed an undercurrent of emotion in Dace. He thought about it for a moment, but could find no reason. Then Dace spoke again. '*Are we taking the idiot with us?*' The question was asked too casually.

'*By Heaven, Dace. Have you found someone you like?*'

'*He amuses me. When he ceases to do so, I will kill him,*' said Dace. Tarantio heard the lie in his voice, but said nothing.

Suddenly all the birds in the trees took flight, the leaves thrashing under their beating wings. Tarantio felt a quivering sensation under his feet. Forin stumbled into the small clearing. 'I think we should saddle up and move out,' he said. 'I'm getting a bad feeling. Maybe there's a storm coming.'

The horses were skittish, and Tarantio needed Brune's help to saddle the gelding, who tried to buck each time the saddle was placed upon his back.

'What in Hell's name is happening?' asked Forin. 'Nothing feels right.'

The earthquake struck as Tarantio, Forin and Brune moved out onto the plain. The ground vibrating beneath them caused the horses to panic and rear. Brune, who was leading the three spare mounts, was unseated and fell heavily, his horse and the others bolting. A section of hillside close by sheared away and a huge crack, hundreds of paces long, opened up in the earth ahead of them, swallowing the fleeing animals. As suddenly as the crack had appeared, it closed, sending up a shower of dust and earth. Tarantio leapt from the saddle, holding firm to the bridle. 'Easy, boy! Easy!' he said soothingly, stroking the beast's flanks. Forin's horse fell as the ground heaved. The big man rolled clear, then scrambled up and caught hold of the reins.

The tremors continued for several minutes, then died away. Dust hung in the air in great clouds. Tarantio hobbled his mount and ran to the fallen Brune as the young man sat up, blinking rapidly. 'Are you hurt?' asked Tarantio.

'Hit my head again,' said Brune. 'Made it bleed.'

'Luckily your head is the thickest part of you,' observed Forin. 'You lost the horses, you dolt!'

'He could have done nothing to save them,' put in Tarantio. 'And if we had ridden a few yards further we would have all been sucked into the abyss.'

'Have you ever heard of such a thing in Corduin lands?' asked Forin. 'For I have not. Down by Loretheli the earth moves. But not up here.'

Tarantio stared down at his hands; they were trembling. 'I think we all need to rest for a while. The horses are too skittish to ride.' Unhobbling the gelding, he led him towards the ruined hill. Above and to the left of the sheared mound was a stand of trees. Tethering the two horses, Tarantio and Forin sat down while Brune wandered away to empty his bursting bladder.

'I think my heart is beginning to settle down,' said Forin. 'I haven't been that scared since my wife – may she rest in peace – caught me with her sister.'

'I have never been that scared,' admitted Tarantio. 'I thought the earth was shaking apart. What causes it?'

Forin shrugged. 'My father used to talk of the giant, Premithon. The gods chained him at the centre of the earth, and every once in a while he wakes and struggles to be free. Then the mountains tremble and the earth shakes.'

'That sounds altogether reasonable,' said Tarantio, forcing a smile.

Brune came running up the hill. 'Come see what I've found,' he shouted. 'Come see!' Turning round he ambled down the ruined hill. Tarantio and Forin followed him to where the hillside had been cut in half, exposing two marble pillars and a cracked lintel stone.

'It is an ancient tomb,' said Forin, scrambling up over the mud which half-covered the entrance. 'Maybe there's gold to be found.' Tarantio and Brune followed him, sliding over the mud and into the entrance. All three men halted before a huge statue, which stood guard over a broken stone doorway.

The sunlight shone down on the marble of the statue and Tarantio stood staring at the carving, trying to make sense of it. The statue stood almost seven feet high. On its left arm was a triangular shield, in its right hand a serrated sword. But Tarantio's attention was not taken by the armour but by the face, which was not human. The bony ridge of its curved nose extended up and over the bald cranium, curving down the thick neck to disappear beneath the sculpted armour. The creature's eyes were large, protruding, and slanted up towards the thick temples. The mouth was lipless and open, showing pointed teeth behind a ridge of sharp bone, like the beak of a hunting bird . . .

'It is a demon,' said Brune fearfully.

'No,' said Forin. 'It is a Daroth. My father described them

perfectly. Six-fingered hands, and eyes that can see in a two-hundred-degree semi-circle. The neck is heavily ridged with bone and sinew. It does not articulate like the human neck, therefore the Daroth needed better all-round vision.'

'You mentioned them back in the cave,' said Tarantio. 'I have heard of them. But they are just myths, surely?'

'No, not myths. They existed before man came to this land. They were great enemies of the Eldarin, who destroyed them utterly. They came from the Northern Desert. Have you ever travelled there?'

'No.'

'Barely an ounce of soil over twenty thousand square miles. According to the legend, the Eldarin used great magic to annihilate the seven cities of the Daroth. Fire from the sky, and all that. The same magic that later destroyed the Eldarin themselves, searing the earth away.'

'They look very fierce,' said Brune.

'They were all mighty warriors,' Forin continued. 'They had two hearts and two sets of lungs. The bones of their chest and backs were twice as thick as ours, and no sword, nor arrow, could pierce their vital organs. A heavy spear could injure them, but it would need a strong man to plunge it home.' He paused and looked up at the cruel, beaked face. 'Hell's teeth, would you want to fight anything that ugly?' he asked Tarantio.

'*I would*,' said Dace.

'I dread to think what the females looked like,' said Tarantio to Forin.

'From what my father said, this could be one of the females. There was little difference between them; they bred like insects and reptiles, laying eggs, or pods. There was no physical union between mating pairs – and little apparent physical difference between the sexes.'

'Why would anyone want a statue of a Daroth guarding their grave?' asked Tarantio.

Easing past the statue, they pushed their way into the main burial chamber. The sunlight was weaker here, but they could see a massive lidless coffin set by the far wall. The answer to Tarantio's question lay within. The coffin contained a massive skeleton, taller even than the statue guarding the tomb. Shocked, Tarantio gazed down on the colossal bones of the chest and back. The body had been laid on its side and the immense ridge of the spine could clearly be seen extending up the neck and over the cranium. Reaching inside, Tarantio lifted clear the immense skull. Dust and grit trickled from it. More than ever, the ridge of bone above the mouth looked like the beak of a hunting bird. 'Incredible,' whispered Tarantio. 'He must have been awesome in life.'

'He's pretty awesome dead,' muttered Forin, reaching out and taking the skull. 'And this is a rare find. The Daroth were virtually immortal, reborn through the eggs. At the time of rebirth the body of the dying adult would shrivel away, bones and all, then the same Daroth would emerge from the pod.'

'Well, this one didn't shrivel away,' said Tarantio.

'Indeed he didn't. I wonder why. Perhaps he chose not to mate, and there was no pod for him to return to.'

'*I can feel the evil here,*' said Dace. '*Like a cold flame waiting for life.*'

Symbols had been carved into the walls, but Tarantio could not decipher them. There were no paintings, no boxes, no possessions of any kind – with the exception of three bizarre pieces of furniture set against the wall. They resembled chairs, save that the seating area was in fact two curved, horsehair-padded slats set six inches apart and crafted at a rising angle from just above the floor. The back of the chair was low; this was also padded, but only along the top of the back-rest.

Brune tried to sit down on one and he looked ludicrous – too low to the ground, his legs splayed, his back bent. 'No, no,' said Forin. 'Let, me show you.' Striding to the chair, he pulled Brune upright and then knelt on the slats, leaning forward to rest his massive forearms on the top of the back-rest. 'The Daroth spine was not suited to conventional chairs.' Rising, he tucked the skull under his arm.

'In times of peace,' he said, his voice echoing eerily inside the enclosed chamber, 'the bones here would have been worth a sack of gold, and the statue outside would have fetched a fortune. Now we'll be lucky to get the price of a meal for the skull.'

'You keep it,' said Tarantio. 'I'm sure there will still be people interested in acquiring it.'

He swung on his heel and walked from the chamber, clambering up over the mud and out into the sunlight. Forin and Brune followed him. In the bright light of earthly reality the skull looked somehow even more eerie, out of place, out of time.

'The Eldarin must have possessed great magic indeed to wipe out a people so formidable,' said Tarantio.

Forin nodded. 'According to legend they annihilated them in the space of a single hour. Perhaps that is what the Eldarin were trying to do to our army, and their magic betrayed them.'

'Perhaps,' Tarantio agreed.

'I wonder what they ate,' said Brune.

Forin chuckled and lifted the skull. 'Beneath this beak there are sharp teeth, the front canines pointed like spikes. At the rear . . . here, look . . .' he said to Brune, beckoning the young man forward, ' are the molars . . . the grinding teeth. They were like us, meat and plant eaters.'

Once more the ground beneath their feet trembled. Forin swore, but the tremor died away swiftly. The three men stood nervously for a few seconds. Then a second quake hit, hurling them from their feet. The skull flew from Forin's hand and struck a boulder, shattering into a hundred pieces.

Tarantio lay hugging the earth, nausea swamping him. For several minutes the rumbling continued, then silence settled on the land and he rose shakily. Forin rolled to his knees and looked down at the shattered skull. 'Who'd have my luck?' he said, then pushed himself to his feet.

By mid-morning the following day they sighted the spires of Corduin. Tarantio found that he knew the guard on the main gate, and there was no problem entering the city. At the first cross-roads within, he bade farewell to Forin. They clasped hands. 'Good luck to you, big man.'

'I hope fortune favours you, Tarantio,' answered Forin with a wide smile. 'Look after the simpleton. If you cut him loose, he'll starve to death within a week.'

As he rode away Brune, who was holding onto Tarantio's stirrup, looked up and asked: 'Where are we going now?'

'To a merchant who will give us money.'

'Why would he do that?'

'It is my money,' said Tarantio.

'What will we do then?'

Tarantio sighed. 'I will teach you how to use a bow and

a sword. When I have done that, you will join a mercenary unit.'

Brune thought about this for a moment. 'I'm not a fast learner,' he said, with a wide grin.

'That isn't a surprise, Brune.'

CHAPTER FOUR

SIRANO, THE FIFTH DUKE OF ROMARK, WAS THE IMAGE OF THE man who had sired him – tall, athletic, handsome, his hair black and his eyes a deep ocean blue. It was for this reason that his father, a short, burly blond-haired man, hated him. The fourth Duke of Romark was a bitter man, who had married for love only to find that his feelings were one-sided. His wife betrayed him with the Captain of his Guards, and fell pregnant by him in the third year of their unhappy marriage.

The captain died in mysterious circumstances, stabbed to death in what appeared to be a drunken brawl. The wife was said to have fainted and drowned in her bath three days after giving birth to Sirano. Everyone agreed it was a tragedy, and there was great sympathy for the fourth Duke.

The child was raised by a series of nurses. Quick and alert, he was always desperate for his father's affection, which was never forthcoming. He never knew why. At school Sirano was the best in his year, and swiftly grew to understand the intricacies of language and the arts. By the age of twelve he could lead discussions on the merits of the great sculptors, debate the philosophical attitudes of the Three Teachers, and had written a thesis on the life and work of the soldier-king, Pardark.

Those who knew him as a young man claimed his father's coldness finally turned the boy's heart to ice on his fifteenth birthday. On the night of the celebrations he was heard to have a terrible row with the fourth Duke, who was heavily drunk.

It was after this that Sirano became fascinated by the wonders of sorcery. He studied day and night, forsaking the normal noble pursuits of hunting and whoring, and gathered to himself books and scrolls. His first spell, involving the sacrifice of a pet rabbit, went awry, the headless creature running down the long corridor of the east wing, spraying blood onto the hanging velvet drapes. His second spell was more successful and ultimately damning.

In a bid to discover why his father loathed him, the sixteen-year-old Sirano wrought the ancient spell of summoning, and called upon the spirit of his dead mother. He conducted this rite in the marble bathroom in which she had died. No spirit came, but what did occur changed the young man's life.

Somewhere during the spell he made a small mistake and instead of summoning a spirit, his spell became one of revelation. In an instant the room grew cold, and Sirano felt a curious sensation of dizziness and weightlessness. Bright colours shone in his eyes, and his body fell to the floor. His spirit, however, floated free and he found himself staring down at a beautiful woman taking her bath. Her eyes were sad, her cheeks tear-stained, and Sirano noted that her belly was still stretched and slack, evidence of a recent birth. The door opened and his father stepped inside. He was slimmer and younger, his hair thicker, and his face was white and angry.

'Did you think I would not find out?' he said.

'You have killed him,' she answered. 'What more can you do to me?'

'Much more!' he hissed. Without another word he punched her full in the face, then thrust her down below the water.

The spirit of Sirano recoiled from the sight. Her legs kicked out, thrashing water over the floor, but the fourth Duke maintained his grip until all struggles ceased.

The room spun and Sirano opened his eyes. He was lying on the floor of the empty bathroom, a small cut on his temple from where his head had struck the edge of a marble sink.

Slowly he rose.

For two years he continued to study, mastering all that he could of spell-making. On the night of his eighteenth birthday he lit the black candles in his room and, placing a grass snake in a round glass jar along with a lock of his father's hair, he painstakingly worked through the Five Levels of Aveas. There was no feeling in him, no anger, no sorrow. When at last he had completed the spell, he rose from his knees and, carrying the snake in the jar, walked slowly along the corridor to his father's apartment.

There were two young serving maids in his bed. Sirano whispered two Words of Power and touched each of them on the forehead. Both rose silently, eyes flickering, and deep in a trance returned to their own beds. Drawing up a chair, Sirano gestured towards the lanterns set in brackets on the walls. They flared into life, casting flickering light on the sleeping man. His face was fat now, bloated with rich living, and a vein throbbed at his temple.

'Wake up, Father,' commanded Sirano. The Duke jerked as if slapped.

'What in Hell's name?' He glanced to his left and right. 'Where are . . . ?'

'Gone. Tell me why you killed my mother.'

'Get out! Get out before I fetch my whip!'

'No more whips,' said Sirano softly. 'No more beatings or cold words. Just answer my question.'

'Are you mad?'

'As in insanity, you mean? I do believe that I am. It is not an unpleasant feeling. In fact there is some comfort in it. But let us get back to the question at hand. When you walked into that bathroom she said, "You have killed him. What more can you do to me?" You said, "Much more." Then you drowned her. Why?'

Colour drained from the Duke's face as his mouth opened, then closed. 'How . . . ?' he whispered at last.

'It doesn't matter, Father. Nothing matters except your answer. Speak.'

'I . . . she . . . I loved her,' he said. 'Truly. But . . . it wasn't enough for her. She took a man to her bed. One of my Guards. They were planning, I think, to have me killed. Yes, to kill me.

I found out.' Anguish twisted his face. 'Why do you want to hear this?'

'The man you killed. Was he tall and dark, with blue eyes?'

'Yes. Yes, he was.'

'I see,' said Sirano. 'I have often wondered why your mistresses never swell with child. Now I know. Your seed is not strong. And you are not my father.'

'No, I am not!' shouted the older man. 'But you will be the Duke when I am dead. I raised you as my own. You owe me for that!'

Sirano smiled. 'I think not. That was just ego on your part. You robbed me of the love of a mother and a father. You have made my life miserable. But I am eighteen now, and a man. I am ready for a man's duties. Goodbye, Father. May your soul burn!'

Rising, Sirano spoke a single word. The snake in the glass shimmered, then was gone. The old Duke made to speak, but something swelled in his windpipe. He scrabbled at his throat and his body writhed; his hand lashed out, striking the wall with a dull thump. His legs thrashed below the sheets, a low gurgling choke came from him. Sirano watched him die, then reached down and opened the old man's mouth.

The head of the snake was just visible. Wrenching open the Duke's jaws, Sirano pressed his fingers down into the throat, drawing out the serpent. It flapped and writhed around his wrist. Moving to the window, he flung the creature out into the garden.

After the official seven days of mourning, Sirano took the Blessing and donned the mantle of the Duke of Romark. The ceremony over, he took his advisors to the ramparts of the high west wall and pointed at the mountains of the Eldarin.

'There is great danger there, my friends,' he said. 'They are sorcerers and shape-shifters. What are they planning, do you think?'

*

Eight years later the twenty-six-year-old Sirano sat listening as his captains made their reports. The forces of the Duke of Corduin had been repulsed, with heavy losses on both sides, on the western border. The renegade corsair, Belliese, had savaged a Romarkian supply fleet in the southern seas, and captured two war galleons. Elsewhere there was only one victory that could be described as anything but pyrrhic.

Karis and her lancers had smashed a mercenary force heading to relieve a small fortress town eighty miles north of Loretheli. Two hundred and forty enemy soldiers were killed for the loss of fifteen dead and thirty-one wounded. The town had surrendered to Karis a day later, its treasury of 12,000 gold coins now swelling the Romark coffers. As the officers discussed tactics, Romark found his mind wandering, his gaze focusing on Karis. Tall and slim, her long dark hair held in place by a silver circlet, she radiated a martial beauty that Sirano found intoxicating. She was not classically beautiful, for her nose was long, and her face somewhat angular. Yet there was something about this warrior woman that stirred his blood as no other could.

Dismissing the captains, Sirano gestured for Karis to remain. Rising from the table, he moved to a beautifully crafted cabinet at the window wall of the large study, removing a cut-glass decanter. Half filling two crystal globe glasses he passed one to Karis.

'My congratulations, Karis. Your raid was an exemplary lesson in tactics.'

Karis gave a short bow, her large dark eyes holding to his own. 'This is what you wished to discuss?' she asked him.

'I have nothing to discuss,' he said, 'but I enjoy your company. Sit for a while.' Karis stretched out on a couch, leaving no room for the Duke to join her. But she lay back with one foot on the floor, the other leg straight, and Sirano did not try to stop his gaze from dwelling on her open legs and the cut of her blue silk leggings. Resisting the urge to run his hand along her thigh, he drew up a chair close to her and sat, sipping his brandy. Karis smiled at him, her expression cat-like.

'I hear you have a new mistress,' said Karis. 'Is she sweet?'

'Indeed she is,' he told her. 'She even tells me she loves me.'

'And does she?'

'Who can say? I am rich, and I am powerful. Many women would find that attractive in itself.'

'So modest, Saro,' she chided him. 'You are also handsome and witty. I don't doubt that you provide your partners with great physical joy.'

'How kind,' he said. 'Are you still cavorting with that mercenary lieutenant . . . Giriak?'

She nodded, then sat up and drained her brandy. 'He is young and strong.'

'And has he fallen in love with you?'

She shrugged. 'He uses the words wonderfully, with exquisite timing. I think that might be the same thing, don't you?'

'It certainly is for me,' he conceded. 'But then I am not entirely sure I know what love is. Neither do you, dear heart . . . unless of course we are talking of your first love, battle.'

Her eyes narrowed. 'You misread me, Sirano.'

He chuckled with genuine humour. 'I do not believe that I do. There are many in all the Duchies who wish for this war to be ended, but you are not among them. War is life to you. The day peace comes – and come it will one day when I win – you will know panic.'

'I think not. Panic is alien to me. However, this conversation is entirely hypothetical. The forces are too even for there to be a decisive end to the conflict. Added to which there are the mercenary armies; they follow only gold. When you Dukes seek to end the battles, what do you think will become of them? Will they lay down their arms and return to the land? No, Saro. You and your noble friends and enemies have loosed the wolves. You will not round them up easily.'

He shrugged. 'These are problems for another day.' His gaze returned to her silk-clad limbs. 'You really are very attractive,' he said. 'One day we should get to know one another a little better.'

'One day,' she agreed. For a moment neither of them spoke, then Karis rose and refilled her brandy glass. 'Have you unlocked the secrets of the Pearl?' she asked him.

'I think we are close,' he said. 'I believe it to be a power source of some kind.'

'You said the same thing two months ago,' she reminded him.

'Patience is one of my virtues,' he replied. 'So far we have tried probe spells of increasing power. Nothing pierces the Pearl. Yet even as we speak my sorcerers are preparing themselves for the ritual of Aveas. I think we will have answers today. It is one of the reasons I asked you to wait with me.'

Karis sipped her brandy, then returned to the couch. This time she did not stretch herself out, but sat on the edge of the seat. 'I am not a magicker, Saro, but do the spells of Aveas not require a death?'

'I am afraid that they do. But needs must when demons threaten, as they say.'

'And what will it achieve, this murder?' she asked him.

'That is hard to say. I tend to think that when wizards talk of human sacrifice they are at their wits' end. But I have studied enough to know that great magic can be conjured from terror. And there is nothing more terrifying than to be chained to an altar, with a knife raised above your heart.'

Before she could answer, there came a knock at the study door. 'Enter!' he called.

A tall, thin man wearing long robes of blue velvet entered and bowed. He was bald, the skin of his face stretched tight around a large skull. 'It would be good,' Sirano told him, 'if you have brought me welcome news.'

'Something of interest has occurred, lord,' answered the man, his voice low and deep. 'It is something I think you should witness for yourself.'

'We will join you presently,' said Sirano, waving his hand and dismissing the wizard. After he had left, Karis rose to leave. 'Wait!' Sirano ordered.

'I do not wish to see it,' she said. 'Human sacrifice does not interest me.'

'Nor me,' he agreed. 'Come with me anyway.'

'Do you order it, lord?' she asked him, her tone faintly mocking.

'Indeed I do, Captain,' he said, moving alongside her and laying his hand on her shoulder. Leaning towards her he tenderly kissed her cheek. 'I adore the perfume of your hair,' he whispered.

Together they walked the long corridor, descending the circular stairs to the lower levels. Torches shone on the bare stone walls and a sleek, fat rat ran across their path as they moved towards two double doors. Sirano paused. 'That rat was altogether too well-fed for my liking,' he said. 'Remind me to send for the quartermaster when we are finished here.'

'Perhaps the rat is a pet,' she said, with a grin.

'Perhaps. More likely the vermin have found a way into the grain store, which I ordered sealed tight.'

Sirano pushed open the double doors and they entered a large circular room, ablaze with the light of twenty lanterns. Three sorcerers in robes of velvet stood around a flat table to which a naked young girl was strapped by her arms and legs. Just beyond the altar, set on an upturned eagle's claw of bronze, rested the Eldarin Pearl. Karis had never seen the jewel, and was stunned by its beauty. It seemed to pulse with living colour, and she could feel warmth emanating from it.

'Oh, please, my lord, save me!' wailed the girl tied to the altar table. Karis swung to look at her. She was no more than fourteen.

'Be silent, child,' ordered Sirano. Swinging to the tall bald sorcerer, he asked, 'Why has the ritual not yet been completed?'

'It has, my lord. That is, what is of interest.'

'Spare me the riddles, Calizar.'

'Observe, lord.' The tall man raised his left hand and began to chant. Red smoke flowed from his fingers, oozing out towards the milky beauty of the Pearl. As it came closer the smoke shifted, forming what appeared to Karis to be a large four-taloned claw which descended towards the Pearl. Just as the red smoke was about to touch the globe, a jagged spark of lightning lanced up. Blue fire exploded within the smoke, flaring in an intricate web of light. The red claw disappeared.

As the smoke faded, the sorcerer raised his right hand. The curved dagger he held flashed down, plunging into the young girl's heart. Her slender body arched up, and a strangled cry was torn from her lips. Calizar dragged the knife clear. A white cloud billowed from the Pearl and swept out over the murdered girl, masking her completely. The huge room filled with the scent of roses. Sirano watched with interest. Karis stood by, her distaste for the attempted sacrifice washed away by a sudden feeling of prescience as she stared intently at the child on the altar.

After several seconds, the white cloud rose from the girl and flowed back into the Pearl.

'No more, please!' wailed the child. Sirano stepped in close, his hand pressing down on the white flesh of her small breasts. There was not a mark, nor a speck of blood to show where the knife tore into her heart.

'How many times has this happened?' asked Sirano.

'This was the fourth, my lord. The Pearl will not, it seems, allow a human sacrifice.'

'Fascinating! What do you make of it, Calizar?'

'It is quite beyond me, Lord Sirano.'

'Give me the dagger and cast the talon-smoke.' Calizar handed him the blade, then began to chant. The girl on the altar started to cry. Sirano smiled at her, and stroked her hair.

'Don't hurt me!' she begged him.

He did not reply. The red smoke closed around the Pearl, lightning and blue sparks came out once more in response.

'Now!' whispered Calizar.

Sirano turned . . . and slammed the dagger into the wizard's chest, driving in the blade up to the hilt. Calizar staggered back and then fell to his knees, his long upper body slumping forward until his brow thudded against the cold stone of the floor.

The white cloud issued from the Pearl, sweeping over the wizard. But as it touched him it recoiled and returned instantly to the globe, seeping through the multicoloured outer layer.

Sirano knelt by the corpse and pushed it to its back. 'I have no time', he said, 'for wizards who find new magic beyond them.' Rising, he turned to the other two sorcerers. 'Do you find this utterly beyond you?'

'Not at all, my lord. But it will require a great deal of study,' replied the first. His colleague nodded agreement.

'Good,' said Sirano. 'So what have we learned today?'

'The Pearl is sentient,' said the first sorcerer, a small man with close-set eyes and a long pointed beard.

'What else?'

'That we can establish some kind of control over it. We made it heal the child. But if you will forgive me for saying so, lord, I do not – yet,' he added swiftly, 'understand why it brought the girl back to life and not my brother Calizar.'

'Ah, but I do,' said Sirano. 'Continue your work.'

'What about the girl, lord?'

'No more sacrifices for the moment. Give her ten gold crowns and send her home.'

Swinging away from them he led Karis back to the upper study.

'Well?' she asked him. 'Are you going to tell me why it saved the girl.'

'She was innocent,' he said.

'How does that help you unlock the Pearl's secrets?'

'It made a choice, my beauty. Don't you see? It is sentient. So we will offer it more choices. And very soon I will have more power than any man who ever walked this land.'

*

For six days Karis saw no sign of Sirano. At midnight on the seventh day a tremor ran through the castle. Karis, who was lying in bed nursing a goblet of wine in her hands, leapt to her feet and ran to the balcony. Bright lights were blazing from the highest rooms of the keep, and lightning forked up from the top turret. Blocks of stone cascaded down to the courtyard below, some smashing through the stable roof.

The naked man who moments before had been lying alongside Karis moved out onto the balcony. 'His magic will kill us all,' he said, gripping the bronze balcony rail. Darkly handsome, his strong face now showed signs of fear. It was not an attractive sight, thought Karis.

'He says he is close to the secrets of the Pearl,' Karis told him.

Giriak swore. 'You told me that a week ago. Yesterday a section of the main wall came crashing down – killed three of my men. He'll wreck the entire city if this goes on much longer. Have you seen the columns of refugees? They're leaving the city in droves.'

Karis shrugged. 'What do you care?' she asked him. 'He gives you gold.'

'I'd like to live to spend it.'

Another tremor struck, and a small crack appeared on the facing wall of the balcony. 'Son of a whore!' hissed Giriak, leaping back into the main room. Karis grinned as she turned to face him. Holding out her arms, she gestured to him.

'Come!' she called. 'Make love to me on the balcony, before it falls.'

'Don't be foolish,' he urged her. Karis let fall the green robe she wore, her naked body glistening in the moonlight. Another tremor struck and the crack in the stone opened wider, tracing a thick black line all the way to the wall. 'Come in!' yelled Giriak.

'Come out,' she taunted. 'Show me you are a man.'

'You are mad, woman! Do you want to die?'

'Collect your clothes and get out,' she said, contemptuously turning from him and climbing to the bronze rail. Balanced delicately, she walked along it, feeling the cold, smooth metal beneath her feet. One more tremor and she would fall. She knew it, and a delicious sense of excitement swept through

72

her. This was life! For some moments she stood there with arms raised.

Lightning swept up from the turret, followed by a clap of thunder that shook the foundations of the building. Karis lost her balance, then spun and launched herself back into the bedchamber, landing on her shoulder and rolling to her feet. Behind her the balcony sheared away and crashed to the courtyard below.

Karis shivered, then glanced around the room. Giriak had gone.

Gathering the wine jug and a goblet, she sat down on the round embroidered rug at the centre of the room. Giriak was a disappointment. Like all the men she had known. Is it a fault in men themselves, she wondered, or merely a flaw in the kind of men I find exciting? Indeed, is the flaw in me?

Her father had maintained that it was. He claimed she was devil-possessed, and tried for years to thrash the devil from her. He would drag her from the cabin and tie her to a post in the barn. The words that followed were always the same. 'Recant! Open your heart to the Source. Beg for forgiveness.' Karis had tried all that, but it made no difference. If she proclaimed her innocence, he would beat her. If she admitted guilt and called upon the Source to forgive her, her father's rage would grow incandescent. 'You lie and mock me!' he would shout. Then he would beat her legs and buttocks with the birch until she bled. So she learned to stay silent through it all, head twisted, her deep brown eyes holding to his insane gaze.

There was no knight at hand to rescue the child, no hero to stride through the forest and pluck her away. Just her and her world-weary mother, a woman old before her time, beaten down by the years and the cold fists of her husband.

'One day I will go back and kill him,' she thought, swilling down the last of the wine. Lying on her back, she stared up at the ornate, painted ceiling. Cracks were showing here too. Giriak was right, Sirano was destroying his own city. 'It is nothing to me,' she said.

Does anything matter to you, she asked herself? Or does life have nothing more to offer than a stunning victory in battle or a sweaty rut with a powerful man?

'Both are one and the same thing,' she said aloud. The ceiling shifted and swam. At first she thought it was another tremor, but then, as her stomach lurched, she realized it was the effect of the wine. Rolling to her knees, she forced herself upright. Taking a deep

73

drink from a pitcher of water, she moved to the bed and sat down. As always her powerful constitution began to override the alcohol in her system.

Weariness flowed over her, and she wished now that she had not sent Giriak away. It would have been pleasant to lie close, feeling the warmth of his body as she drifted into sleep.

The bedroom door opened and she felt the touch of a cool breeze. Opening her eyes, she sat up. But it was not Giriak who entered.

Sirano stood in the doorway, and Karis was surprised by the change in the man. His handsome face was thin and drawn, his cheeks covered by black stubble, his eyes dark-rimmed and weary. His clothes, so beautifully fashioned from black silk, were sweat-stained and creased, and his black hair was lank and dark with sweat. Moving to the bedside, he gave a tired smile.

'You are beautiful naked, Karis,' he said. The words were forced, no more than echoes of what would only a few days before have been genuine emotion.

'You look dreadful,' she told him. 'How long since you slept?'

'Days. I swear I am close though. The Pearl's defences are thin. If I had the energy, I would have stayed for the breakthrough tonight. The Spell of Seven almost made it. It could not save all the victims. That's when I knew.'

'How many did you kill, Saro?'

'Kill? Oh, the girls . . . two. Five survived. But I am almost there, Karis.'

'You will ruin your city and destroy yourself in the process. Do you know the quakes are spreading further? A rider came in today. He said Corduin was struck three times in the last month. Is this your doing?'

He nodded. 'Do not concern yourself. With the power of the Pearl, I can rebuild and Morgallis will be a hundred times more beautiful than before. And we will have eternity to make it even better. Immortality lies within that sphere.'

'We?' she countered.

'Why not, Karis? You and I. Young for ever.'

'Perhaps I do not want to be young for ever,' she told him.

'You say that only because you have not yet felt the winter fingers of the grave upon your skin.' His eyes were bright and feverish. Karis rose from the bed and filled a goblet with water, which she offered to him. 'Wine,' he said. 'Give me wine.'

Hurling the water to the floor, she poured the last of the wine into the goblet. He took it from her with a trembling hand and drank deeply. 'I am so tired.'

'Then go to your room and sleep.'

For a moment he was silent, his expression thoughtful. 'I am not a vain man,' he said at last. 'I know that you find me attractive. And I truly believe you are the most divine of women. Why then do we never sleep together?'

'This is not the time to talk of it, Saro,' she told him.

He smiled. 'I know the answer – but I wanted to hear you say it. You are a mercenary. When your contract is finished, you move to the highest bidder. It would complicate matters if you were emotionally involved with one of the four Dukes. Not so?'

'Exactly so,' she agreed. 'Knowing this, why do you persist?'

'I yearn for the unattainable,' he said. His expression softened. 'Do you trust my word, Karis?'

'I have no reason to doubt it.'

'Then grant me permission to stay until dawn. I have the need to feel the warmth of human skin against my own. I shall not make any attempt to seduce you – that I swear.'

'What of your mistress? Is her skin not soft and warm?'

'May I stay?' he said.

She looked at him, then sighed. 'You may stay – until dawn.'

Sirano rose and slowly stripped away his clothes before stumbling to the bed. When Karis pulled back the coverlet and slipped in beside him his body was cold to the touch. Putting her arms around him, she drew him close.

'She is dead, Karis,' he whispered. 'Her body is no longer soft and warm.'

'You sacrificed her?'

'With my own hand.'

Karis did not speak. His breathing deepened and soon he was asleep in her arms. But no sleep came to Karis. The girl had been no more than eighteen, and was besotted with Sirano, her doe-eyes never leaving his face. She lived to please him. Now she had died to please him.

Karis lay still for some time, then eased herself away from the

75

sleeping man. Rising silently, she moved to where her clothes lay discarded on the floor. Slipping her dagger from its sheath, she returned to the bed. One thrust was all it would take.

In the lantern light his face looked very young, boyish and innocent. You are not innocent, she thought. You are a killer, succumbing to evil.

A brilliant light shone down upon the bed, illuminating his face, and Karis swung round. The western wall was glowing bright, as if lit from within. A tall figure emerged from it; his face was slender, and framed with white fur save around the eyes and nose. Karis flipped the dagger, then hurled it. It sailed through the figure and clattered against the far wall.

'You have nothing to fear, child,' whispered a voice inside her head.

'Who are you?' she asked, aloud. Beside her Sirano stirred and woke.

'I am Ranaloth,' said the apparition.

'The spirit of the Pearl,' said Sirano. 'Are you ready to give me what I want?'

'I cannot. Nor should you make any more attempts to steal it.'

'I will beat you, Eldarin. Just as I destroyed your people. You cannot stop me.'

'You are not quite correct. I could stop you. I could kill you, child. Instead I appeal to you, Sirano, not to continue. The Pearl is more important than your ambition. And should you succeed, you will unleash a terror you cannot control.'

'Empty words,' sneered Sirano.

'The Eldarin do not lie, Duke of Romark; we put that behind us a thousand years ago. You see the Pearl as a weapon, as an aid to your dreams of conquest and immortality. But it is not a weapon. And it will not, even if pierced, give you what you desire.'

'Do not seek to fool me, old man,' said Sirano. 'I am a Master of Spells. I can feel the power within the Pearl, and soon I will draw it to me.'

The figure stood silently for a moment, then Ranaloth spoke again. 'A long time ago the Eldarin faced another evil,' he said. 'We contained it, removed it from the world. The Pearl holds that evil at bay. Do not . . .' Suddenly the light around the apparition flickered and the old man staggered. 'Your sorcerers continue to attack us,' he said. His shoulders slumped, and he spread his hands in a gesture of hopelessness. 'Now,' he said, an infinite sadness in his voice, 'it is too late.' Turning to Karis, he told her, 'Leave this city and take to the high places. Your world is finished. Desolation and horror await you.'

The light dimmed and the figure disappeared. The two humans sat in silence for several moments, then Karis rose from the bed. 'What have you done, Saro? What has your evil brought us to?'

'Evil?' he sneered. 'What is evil? All men of power are called evil by their enemies. It means nothing, it is just a word.'

'The Eldarin said our world is finished. He promised desolation and horror.'

'He lied!'

'Why would he lie? What would be his purpose?' Karis shook her head. 'No, Sirano, his words rang with the truth. You destroyed the Eldarin. You plunged the world into war. And now you have unleashed an evil force that might destroy us all.'

'What evil force? I tell you he lied, and I'll tell you why. It was because he knew I had him! And I will have his power!'

'I don't think so,' said Karis. 'And you no longer have me.'

'We have a contract!'

'The unearned monies will be returned to you. My men and I will leave with the dawn.'

'As you will,' he said. 'Perhaps when you come back to me on bended knee I will forgive you, Karis.'

She laughed at him. 'You will need to be immortal, Saro, to live long enough to see that day. Now be so kind as to leave me in peace. I need some sleep.'

*

The door closed behind Sirano and Karis stood silently, listening as the sound of his footsteps receded. Once sure he was not coming back, she moved swiftly to the large wardrobe and took from it her riding clothes: breeches of brown oiled leather and a shirt of thick, cream-coloured wool, knee-length boots with a two-inch heel, and a sleeveless leather jerkin, the shoulders and upper back reinforced by a delicately wrought cape and hood of tiny mail rings. Moving to the mirror by the bedside she brushed back her shoulder-length black hair, drawing it tightly into a ponytail which she tied at the nape of her neck. Without the softening effect of her hair hanging loose Karis looked older, and she stared hard at her reflection. The dark eyes had seen too much pain, and it showed in the guarded gaze. Leaning forward, she lifted her hand to her temple. A single grey hair shone there. Angrily she plucked it out. Twenty-eight is not *so* old, she reminded herself.

'Move yourself,' she said, aloud. 'You don't have time to stare into mirrors.'

Once the shock of her defection had worn off, Sirano would take steps to stop her. Of all the mercenary leaders Karis was, quite simply, the best. She knew it. He knew it. He would not allow her to join one of his enemies, and Karis had no wish to be strapped to an altar and sacrificed to the Pearl.

Looping her sword-belt around her slender waist and twirling her sheepskin riding cloak about her shoulders, she took a last look around the room. The dagger she had hurled at the Eldarin ghost lay against the far wall. She sheathed it in the hidden scabbard of her right boot. Lastly she opened the small chest by the far wall and took from it a heavy pouch containing forty gold pieces, which she thrust deep into a hidden pocket inside her jerkin. Gathering her hunting-bow and quiver, she walked from the room, moving silently along the corridor and down the winding stairs to the courtyard door.

At the stables she bridled and saddled Warain, the strongest and fastest of her geldings. It irked her to leave behind the other two, but they were stabled at the barracks and fetching them would add an hour she could not afford. Warain's great grey head nuzzled her, and she rubbed his broad brow with her knuckles and then led him from the stall.

A bleary-eyed stableboy rose from his bed of straw. 'Can I help you, sir?' he asked.

Karis loomed over the child, then took his chin in her hand. 'Do I look like a man to you, boy?' she asked him.

He blinked nervously. 'I'm sorry, ma'am. I was half asleep.'

Karis shook her head, annoyed at the irritation she felt. The boy was probably not yet past puberty, but even so . . . 'Go and fill me a small sack of grain,' she ordered him. He ran off to the far end of the stable, returning with the feed-sack moments later. Looping it over the high pommel of the saddle, Karis ruffled the boy's hair. 'Do not mind me, child. It has been a long and exhausting day.'

'I saw only the boots and the sword, ma'am. You are very beautiful,' he said gallantly.

'Tell me that in ten years, and I'll promise you a night to remember!' Karis swung into the saddle as the boy opened the stable door. She ducked down into Warain's neck and steered the gelding through the open doorway. Warain was over sixteen hands tall and the lintel stone above the door brushed her shoulders.

Sitting up, she heeled Warain forward and rode slowly down Long Avenue towards the Western Gate. She had left behind all of her clothes, and various gifts and souvenirs that others would have considered of sentimental value. But Karis was not a sentimental woman. She had only one regret – not being able to say goodbye to the veteran warrior, Necklen. The old man had become a friend – and friendship with a man was rare for Karis. He loved her like a man should love a daughter. Anger flared as old memories burst to life. If she had known a father like Necklen, maybe now she would be happy.

Tugging on the reins, she halted Warain. There was still time to find Necklen and urge him to ride with her. He would come willingly. Karis was torn. His company always lifted her spirits, but the perils would be great and she had no wish to lead the old man to his death. 'I will send for you,' she whispered, 'when I have a new command.'

The streets were deserted as she rode, but everywhere there were signs of Sirano's obsessive desire to open the secrets of the Pearl. Huge cracks showed on the sides of buildings and several walls had fallen. The road ahead was buckled, sharp paving stones twisted up from the surface like broken teeth. She could see the main gates now, and the two sentries standing below the tall arch. She had timed her departure well, and the dawn light was just creeping above the eastern mountains. No-one was allowed out of Morgallis at night without a pass.

'Good morning,' she said, as she drew abreast of the men.

'Good day to you, Karis,' said the first guard amiably. He gave her a wide smile. His face was familiar, and she struggled for a link. The name came first.

'You are looking well, Gorl. Perhaps too well,' she added, pointing at the man's paunch. 'How long since you marched on a campaign?'

79

'Almost a year – and I don't miss it. Got me a wife now, and two nippers.'

'A wife? And you swore no one woman could satisfy you.'

He shook his head, and grinned. 'That was afore I knew you, lady. You taught me different.' Then she remembered: Gorl had been one of her many lovers. Was it on the Mountain Campaign, she wondered? No, that was the slim bowman who had died near Loretheli. 'Where are you riding to, this chilly morning?' asked Gorl, the question cutting through her thoughts.

'I quit Sirano's service last night. I think I'll ride for the sea. Rest up with a few sailors.'

Gorl chuckled. 'By the Gods, you're a wonder, Karis! Live like a whore, fight like a tiger, look like an angel. It was two years before I got you out of my blood. Or thought I had.'

'I think of you fondly too,' she said. 'Now open the gate.'

Stepping back, he winched the bar out of its broad sockets while the other guard pushed open the gate of oak and bronze. 'You stay healthy, you hear?' shouted Gorl as she heeled Warain into a canter. Karis waved and rode out into the hills.

Maybe it was after the siege of that garrison fort near Hlobane . . . No. A fleeting memory touched her, and she recalled making love to Gorl in the shade of a willow tree beside a fast-flowing stream. There were no willows near the garrison. Oh well, she thought. It will come to me or it won't.

Once out of sight of the city, she swung to the west, and by midday had ridden almost a complete semi-circle, the city now south-east of her. It would not fool any pursuers for long, but by the time they figured out her true direction she would be long gone. How far would Sirano go to see her captured or slain, she wondered? A long, long way, she decided. Then she laughed aloud. 'You arrogant strumpet,' she told herself. 'Maybe he has forgotten you already.'

To the best of her recollection it was around 240 miles to Corduin, much of it over rough country. The fastest route would be north and west, skirting the line of the Great North Desert. She smiled at the memory of her mother's stories. The desert was a place of myth and magic, a haunted land. Tribes of giants had once wandered there, eaters of human flesh, violaters of young girls. But with the memories came the sadness of reality, and she remembered her mother's bruised face, the blackened eyes, and the terrible sorrow that rules when love is replaced by fear.

'Just you and I, Warain,' she said, with a sigh. 'Come, let us work some of that fat from you.' The big grey bunched his muscles and broke into a run.

*

High on a hillside overlooking the city of Corduin, a beautiful raven-haired girl beside him, Duvodas sat on a broken wall beside a trickling stream. His harp glinted in the sunlight as it lay on the green silk shirt he had removed to allow the sun's autumn warmth to his skin. 'What are you thinking, Song-man?' asked Shira. Her crippled leg was hidden by the folds of her rust-coloured skirt, and her beauty was now unsullied. Duvodas slid off the wall to sit beside her on the grass.

'I was thinking of far-off days and gentle music, Shira. Of sunshine on meadows, of laughter and song. There was magic there – a magic born of love and caring. Where I grew up, they would have healed your leg. Then you would have been able to run across these hills.'

'Sometimes I try to forget about my leg,' she said, sadly. 'Especially when I am sitting down.'

He was instantly contrite, reaching out and stroking her cheek. 'I am sorry,' he said. 'That was thoughtless. Forgive me?'

She smiled, and he was lost in wonder at the beauty of it. Joy radiated from her, as powerfully as any music from his harp. Her hair was dark and long, her skin ivory fair. But the magic of her was in that radiant smile; it was both enchanting and contagious. Taking her hand, he lifted it to his lips. 'You are a beautiful woman, Shira.'

'And you are a rogue, Song-man,' she chided him.

'How can you say that?' he asked her, genuinely puzzled.

'A woman can tell. How many other girls have you complimented so prettily?'

'None,' he said. 'I have never met one with a smile like yours.' She wagged her finger at him, but he knew she was pleased. Twisting round, she opened the picnic hamper and produced two plates, some fresh-baked bread and two sealed pottery jars, one containing butter and the other a strawberry preserve.

'Customers have been asking Father where he purchased his new ale and wines. They say they have never tasted finer.'

'Music has that effect on appetites,' he said. 'How is your father's gout?'

'You are changing the subject again. You do that every time I talk about the effect of your music. Are you embarrassed by your talent?'

He smiled and shook his head. 'I love my music. It is just . . . when I am with you, I don't want to think about taverns and customers. I want to enjoy the freshness of the fields, the smell of the flowers, and – most of all – your company.' It was astonishing to Duvo that Shira, soon to be nineteen, was unmarried. He had understood the words when one of the tavern regulars told him: 'Shame about the leg. She's a wonderful girl, but she'll get no man.' How, he wondered, could a physical injury to a limb have such an effect? It was a mystery to Duvo. It was true that she walked clumsily, but her spirit was a delight and her personality extraordinary. She was kind and caring. What was it then that she now lacked in the eyes of suitors?

They ate in pleasant silence, finishing the meal with a jug of apple juice. Replete, Duvodas lay back on the grass, staring up at the sky. 'There was a fight outside the tavern last night,' she told him. 'People were queuing to get in. Father cannot believe his luck. And, to answer your question, his gout seems to have disappeared.'

'That is good news.'

'Where are you from, Duvo? Where is this land where my leg could be straightened?'

'It is in a far place,' he said softly, sitting up. 'A place we can no longer journey to. It exists only in here,' he said, tapping his temple. 'But I remember the joy of it. I will always treasure those memories.'

'Where was it?'

'It is better not to speak of it.'

She leaned in close to him, so close he could smell the perfume of her hair. The effect was disconcertingly pleasant. 'You lived with the Eldarin, didn't you?'

He sighed. 'Yes. With the gentle Eldarin.'

'They were going to destroy us all – that's what our schoolteacher told us.'

He shook his head. 'The Eldarin were peaceful; they had no wish to dominate others. But truth counts for nothing against the evil lies of men like Sirano. What I will never understand is the reason behind it all. What did Sirano and the others hope to achieve by destroying the Eldarin? The world has been at war ever since. Thousands have died. And for what? Did they envy the Eldarin their civilization, their knowledge? Was it just greed? I don't know. Hate seems so much stronger than love. A sculptor can spend years fashioning a statue from a single piece of marble. Another man can wreck it in a heartbeat with a heavy hammer. Love and hate.'

'I am sorry,' she said. 'Now I have saddened you.'

'You must not mention the Eldarin to anyone. I like my life as it is. Quiet.'

'Your secret is safe with me. All your secrets are safe with me.'

Leaning in he kissed her cheek. 'So chaste, Song-man,' she whispered. 'Is that all you wish for?'

'I wish for many things,' he told her, drawing her close. 'Most of them I cannot have.'

'You could have me,' she told him. He looked into her eyes and saw the fear of rejection there.

'Please do not fall in love with me, Shira,' he said. 'Soon I will be moving on.'

'Why must you go? Are you not happy here?'

'It is not a question of happiness.'

She pulled away from him, but as she did so she raised her hand and ran her fingers through his long blond hair. 'You cannot ask someone not to love you,' she said. 'It lessens love if you believe it can be controlled by mere will. I have loved you from the moment I saw you. You remember when you came into the tavern? Father said he had no need of a singer, and you told him that you would double his takings in the first week?'

'I do. I didn't know you were there.'

'I was in the kitchen doorway. When you came in the sun was at your back, and your hair shone like gold. I'll never forget that day.'

Drawing her down to the grass, he kissed her gently on the lips. Then he sat up. 'There is no deceit in me, Shira. I love you as I have loved no other. That is the truth. But there is another truth.'

'You have a wife?'

'No! That is something I cannot have. What I mean is that it will not be long before someone – as you have – begins to question my music and the spells it weaves. Then I will be forced to flee into the night.'

'I would go with you.'

Tenderly he took her hand. 'What kind of life could I offer you? I am a wanderer with no home and no people.'

She sat in silence for a moment. 'Would you have taken me with you had I been able to run across these hills?' she asked.

'No, never that. I love you, Shira. I love you for everything you are; for your sweetness and your love of life, for your caring and your courage.'

'You speak of courage, Duvo. Where is yours? I know how hard life can be. Two of my brothers have died in this senseless war, and I have spent my life in constant pain. From the day the wagon wheel crushed my leg – until you played for me – I have rarely known a moment when I could not feel the scraping of bone as I moved. But I go on, Duvo. We all go on. Life is harsh, life is cruel, life is uncaring. But we go on. I could take it with better heart if you did not love me. You could say farewell then, and I would be sad for a long while. But I would recover, I would take the wound and let it heal. Yet to love me, and still leave me . . . that is hard to bear.'

Duvodas sat very still, staring into her large, dark eyes. All tension flowed from him, and he raised her hand to his lips and kissed her palm. Then he sighed. ' None of us can help the way we are, Shira.'

They returned the plates and cups to the hamper and Duvodas lifted it to his shoulder. Shira gathered up his green shirt and his harp and took his arm. Her twisted left leg, several inches shorter than the right, made her movements ungainly and clumsy. Slowly they made their way down the hillside and on to the path towards the gates. Several children ran by and two of them stopped and laughed at Shira. She did not seem to mind, but the sound cut through Duvodas.

'Why do they laugh?' he asked her.

'My walk is comical,' she said.

'Would you laugh at another's misfortune?'

'Last winter the merchant Lunder, a large man and very pompous, came to collect a debt from father. As he left, his foot slipped on the ice. He struggled to stay upright, then his legs flew up in the air and he fell into a ditch. I laughed so much there were tears running down my face.'

'I don't understand where the humour lies,' he told her.

'Did the Eldarin not laugh?'

'Yes. They knew great joy. But it was never as a result of brutality or derision.'

They fell silent and walked on. Outside the gates they turned on to the main street and on through the square. There were four fresh corpses hanging from the gibbet there. Three had placards around their necks proclaiming the single word: THIEF; the fourth placard said DESERTER. Several women were standing in front of the gibbet. Two were weeping.

'So much pain in the world,' said Shira. Duvodas did not reply. Few were the days when the gibbet went unused.

They moved on, reaching the tavern just before dusk. Shira's father stepped out to meet them. Fat, tall and bald, Ceofrin was every inch the tavern-keeper, his face ruddy with good health, his smile swift and reassuring. Duvodas sensed that Ceofrin was hoping for good news, and his heart sank.

'Did you two have a good picnic?' he asked.

'Aye, Father,' said Shira, letting go of Duvo's arm. 'It was very pleasant.' Slipping past him she limped into the tavern.

Ceofrin took the picnic hamper from Duvo. 'You two make a fine couple,' he said. 'I've never seen her so happy.'

'She is a wonderful girl,' Duvo agreed.

'And she'll make a fine wife. With a handsome dowry!'

'With or without the dowry,' said Duvo. Shira had placed his harp on a nearby table. Now he gathered it up and began to walk towards the stairs.

'Wait,' said Ceofrin. 'I'd like a word with you, lad – if you don't mind.'

Duvo took a deep breath and turned back, his grey-green eyes focusing on Ceofrin's blunt, honest face. There was no hiding his emotions; the innkeeper was worried, and it showed. He sat down at a table by the leaded glass window and gestured to Duvo to sit opposite. 'This is not easy for me, Duvodas.' He licked his lips, then rubbed the back of his hand across his mouth. 'I'm not a fool. I know the world is a harsh, cruel place. Two of my sons are buried in unmarked graves somewhere south of Morgallis. My daughter – the most beautiful child you ever saw – was crippled beneath a wagon. My wife died of the Eldarin Plague – as did nearly a quarter of the people in Corduin five years ago. You understand what I'm saying? I don't see life like one of your songs.'

'I understand,' said Duvo, softly, waiting for the man to get to the point.

'But Shira now . . . she's different. Never complained about the leg, did you know that? Just took the hurt and got on with her life. Everyone loves her. She's like a . . . a living embodiment of your music. When she is around people smile. They feel good. She's nineteen now, an old maid. All of her school friends are married; some with babes. But not many suitors will consider a crippled wife. Shira understood this, yet still she fell in love. Not with a baker, or a tailor's clerk, but with a handsome musician. I am a plain man, and not good with the ladies. I can tell those who are, though. You could have your pick. You understand what I'm saying? She loves you, man, and that means you have it in your power to destroy her.' Ceofrin rubbed his hand across his mouth, as if trying to wipe a bad taste from his lips. 'So where do you stand?' he said at last.

'I love her,' said Duvo simply. 'But she and I have spoken of this. I cannot wed. There is much that I cannot speak of, Ceofrin. I would be a danger to her.'

'You are a spy?' Ceofrin's voice dropped to a husky whisper, fear shone in his eyes.

Duvo shook his head. 'No. This . . . petty war means nothing to me.' He leaned forward. 'Listen to me, Ceofrin, I would never willingly do anything to harm her. And I have not . . . nor will I . . . take advantage of her love. You understand that? I'll not be leaving her with a swollen belly. But I will be leaving come the spring.'

Ceofrin was silent for a moment. When at last he spoke his voice was edged with bitterness. 'A curse on love!' he said. 'Like life, it always ends in unhappiness.' Pushing himself to his feet, he strode away towards the kitchens. Duvo hefted his harp and lightly ran his fingers over the twenty-five strings. Light notes echoed around the room and a host of dust motes, lit by a sudden shaft of sunlight, seemed to dance in rhythm to the sweetness of the sound.

'No man should curse love,' said Duvo. 'Ultimately, love is all there is.'

*

Brune had never been in a city as large as Corduin, and as he walked along beside Tarantio's horse he tried to remember landmarks. There were scores of roads and alleys, crossing and re-crossing wide avenues, lines of shops and stalls, and beyond them workplaces and factories. There were, it seemed to Brune, hundreds of statues, most of them portraying lions – some with wings, some with two heads, some wearing crowns.

They had journeyed less than a mile and Brune was hopelessly confused. Confusion was a major fact of Brune's life, and it scared him. He glanced nervously up at Tarantio. 'Do you know where we are?' he asked.

'Of course.'

The answer reassured Brune, and his panic vanished. 'There are lots of lion statues,' he said.

'It is the symbol of Corduin's ruling house.' Tarantio swung the horse to the right, down a narrow cobbled street. Brune's boots were thin, and the cobbles dug into the soles of his feet.

'Are we nearly there?'

'Nearly,' agreed Tarantio, turning left into an even narrower alley which opened out into a circular stable-yard. Several horses were in their stalls: others were being exercised in a field nearby. A short, wiry, elderly man with a drooping grey moustache approached the two men. Tarantio swung down from the saddle.

'A fine beast,' said the newcomer, eyeing the horse. 'Just a small cow-hock short of greatness. My name is Chase. What can I do for you?'

'I'd like to winter him here,' said Tarantio.

'There are cheaper places, my friend,' said Chase amiably.

'The best rarely comes cheap,' said Tarantio. 'What down payment do you require?'

'Who recommended you to me?'

'The merchant, Lunder. I came here last year to view his prize mares. Liked what I saw.'

'Will he guarantee your payment?'

'I need no guarantees. My word is iron.'

Chase looked hard at him, his flinty eyes raking Tarantio's lean face. 'I think that's probably true, warrior. Therefore, from you, I'll take two gold pieces. That will keep him in grain and grass for two months. Then I shall require a further five to last until the spring.'

Tarantio opened his coat and reached inside, producing a small pouch from which he took seven small gold coins. Each was embossed with two crossed swords on the face, the reverse showing a spreading oak. He passed the coins to Chase.

'You are a trusting man, I see,' said Chase.

'Indeed I am. But not blindly so. You say your name is Chase. Once you were called Persial, the Fleet One. For twenty-five years you were the finest horse-racer in the Duchies. Your career ended when you were fifty. Someone offered you a fortune to lose a race, but you refused. Your hands and feet were broken with hammers. Now you are Chase, the horse-trainer.'

Chase smiled grimly. 'Men change, stranger. Perhaps now I am wiser.'

Tarantio shook his head. 'Men don't change. They just learn to disguise the lack of change. I'd like him grain-fed, and I shall be visiting regularly.'

'Whenever you like.'

'Can you recommend a place to stay for a few nights?'

'There's a tavern close by. They have rooms, and the finest food you'll ever eat. They also have a musician who plays the sweetest music I ever heard. The place is called the Wise Owl. Turn south outside the entrance and it's in the third street on the left. You'll not find better. Mention my name to Ceofrin, the owner.'

'Thank you,' said Tarantio, turning to lift his saddlebags and blankets from the gelding.

'Do you have a name, son?' asked Chase.

'I am Tarantio.'

Chase grinned. 'I'll have the gelding's saddle close by him, day and night.'

Hefting his saddlebags to his shoulder, Tarantio strolled away, Brune following. 'That was a lot of money,' said Brune. 'I have never seen seven gold pieces together before. I saw one once. Lat had one; he let me hold it. It was heavier than I thought it would be.'

'Gold is a heavy metal,' said Tarantio.

They reached the Wise Owl just before dusk and tapped on the main doors. 'We open in an hour,' a tall, burly man shouted from an upper window.

'We are seeking a room for a few days,' Tarantio told him.

'I'm not letting rooms at the moment.'

'Chase sent us to you,' said Tarantio.

'Well, why didn't you say that in the first place? Wait there and I'll be down.'

Two log fires had been recently lit, one at each end of the wide dining area inside, and two serving girls were cleaning the wicks on the wall lanterns. There was a raised dais to the right of the long bar, upon which a blonde young man, dressed in a shirt of green silk and leggings of brown wool, was tuning the strings of a hand harp. 'I have just the one room,' said Ceofrin, ushering the two men inside. 'Two beds and a good fireplace. It overlooks the main square. The price is a quarter silver a night, but that also buys you breakfast and an evening meal. Wine or ale is extra. How many nights are you staying?'

'Probably no more than four. I'm looking to rent a small house for the winter.'

'There's lots empty in the North Quarter. That's where the Eldarin Plague hit hardest.' Suddenly a series of shimmering notes filled the room and Tarantio jerked as if stung. Brune looked at him quizzically, but nothing was said, and the two men followed Ceofrin up the wide staircase. 'Do you want to book a table for tonight? It'll be busy and if you don't book you'll miss the music.'

'Have some food brought to the room,' said Tarantio. 'I am not in the mood for music.'

'I am,' said Brune. 'He sounds very good.'

'You'll not believe it until you hear it,' said Ceofrin confidently.

As they moved along an upper corridor, a beautiful, dark-haired girl stepped out of a room and walked towards them, limping heavily. 'My daughter, Shira,' said Ceofrin, pride in his voice. 'She will be cooking tonight.'

Tarantio bowed. Brune stood, mouth open, as Shira smiled at him. His mouth was dry, his mind reeling. In that moment he realized his hands were dirty, his clothes travel-stained, his hair a tangled, greasy mop. 'Hello,' she said, holding out her hand. Brune looked at it, then realized with a jerk that he was supposed to shake it. He glanced down at his own grubby palm, and wiped it quickly down the side of his leggings. Then he took her hand and gently squeezed it. 'And you are?' she prompted.

'Yes,' he said. 'I am.'

'He is Brune,' said Tarantio, with a wide smile.

'Yes . . .' he said. 'I am Brune. Pleased to meet you.'

'And I am Tarantio,' said the swordsman, taking her outstretched hand and raising it to his lips. With another dazzling smile she eased past them and made her slow, ungainly way down the corridor.

'This way,' said Ceofrin, leading them into a wide room with two well-crafted beds of pine. The ceiling was white and low, supported by long oak beams, and there was a stone-built fireplace set against the northern wall. The wide windows were leaded and Tarantio moved over to them, glancing out and down on the cobbled square. 'It is cold now, but I'll get a maid up to light the fire. Then it'll be cosy, you mark my words.'

'It is fine,' said Tarantio, reaching into his pouch and producing his last gold coin. He flipped it to Ceofrin and the tavern-keeper hefted the coin. 'This will leave you with nineteen silvers,' he said. 'I will have a servant bring the remainder to you.'

'Is there a bath here?' asked Tarantio.

'Aye. I'll get the water heated – it will take around half an hour. It's on the ground floor – the door behind where the harpist is practising.'

As Ceofrin left the room Brune walked to the first of the beds and sat down. 'Oh,' he said, 'wasn't she beautiful?'

Tarantio dropped his saddlebags by the far wall. 'A vision,' he agreed. 'Shame about the leg.'

'Did I seem very stupid to her, do you think?'

'A man who suddenly can't remember his own name is very rarely considered a genius,' said Tarantio. 'But I think she was pleased by your reaction to her beauty.'

'You really think so?'

Tarantio did not reply. Shucking off his coat and tugging off his boots, he lay down on the second bed.

Brune lay back, picturing Shira's smile. Life was suddenly full of sunlight.

*

One hundred and twelve miles north-east, above the flanks of the highest mountain of the Great Northern Desert, a black vulture banked on the thermals, gliding towards the south, its keen eyes scanning the desert for signs of movement. It banked again, this time towards the west. The vulture did not hear the low, rumbling sounds from the peak of the mountain, but it saw boulders shiver and tremble. One huge stone rolled clear, bouncing down the red slope, dislodging hundreds of smaller stones and sending up a cloud of crimson dust. The vulture dipped its wings and flew closer.

A fissure opened, and the bird saw a small, dark object exposed to the light.

It was the last sight the vulture would ever experience . . .

A fierce wave of freezing air erupted from the mountain-top, striking the bird and ripping away its feathers. Dead in an instant, the vulture fell from the sky.

On the mountain-top a black pearl shimmered in the sunlight. The spell holding it wavered and shrank, then fell away like a broken chain.

In the warmth of the sun the black pearl swelled to the size of a large boulder. Blue flames crackled around it, hugging to the surface, flaring into lightning bolts that blazed in every direction.

Sixty miles away a young shepherd boy, named Goran, watched the display from the green hills south of the desert. He had seen dry storms before, but never one such as this. The sky was not dark but brilliantly blue and clear, and the lightning seemed to be radiating from a mountain-top like a spiked crown of blue-white light. He climbed to a high vantage point and sat down. As far as the eye could see, the dead stone of the desert filled his vision.

The lightning continued for some time, without thunder or rain. The boy became bored with the lights, and was about to descend to his flock of sheep when a dark cloud rose up from the distant mountain. From here the cloud looked no larger than a man's head but, considering the distance, Goran guessed it to be colossal. He wished his father were here to see it, and perhaps explain the phenomenon. As the cloud continued to rise, swelling and growing, filling the sky, Goran realized that it could not possibly be a cloud. It was perfectly round, the perimeter sharp and clearly defined. Like the moon. Like a black moon – only twenty times the size.

No-one back at the village was going to believe this, and Goran could feel his irritation rising. If he told them they would laugh at him. Yet, if he said nothing, he might never learn the reason for the phenomenon. He was only thirteen. Perhaps colossal black moons had been seen before in the desert. How could he find out without risking derision?

These thoughts vanished as the black moon suddenly fell from the sky, striking the point of the seemingly tiny mountain peak like a boulder crushing an anthill. But the black moon did not crush the mountain. Instead it burst upon the stone.

Goran scrambled to his feet, fear causing his heart to pound. No longer solid, the moon had become a gigantic tidal wave, hundreds of feet high, roaring across the desert, sweeping towards the hillside on which he stood. Too frightened to run, Goran stood petrified as the black wall advanced, engulfing the red rocks of the desert. On the hillside the flock of sheep panicked, and ran. Goran just stood there.

As the tidal wave devoured the miles between them Goran saw that it was shrinking, and from his high vantage point he found he could see beyond the advancing black wall. Behind the wave, the land was no longer dead rock and shimmering heat hazes; there was the pale green of pastures and meadows, the deeper hues of forests and woods. And more incredible yet, as the shrinking black wave grew closer he saw a strange city appear behind it, a city of dark domes like thousands of black moons wedged together.

The tidal wave shrank and slowed as it neared him, until at last it gently lapped at the foot of the hills, seamlessly joining to the grass where his sheep fed.

Goran sat silently, jaw agape. There was no desert now, no hint of the gloomy, depressing stone. Verdant hills and valleys greeted his gaze, and away to the right a glistening stream rippled down over white rocks, joining to a river that vanished into deep woods.

Leaving his sheep to feed on the new grass he ran back down the hills and up along the deer trail, his heart thumping. Cresting the last rise before the village, he ran down to the main street and found his father, the farmer Barin, taking lunch with the blacksmith, Yordis, outside the forge.

Swiftly the boy told the men what he had seen. At first his father laughed and, leaning forward, smelt his son's breath. 'Well, it is not wine you've been drinking,' he said, ruffling Goran's hair.

'Perhaps he fell asleep, Barin,' offered the blacksmith, 'and dreamt the whole affair.'

'No, sir,' insisted the boy. 'But even if I had, I would have had to be awake to run back and tell you about it. I swear the desert is gone, and there is a city no more than five miles from our hills.'

'It is a dull day,' said Barin, 'and a ride will make it more interesting. But be warned, Goran, if there is no city I shall take off my belt and flay your buttocks till they bleed!' Swinging to the blacksmith, he said, 'You wish to see this city, my friend?'

'I wouldn't miss it for the world,' said Yordis. The two men saddled their mounts and, the boy riding behind his father, set out for the hills.

Once there, the good humour vanished, and the two men sat their horses and gazed silently at the distant city.

'What in Hell's name is going on?' asked the smith.

'I don't know,' Barin replied. 'Ride back and fetch the others. The boy and I will wait.'

The smith rode off as father and son dismounted. 'It is a magical city,' said the boy. 'Perhaps the Eldarin have come back.'

'Perhaps,' his father agreed.

Yordis returned with some twenty villagers, and the group rode down to the rich grassland. Dismounting, they walked around in silence for a while, then gathered together and sat in a circle. 'Someone should ride to the garrison; they could send a rider to Corduin to let Lord Albreck know what has occurred,' said Barin.

'Who would be believed?' asked a village elder. 'I have seen it and I still do not believe it.'

'Should we go to the domed city and make ourselves known to them?' asked another.

'That will not be necessary,' said Barin. 'It seems they are coming to us.'

The men rose and turned to see a hundred horsemen galloping across the grassland. The horses were huge, taller by six hands than anything the villagers had ever seen, and the riders were large, powerful warriors, seemingly wearing helms of white bone. But as they came closer, Barin realized that they were not helms at all. The riders were not human. Fear rose in him and, grabbing his son, he lifted him to the saddle. 'Get to the Duke Albreck,' he hissed. Then he slapped his hand hard on to the rump of the horse, which half-reared and then bolted towards the south.

The riders ignored the fleeing boy and formed a circle around the villagers. One of them dismounted and walked up to Barin. The warrior was more than seven feet tall, huge across the shoulder. His face was flat, the bone of his ridged nose flowing up over his hairless cranium. The eyes were huge and black, showing no evidence of a pupil, and the beaked mouth was a curious M-shape, curving downward, lipless and cruel.

The creature loomed over the farmer, and a series of guttural clicks came from its mouth. Barin blinked and licked his lips nervously. 'I . . . I do not understand you,' he said. The creature paused, then made a motion with his hand, touching his own lipless mouth and then pointing to Barin. 'What is it you want?' asked Barin. The creature nodded vigorously, then gestured him to continue.

'I do not know what to say, nor whether you can understand my words. I fear you cannot. We are all villagers here, and we came to see the miracle of the desert. We mean no harm to anyone. We are peaceful people. The reason we came so far north was to avoid the wars that plague our lands.' Barin spoke on for some time, his eyes shifting nervously from the monster before him to the other riders who sat motionless. After some time the creature before him lifted his hand. He spoke, but the words were strange and – largely – meaningless. But there were some familiar sounds now. He seemed to be asking Barin a question. Barin shook his head. The monster motioned him to speak again and he did so, telling them of problems with crops, of raising buildings on marsh land, of the plague that stopped short of their village but almost obliterated three others. Just as he was running out of things to say, the monster spoke again.

'What are you?' it asked, the voice deep and harsh, the dialect perfectly pronounced.

'We are villagers from the south. We mean no harm, sir.'

'You serve the Eldarin?'

'No, sir. We serve the Duke of Corduin. The Eldarin are no more; there was a war and they . . . disappeared. Their lands became a desert, like this one . . .' he tailed off lamely.

'A desert, you say? What is the desert?'

'Barren . . . empty . . . devoid of life. No water or earth. No grass or trees. That is a desert. Until this very morning the desert was all around here. Red stone, not a handful of earth for thousands of square miles. But today – and my son saw this – a great black cloud

94

rose up and everything . . . the city, the trees, flowed from it. That's why we came here.'

The huge warrior stood silently for a moment. 'There is much here to think on,' he said at last. 'And our mastery of your language is . . . not good. This morning the sun rose . . . wrong. I think you . . . truth speak. Eldarin did this to us with . . . magic.'

'You are mastering the language wonderfully, sir,' said Barin. 'And with such speed . . . swiftness. In my judgement that is amazing.'

'We have talent for tongues,' said the creature. 'Your . . . people . . . killed Eldarin?'

'Yes. Well . . . no one knows what happened to them. Their land was destroyed. Our army was there to fight them, but what happened there was the . . . opposite of what happened here. The grass and trees and water disappeared. So did their cities.'

'You and I will . . . discuss . . . this further. But let us deal first with matters we *can* make judgement upon. Which of you here is the strongest?'

There was silence as the villagers stood by, frightened. 'I am,' said the smith at last, stepping forward.

The leader approached him, towering over Yordis by more than a foot. 'What is your race called?' he asked.

'We are just . . . men,' the smith answered.

The leader called to one of his riders, who dismounted and approached. 'Fight him,' the leader ordered Yordis.

'We are not here to fight, sir,' put in Barin. 'We are none of us warriors.'

'Be silent. I wish to see your man fight against a Daroth warrior.'

Drawing his sword the leader tossed it to the smith, who caught it expertly by the hilt but then sagged under the weight of the weapon. Instantly his opponent drew his own sword and attacked. Yordis blocked the first blow, and sent a two-handed sweep that hammered against the warrior's shoulder, cutting deep into the white flesh. A milky fluid began to stream from the wound. The smith attacked again, but the warrior ducked under a slashing cut and rammed his own blade deep into the smith's belly, wrenching it up through the heart. Blood and air hissed from Yordis's open lungs, and his body fell to the earth. The wounded warrior sheathed his sword and drew a curved dagger; with this he cut a strip of flesh from the

95

smith's forearm, and ate it. Blood staining his ghost-white face, the warrior turned to his leader. 'They taste of salt,' he said. A hissing staccato sound came from the other warriors, which Barin took to be a form of laughter. Yordis had been a dear friend, but the farmer was too shocked and frightened to feel despair at his parting. In that moment all he felt was relief that it was not him lying on the soft earth, with blood pooling beneath him.

The leader took Barin by the arm. 'Mount your pony and follow us,' he said. 'We need to speak further.'

'What of my friends?' he asked.

The leader barked out an order, whereupon the warriors drew their serrated swords and closed in. The villagers tried to run, but the circle of horsemen hemmed them in and they died screaming. Within the space of a few heartbeats all the villagers were slain, the grass stained red by their blood.

Barin stood by, mesmerized by the slaughter. 'We meant you no harm,' he said. 'They are . . . were . . . peaceful people.'

The leader loomed above him, his huge dark eyes staring down unblinking. 'They were nothing, for they were not strong.'

It took Barin three attempts to mount his gelding, his limbs were trembling uncontrollably. The leader stepped into the saddle of his enormous stallion. Around him the Daroth warriors were dismounting; they ran to the bodies and began to strip away the clothes.

'Your friends' lives will not be completely wasted,' said the leader. 'Salt flesh is a great delicacy.'

CHAPTER FIVE

Duvodas was troubled. Eyes closed, he stroked the harp strings, sending out a fluted ripple of notes. 'That is very pretty,' said Shira.

'It is wrong,' he said, opening his eyes and looking at the girl. Dressed in a skirt of russet brown and a blouse of cream-coloured wool, she was sitting on the round wall of the well. Putting aside his harp, Duvodas walked to her and kissed her cheek. 'I am not good company today,' he told her.

'You are always good company, Duvo. And what do you mean, it is wrong? What is wrong?'

'I don't know – exactly. I saw a painting once of three women on a castle wall, staring down over the sea. I remembered it for years. But when I saw it again one of the women was wearing a green dress, though I had remembered it as blue. Suddenly the picture looked wrong to me, as if an artist had changed it.' He paused, then returned to his harp. Balancing it to his hip, he played the chorus notes of the Love Song of Bual. When he had finished, Shira clapped her hands. 'I love that,' she said. 'You played it the first night you were here.'

'Not like that,' he told her. 'The music has changed.'

'How can music change?'

He smiled. 'I draw my music from the magic of the land. Either the magic has changed, or my ability to channel it has altered. The first time you heard the love song you wept. Tears of happiness. That is the magic of Bual. But you did not weep today. The magic touched you differently. Your reaction is more of the mind than the heart.'

'Perhaps that is because it is no longer new to me,' she suggested.

'No. The magic should have brought tears. Something is wrong, Shira.'

'You are very tired. You performed for over two hours last night.'

'You have put the cart before the horse, pretty one. I performed for two hours because something had changed. You remember the group who complained about the pies? Said they were tasteless? The food should have tasted exquisite. I know my skills remain, and I trust my abilities. I have eaten no meat, drunk no wine. It is a mystery. I have long understood that magic does not swell brightly within cities. The stone walls, streets, roads and foundations close us off from the land and its power. The murders, the hangings, the robberies, the violence – these also taint the purity. But I know how to deal with that, Shira. I make myself immune to the pettiness of the world, to its dark side.' He fell silent for a moment, then he took her by the arm. 'Will you walk with me to the hillside? Perhaps I can find the answer with grass below my feet.'

'I cannot today. Two of the cooks have fallen ill and Father needs me.'

'Were the cooks here last night?' he asked.

'Yes.'

'Then they should not be ill. They heard the music.' Without another word he strode from the yard and out into the streets of Corduin. Back in Eldarisa he would have sought out one of the many seers, and received his answer within moments. Here, in this giant sarcophagus of a city, there were no seers of worth. There was no magic, save his own. There was sorcery. Sometimes he could feel its emanations coming from the palace of the Duke. But it was small sorcery, childishly malevolent. His music was stronger.

What then, he wondered, was drawing the life from his songs?

98

Duvo wandered on through the streets. The gates of the park were open and he strolled through, following the path to the High Hill, then leaving it and walking upon the grass. He lay down on his back, stretching out his arms and closing his eyes, feeling the power of the land like a gentle voice whispering to his soul. Yet even here it was changed in an – as yet – indefinable way.

His upbringing in Eldarisa had taught Duvo never to worry at a problem, but to let his mind float around it. Master Ranaloth had told him many times that lack of focus was the key.

'That does not seem to make sense, sir,' the ten-year-old Duvo had told him, as they strolled through the scented gardens of the Oltor Temple.

'Focus is only required, young human, when the core of the problem is identified. You are angry because of what Peltra said to you this morning. You are focusing now on what made her say it, and this might help you. But lose your focus, and let your mind free, and you will find yourself asking why the words hurt you, and what it is in you that drew the words from her.'

'She hates me because I am human. She calls me an animal, says that I smell.'

'That is still your anger speaking. Lose it. Float above it.'

Duvo sighed. 'I don't think I can do what you require of me, Master Ranaloth. I am not Eldarin.'

'But Peltra is, and she cannot do it either . . . yet.'

'I do not know why she is angry with me. I have never harmed her. Equally, I cannot say why her words hurt me. I am a human. I am an animal – as we all are. Perhaps I even smell.' He laughed. 'Why did it hurt me, sir?'

'Because it was intended to. And because you care about what Peltra thinks of you.'

'I do care. She is normally a sweet person. I thought she was fond of me.'

'Your essay on the healing powers of mountain herbs was very fine, Duvo. Well researched.'

'Thank you, sir. The library is wonderfully well equipped.'

'And what led you to the Book of Sorius?'

Duvo thought about it. 'It was Peltra. We were walking on the hillsides and she was telling me about it.' He reddened. 'I won the prize, but I wouldn't have won if she hadn't told me about the Book.'

'There is no shame in that,' said Ranaloth softly.

'I think perhaps there is, sir. I didn't think. She was so proud of discovering the mystery you set that she bragged to me of it. Then I too studied the text – and won the prize.'

'Your perception, then, is that you were at fault?'

'I believe that I was. But it was not intended, it was merely thoughtlessness.'

Now on the hillside Duvo tried to float free of the problem, letting his mind wander. Many things could alter the flow of magic from the land: death, violence, disease, fear – even joy. Equally, the mind or body of the musician could be out of harmony with the magic. Calmly and carefully Duvo examined his thoughts. His mind was sharp, and attuned to the flow. Likewise his body had been fed no flesh, consumed no alcohol. Nor had he succumbed to his physical desire for Shira. Confident that he was not the problem, Duvo relaxed and took up his harp, playing the ancient lay of the Far Time, and the Dying of the Light. As he played he felt the power of the land flowing through him, filling his veins and drawing him in. He was at one with the grass and the earth, with the trees and flowers, feeling the heartbeat of life swelling around him.

The land welcomed his music. As the lay ended, Duvo took a deep breath.

At eighteen Master Ranaloth had taken him to a glade at the centre of Oltor Forest, where together they had sat upon a flat boulder. 'What music would you play here?' asked Ranaloth.

'That is simple, sir. There are three. Each would be apposite. A forest song, a river song, or a mountain song.' He shrugged. 'Is there more to the question than I can see? Is it a riddle of some kind?'

'You will not know until you play, Duvo.'

Taking up his harp, Duvo reached out for the forest music. There was nothing. Rising he glanced down at the boulder. Perhaps the stone was blocking the flow. He took two steps, then reached out again. Nothing. He glanced at Ranaloth, and saw the sorrow in his golden eyes. 'Am I doing something wrong, sir?'

Ranaloth shook his head. 'You know the history of Oltor Forest?'

'This is where they all died.'

'Yes,' said the Eldarin sadly. 'This is where a race was obliterated. The Oltor were a gentle, independent people, but they could not stand against the Daroth. Their cities were systematically destroyed and the last remnants of their people fled here, to this forest. A Daroth army surrounded it – sixty thousand strong – and the slaughter began. The last Oltor, twenty women and more than a hundred children, managed to reach this glade. They went no further.'

'And now there is no magic in the glade?' whispered Duvo.

'No magic,' agreed Ranaloth. 'Bring it back, Duvo.'

The elderly Eldarin rose, patted the young man's shoulder and walked away. Duvo sat down. A race died here, he thought. Not just a tribe, or a clan, or even a nation. But a race. He shivered, and felt the enormity of the task he had been set. How does a man restore magic after such an act?

Holding his harp to his hip, Duvo tried to play, but there was no music to be found. For several hours he sat in the glade. The sun fell, and the moon rose; still the young man waited for inspiration. An hour before the dawn he rose and moved across the glade, reaching the edge of the trees. Here he could feel the tiniest tremor of magic, like the breeze from a butterfly's wing. Slowly he circled the glade; then he began to play as he walked, the softly lilting Song of Birth. As the music swelled he edged away from the magic, towards the centre of the glade. Three steps he made before the music died away. Again and again Duvo returned to the trees, drawing the magic forward, letting it flow through him into the earth below his feet. Inch by weary inch, he slowly created a magical web that criss-crossed the glade.

The dawn came, the sun rising towards noon. Exhausted now, Duvo played on. Moving to the centre of his web, he calmed himself for the Creation Hymn. He stood silently for several minutes, breathing deeply, calming his mind. Then his fingers danced upon the strings and his strong clear voice sang out. Sunlight shone down upon the glade, and several birds flew into the branches of nearby trees. Duvo walked as he sang, and not once did the music waver.

The magic was back!

He slumped down upon the boulder and laid his harp beside him, his fingers cramped and trembling.

Master Ranaloth emerged from the tree-line, sunlight shining on his snow-white fur. His own harp was slung across his shoulder.

'You did well, Duvo,' he said, pride in his voice. 'You are a human beyond compare. And in you I see hope for your race.'

'Thank you, sir. It was harder than I could have believed. Tell me, though, why only this glade? Is it because the end came here?'

'It was not just this glade,' said Ranaloth. 'It was the whole forest. The glade was the last point of emptiness.'

Duvo stared at him. 'The forest covers hundreds of square miles. And you . . . ?'

'It took many centuries, Duvo. But it was necessary.'

'But you could not have done it alone?'

'It is my gift. And now it is yours. Without magic the land dies. Oh, you can still grow crops upon it, but it is spiritually dead nonetheless. The evil of the Daroth is that they live to kill – and they destroy not only races, but also the soul of the lands they inhabit. That is a crime beyond comprehension. You humans do it also. Though you do it more slowly, with your cities of stone, your lusts and your greed. But among you are those who care. Among the Daroth there are none.'

'You speak as if the Daroth still live. But the Eldarin destroyed them centuries ago.'

'The Eldarin do not destroy, Duvo. The Daroth live.'

'Where?'

'Where they can do no harm.'

Duvo had asked many questions, but Ranaloth would say no more. 'But what if they return?' Duvo asked.

'As long as the Eldarin survive, they will not return.'

Now, on the grass of the hillside above Corduin, Duvo rose and stared towards the north. His throat was dry, his heart hammering. He knew now why the magic of the land was changed. He could feel it; the slow, almost imperceptible pull towards the north, the power seeping away like water through a cracked jug.

The Eldarin had not survived.

And the Daroth were back . . .

*

Tarantio sat at a corner table, his back to the wall, and finished the last of the meat pie. The gravy was thick and rich, the meat tender. The atmosphere in the Wise Owl was tense, for the musician had not appeared this evening and many of the guests were complaining.

Ceofrin moved among the tables, making his apologies and assuring his customers that the harpist would appear momentarily. One group of four young nobles rounded on the innkeeper, claiming that the food tasted like dung and they had no intention of paying. Shira moved to the table and spoke to them, and they settled down, explaining they had travelled across the city to hear Duvodas play. Then they apologized for the outburst. Tarantio was impressed by the harmony she radiated, and he glanced across at Brune, who was staring at her with undisguised admiration. Ceofrin backed away from the table, relief showing on his round, fat face. Shira refilled the wine goblets and then, with a last dazzling smile, returned to the kitchen.

'I hope the harpist does appear,' said Brune.

'I don't think he is in the building,' Tarantio told him. Brune's disappointment showed.

Dace, however, was delighted. *How do people listen to that dreadful screeching?*' he asked.

'*Because it is beautiful,*' Tarantio told him. It was impossible to lie to Dace, and he could feel his confusion at the answer. '*Explain it to me,*' Dace insisted.

'*I don't think that I can, brother. I hear it and it moves me to tears. Yet I can feel your discomfort.*'

'*Well, he's not here now, for which I am thankful. And tell the idiot he has gravy on his chin.*'

'Wipe your chin, Brune.' The young man grinned at Tarantio and rubbed his hand across his face, licking the gravy from his palm.

'It's good food here. Shira cooked it, you know. Ah, but she's a wonder.' He glanced towards the kitchen, hoping for a glimpse of the girl, but the door was now closed. 'Did you see that man about your money?' he asked in a loud voice.

'Perhaps you should speak a little louder,' advised Tarantio. 'I don't think all the people in the tavern could hear you.'

Brune swung round. 'Why would they want to?'

'It doesn't matter. It was sarcasm, Brune. I was trying to point out that it is not wise to talk so loudly about money; it could be that there are robbers close by.'

'You don't need to tell me twice,' said Brune, tapping his nose. 'So, did you see him?'

'Yes. We have done rather well. My investments have brought me almost two thousand silver pieces.'

'Two thousand!' exclaimed Brune. 'In silver?' Several people close by turned to look at the two men. Dace's laughter echoed inside Tarantio's mind. *'I am so glad we brought him with us,'* said Dace.

'What will you do with all that money?' Brune asked.

'Let's talk about something else,' Tarantio told the sandy-haired youngster. 'Anything you like.'

Brune thought long and hard. 'Shame about the harp-man,' he said, at last. 'You should have been here last night. He was amazing. Can I fetch you some more ale?'

Tarantio nodded. *'Let me enjoy this one,'* said Dace. *'It is a long time since I tasted good ale.'*

'No. I don't want to see bloodshed here.'

'I promise, brother. No blades. Just a jug of ale, and then I shall sleep.'

Tarantio relaxed and faded back as Dace stretched and finished the last of the pie. Brune was on his way back to the table when a tall man, one of the troublesome nobles, turned suddenly, colliding with him. Ale swished from the two jugs Brune was carrying, splashing the man's black silk shirt.

'You clumsy dolt!' he shouted.

'Sorry,' said Brune amiably, trying to move past the man. 'But you did bump me.'

As Brune walked on the tall man's fist struck him behind the ear, punching him from his feet. Brune fell against a table, striking his head on the back of a chair before pitching unconscious to the floor.

Dace vaulted the table and reached the scene just as the tall man was unleashing a kick against Brune's body. Dace's foot lashed out to hook under the man's leg; then with a flick he sent the tall man crashing to the floor. The man rolled to his knees and drew a dagger. Dace grinned and reached for his own; then he stopped.

'You are a bore, brother,' he said aloud.

The tall man rose, eyes narrowed. 'I'll gut you for that, you whoreson!'

'Don't tell me, show me,' said Dace contemptuously. The man lunged. Dace side-stepped, grabbing the knife wrist with his left hand,

104

his right arm moving under the man's elbow. Dace slammed down with his left and up with his right. A sickening crack echoed around the room as the tall man's arm snapped at the elbow; the victim's scream was awful. The tall man fell back as Dace released him, the knife falling from his fingers. White bone was jutting through the sleeve of his black shirt, which was now stained with blood. He screamed again. 'Oh, shut up!' snapped Dace, ramming the heel of his palm into the man's nose and following up with a right uppercut that lifted him to his toes. Stepping back, Dace let the man fall and then walked to Brune, who was groaning and trying to rise.

A movement from behind caused Dace to spin. Three men were approaching, knives in their hands. Dace laughed at them, then he walked towards them.

'Happily for you, I promised a friend I'd kill no-one tonight. However, that does not mean I cannot cripple you – like your friend on the floor, who will be lucky to use that arm again. So who is first? I think I'll smash a knee-cap next time!'

He advanced again and the men fell back, confused. 'What is the problem, children? Can't make up your minds about who will be the first? What about you?' he asked, stepping in close to a lean, bearded man. The knife-man jumped back so suddenly he fell over a chair. The other two sheathed their knives and backed away. Dace laughed at them. 'What a trio of buttercups,' he said. 'Pick up your friend and get him to a surgeon.' Swinging towards the bar, he called out, 'Two more jugs of ale, if you please.'

The men carried the unconscious attacker from the tavern and Dace helped Brune to his feet. 'How are you feeling?' he asked.

'My head hurts,' said Brune.

'Ah well, you're used to that,' said Dace happily. Ceofrin brought the jugs, and leaned in to Dace.

'I think you had better move on, my friend. The man you . . . injured . . . is highly connected.'

'His arm isn't,' said Dace, with a wide smile.

'I mean it, Tarantio. He is a cousin of the Duke and a close friend of Vint, the Duke's Champion.'

'Champion, you say? Is he any good?'

'It is said he has killed thirty men. That makes him good – to my reckoning, anyway.'

Dace lifted his jug and half drained it. ' It makes him interesting,' he agreed. Ceofrin shook his head and moved away.

'*You promised,*' said Tarantio.

'*I kept my promise. I didn't know someone was going to punch the idiot. And I didn't kill him, brother.*'

'*You crippled him!*'

'*You said nothing about crippling people. Did you hear what he said about Vint?*'

'*Yes. And we are going to avoid him.*'

'*There is no sense of adventure in you.*' The door opened and Duvodas stepped in. The crowd saw him, and began to cheer. '*Damn!*' said Dace. '*Just when I was beginning to enjoy myself. I think I'll sleep now.*'

Tarantio took a deep breath. 'Where is the man who hit me?' asked Brune.

'He's gone,' replied Tarantio.

'Did you hurt him?' asked Brune.

'I think I did,' said Tarantio.

*

Goran, the shepherd boy, was forced to wait at the garrison for a full day as he tried to make his report. As night fell he sat shivering beneath an archway at the main gate. A kindly sentry shared his supper ration with the boy, and found him an old blanket to wrap around his slender frame. Even so the cold autumn winds chilled him. Finally another soldier came to fetch him, and he was taken to a small office inside the garrison where the soldier ordered him to sit down and wait. Moments later a slender, middle-aged officer entered and sat down at a narrow desk. He looked tired, thought Goran, and bored. The officer looked at him long and hard. 'I am Capel,' he said. 'For my sins I am the second in command of this . . . outpost. So tell me, child, your important news.' Goran did so, and Capel listened without expression until the boy concluded his tale of black moons and monster warriors on monster horses.

'You understand, child,' he said, 'that such a fanciful tale is likely to see you strapped to the post for twenty lashes?'

'It's true, sir. I swear it on my mother's grave.'

The officer rose wearily to his feet. 'I'll take you to the captain.

But this is your last chance, boy. He is not a forgiving man, and certainly not noted for having a sense of humour.'

'I must see him,' said Goran.

Together they walked through the corridors of the garrison keep, and up a flight of winding stairs. Capel tapped on a door and entered, bidding the boy to wait. After several minutes, the door opened and Goran was called inside. There he told his story again to a young, fat man with dyed blond hair and soft eyes.

The fat man questioned him at even greater length than the older officer. Goran answered every question to the best of his ability. Finally the captain rose and poured himself a goblet of wine. 'I would like to see this miracle,' he said. 'You will ride with me, boy. And if it proves – as I think it will – a grand nonsense, I shall hang you from a tree. How does that sound?'

Goran said nothing and was taken to the barracks and allowed to sleep on a pallet bed within a cold cell. The door was locked behind him. At dawn Capel woke him and they walked to the courtyard stables where a troop of forty lancers were standing beside their mounts. They waited for an hour before the fat captain appeared; a young soldier helped him mount a fine grey stallion, and the troop cantered out of the garrison, Goran riding beside Capel.

'Tell me again about these monsters,' said the soldier.

'They were huge, sir. White hairless heads, and strange mouths. Their horses were giants.'

'You describe their mouths as strange. Like a bird's, perhaps?'

'Yes, sir. Like a hawk's beak of bone beneath the nose, sharp and pointed.'

The troop stopped at mid-morning to rest the horses, and the men took bread and cheese from their saddlebags. Capel shared his breakfast with Goran. The fat captain drank wine from a flask to wash down a whole, cooked chicken; then a soldier brought water from a stream for him to wash his hands, which he dried with a white linen towel.

After half an hour they continued on their way, reaching Goran's village an hour after noon. It was deserted.

Capel dismounted and searched the area, then he moved alongside the captain's mount. 'Hoof prints everywhere, sir. Huge. Just as the boy said.' The captain looked around nervously.

'How many in the raiding party?' he asked, sweat breaking out on his plump face.

'No more than thirty, sir. But there are also footprints larger than any I've seen.'

'I think we should go back, don't you?' said the Captain.

'We could do that, sir, but what report would we then make to the Duke?'

'Yes, yes. Quite right, Capel. Well . . . perhaps you should take the men on. I have much to do back at the garrison.'

'I do understand how busy you are, sir. One thought strikes me, however. What if this raiding party has moved south? It could now be between us and the garrison.'

The fat man's eyes widened and he glanced back nervously. 'Yes, of course. You think then we should . . . push on?'

'With care, sir.'

The troop moved off into the higher hills, the fat captain positioning himself at the centre of the troop. Goran edged his mount alongside Capel. 'The captain doesn't seem much like a soldier,' he said.

'He's a nobleman, lad. They're a different breed – born to be officers.' He winked at the boy. They rode for almost an hour, finally cresting the rise before what had been the Great Northern Desert. The men sat their horses in silence, staring out over verdant hills and valleys, woods and plains.

The fat officer moved alongside Capel. 'It is like a dream,' he said. 'What can it mean?'

'When I was a lad our village storyteller told tales of ancient days. The Three Races – you remember, sir? The Oltor, the Eldarin and the Daroth?'

'What of it?'

'Our storyteller's description of the Daroth matches what the boy saw. Huge, powerful heads of white, ridged bone. A beak of a mouth.'

'It cannot be,' said the captain. 'The Daroth were destroyed by the Eldarin centuries ago.'

'And a few days ago this was the Great Northern Desert,' pointed out Capel. Around them the thirty men were sitting their horses nervously. There was no conversation, but Goran could feel the tension.

'And that looks like no human settlement I have ever heard of,' went on Capel, gesturing towards the distant city of black domes. 'Should we send a delegation?'

'No! We are not politicians. I think we have seen enough. Now we will ride back.'

One of the soldiers pointed to a small hollow at the foot of the hills, where the remains of a fire-pit could clearly be seen.

'Go down and check it,' the captain ordered Capel. 'Then we'll leave.'

The officer beckoned three men to follow him and rode down the slope. Goran heeled his horse forward and followed them.

At the foot of the hill Capel dismounted. Bones were scattered around the pit, and a small pile of skulls had been carelessly kicked into the ashes. A little way to the right was a mound of torn and bloody clothing. Goran jumped from his horse and began to search through the clothes. His father's tunic was not among them.

'Riders!' shouted one of the three soldiers. Goran saw some twenty monsters approaching from the south. Running to his horse, he vaulted to the saddle.

'Let's get out of here,' said Capel. Turning his mount towards the slope, he glanced up to see, far above them, the captain's horse rear suddenly, pitching him to the ground. The sound of screaming horses filled the air. One gelding toppled head-first over the crest with a long black spear through its neck. Capel dragged on the reins of his mount, his mind racing. Above him now he could see scores of white-faced warriors moving out onto the slope – behind him twenty more riders were bearing down. With three men he could make no difference to the battle being waged above, and if he tried he would be caught between two forces. To be forced to run from a fight was galling, but to stay would be certain death. Death did not frighten Capel, but if no-one escaped there would be no-one to raise the alarm back in Corduin.

Capel swung his horse towards the east. 'Follow me!' he shouted. The three soldiers and Goran obeyed instantly, and they galloped back down the slope to the level ground of the plain. The huge horses of the enemy could not match the speed of the Corduin mounts. They did not try. Capel glanced back to see the Daroth riding slowly up the slope.

109

And just for a moment he glimpsed the fat captain running witlessly along the crest. But then he was gone.

*

The dream was subtly different. The child was still crying and Tarantio was trying to find him – deep below the earth, down darkened tunnels of stone, he searched. He knew the tunnels well; he had worked them for four months as a miner in the mountains near Prentuis, digging out the coal, shovelling it to the low-backed wagons. But now the tunnels were empty, and a gaping fissure had opened in the face; through this came the thin, piping cries of terror.

'The demons are coming! The demons are coming!' he heard the child cry.

'I am with you,' he answered. 'Stay where you are!'

Easing himself through the fissure, he moved on. It should have been pitch-dark in here, for there were no torches, yet the walls themselves glowed with a pale green light, strong enough to throw shadows. As always he emerged into a wide hall, the high ceiling supported by three rows of columns. The ragged men with opal eyes advanced through the gloom, hammers and pickaxes in their hands.

'Where is the boy?' he demanded, drawing his swords.

'Dead. As you are,' came the voice in his mind.

'I am not dead.'

'You are dead, Tarantio,' argued the voice. 'Where is your passion? Where is your lust for life? Where are your dreams? What is life without these things? It is nothing.'

'I have dreams!' shouted Tarantio.

'Name one!'

His mouth opened, but he could think of nothing to say. 'Where is the boy?' he screamed.

The voice fell silent and Tarantio moved forward. The line of ragged men parted, and beyond them he saw a swordsman waiting for him. The man was lean, his face grey, his eyes golden and slitted like those of a hunting cat. His hair was white and spiky, standing out from his head like a lion's mane. In his hands were two swords.

'Where is the child?' asked Tarantio.

'Will you die to find out?' the demon asked in return.

*

Tarantio awoke and swung his legs from the bed. The sound of Brune's soft snoring filled the room. Tarantio took a deep, calming breath. Dawn light was shining through the leaded glass of the windows, making geometric patterns on the floor of the room. Tarantio dressed swiftly and went downstairs. One of the two fires in the dining hall had died, but the other was still flickering. Adding two thin logs to it, he blew the blaze to life and sat quietly before the flames.

'You look troubled,' said Shira, limping in from the kitchen.

'Bad dreams,' he said, forcing a smile.

'I used to have bad dreams,' she said. 'Would you like some breakfast? We have eggs today.'

'Thank you.'

She left him with his thoughts, and he pictured the dream again and again. Still there was no sense to it. Tarantio shivered, and added more fuel to the growing fire.

Shira returned with a plate of fried eggs and a slab of steak. Tarantio thanked her and devoured the meal. She sat down beside him when he had finished, and handed him a mug of hot, sweet tisane.

Tarantio relaxed. 'This is good,' he said. 'I don't recognize the flavour.'

'Rose-petal, lemon mint, and a hint of camomile, sweetened with honey.'

Tarantio sighed. 'The best time of the day,' he said, trying to make conversation. 'Quiet and uncluttered.'

'I have always liked the dawn. A new day, fresh and virgin.'

The use of the word 'virgin' unsettled Tarantio, and he looked away into the fire. 'You were very frightening last night,' she said.

'I am sorry you witnessed it.'

'I thought someone was going to die. It was horrible.'

'Violence is never pleasant,' he agreed. 'However, the man brought it upon himself. He should not have struck Brune, nor should he have attempted to kick him thereafter. It was the act of a coward. Though he will, I think, be regretting his actions now.'

'Will you be taking Father's advice, and leaving us?'

'I have not yet found a dwelling that suits me.'

'This tavern never made any money,' she said suddenly, 'not

111

until Duvo came with his music. Father worked hard, and we scraped by. Now he is on the verge of success, and that means a lot to him.'

'I am sure that it does,' agreed Tarantio, waiting for her to continue.

'But taverns with a reputation for violence tend to lose their customers.'

He looked into her wide, beautiful eyes. 'You would like me to leave?'

'I think it would be wise. Father didn't sleep last night. I heard him pacing the room.'

'I will find another tavern,' he promised her.

She made to rise, then winced and sat back. 'You are in pain?' he asked.

'My leg often troubles me – especially when it is going to rain. I shall be all right in a moment. I am sorry for having to ask you to leave. I know that what happened was not your fault.'

He shrugged, and forced a smile. 'Do not concern yourself. There are many taverns. And I will not need more than a few days to find a place of my own.'

Taking his empty plate, she limped back to the kitchen.

'*Such a sweet child,*' said Dace. '*And you fell for it, brother.*'

'*What she said was no more than the truth. Vint will come here looking for you . . . me.*'

'*I'll kill him,*' said Dace confidently.

'*What is the point, Dace? How many deaths do you need?*' asked Tarantio wearily.

'*I don't need deaths,*' objected Dace. '*I need amusement. And this conversation is becoming boring.*' With that Dace faded back, leaving Tarantio mercifully alone.

Returning to his room, he filled a pewter bowl and washed his face and hands. Brune yawned and stretched. 'I had a lovely dream,' he said, sitting up and scratching his thick fingers through his sandy hair.

'Lucky you,' said Tarantio. 'Pack your gear. Today we look at houses.'

'I'd like to stay here and talk to Shira.'

'I can see the attraction. However, the man I fought last night is likely to come back with a large number of friends – including a

112

sword-killer named Vint. They'll be looking for you and me. You're welcome to stay here, of course. But keep your dagger close by.'

'No,' said Brune. 'I think I'd like to look at houses. I don't want to meet any sword-killers.'

'Wise choice,' Tarantio told him.

'*Boring – but wise,*' added Dace.

*

The twelve targets were circles of hard-packed straw, four feet in diameter, placed against a wall of sacks filled with sand. The archers stood some sixty paces from the targets, their arrows thrust into the earth.

Tarantio and Brune had waited for almost an hour for a place to become free, and stood now on the extreme right of the line. 'Let me see you strike the gold,' said Tarantio.

Brune squinted at the circle. It was painted in a series of rings, yellow on the outer, followed by red, blue, green, and lastly a gold centre. 'I don't think I can,' he said.

'Just cock the bow, and we'll make judgements later.' Brune pulled an arrow from the earth and notched it to the string. 'Wait,' said Tarantio. 'You did not check the cock feather.'

'The what?'

'Put down the bow,' ordered Tarantio and Brune obeyed. Tarantio lifted an arrow and showed the flights to the bewildered young man. 'See how feathers are set into the shaft. Like a Y. Two sets of feathers are set close together, the third stands alone. This is the cock feather. When archers are told to cock their bow, this means that the cock feather should point away from the bow. Otherwise, it will strike the bow as it is loosed and deflect the arrow.'

'I see,' said Brune, taking up his bow again. Drawing the string back to his chin, the young man let fly. The shaft soared high over the target, striking the top of the sand-sack wall. 'Was that good?' he asked.

'Had your opponent been fifteen feet tall, it would have scared him,' said Tarantio. 'Let me see the bow.'

It was cheaply made from a single piece of wood some four feet long. The best bows were constructed of elm or yew, and often skilled bowyers would create bonded versions incorporating both woods. Tarantio cocked an arrow and drew back the string. The pull was no more than twenty pounds. Loosing the shaft, he watched it punch weakly home in the blue inner ring.

'You're very good,' said Brune admiringly.

'No, I'm not,' said Tarantio, 'but even a master archer would have difficulty with this bow. You'd probably be better off throwing a stone at an advancing enemy. This does not have the power to punch through armour.'

'I made it myself,' said Brune. 'I like it.'

'Have you ever hit anything with it?'

'Not yet,' admitted the young man.

'Trust me, Brune. If you are ever hunting deer with it, just run up and use it like a club.'

Several men approached them. The first, a tall slim bowman in a tunic of fine leather, bowed to Tarantio. 'Are you planning to practise further, sir?' he enquired. 'I have little time myself and was hoping to loose a few shafts.' His dark hair was close-cropped, his head shaved in two crescents above the ears, and he sported a thin trident beard. His clothes were expensive, and he was obviously a nobleman. Knowing how arrogant the nobility could be, Tarantio was impressed by the courteous way he phrased his question.

'No, you may have the target,' said Tarantio amiably. 'My friend and I are finished here. Where can I purchase a good bow?'

'For you, or your friend?' enquired the man.

'For him.'

'Have you considered a crossbow? I saw your friend shoot, and – with all respect – he does not have an eye for it.'

'I fear you are right,' agreed Tarantio. The slim bowman turned to one of his companions, calling him forward. The man held a black crossbow, its stock engraved with silver, which the bowman took and offered to Tarantio.

'Let him try a shot or two with this,' he suggested.

'You are most kind.'

'It is very pretty,' said Brune. 'How does it work?'

Tarantio touched the top of the crossbow to the ground, placing his foot inside the iron stirrup at the head, then drew back the string. Taking a small black bolt from the bowman he slid it home. 'Aim it towards the target, then squeeze this lever under the stock,' he told Brune. Brune lifted the crossbow and squeezed. The bolt vanished into the sand-sacks some eight feet to the left of the target.

114

'That was closer,' said Brune. 'Wasn't it?'

The men with the bowman laughed. The bowman himself moved to stand before the sandy haired Brune, looking closely into his eyes. 'Which is your bad eye?' he asked.

'This one,' said Brune, tapping his right cheek.

'Can you see out of it at all?'

'I can see colours with it, but it doesn't work very well.'

'Have you always had this problem?'

'No. Only since someone hit me with a lump of wood.'

'Your friend is almost blind in the right eye,' he told Tarantio. 'Take him to Nagellis, in the North Quarter. There is a magicker there named Ardlin, who has a house beside the Three Heads fountain. You can't miss it – it has a huge stained-glass window showing the naked form of the Goddess Irutha.' The man smiled. 'It is a fine window. Ardlin is a healer of great talent.'

'Thank you,' said Tarantio. 'You are most kind.'

'Think nothing of it, my friend.' The bowman offered his hand. 'My name is Vint.'

Tarantio looked into the man's smoke-grey eyes. 'And I am Tarantio,' he told him, accepting the handshake.

Vint's face hardened. 'That is a pity,' he said. 'I was rather hoping that when we finally met I would dislike you.'

'There is much to dislike,' said Tarantio. 'You just don't know me well enough yet.'

'Let us hope that is true,' said Vint. 'Where may I call upon you?'

'I have rented a house not far from here. I believe the street is called Nevir North. The house has red tiles and two chimneys. The owners placed a stone wolf to the right of the gate.'

'This afternoon then, an hour before dusk?' offered Vint.

'That is suitable,' agreed Tarantio.

'Sabres?' asked Vint.

'Bring two,' said Tarantio. 'I prefer short swords, but I'll gladly borrow one of yours.'

'No, no. Short swords it is. Would you object if I brought some of my younger students?'

'Not at all.'

'*They can carry his body back*,' said Dace.

Tarantio turned away. Brune handed back the crossbow and hurried after him. 'What is happening?' he asked.

115

'Let's find this magicker, Brune,' said Tarantio. 'I can't teach the bow to a half-blind archer.'

'Why is that man going to fight you?'

'It is what he does,' Tarantio told him.

*

Karis was not easily shocked. Her early life of pain, betrayal and brutality at the hands of her father had birthed in her a cynicism that allowed her to accept the outrageous as if it were commonplace. But when she crested the last rise before the Great Northern Desert, she was stunned. Expecting a vista of bare rock and drifting sand, she was met by a landscape of verdant green dotted with woods and streams.

She knew this area well, having fought two skirmishes here last year. There was no way she could have lost her bearings. To her left, the sun was low in the sky. Ahead, therefore, was north. No question of it.

Guiding the great grey gelding down the slope, she rode to the grasslands and into a grove of trees beside a rippling stream. Dismounting, she loosened Warain's saddle-girth, but did not remove the saddle. Then she let him wander and graze. Warain was well trained, and would come to her fast at a single whistle. Sitting beside the stream, Karis drank deeply, then emptied her water canteen and refilled it.

Perhaps the Eldarin have come back, she thought. What had happened here was the very opposite of the disaster that had struck Eldarin lands during the short-lived war. But the instant the thought came she dismissed it, recalling the words of the Eldarin spirit which had appeared in her room. 'A long time ago the Eldarin faced another evil,' he said. 'We contained it, removed it from the world. The Pearl holds that evil at bay.'

This place does not feel evil, thought Karis. The water is sweet and good, the grass rich and green. What evil, then?

Karis was tired. She had been riding for three days, and had eaten little. Yesterday all she had found was a bush of sweet berries, but these had given her a sour stomach. The day before that she had brought down a pheasant, and cooked it in clay. But there was little meat on the bird.

Allowing Warain to graze for an hour she slept briefly, then summoned the gelding, tightened the saddle and rode back into the dry hills. Ordinarily she would have camped by the stream, but her mind was troubled.

She built a small fire and lay down beside it. It was not cold enough to require a camp-fire, but the flames comforted her, inducing a feeling of safety.

What was the evil the Eldarin had contained?

Karis wished she remembered more of her mother's stories. The flesh-eating tribes of giants had a name, but she could not recall it. She awoke in the night as Warain's front hoof pawed at the ground. Rising, she pulled her bow from the back of the saddle and strung it. 'What is it you hear, grey one?' she whispered, notching an arrow to the bow. In the distance a wolf howled. Warain's head swung towards the sound.

In the bright moonlight Karis scanned the area. There was no sign of movement. 'The wolves will not trouble us, my friend,' she said, moving to the horse and patting its long, sleek neck. Warain nuzzled her shoulder. 'You are the most beautiful male in my life,' she whispered. 'Strong, and true. When we get to Corduin, I'll winter you with Chase. You remember Chase, don't you? The crippled rider.' She scratched the grey's broad brow. 'Now settle down and rest.'

The fire had died and she lay down beside the embers, wrapping her cloak about her.

Just before dawn she woke, and sat up, hungry and irritable. Yesterday she had spotted a deer, but had not killed it. It seemed a great waste of life and beauty to slay such a magnificent beast for the sake of a meal or two. Now she regretted it. Drinking deeply from the canteen, she rose and saddled the gelding. 'If we see a deer today,' she told the horse, 'it dies. I swear my stomach has wrapped itself around my backbone.'

Stepping into the saddle, she rode down once more into the new grassland, heading for Corduin.

The memory of the guard back at the gate was beginning to irritate her. She remembered he was a ten-heartbeat lover – grunt, thrust, sweat and collapse. But where? What had he said – fight like a tiger, live like a whore, look like an angel? He meant it as a compliment, but the word whore did not sit right with Karis. She used men as she used food: to satisfy a hunger, a need she could not – would not – rationalize. Unlike food, however, the men rarely satisfied her.

Even as the thought came to her she remembered Vint, the pale-eyed swordsman. He knew how to satisfy a woman's hunger. His body was lean and hard, his caresses soft and gentle. And, as an added bonus, there was no emotion in him – no fear of love, or jealousy. She had heard that he became the Duke of Corduin's Champion after Tarantio had refused the post. So far he had killed five men in duels. If he was still in Corduin . . .

The sun was high, the sky cloudless as she rode through the green hills. To her right she saw a red hawk swoop down on a luckless rabbit. Hauling on the reins, she scanned the area for a falconer. Hawks, she knew, preferred feather to fur; they had to be wedded to it. But there was no man in sight. The hawk struck the rabbit, sending it tumbling, then settled down to feed as Karis rode on.

Then she remembered the night she had seduced the sentry, Gorl. She and her mercenaries had struck a wagon convoy sixty miles south of Hlobane, when she was under contract to Belliese. That's where the willows were, and she had chosen Gorl because of the lustre of his beard and his deep, soft eyes. Her spirits lifted. Having remembered, she filed him away to be forgotten once more.

'I hope you find a good man,' her mother had said, as Karis prepared to run away into the night. Her father was stretched out on the floor in a drunken stupor.

'You should come with me,' she urged the tired woman.

'Where would I go? Who would have me now?'

'Then let me kill him where he lies. We'll drag the body out and bury it.'

'Don't say that! Please. He . . . was a good man once. He truly was. You just go, my dear. You can find employment in Prentuis – you're a good girl, with a fine body. You'll find a good man there.'

Karis had walked away without a backward glance. Find a good man? She had found scores. Some who made love tenderly, whispering words of endearment, and others who had been rough and primal. Never had she considered wedding any of them. Never had she made the mistake of loving any of them. No, the men who made her stomach tremble she avoided. Sirano had been one.

Tarantio another . . .

'You I will never forget,' she said aloud. She had first seen him swimming in a lake with twenty or so soldiers. It had been a long, dry, dusty march, and when they camped by the lake the men threw

118

off their armour and clothes and ran into the water, splashing each other like children. Karis had dismounted and sat at the lakeside watching them whoop and dive and laugh. But one slim young man did not join in the revelry. He swam away from the group, then walked naked into the undergrowth, emerging moments later with handfuls of lemon mint which he rubbed across his skin. His face and arms were tanned gold, but his chest and legs were white. He was lean, and beautifully muscled, the dark hair on his chest tapering down to a fine line pointing like an arrow to his loins.

'I will have you,' Karis had decided. She had called him over, and he waded to where she sat.

'What is your name, soldier?'

'I am Tarantio.'

'My captain spoke of you.' His eyes were a deep, dark blue, his hair thick and tightly curled. 'He said you were a ferocious fighter. With a thousand like you, he says he could conquer the world.'

He had smiled then and turned from her to swim away. The smile had been dazzling, and in that moment Karis knew she would never take him to her bed.

Warain pulled up now, his ears pricked and his nostrils flaring. Karis looked around, but could see nothing untoward. But she trusted Warain. Angling to the right through the trees she came to a rise and looked down upon the green plain. In the distance four riders were heading towards the hills where she waited. They were being pursued by a score of warriors wearing huge white helms. Karis shaded her eyes.

Below her, hidden in a gully, was another group. These were closer, and she saw the reality – not helms at all, but heads of stark white bone. They were armed with serrated swords, and the fleeing riders were heading straight for them.

Karis pulled her bow clear, strung it, and notched an arrow. Then she heeled Warain into a run down the slope.

The pounding of the gelding's hooves alerted the warriors below and they swung as she thundered towards them. Her arrow slammed into a white neck, then Warain leapt the gully and galloped on towards the riders. Karis pointed to the hills. 'You are in a trap!' she shouted. 'Follow me!' Swinging Warain, she rode hard for the high ground. The riders turned after her, and together they made the long, slow climb.

The pursuing enemy angled up the slope to cut off the escape. Heat flared inside Karis's head, and she felt the onset of a terrible fear. The horses were affected also, and Warain almost stumbled. The grey gelding righted himself, but he slowed almost to a stop and Karis could feel him trembling with terror. 'It is sorcery,' she thought. 'On, Great One!' she shouted, touching her heels to Warain's flanks. At the sound of her voice, his muscles bunched and he surged forward. Three of the enemy riders had cut across the line of escape, and their huge mounts bore down on the fleeing group.

Warain galloped on. Karis angled him towards the first of the massive horses. He needed no urging; he could see the enemy mounts – they were larger and more powerful than he – but Warain was a war-horse of enormous pride. Striding out even faster, the great grey charged at the enemy, his mighty shoulder striking the first horse with tremendous power. With a whinny of pain and terror the enemy horse toppled, pinning its rider beneath it. Warain surged through the gap, and on to open ground, the four smaller horses coming through in his wake.

Karis swung to see the warriors scrambling out of the gully. One still had her arrow in his neck, and she watched him tear it clear and throw it aside.

Then she was over the crest and out of sight of the pursuing horsemen. Outpacing their pursuers, the group rode on for an hour heading south-west. At the top of a high hill Karis pulled up and looked back. From here she could see for miles; the pursuit had been abandoned. Leaning over Warain's neck, she stroked her fingers through his white mane. 'I am proud of you,' she whispered. A middle-aged man, wearing the armour of a Corduin lancer, approached her. 'My thanks to you, Karis,' he said. 'The Gods alone know what would have become of us had you not been to hand.'

She remembered him from her time in the Duke's service – a good man, sound and cautious, but not lacking in courage. 'What were they, Capel?' she asked him.

'They are Daroth. And I fear the world has changed.'

CHAPTER SIX

ARDLIN STOOD AT HIS HIGH BALCONY WINDOW, GAZING OUT towards the north. The trembling had stopped now, but the fear remained. The dream had been vivid, rich with colour: the colour of blood, red and angry. Ardlin had found himself floating above the scene, watching a group of soldiers attacked by Daroth warriors. There was a fat officer, who fell from his horse and tried to run. The Daroth caught him and stripped him naked; then they dug a fire-pit. What followed was stomach-wrenchingly awful. Ardlin had jerked awake, his face and body sweat-drenched.

At first he had felt an overpowering sense of relief. It was a dream. Just a dream – born of his fascination with the ancient races. But as the morning wore on his concern grew. He was a magicker with a talent for healing; he knew spells, and could concoct potions. Above it all, however, he was a mystic. A Sensitive, as the Elders would have said.

Ardlin had tried to put the dream behind him, but it nagged and tugged at his thoughts.

At last, around mid-morning, he sat on the floor of his sanctum and induced the Separation Trance. Floating free of his body he flew to the north, across the rich hills and valleys towards the mountains of the desert. He did not consciously direct his flight, but allowed the memory of the dream to draw him on.

In the hills he found the fire-pit, and the remains of several corpses. The head of the fat officer lay beneath a bush, dead eyes staring up at the sky, flies crawling across the bloody stump that lay exposed beneath the chin.

Ardlin fled for the sanctuary of his body.

The Daroth were back.

For thirty years Ardlin had been a collector of ancient tomes and artefacts, and had spent many long, delightful hours studying the clues of the past. His main fascination had been with the Oltor. No-one now living had any idea how their society had been structured, nor how their culture had flourished. Ancient writings merely stated that they were a gentle golden-skinned race, tall and slender, and gifted with an extraordinary talent for music. It was said they could make crops grow through the magic of their harps. According to one tome, it was with this magic that they inadvertently opened two gateways – one to the desolate world of the Daroth, the other to the world of the Eldarin.

Ardlin remembered the story well. The Oltor had welcomed the new races, holding the barrier open so that great numbers of Daroth could move through. Their own land had become a desert, and the Daroth were dying in their multitudes.

The Oltor granted them a huge tract of land in the north, so that they could grow crops and build cattle-herds, in order to send the food back to their own world. But more and more Daroth came through the gateway, demanding ever more land. Being gentle and trusting, the Oltor allowed the migration to continue.

Several hundred Eldarin also came through, and built a city in the southern mountains, near the sea.

As the years passed the Daroth grew in numbers, and the land they had been granted became less fertile. Forests had been ruthlessly cut away, exposing the earth to the full force of the hot summer winds which seared the grass and blew away the topsoil. Over-grazed and badly used, the grassland began to fail. Then the Daroth dammed the three major rivers, bringing drought to the Oltor.

They sent representatives to the Daroth, urging them to reconsider their methods. In return the Daroth demanded more fertile land. The Oltor refused. And died . . .

Huge and powerful Daroth warriors had sacked the cities of the Oltor, destroying them utterly. Ardlin remembered the chilling line from the Book of Desolation. *Invincible and almost invulnerable, the Daroth could not be slain by arrow or sword.*

Now he stood on the balcony, wondering how he could escape the holocaust that would follow. Most men who knew him assumed him to be rich and, indeed, he had been. Fortunes had been paid for his skills, enabling him to build this fine house and to keep three mistresses. The fortunes had also funded his other great pleasure: gambling. There was no greater thrill than to wager on the roll of the dice, watching the cubes bounce across the ivory-inlaid walnut table – seeing the twin green eyes of the leopard and the staff of the Master appear as the dice came to rest. The ecstasy of that moment left a taste in the heart that was stronger than any opiate – better than the joys in the arms of his mistresses. It seemed to Ardlin that it was the very taste of life itself.

Unfortunately the eyes and the staff appeared all too infrequently when Ardlin threw. And he had wagered greater and greater sums.

Now he had nothing left to wager, and instead of possessing fortunes he owed them.

On the balcony, he ran his slender hand through his thinning hair and sighed. Fortunes meant nothing now. What he needed was a good horse, some supplies, and enough gold to purchase passage on a ship from Loretheli to one of the larger, settled islands.

Heavy and huge, the Daroth were said to fear crossing water and on an island he might be safe. At least he would be a lot safer than here, in this doomed city.

The problem was that he had no horse, nor money to purchase one. The great house was now empty of all valuables, and all of the friends he had made during his stay in Corduin had been sucked dry. He could think of no-one who would advance him a single copper piece.

How long, he wondered, until the Daroth army reaches the gates of Corduin? Two days? Five? Ten? Panic caused him to tremble once more. In the old days he would have gone to his medicine store and chewed on the Lorassium leaf. That would have calmed him. But there were no leaves now, and no money to buy them.

Leaving the balcony, Ardlin walked down to the kitchen and pumped water into a jug. Then he filled a goblet and drank. The water only highlighted his hunger . . . and there was nothing to eat.

A loud knock came at his front door, causing him to jump. Silently he made his way to the observation panel and slid it open.

There were two men standing outside, one lean and slim, his hair dark and short-cropped to the skull; he was dressed in a black leather jerkin, dark leggings and boots. Beside him was a gangling young man carrying a longbow. They were not creditors . . . but they could be collectors. The dark one looked like a collector – hard and lean. On the other hand they might be in need of his services, which meant money. Ardlin bit his thin lower lip. What to do?

'There's no-one here,' he heard the hulking young man say. 'Maybe we should come back later? Anyway, I'm not sure I want someone poking around in my eye. Maybe it will get better on its own.'

Ardlin ran to the front door, took a deep breath to compose himself, then smoothed down his silver hair. He opened the door. 'Good day, my friends,' he said, his voice deep and resonant. 'How may I be of service to you?'

The dark-haired young man had eyes of the deepest blue. 'My friend here has an injury to his eye. We were recommended to you.'

'Indeed? By whom?'

'Vint.'

'A charming fellow. Do come in, my friends. Despite this being my day of rest, I will see you – as a mark of respect to the noble Vint.'

He led them through to his sanctum and seated Brune on a low chair by the window. From a mahogany box he took a thick piece of blue glass which he held over Brune's right eye, peering through it for some moments. 'The injury was caused by a blow to the head, yes?' he said.

'With a lump of wood,' said Brune.

'Tell me, do you experience stabbing pains behind the eye?'

'In the mornings,' admitted Brune. 'But they go away quick.'

Ardlin returned the glass to its box, then sat down behind an elaborately carved desk of oak. 'The damage to the eye is extensive,' he said. 'I cannot make this any easier for you. You will lose the sight in that eye completely.'

'Got the other one, though, eh?' said Brune, his voice shaking.

'Yes. You will have the other one.'

'There is nothing to be done?' asked the dark-haired young man.

'Not with the eye in its present condition. I could . . .' Ardlin paused for effect. 'But no, such a solution would be far too costly, I fear.'

'What is the solution?' asked the man. Ardlin's heart leapt.

'I have in my possession an orb, a magical orb. I could replace the eye. But the orb is an ancient piece, and its worth incalculable.'

The young man rose and stood facing Ardlin. In the light from the window it seemed to the magicker that the man's eyes had changed from dark blue to arctic grey. 'My name is . . . Tarantio,' he said. 'Have you heard the name?'

'Sadly, no.' Ardlin felt a touch of fear as he gazed into those eyes.

'Like Vint, I am a swordsman.'

'Each to his own,' said Ardlin smoothly.

'Now you name a price, magicker, and then we will dicker over it.'

'A hundred gold pieces.'

Tarantio shook his head. 'I do not think so. Ten.'

Ardlin forced a laugh. 'That is ridiculous.'

'Then we will trouble you no further. Let's go, Brune.'

Ardlin waited until they had reached the door. 'My friends, my friends,' he called, 'this is no way to behave. Come back and sit down. Let us discuss the matter further.'

In his heart he knew he had lost.

But ten gold pieces would get him to a safe island . . . and that was worth a dozen fortunes.

*

'Will it hurt?' asked Brune.

'There will be no pain,' Ardlin assured him.

'How long will this take?' asked Tarantio. 'I am meeting Vint later today.'

'The process will take around two hours. Do you have the gold with you?'

'Yes. I'll pay you when I have seen the results.'

'Not a trusting man, then? Very well, you can wait here. Follow me, young man,' said Ardlin.

'You're sure this isn't going to hurt?' asked Brune, rising.

'I'm sure.' Ardlin took him through to a back room and bade him lie down on the narrow bed by the window. Brune did so. Ardlin touched the young man on the brow, and instantly Brune fell into a deep sleep.

The magicker moved to the wall, opening a secret panel and removing a pouch. Opening the drawstrings, he tipped out the contents into the palm of his hand. There was a silver ring, a copper locket, a lock of golden hair wrapped in silver wire, and a small round piece of blood-red coral. Each of the items was of great value to his profession. The ring aided him in the Five Spells of Aveas; the locket kept him free of the diseases which afflicted many of his clients, and the lock of hair boosted his mystic insight into the cause and cure of most ailments. The Oltor coral, however, was the masterpiece in his collection. It could rebuild ruined tissue, muscle and bone. When first he had acquired it, the coral had been the size of a man's head. But each time it was used it shrank. Now it was no larger than a pebble.

The damage to the eye would make no perceptible difference to the coral, he knew, for though extensive in human terms, the injury covered only a small area of tissue. Holding the coral above the sleeping Brune's right eye, Ardlin focused his concentration, feeling the coral grow warm in his hand. Lifting the eyelid, he took the round glass magnifier and examined the eye. All the damage had been repaired. However, he had promised them a magical orb in place of an eye, and it would take but a small spell to recolour the iris. Green would be pleasant, he thought. Holding the coral once more over Brune's face he began to speak one of the Five Spells of Aveas: the Spell of Changing. As he was almost finished he heard footsteps outside the room, and the creak of the door opening. In a rush he finished the spell, his whispered words tumbling out. The heat of the coral surged in his hand.

Ardlin's jaw dropped. Opening his hand, he stared down at the pink skin of his palm.

The coral had vanished.

It was impossible! There was enough power left to heal the wounds of twenty, perhaps thirty men. How could it have exhausted itself

126

with such a simple transformation? He heard Tarantio speak, but was too stunned to understand the words. The swordsman repeated them.

'Is he cured, magicker?'

'What? Oh, yes.' Ardlin lifted Brune's eyelid. His right eye was now covered with a golden sheen, the pupil hidden beneath it. Ardlin was both surprised and relieved. How had he made the mistake? And would the young man be able to see? Sweat broke out on Ardlin's face.

'What is troubling you?'

'What *troubles* me? You have witnessed the end to my career as a healer. I had a magic stone, but now it is used up, the power gone. Ten gold pieces!' He gave a wry laugh and shook his head. 'A man once paid a thousand pieces of gold to heal a crooked arm. It took less power than your friend's eye.' Ardlin sighed and fell silent as Tarantio counted out the coins and dropped them into his outstretched palm. 'Tell me, swordsman, why were you so confident that I would take such a paltry sum?'

'Look around you, magicker,' answered Tarantio. 'This grand house is empty of ornament. There are indentations in the rugs where furniture once stood. You are poorer than a blind beggar, and in no situation to haggle.'

'Sadly true,' admitted Ardlin. 'But at such times is it not cruel to take advantage of a man's misfortunes? The work I have done for your friend is worth far more than ten coins. He has the eye of an eagle now.'

'Aye, maybe it is,' admitted Tarantio. 'But that was the bargain. And I have honoured it.'

Ardlin's thin face sagged. 'I need to get out of the city, Tarantio. These coins will book me passage on a ship from Loretheli. But I have no means to purchase a horse to get there. I beg you to reconsider. My life depends upon it.'

Brune awoke and sat up, blinking. 'I can see everything,' he cried happily. 'Better than ever before!' He moved to the window and stared at the trees outside. 'I can see the leaves, one by one.'

'That is good,' said Tarantio. 'Very good.' Turning to the magicker, he stood for a moment in silence. Then his face relaxed and he smiled. 'Go to the merchant, Lunder. Tell him I sent you.

Tell him Tarantio says to supply you with funds for a good horse and supplies.'

'Thank you,' said Ardlin humbly. 'In return, let me offer you this advice: Leave the city. It is doomed.'

'The armies of Romark won't lay siege to Corduin,' said Tarantio. 'Too costly.'

'I am not talking about the wars of men, swordsman. The Daroth have returned.'

*

Karis, Capel and the boy, Goran, were led into the Duke's private rooms. The ruler of Corduin looked older than Karis remembered; his thin beard, closely shaved to his chin, was salt and pepper now, but his dark hooded eyes were as coldly alert and intelligent as ever. He sat on his high-backed chair, leaning forward, his slender arms resting on his knees as Capel gave his report. Then he turned his hawk eyes on Karis.

'You saw all this?' he asked her.

'I did not see the attack on his men, nor the dark moon rising. But I saw the Daroth. He speaks the truth, my lord.'

'And how was it that you were riding into my lands, Karis? Do you not serve Sirano?' He almost spat out the name.

'I did, my lord.' Swiftly Karis told him of the experiments with the Pearl, and of the ghostly vision of the Eldarin. 'He warned Sirano that a great evil would be unleashed. Sirano did not listen. I believe the Daroth were the evil he spoke of.'

Turning to a manservant standing close by, the Duke ordered his Council to be gathered. The man ran from the room. 'I have studied history all my life,' said the Duke. 'History and myth. Often have I wondered where the two meet. Now, thanks to the insane ambition of Romark, I am to find out.' Rising from his chair he walked to the bookshelves lining the far wall, and selected a thick leather-bound tome. 'Come with me to the Meeting Hall,' he said. With the book under his arm he made for the door, where he stopped and waited; just for a moment the ruler of Corduin seemed lost and confused. Karis suppressed a smile, wondering how long it had been since he had been forced to open a door for himself. Then she moved forward to open it for him. The Duke strode out into the hallway beyond and led them deep into the palace. There was a huge, rectangular table

128

in the Meeting Hall, and seats for thirty councillors. The Duke sat at the head of the table and opened the book, tracing the words with his fingers as he read. Karis, Capel and the boy, Goran, stood silently beside him.

The first of the councillors arrived within minutes, but they did not disturb the Duke; they merely sat quietly in their places. Gradually the chairs began to fill. The last to arrive was the swordsman, Vint, the Duke's Champion. Dressed in a stylish tunic of oiled leather embossed with silver swirls, he looked just as cruelly handsome as Karis remembered. He had not sported the shaved crescents above his ears when last she had seen him, nor the two silver earrings in his left ear. But then fashions among the nobility changed faster than the seasons. He flashed her a broad smile, and gave an extravagant bow. 'Always a pleasure to see you, my lady,' he said.

The Duke looked up. 'You are late, Vint.'

'My apologies, my lord. I was on my way to a duel, but I got here as fast as I could.'

'I don't like you fighting for anyone but me,' said the Duke. 'However, that is a small matter. I hope the man you killed was not a friend of mine?'

'Happily no, my lord. And there was no duel. Your servant found me as I was on my way to his home. I have, of course, sent a message to him, apologizing for the necessity of postponing our meeting.'

'Well, sit you down,' said the Duke. 'I think you will find the duel postponed indefinitely.' He glanced up and scanned the faces of his councillors. 'All of you listen well to what you are about to hear. Understand that this is no jest. The decisions made here today will affect us all for the rest of our lives. Those lives, I should add, might not be very long-lived.' Turning his head, he glanced at Goran. 'You speak first, boy. Tell it all as you told me.'

Nervous and trembling in such company, Goran began to speak at speed, his words tumbling out. Karis stopped him. 'Slowly, boy. Take it from the beginning. You were looking after your sheep, and then you saw something. Go from there.'

Goran took a deep breath, then told of what he had seen. Then Capel addressed them, outlining the tragedy that had befallen his captain and most of the men. Lastly Karis spoke, describing the actions of Sirano and the words of the Eldarin ghost.

Then there was silence. It was Vint who broke it. 'I know

nothing of these Daroth,' he said, 'but if they can bleed I can kill them.'

'Do not be too sure,' warned Karis. 'When my horse leapt the gully I put an arrow into the throat of one of them. It was a lucky shot, but it struck true. Not only did it not kill him, but he clambered out of the gully, tore the arrow loose and threw it aside. They are huge, these Daroth, and mightily muscled.'

'Karis is quite correct,' said the Duke. 'No arrow or sword can kill them. That's what it says here, in this ancient book. In war they are sublime killers, impervious to pain. Their strength is prodigious. Many of the stories here are – in essence – myths. But all myths contain a grain of truth. According to this source there were . . . are? . . . seven cities of the Daroth. Twenty thousand or so Daroth live in each city. There is a map here. Five of the Daroth cities are too far away to trouble us now. One other is more than two months' ride from Corduin. That leaves only the last; it has no name, but we will call it Daroth One. Let us assume that there are twenty thousand Daroth living there. What size of army could they muster? And what must we do to combat them?' His dark eyes scanned the assembly. 'Let us begin with reaction to what we have heard.'

One by one the councillors spoke, asking questions of Capel, Goran and Karis. The warrior woman coolly read the mood of the councillors: they were stumbling in the dark, confused and uncertain. After the meeting had been in progress for an hour, she stepped up to the Duke. 'If I may, my lord?' she said, with a bow. 'I do have a suggestion.'

'I would be glad to hear it,' he told her.

'There is little we can do to plan until we know the intentions of the Daroth. This we cannot ascertain until we have sent a delegation to them. I propose that a small group should be selected to ride north and meet with their leaders.'

'We do not even know the language they speak,' objected Vint. 'And from the way they attacked Capel and his men, one would surmise they are in no mood to negotiate.'

'Even so,' said Karis, 'there is really no alternative. We need to know their numbers, their fighting style, their weaponry, their strategies. Do they have siege-engines? If not, no matter how strong they are they will not breach the walls of Corduin. Language is not the greatest problem here. Lack of knowledge is what could destroy us.'

'Would you lead this group, Karis?' asked the Duke.

'I would, my lord – for a thousand in silver.'

Vint's laughter boomed out. 'Ever the mercenary, Karis!'

*

Albreck, Duke of Corduin, entered his private apartments and sat down on a richly embroidered couch. One of his manservants knelt before him, pulling off the Duke's boots. Another brought him a crystal goblet filled with cooled apple juice; Albreck sipped the drink, and handed the goblet to the servant.

'Your bath is prepared, my lord,' said the man.

'Thank you. Is my wife in her apartments?'

'No, my lord, she is dining with the Lady Peria. She has ordered her carriage to be ready for her return at dusk.'

Albreck stood. The two servants undressed him and removed his rings; then he strode naked to the rear rooms and slowly descended the steps into the sunken bath. Servants scurried around him, bringing buckets of warmed, perfumed water which they added to the bath, but the Duke was oblivious to them.

The War of the Pearl was a costly nonsense, which Albreck had tried hard to avoid. But there was no escape from Sirano's ambition, and the army of Hlobane had been drawn into the conflict. Now, his army depleted and supplies short, he faced an enemy of unknown power.

'Close your eyes, my lord, and I will wash your hair,' said a servant. Albreck did so, momentarily gaining enjoyment from the rush of warm water to his crown. Nimble fingers massaged his scalp.

All the ancient stories told of the horrors of the Daroth, their ferocity, their malevolence and their cruelty. Not one spoke of art, or love. Was it possible that an entire race could be devoid of such feelings? Albreck doubted it – and in that doubt there was a seed of hope. Perhaps a war could be avoided? Perhaps the old stories were exaggerated.

The servant rinsed his hair, then dried it with a warmed towel. Albreck rose from the bath and donned an ankle-length white robe held out for him. Then he returned to his room and sat beside the fire.

Even if the stories were exaggerated, the truth came through like a searing flame. The Oltor had been wiped out, their race annihilated,

131

their cities rendered to dust. No-one now knew for sure what the Oltor had looked like, nor what kind of race they were. They had saved the Daroth, and in return the Daroth had destroyed them. There was not a great deal of hope to be found in such deeds.

A burning log fell to the hearth. A servant stepped forward swiftly, taking up a pair of brass tongs and lifting it back to the flames. Albreck glanced up. 'Fetch the Chief Armourer,' he told the man.

'Yes, my lord.'

'And bring me the Red Book from my study.'

'At once, my lord.'

Albreck sighed. All his life he had loved the arts: music, painting, poetry. But he also had a passion for history, and would have liked nothing better than to spend his days in study. Instead he had been born to this title, with all its concomitant burdens.

The servant returned within moments, carrying a large book bound with red leather. Albreck thanked him and opened it, scanning the pages which were filled with a neat, flowing script. Each page bore a date, and Albreck found the entry he was looking for. The Chief Armourer had introduced a Weapon Maker to him last summer. The man had designed a new siege engine, which he claimed would help Albreck win the war.

Albreck had long since decided the situation would be resolved – once men realized the true futility of the exercise of war – around a negotiating table, and had no desire to invest in new weapons of destruction. He recalled the Weapon Maker as a large man, brilliant of mind, with a pompous turn of phrase. The pomposity he could ignore, the brilliance was what was required.

The Chief Armourer arrived, breathless and red from running. Albreck thanked him for arriving so swiftly, and asked him if the Weapon Maker was still resident in Corduin.

'Indeed he is, my lord. He is currently working on a new sabre for the swordsman, Vint.'

'I would like to see him. Bring him to my apartments this evening.'

'Yes, my lord. Are we then to build the new siege-engines?'

The Duke ignored him and returned to his reading. He did not see the man bow, nor hear the door click shut behind him.

*

Karis was given a suite of apartments on the first floor of the palace. At her command, servants prepared a perfumed bath for her; then she dismissed them. Vint arrived soon after, just as Karis was undressing.

'May I join you?' he asked.

'Why not?' she answered, lowering her lean frame into the water. Vint chuckled, then doffed his boots, leggings and shirt.

'By Heaven, Karis, you are still the most desirable woman I've ever known.'

'Beautiful sounds better,' she admonished him.

He paused and stared at her critically. 'Well . . . you're not a great beauty, my dove. Your nose is too long, and your features too sharp. Also – to be frank – you are a little too lean. However, that said, I never knew a better bed partner.'

'How coy,' she said, with a smile. 'As I recall, we have not yet rutted in a bed. The back of a wagon, the bank of a river, and . . . oh yes, the hay-loft of a barn. No bed that I can recall.'

'Nakedness and pedantry do not go together,' he said, sliding into the water beside her. 'And now it is your turn to compliment me.'

Reaching out, she stroked the skin of his shaved temples. 'I preferred it when it was long and braided,' she told him.

'One has to remain in style, Karis. It shows the populace where true wealth lies. Now play the game and offer me a compliment.'

'You are among the top fifty lovers I have known.'

His laughter pealed out. 'Ah, but I have missed you, lady. You help to remind me that I am – despite my talents – merely mortal. But you do not fool me. I am in the top ten.'

'Arrogant man,' she said, allowing him to move closer to her.

'Arrogance is one of my many virtues. Will you allow me to accompany you on your mission?'

'Yes. I would have requested you.'

'How pleasing.' Leaning in, he kissed her lips, gently at first and then with increasing ardour. His hand caressed her breast, then his arm circled her waist, lifting her on to him. They made love slowly, and Karis allowed her mind to relax. He was right; he was high on the list of good lovers. But, as enjoyable as it was, there was no time to fully appreciate his skills. Karis increased the rhythm, then began to moan, her breath coming in sharp gasps. Vint's hands gripped her hips, and he too began to move with greater urgency. He sighed as he climaxed. Satisfied that she had fooled him, Karis kissed his cheek, then moved away.

'I needed that,' he said, with a smile. 'I was prepared for a duel, and the blood was up. Sex is certainly a fine substitute for fighting. Not perfect, mind, but close.'

'Who was the lucky opponent?'

'A man named Tarantio. Said to be something of a swordsman.'

Karis laughed aloud. 'Ah my dear, dear Vint. You are the lucky man. Tarantio would have cut your ears off.'

His face hardened, and no sign of humour remained. 'Don't mock me, darling. There is not a man alive to best me with any kind of blade.'

'Trust me, Vint,' she said, her face serious. 'I have seen you both fight and there is in you a quality of greatness with the blade. But Tarantio . . . ? He is inhuman. You were not here when he fought Carlyn; it was awesome.'

'I remember the story,' said Vint. 'Carlyn killed the legendary Sigellus and was challenged by one of his pupils. It was said to have been some fight.'

'It wasn't a fight, Vint, not even close. Tarantio cut him to pieces; he sliced off both the man's ears, cut his nose, then criss-crossed his face with deep cuts. Each one could have been a death stroke, but Tarantio was playing with him. And Carlyn was almost as good as you, my dear.'

'I think you underestimate me, Karis. I am not without a few tricks of my own.'

'I wouldn't want you to be killed. Where would I go for good love-making?'

'I take it Tarantio is also among the top ten of your lovers?'

Karis forced a laugh. 'You will never know. Now tell me where I can find him.'

'You will invite him on to our quest?'

'Yes. And pay him anything for the privilege.'

Vint rose from the bath. Robes had been left draped across a bench seat. Donning one, he passed the other to Karis. 'Are you doing this to stop me from carrying out my duel?'

'Not at all,' she assured him. 'I do not interfere in the lives of my

men. If you wish to die young, then make good on your challenge
– but not until we return.'

Vint smiled. 'Who could deny you anything, Karis?'

There was a discreet tap at the door. When Karis opened it, the
dark-haired boy Goran stood outside. Karis ushered him in and he
stood on the threshold looking nervous and ill at ease. 'What did
you want?' she asked him.

'Can I come with you tomorrow?'

'I do not think that would be wise, boy. Our chances of returning
alive are not great.'

'They took my father. I . . . I need to find out whether he lives.'

'You were close?' she asked.

'He is the finest man who ever walked,' said Goran, his voice
thickening and tears forming in his eyes. 'Please let me come.'

'Oh, let him come, Karis,' said Vint. 'The boy has spirit, and
wouldn't you want to look for your own father?'

Karis's eyes were cold as she turned to Vint. 'If it was my father,'
she said, 'I'd help the Daroth skin him!'

*

Brune sat quietly in the garden behind the house, watching a line
of ants moving up a rose-bush. They filed slowly up the stem of
a late-flowering bud, then down again. Brune focused on the bud,
which was covered with greenfly. The ants were moving up, one
at a time, behind the greenfly, and appeared to be stroking the
aphids. This puzzled Brune: it was as if the tiny black insects were
paying homage to their larger green cousins. But that was ridiculous.
Narrowing his eyes, Brune looked closer. Then he smiled. The ants
were feeding. Stroking the greenfly caused the aphids to produce a
viscous discharge. Brune clapped his hands and laughed aloud.

'What is so amusing?' asked Tarantio, stepping out into the
sunshine. He was carrying a black crossbow with a slim stock and
wings of iron, and a quiver of stiffened leather containing twenty
short black quarrels.

'The ants are milking the greenfly,' Brune told him. 'I didn't know
they did that.'

'What are you talking about?' Tarantio laid bow and quiver on
the stone table beside the bench on which Brune was sitting.

'The rose-bush. Look at the ants.'

Tarantio walked the length of the garden, some sixty paces, and knelt down by the bush for a few moments. Then he returned to the seated Brune. 'I see they are swarming near the greenfly, but what makes you believe they are milking them?' he asked.

'You can see it. Look, there's one feeding now; he's filling his food sac.'

'Are you mocking me, Brune? I can hardly see the bud from here.'

'It's my new eye,' said Brune proudly. 'I can see all sorts of things with it, if I try hard. I was watching the ants earlier. They swap food. Did you know that? They rear up in front of each other, then one vomits . . .'

'I am sure it is fascinating,' said the swordsman swiftly. 'However, we have work to do. I have purchased this crossbow and I'd like to see how your new eye affects your aim.'

Tarantio showed Brune how to cock the weapon, then bade him shoot at the trunk of a thick oak some twenty paces away.

'Which part of the trunk?' asked Brune. Tarantio laughed and moved to the tree, scanning the bark. There was a small knot no more than an inch in diameter. Tarantio touched it with his index finger.

'Just here,' he said. As he spoke, Brune hefted the weapon. 'Wait!' cried Tarantio. The black bolt slammed into the knot, barely inches from Tarantio's outstretched hand. Furious, he stormed back to where Brune stood. 'You idiot! You could have killed me.'

'I hit the knot,' said Brune gleefully.

'But the bolt might have ricocheted. It happens, Brune.'

'I'm sorry. It was just so easy. Don't be angry.'

Tarantio took a deep breath, then sighed. 'Well,' he said at last, 'we know the gold was well spent. The magicker did a fine job. Perhaps a little too fine.' Leaning in close to Brune he stared into the young man's eyes.

'What are you looking at?' asked Brune nervously.

'Your left eye. I could have sworn it was blue.'

'It *is* blue,' said Brune.

'Not any more. It is a kind of golden brown. Ah well, maybe it is just part of the magic from the golden orb.'

'He wasn't supposed to change the colour,' objected Brune, worried now. 'He wasn't, was he?'

'I don't suppose that it matters,' replied Tarantio, with a smile. 'Not if you can see ants feeding. Anyway, it is a good colour. And it better matches the gold of your right eye.'

'You think so?'

'Yes.'

They heard the sound of horses on the road outside. Tarantio's face hardened as Vint came riding to the gate. The Corduin swordsman gave a broad smile and waved as he dismounted. He opened the gate wide, and a second rider came through. Tarantio watched as Karis dismounted, tethering her grey to the gatepost.

'Good to see you again, Chio,' she said.

'And you, Karis. Come to see him die?' he asked.

'Not today. What brings you to Corduin?'

'I grew tired of war,' he told her. 'Added to which I was with the mercenaries your lancers destroyed. I barely got away. Did life prove too dull with Sirano?'

'Something like that,' she agreed. Karis glanced at Brune. 'What is the matter with his eye?'

'Nothing. He sees better than any man alive. What is it you want?'

Karis smiled. 'A little hospitality would be pleasant. A drink perhaps? Then we can talk.'

Tarantio sent Brune inside to fetch wine. Vint sat perched on the edge of the stone table, while Karis sat down opposite Tarantio. She told him of the return of the Daroth, and the murder of the villagers and the soldiers from the northern garrison. Tarantio listened, astonished. Brune returned with a pitcher of wine and four clay cups, but no-one touched the drink.

'You saw them yourself?' asked Tarantio.

'I did, Chio. Horses of eighteen hands or more, huge warriors with white, naked skulls and twisted faces. And the desert is no more. Trust me. The Daroth are back.' She told him of Sirano's assault on the Pearl, and of the ghostly Eldarin. Lastly she outlined the decision of the Council to send a group of riders to meet with the Daroth. 'I will be leading the group,' she said. 'I want you with me.'

'Who else have you chosen?'

'Vint, the boy Goran, and a politician called Pooris. But it must be a small group.'

137

'Forin is in Corduin,' he told her. 'He is a good man – and he knows many stories of the Daroth. He could be useful.'

'I will have him found. Will you come?'

'You have not mentioned a price,' he pointed out.

Karis grinned. 'One hundred in silver.'

'That is agreeable. And what about him?' he asked, gesturing at the green-clad swordsman.

'What about him?' countered Karis.

'He wants to kill me. I do not relish being stabbed to death as I sleep.'

'How dare you?' snapped Vint. 'I never murdered a man in my life. You have my word that our duel will wait until we return. Or is my word not good enough for you?'

'Is his word good, Karis?' asked Tarantio.

'Yes.'

'Then I agree. I won't kill him until we return.'

Vint's handsome face lost its colour. 'You are an arrogant man, Tarantio,' he said, 'but it would be wise to remember the old adage – never a horse that couldn't be rode, never a man that couldn't be throwed.'

'I'll remember that when I find a horse I can't ride.'

'Would either of you mind,' put in Karis, 'if I enquired as to what caused this enmity?'

'A friend of his attacked Brune. Hit him from behind, then tried to kick him while he was unconscious. I stopped him. He drew a knife on me and I broke his arm. Should have killed him, but I didn't.'

'That is not how it happened,' said Vint to Karis. 'My friend was dining when this . . . drunken savage . . . attacked him for no reason.'

'For what it is worth, Vint, I have never known Tarantio to lie. Nor have I ever seen him drunk. But that is beside the point. You are both strong men, the kind I would want with me on this mission. I will not however take either of you if you do not grip hands now, and swear to be sword brothers until we return. I cannot afford such hatred. While we are in Daroth lands, you must each be willing to risk your life for the other. You understand me?'

'Why would he need a sword brother?' asked Vint. 'Surely he could master the Daroth on his own.'

'That is enough!' snapped Karis. 'Shake hands and swear your oath. Both of you.'

For a moment the two men sat in stony silence, then Tarantio rose and offered his hand. Vint stared at it for several heartbeats, then thrust out his own, and the two men clasped each other wrist to wrist. 'I will defend your life as my own,' said Tarantio.

'And I likewise,' hissed Vint.

'We will depart at dawn,' said Karis. 'If your man Forin has not been found by then, we will leave without him.'

'I would like to bring my . . . friend . . . Brune,' put in Tarantio, as Karis moved towards her horse.

She swung back. 'Can he fight?'

Tarantio shrugged. 'No, general, but he has the eyes of an eagle. Trust me on this.'

'As you wish,' she said.

CHAPTER SEVEN

Of all the joys Duvodas had ever known, this was the most intense, the most beautiful. In his young life he had summoned the music of the earth, and watched its magic flow across the land. He had healed the sick, and felt the lifeblood of the universe flowing in his veins. But here and now, as he lay beside his new bride, he felt complete and utterly happy. He stroked her long dark hair as she slept, and stared down at her beautiful face lit by the virgin light of a new dawn. Duvo sighed.

The wedding had been joyous and raucous. Ceofrin had opened his tavern to friends, family and loyal customers. The food and drink were free, and Duvo had played for them. The priest had arrived at noon, the guests pushing back the tables so that he could lay the ceremonial sword and sheaf of corn upon the freshly swept floor. Duvo had put aside his harp and led Shira to the centre of the room. The words were simple.

'Do you, Duvodas of the Harp, agree to this binding of soul and flesh?'

'I do.'

'Do you swear to value the life of this, your beloved, as you value your own?'

'I do.'

'Will you honour her with the truth, and bless her with love for all the days of your life?'

'I will.'

'Then take up the sword.'

Duvo had never before held a blade, and he was loath to touch it. But it was a ceremonial piece, representing defence of the family, that had never been used in combat, and he knelt and lifted it by the hilt. The crowd cheered and Shira's father, Ceofrin, stood by misty-eyed as he did so.

'Do you, Shira, agree to this binding of soul and flesh?' asked the priest.

'I do.'

'Do you swear to value the life of this, your beloved, as you value your own?'

'Always.'

'Will you honour him with the truth, and bless him with love for all the days of your life?'

'I will.'

'Then take up the sheaf, which represents life and the continuation of life.'

She did so, then turned to Duvo, offering it to him. He took it from her hand, then drew her to him, kissing her. The crowd roared their approval, and the revelry began again.

Now it was dawn, and Shira slept on. Dipping his head, he kissed her brow. Sorrow slipped through his joy like a cold breeze, and he shivered.

The Daroth were coming.

That was why he had changed his mind about marrying the girl beside him, for only thus could he guarantee her safety. Now when he left Corduin, she would be beside him, and he would take her far from the threat of war and violence.

Rising from the bed, he took up his harp and sat by the window. Nervously he stroked the strings, reaching out for the harmony. He quite expected to feel nothing, and remembered a walk with Ranaloth through the gardens of the Temple of the Oltor.

'Why did you raise me, Master Ranaloth?' he had asked. 'You do not like humans.'

'I do not dislike them,' answered the Eldarin. 'I dislike no-one.'

'I understand that. But you have said that we are like the Daroth, natural destroyers.'

Ranaloth had nodded agreement. 'This is true, Duvo, and many among the Eldarin did not want to see a child of your race among us. But you were lost and alone, an abandoned babe on a winter hillside. I had always wondered if a human could learn to be civilized – if you could put aside the violence of your nature and the evils of your heart. So I brought you here. You have proved it possible, and made me happy and proud. The triumph of will over the pull of the flesh – this is what the Eldarin achieved many aeons ago. We learned the value of harmony. Now you understand it also, and perhaps you can carry this gift back to your race.'

'What must I beware of, sir?' he had asked.

'Anger and hatred – these are the weapons of evil. And love, Duvo. Love is both wondrous and yet full of peril. Love is a gateway through which hatred – disguised and unrecognized – can pass.'

'How can that be so? Is not love the greatest of the emotions?'

'Indeed it is. But it breaches all defences, and lays us open to feelings of great depth. You humans suffer this more than most races I have known. Love among your people can lead to jealousy, envy, lust and greed, revenge and murder. The purest emotion carries with it the seeds of corruption; they are hard to detect.'

'You think I should avoid love?'

Ranaloth gave a dry chuckle. 'No-one can avoid love, Duvo. But when it happens you may find that your music is changed. Perhaps even lost.'

'Then I will never love,' said the young man.

'I hope that is not true. Come, let us walk into the Temple and pay homage to the Oltor.' Together they had strolled through the entrance. The vast circular building housed hundreds of thousands of bones, laid upon black velvet cloths. Every niche was filled with them – skulls, thigh-bones, tiny metatarsals, fragments and splinters. There was little else here, no statues, no paintings, no seats. On a high table, laid upon a sheet of satin, were a dozen red stones. 'The blood of the Oltor Prime,' said Ranaloth. 'One of the last to die. His lifeblood stained the rocks below him.'

142

'Why did the Eldarin gather all these bones?' Duvo had asked.

Ranaloth gave a sad smile. 'They were a fine people, who knew the songs of the earth. We learned their songs; you now sing many of them. But the Oltor will sing no more. It is fitting that we can walk here and see the result of evil. This is what it means to confront the Daroth. How many hopes and dreams are trapped within these bones? How many wonders lie never to be discovered? This is what war is, Duvo. Desolation, despair and loss. There are no victors.'

Now, in the quiet of the dawn, Duvo began the Song of Vornay – sweet and lilting, soft as the feather of a dove, gentle as a mother's kiss. The music filled the room, and Duvo was amazed to find that not only was the magic still there, but it had changed for the better. Where the power had been passive and impersonal, it was now vibrant and fertile. He was hard pressed to contain it, and found himself playing the Creation Hymn. As his fingers danced upon the strings he became aware of a nest upon the roof outside the window, and the young chicks within it. And below, from the alley, he felt the tiny, irrepressible music in the heartbeat of three new pups, born in the night. Duvo smiled and continued his song.

Suddenly he faltered.

The sense of magic was strong upon him and he realized, with both dread and longing, that new life was closer still . . . within the room. Putting aside his harp, he returned to the bed and lay down beside the still sleeping Shira. As the magic faded from his mind, he reached out one last time, and felt the tiny spark of what in nine months would be his child.

His son . . . or daughter. A sense of wonder flowed through him, and an awesome feeling of humility linked with mortality filled his mind.

Shira awoke and smiled sleepily. 'I had such wonderful dreams,' she said.

*

Sixty miles north-east of Corduin, in a moonlit hollow, Karis studied the ancient map. According to the coordinates they were less than twenty miles from Daroth One. They had seen no Daroth warriors in the four days since they left Corduin, but everywhere there were signs of panic: small villages deserted, columns of refugees fleeing for what they perceived as the safety of the city.

The others were still asleep as the dawn sun rose. Karis added dry wood to the embers of last night's fire and gently blew it to fresh life. Autumn was fast becoming winter, and a chill breeze was blowing down from the mountains.

The politician, Pooris, rose from his blankets, saw Karis by the fire and moved across to her. He was a small, thin man, bald – save for a thin circlet of silver hair above his ears. 'Good morning to you, Karis,' he said, his voice smooth as winter syrup.

'Let us hope it proves so,' she said. He smiled, but the action did not reach his button-bright blue eyes.

'May we speak – privately,' he asked her.

'It does not get much more private than this, Pooris,' she pointed out.

He nodded, then swung a glance to the sleeping warriors. Satisfied they could not hear him he turned again to the warrior woman. 'I am not blessed with physical bravery,' he said. 'I have always been frightened of pain – suffering of any kind. I fear the Daroth.' He sighed. 'Fear is not a strong enough word. I cannot sleep for worrying.'

'Why tell me this?'

'I don't know. To share, perhaps? Is there some secret to your courage? Is there something I can do to bolster my own?'

'Nothing that I know of, Pooris. If trouble comes, stay close to me. Follow my lead. No hesitation.' She looked at him and smiled. 'Bear this in mind also, councillor – not many cowards would volunteer for a mission such as this.'

'Are you frightened, Karis?'

'Of course. We are all riding into the unknown.'

'But you think we will survive?'

She shrugged. 'I hope that we will.'

'I have often wondered what constitutes heroism,' he said. 'Tarantio and Vint are sword-killers. Most people would call them heroes. But does heroism come naturally to swordsmen?'

Karis shook her head. 'Heroes are people who face down their fears. It is that simple. A child afraid of the dark who one day blows out the candle; a woman terrified of the pain of childbirth who says, "It is time to become a mother." Heroism does not always live on the battlefield, Pooris.'

The little councillor smiled. 'Thank you, lady,' he said.

'For what?'

'For listening to my fears.' He rose and walked away through the trees and Karis returned to studying the map. While the Duke's men searched for Forin she had spent her time in the library, reading everything she could find about the Daroth. It wasn't much. She had widened the scope, investigating stories – myths mainly – of a race of giant warriors said to have inhabited the north country. Perhaps these tales were also of the Daroth.

None of the research material she had found had supplied a clue as to what action she should take when they approached the Daroth city. Pooris had suggested riding with a flag of truce. Why should the Daroth recognize this convention, she had asked him?

Forin – who, as Tarantio had told her, knew many stories of the Daroth – had only one suggestion. 'Take salt as a gift,' he said. 'According to my father, who heard it from the Eldarin, the Daroth adore the taste. It works on their system like wine does with us.'

Karis had taken heed. But in order to offer salt to the Daroth, they must first agree to speak. They had not spoken with Capel's men, but had attacked swiftly and without mercy.

Pooris returned from the woods and began to neatly fold and roll his blanket. Forin awoke, belched loudly and sat up. He yawned and stretched; rising, he thrust his hand down the front of his leather leggings and scratched at his genitals. Then he saw Karis, and gave a sheepish grin. 'I like to check that the old soldier is still alive,' he said. Then he too strolled from the camp. He did not go as far as Pooris had done, and Karis could hear him noisily urinating against a nearby tree-trunk.

Pooris reddened, but Karis merely chuckled. 'Do not be embarrassed, councillor,' she advised him. 'You are not among the nobility now.'

'I rather guessed that,' he said.

Tarantio and Brune joined her, then Goran and Vint. They breakfasted on oats they had found in an abandoned village. Goran and Vint sweetened theirs with honey; Tarantio ate his with salt; Pooris was not hungry. And Forin refused the oats, chewing instead upon his ration of dried meat. Brune ate his portion, scraping the last of the porridge from the bowl with his fingers.

'I think we will see the Daroth today,' said Vint. 'They must have outriders. Have you come up with a plan yet, Karis?'

145

Ignoring the question, she finished her meal, then cleaned her plate upon the grass. 'When we do see them, not one of you must draw a weapon,' she said at last. 'You will sit quietly while I ride forward.'

'And if they attack?' asked Pooris.

'We scatter and meet again here.'

'It has the merits of simplicity,' observed Vint. Drawing his knife, he began to scrape away the bristles on his cheeks and chin.

'Why bother to shave?' asked the red-bearded Forin.

'One must observe certain standards,' pointed out Vint, with a self-mocking grin. 'And naturally,' he continued, ' I want the Daroth to see me in the full bloom of my beauty. They will be so over-awed they will immediately surrender to us and swear fealty!'

'Exactly my plan,' said Karis drily.

She kicked earth over the fire, extinguishing it, then they saddled their horses and rode north. The boy, Goran, heeled his mount alongside Warain. 'Do you think my father is still alive?' he asked Karis.

'There is no way to know,' she said, 'but let us pray so. You are a brave lad. You deserve to find him.'

'Father says we don't always get what we deserve,' he pointed out.

'He is a wise man,' said Karis.

They rode on for more than two hours, cresting the low hills before the mountains and heading down through a narrow pass on to the broad grasslands. From here they could see the distant city. There were no walls around it, and the buildings were round, squat and ugly to the human eye.

'Like a huge mound of horse droppings,' observed Forin.

Karis heeled Warain forward and the small troop cantered on.

As they approached the city, a line of twenty horsemen rode from it to intercept them. Karis felt a tightness in her belly. The horses upon which they rode were huge, eighteen hands, dwarfing even the giant Warain. She felt Warain tense beneath her. 'Steady, now,' she said, patting his sleek grey neck.

The leading Daroth warrior drew his long serrated sword and rode at Karis. Untying the pouch at her belt, she rode to meet him with hand outstretched. His sword was raised, his oval jet-black eyes staring hard at her as she came abreast of him. Smoothly she

146

extended her arm and offered him the pouch. Letting go of the reins, he took it from her and clumsily opened it. Salt spilled out. Placing a large finger into his beaked mouth, his swollen purple tongue licked out, wetting the tip. He dipped it into the salt pouch and tasted it.

Re-tying the pouch, he slipped it into a pocket in his black jerkin, then returned his gaze to Karis. 'Why are you here?' he asked, his voice cold, sepulchral.

'We come to speak with your leader,' she told him.

'He can hear you. All Daroth can hear you.'

'It is our custom to speak face to face.'

'You have more salt?'

'Much more. And we can deliver many convoys of it, fresh from the sea.'

'Follow me,' said the rider, sheathing his sword.

*

The city was unlike anything Tarantio had ever seen. The buildings were all spherical and black, unadorned and dull to the eye, built in a seemingly haphazard manner, yet all linked and joined by covered walkways. There were many levels of them, one atop the other.

'It's like a huge bunch of grapes,' said Forin. 'How do they live in them?'

Tarantio did not answer. As they rode on every building disgorged more Daroth, who stood silently watching the small cavalcade. The road was paved and smooth, the sound of the horses' hooves loud in the silence.

'*They are an ugly people,*' said Dace.

'*Perhaps we look ugly to them,*' observed Tarantio.

Ahead were two tall spires. Black smoke drifted lazily from the top of both, forming a pall above the city. Tarantio sniffed the air. There was an odd smell about the place, sweet, sickly and unpleasant.

The roadway widened and the group rode between two black pillars, heading towards a huge grey dome; the smoking spires were situated behind it. The Daroth riders peeled away, leaving only the leader, who dismounted before the round open entrance to the dome.

'Stay with the horses,' Karis told Goran, as the group dismounted.

'I want to find my father,' objected the boy.

147

'If he is here, I will find him,' she promised.

The Daroth entered the dome; Karis and the others followed. The councillor Pooris kept close to the warrior woman; his face was pale, his hands trembling. Tarantio and Forin were just behind them, followed by Vint and Brune.

The huge building was lit by globed lanterns set into the walls, and Karis was amazed to find that no pillars supported the colossal domed ceiling. There were no statues or adornments. At the far end of the circular hall was an enormous table shaped like a sickle blade. Around it were some fifty Daroth warriors, kneeling on the weirdly carved chairs Tarantio had first seen in the Daroth tomb.

'My father would have liked to see this,' said Forin. Tarantio could hear the fear in his voice, but the big man was controlling it well.

Karis moved forward. 'Who is the leader here?' she asked, her voice echoing strangely. A series of clicks sounded from the Daroth, then a warrior at the centre of the table rose.

'I am what you humans would call the Duke Daroth,' he said.

'I am Karis.'

'What is your purpose here?'

'A delegation such as this is our way of showing our peaceful intentions. Let me introduce the councillor Pooris, who has a message from our Duke.' Turning, she gestured Pooris forward. The little man took a nervous step towards the table and bowed low.

'My Duke wishes it to be known that he welcomes the return of the Daroth people, and hopes that this new era will bring trade and prosperity to both our peoples. He wishes to know if there is anything you desire from us, in the way of trade.'

'We only desire that you die,' said the Daroth. 'We will not coexist. This is now a Daroth world. Only the Daroth will survive. But tell me more of the salt you offer.'

Karis watched as Pooris faltered, feeling sympathy for the little politician. The Daroth's words were certainly not honey-coated, and left little room for further negotiation. 'Might I ask, sir,' said Pooris, 'that you expand upon your decision? War is never without cost. And peace can bring riches and plenty.'

'I have said what I have said,' the Daroth told him. 'Now I wish to hear of the salt you will send.'

Pooris stepped forward. His hands were no longer trembling. 'The salt was offered in the spirit of peace. Why would we send it to an enemy?'

'Trade,' said the Daroth Duke, simply. 'We understand that when you humans desire something that you cannot take by force, you trade for it. We will take the salt as trade.'

'In return for what, sir?' asked Pooris.

'We have more than a hundred of your older humans. We have no use for them; we will trade them for their weight in salt.'

'Do you have a man here named . . .' Pooris swung to Karis and gave her a questioning look.

'Barin,' she said.

'He is here,' said the Daroth Duke. 'He is important to you?'

'His son is with us. That is how we know he was captured by you. We would like him returned.'

'He is owned by one of my captains. He does not wish to trade him; he will, however, allow you to fight for him.' The clicking sound came again from the gathered group. Karis took it to be laughter. All her adult life Karis had been skilled in the reading of men. The skull-faced Daroth were not men, but even so she could sense their contempt for the human embassy. In that moment she realized that their chances of leaving alive were slender at best. Under normal circumstances Karis was a cautious leader, but sometimes, she knew, recklessness could carry the day. Calmly she stepped forward, laying her hand on the shoulder of the councillor and drawing him back.

'We did not come here to kill Daroth,' she said coolly. 'But if necessary we will do this. How does one challenge your captain?'

'You already have,' said the Duke. 'He says he will fight the largest of you – the red-bearded one.'

'I choose who fights,' said Karis, 'and I will not use my strongest warrior. It would be beneath him to fight a single Daroth. Before this duel takes place, however, Lord Duke, what are the rules? When my chosen fighter has killed your captain, do we then have possession of the man Barin?'

'If you kill my captain you own all his possessions, for he is pod-lost and cannot live again.'

'And we will be allowed to leave the city?'

'Why would we keep you here? We know all we need to know of your puny race. Your young ones are sweet and tender, your old ones stringy. Who will you choose to fight for the human?'

'Where is the captain?' she demanded.

A Daroth rose from beside the Duke and Karis looked hard at him. The warrior was huge, barrel-chested and powerful. She swung to Tarantio and he nodded acceptance. 'I think your captain looks old and fat,' she said. 'I will therefore use my smallest warrior.'

'When he dies,' said the captain, 'you will become mine. I will feast on you tonight, female. I will swallow your eyes whole.'

Karis ignored him and walked back to Tarantio. 'Can you take him?' she asked, her voice just a whisper.

'I can take anything that lives,' Dace told her. Drawing his short swords, he stepped out to meet the captain. The Daroth was carrying a long, serrated broadsword. As Dace took up his fighting stance he felt a hot stab of pain in his mind, like a flame searing up from his neck and into his cranium. He staggered back.

'They are telepaths,' came the voice of Tarantio. *'Fight through the pain. I will try to block the fire.'*

Dace's anger swelled. Huge as the Daroth was, still he felt he needed the advantage of magic. You may be big, thought Dace, but you are a coward! The pain flared once more.

'He is in here with us,' whispered Tarantio. *'He can hear us.'*

'I think I'll kill him now,' said Dace. He darted forward, ducking under a ferocious cut to slam his sword-blade into the Daroth's belly. The blade did not penetrate more than half an inch. Dace leapt back, swaying away from a slashing blow that would have opened him from shoulder to belly.

'The armpit,' said Tarantio. *'Remember the tomb. They have no bone protection there.'*

The Daroth backed away, his elbows dropping protectively to his sides. *'Yes, I had remembered, brother,'* snapped Dace. *'So good of you to remind our opponent.'* The Daroth, now holding his blade double-handed, ran forward and sent a wicked sweeping cut which Dace parried. Such was the power of the blow that the smaller warrior was sent hurtling to the floor. As Dace rolled to his knees, the Daroth leapt towards him with sword raised. Dace switched his grip on his right-hand sword, holding it now like a dagger. He waited until the last moment, then surged upright, dancing aside as the serrated sword came down. As his sword slammed into the Daroth's armpit, plunging through muscle and tissue, a hideous croaking scream came from the captain, who stumbled and fell to his knees. Dace plunged his second sword into the Daroth's body, alongside the first blade, then levered it up and down. Milk-coloured liquid sprayed from the wound, drenching Dace. Dragging his swords clear he threw himself upon the dying Daroth's back and smashed again and again at the nape of the giant neck and the raised vertebrae showing there. The white skin peeled away, exposing bone. One of the vertebrae cracked, a second suddenly dislodging. The Daroth's head fell sideways. Dace delivered a tremendous blow to the neck, which snapped with a sound that echoed around the hall. The Daroth captain pitched forward from his knees, his face striking the stone floor. The fiery pain in his mind faded away, but still Dace continued to hack at the neck, his blows frenzied and powerful. The head rolled clear.

'That is enough,' he heard Karis say. Dace blinked. He had an urge to rip out the Daroth's dark eyes and swallow them whole. Tarantio surged back into control.

Karis walked to the sickle table and stood silently for a moment. 'As I thought, old and fat,' she said. 'I would like the man, Barin, brought out now. I will trade the rest of his possessions for the prisoners you hold. Added to this – upon my return to Corduin – I will also arrange a wagon of salt to be brought to the edge of your lands.'

'I accept your trade, female,' said the Duke. 'You have entertained us well today. Come the spring – when the Daroth army descends upon your city – you will entertain us more.'

'We will surprise you, my lord, I think.'

'I do not believe so. The human who fought for you is unique. You do not have enough like him to trouble us.'

Karis smiled. 'That remains to be seen. I look forward to your visit.'

*

There were 107 captives, all of them past middle age, and several white-haired elders. They were herded out to the open ground before the dome, where Karis greeted them. The last to arrive was Goran's father, a burly man with dark curly hair and beard. Goran ran to him, and hugged him. Barin ruffled his son's hair, then looked up at Karis. 'We must leave quickly,' he said, his voice low. 'There is no honour among these monsters. And their word is not iron.'

151

Karis nodded, and led the refugees back along the main street of the city of domes. Daroth came from every doorway to stare at them as they made their way towards the grasslands. Karis noticed that all the Daroth eyes were fixed upon the lean figure of Tarantio. He had killed one of them in single combat, and all had felt the blows of his swords.

They reached the outskirts of the city without incident and headed south. 'You must beware of warmth and pain in your mind,' said Barin. 'This will indicate they are reading your thoughts.'

Karis passed the warning back to the others. 'What do you think they will do?' she asked the man.

'The blood relatives of the Daroth cut down by your swordsman will follow you. They will try to take you alive, and keep you until the entombing. Then you will be fed to the wife of the Daroth your man fought – save for your heart, which will be placed in the coffin with the body of her husband.'

'What did the Duke mean about pod-lost?' asked Karis.

'The Daroth are virtually immortal. They exist in a single body for no more than ten years. Then, when the pods are ripe and a new form emerges, the old body is shed. Your man ended the life of the Daroth captain. Under normal circumstances he would have been born again, but his pod was either flawed in some way, or diseased. Whatever the answer, his immortality ended in that hall. Now his relatives will seek to avenge his passing.'

'But why me?' she asked. 'Why not Tarantio who actually killed him?'

'You are the leader. It was you who instigated the duel.'

'What do you suggest?'

'Head for high ground where the air is thin and cold. It affects the Daroth far more than us; they are heavy, and they do not like the cold.'

'You know of such a place?'

'There is a pass through the mountains – some twelve miles east of here. It is very high.'

Once out of sight of the city, Karis led the column down into a deep gully, then changed the direction of travel from south to east. Vint rode alongside her. 'Where are we going?' he asked.

Karis told him of Barin's warning. 'If they do come after us, I do not see how we can fight,' said Vint.

'There is always a way to fight,' snapped Karis. 'My father had a pet python; he used to feed it with live mice. The python was around six feet in length. He made me watch the snake feed. It was . . . nauseating.'

'What has this to do with the Daroth?' asked Vint.

'One day a mouse killed the snake.'

'I don't believe it!'

'Neither did my father; he accused me of poisoning it. But it was true. I freed the mouse. I hope she had a long life, and gave rise to many legends among her kind.'

Heeling Warain into a run, Karis circled the column and galloped back along the line of refugees where she swung into place between Tarantio and Brune. 'You fought well, my friend,' she said with a smile. 'You will become a legend. The Daroth Slayer, they will call you.'

'Their Duke was right,' said Tarantio. 'We will not stop them in the spring. Shemak's Balls, Karis, they are tough to kill! I cannot see how men can defeat them. Their skin is like toughened leather, their bones stronger than teak.'

'Yet you killed one.'

Tarantio smiled. 'There are not many like me,' he said. 'For which I have – up to now – always been grateful.' When Karis told him of Barin's warning, Tarantio ordered Brune to ride to the crest of a nearby hill and watch for signs of pursuit.

By late afternoon the refugees were exhausted, and the line was stretched out over several hundred yards. Brune had returned with good news, that the pursuing Daroth had headed off into the north. So far the ruse had worked. But they were still several miles from the pass, and Karis was loath to allow a rest stop. Forin and Vint gave up their horses to two old men and the convoy moved on, ever more slowly.

At dusk they came to the foothills of the mountains, where Karis allowed the refugees to rest. Dismounting she walked among them. 'I want you all to listen to me,' she said. 'The Daroth are following us and they are intent on slaughter. Ahead of us is a long climb, but it is a climb to life. I know you are all tired, but let fear add strength to your limbs.'

The fear was there; she could see it in their eyes. One by one they pushed themselves to their feet, and moved out onto the slopes.

Brune galloped his horse from the hills. 'They are three – maybe four – miles away,' he said. 'There are twenty of them.'

Hearing this, the refugees began to run.

Karis rode ahead of them, Tarantio, Brune and Pooris with her. At the top of the steepest part of the rise, she reined in and scanned the shadow-haunted pass. For the first 200 yards it rose gently, but then inclined sharply for another 200. Then the walls narrowed to less than fifteen feet apart. She rode Warain up the sharp incline, then dismounted. Huge boulders were strewn across the trail. Glancing up, she saw there were scores more precariously balanced on both walls of rock. With more time she could have set up an avalanche. But was there time?

The first of the refugees staggered by her. Karis called out to them to help, then put her shoulder to a massive boulder some seven feet in diameter. Ten men sprang to help her, and slowly the huge stone began to move. 'Carefully now,' said Karis. 'We do not want to send it down on our own people.' Slowly they rolled the boulder to the edge of the rise. The refugees were streaming up the narrow incline; behind them, less than half a mile distant, came the Daroth.

More than two-thirds of the refugees were behind her now, but around twenty were still struggling up the slope. Tarantio, Vint and Forin ran down to help the stragglers. Brune rode his horse down and lifted one old man across his saddle, galloping him back to safety.

Bunched tightly, the Daroth charged. Eight people had still not reached the incline, as the Daroth bore down on them. A spear smashed through the back of the last man, tearing out his lungs. Karis swore. The surviving seven were doomed, and if she did not act swiftly the Daroth would reach the crest.

'Now!' she cried, and the men beside her threw their weight against the boulder. For a moment only it refused to move, then it slowly rolled clear. Gathering speed, the enormous stone crashed against the right hand wall of the pass, careering off to thunder down the slope.

The first to die was a refugee, his body crushed to pulp. Half-way up the slope, the Daroth saw the threat and tried to turn – but close-packed as they were, there was no escape. The boulder crashed into their ranks, smashing bones and killing horses and riders. Then it hammered against the wall of the pass, dislodging yet more rocks and stones which showered down on the Daroth below. A section

154

of cliff sheared away, plunging down to block the pass. A cloud of dust billowed up, obscuring the carnage.

One refugee came out of the dust, scrambling up the incline to fall at Karis's feet. The man had a gash to his head, and a broken arm. Friends helped him to stand and supported him.

In the dying light of the sun the refugees watched as the dust cleared. Not one Daroth could be seen.

'Let's go home,' said Karis.

*

Karis led the refugees back to their ruined villages, where the ninety-three survivors picked their way through the debris, seeking what possessions they could find. There was little food, for the Daroth had stripped the storehouse and driven away all the cattle. Tarantio, Forin and Brune rode off into the valley to hunt. Karis, Vint and Pooris remained behind. The small politician had said little since their departure from Daroth One, and he sat with shoulders slumped, his back against the wall of the plundered storehouse.

Karis sat down before him. 'What is troubling you, councillor?'

He gave a weak smile. 'Look at all their faces,' he said, waving in the direction of the refugees as they searched through the wreckage. 'They are lost. Ruined. Not because their village has been attacked – such is the lot of farmers, I am afraid. They are lost because they have seen the enemy, and they know their world is gone for ever.'

'They have not beaten us yet,' she said, but Pooris said nothing and Karis returned to where Vint sat by an open fire.

'You did take a chance, lady,' he told her, with a grin. 'Supposing Tarantio had failed.'

'Then we would be dead. But it wasn't that great a risk. As I told you before, I have seen him fight. Now you have too.'

'He is a madman, Karis. I saw that, right enough. God's teeth, I would swear his eyes changed colour. It was like watching a different man.'

'Still think you could take him?'

He laughed aloud. 'Of course. I am invincible, dear lady.' Karis looked into his eyes, amazed to see that he meant what he said. She shook her head.

'When we get back, if you will take my advice, you should go to the tavern where the incident took place and learn for yourself

155

the truth of the matter. It would be folly to fight Tarantio for the wrong reason.'

'I shall do as you say.'

*

Four days later the farmer, Barin, was led into the library rooms of the Duke's private quarters. Karis and Vint were already seated there, as was the councillor Pooris. Barin had seen the Duke once before, leading a parade through Corduin, but never had he been this close to royalty. Albreck was an imposing man, with shrewd deep-set eyes and a hawk beak of a nose. Barin made a clumsy bow. 'Be at your ease, man,' said Albreck. The Duke turned to a servant standing beside him. 'Bring him a goblet of wine.'

The servant did so and Barin stood staring at the goblet, which was fashioned from silver and inset with grey moonstones. Gold wire had been set into the silver in an elaborate swirl, making the letter *A*. The goblet, Barin realized, was worth more than he could earn in a year from his fields. He sipped the wine, and his spirits were lifted by the fact that it was thin and a little sour. Old Eris made better wine back in the village!

'Now,' said the Duke, 'tell us all you can of the Daroth. It is of vital importance.'

'I hardly know where to begin, sire. You already know they are powerful beyond belief.'

'How do they live, how are they governed?' asked the Duke.

'It is hard to say. They can communicate with each other without speech over large distances. As I understand it, their decisions are made communally. Instantly.'

'Would you describe them as evil?'

'Indeed I would, sire, for they do not understand the concept of evil – and in that alone they are terrifying. In the time I was with them, they killed and ate scores of young men and women. They cooked them over charcoal pits, first smothering them in clay. Most were alive when the cooking began. I will never forget the scenes; they are branded into my memory. They asked me why I did not eat. I told them that for us cannibalism was a vile practice. They did not – or would not – understand.'

'Do they have religious beliefs?' asked Pooris.

'They have no need of such, being virtually immortal. They live

156

for only ten years, and twice in that time they create pods – giant eggs – in which they are reborn.'

'What do you mean, reborn?' queried the Duke.

'As I understand it, sire, when the young Daroth are . . . hatched, they lie still, as if dead. The father, if you like, then moves to the . . . infant and a joining takes place. The old body withers and dies, the young body grows to full manhood in a matter of moments. All that is left is the empty pod and the withered husk of the former Daroth. This cycle happens twice in every Daroth lifetime: once for the father, once for the mother. And they go on . . . and on.'

'They told you all this?' put in Karis.

'No. They drained my mind of all knowledge, but in doing so I could read theirs. I saw it, if you will.'

'One aspect troubles me,' said Pooris suddenly. 'If the Daroth only breed to replace father and mother, how then does their population grow?'

'There is a special season, once every fifty years,' explained Barin. 'I cannot translate their name for it, but my own would be the Time of Migration. At this time the Daroth become hyper-fertile, if you will, and the pods can contain two or sometimes three infants. This last happened – in their time scale – four years ago; it led to the building of the city you call Daroth One. That is why the land around the city is so fertile. It has not yet had its heart ripped out.'

Vint drew up a chair for Barin. 'Sit you down, man. You look exhausted.'

Barin did so. 'Aye, sir, I am tired beyond belief.'

'You say they have no concept of evil. What did you mean by this?' asked Albreck.

Barin tried to gather his thoughts. 'I can answer it only as a farmer, lord. When the blowfly attacks a sheep it will kill it horribly, laying its eggs inside the living sheep. But the blowfly is not evil; it merely wishes to extend its life. The Daroth are like that, with the exception that they know the havoc they cause to other species. But they do not care. They do not love the land. They live only to live again. No music, no culture. They are parasites, their cities ugly and temporary. When they exhaust the land of all nourishment they merely move their cities to fresh ground. They are makers of deserts.'

'What of friendship, camaraderie?' asked Karis. 'Do they have legends of heroes?'

157

'No legends, lady, for they have lived for ever. They love to fight. Without an external enemy, they fight amongst themselves. But if one is slain his body is taken to the pod, and left there until the new body is born.' Barin talked for more than an hour, telling them of the Oltor and of their total destruction. 'They hunted the last of them through a mighty forest. I saw the Daroth slaughter them. The Oltor were a peaceful people, tall and slender, their skin golden. They had no weapons. And they were all exterminated.'

'We are not Oltor, and we do have weapons,' said Karis.

'They will not be stopped, my lady,' said Barin sadly. 'In the far distant past, when they warred upon one another, they created engines of great destruction. Giant catapults that could smash down the walls of a castle, battering-rams to breach any gate. With one blow they can cut a man in half. They are deadly beyond our imagining.'

'Yet we killed them when they came after us,' Karis reminded him.

'You will not hold Corduin, my lady.'

'Let us talk of weaknesses,' said the Duke sternly. 'What do they fear?'

'Deep water, my lord. They are too heavy to swim, and they abhor boats. Also, perhaps because of their great weight, they do not function well at high altitudes where the air is thin. Lastly, there is the cold. They need heat; in winter they become lethargic and slow.'

The evening wore on until at last Duke Albreck rose and approached Barin. 'You have done well, farmer,' he said, tossing a pouch of gold coins which Barin caught. 'You are welcome to stay in the palace until you can find a new home.'

'Thank you, lord,' said Barin, rising. 'But, by your leave, I shall take my son to Loretheli and travel to the islands.'

'As you will. Though I understand it will be safe here until the spring.'

'Not so, my lord. A Daroth army of more than five thousand was sent out two days before the Lady Karis arrived. I do not know their destination.'

'If it had been Corduin, we would know by now,' said Karis.

Albreck walked to the far wall and stared at the ancient map hanging there. 'There can be only one destination,' he said, stabbing

158

his finger towards the map. 'The Lord Sirano is, I fear, about to reap the harvest of his ambitions.' Dismissing the others, he bade Karis stay. That she was a superb leader of men he already knew; that she was a whore was meaningless to him. Men who had a hundred lovers were admired. Albreck could see no reason why the situation should be so different with a woman. What worried him was something far more serious.

She was still dressed in her travel-stained clothes and he bade her sit opposite him. She was a striking woman, he thought, with a leanness that ought to have made her appear masculine, yet somehow emphasized her femininity. 'I shall have my tailor attend you,' he said.

Karis laughed. 'I am not looking at my best, my lord,' she admitted.

'I shall speak frankly. I am considering asking you to conduct the defence of Corduin. Yet I am troubled.'

'I am more suited to moving campaigns,' she said. 'But I do have experience of sieges.'

'That is not what troubles me, Karis. I do not doubt your talents; I doubt your temperament.'

'You are a plain speaker, my lord. How does my temperament offend you?'

'It does not offend me. I am not easily offended. I had an elder brother – did you know that?' Karis shook her head. 'He was a fine man, but he loved danger. When we were children he once climbed to the palace roof, and ran along the top of the parapet. My father was furious, and asked him why he had done it. Did he not realize that one slip, one gust of wind, and his life would have ended? You know what he said, don't you?'

'Yes, he told him that was why he did it.'

'Exactly. The moment of madness, the exultation that comes with spitting in the eye of death.'

'This is something you have experienced, my lord?' she asked him, surprised.

'No. Never. But that is what my brother told me. Two months before my father died my brother travelled with some friends into the high country where there was a mountain which no man had ever climbed. My brother climbed it; he was killed in a rock slide

159

on the way down. There was no need to climb that mountain; it achieved nothing. And he died.'

'And you think I am like your brother?'

'I know that you are, Karis. You live your strange life on the edge of an abyss. Perhaps you are a little in love with death. But my city is in peril. To defend it will require dedication, constancy and skill.'

Karis was silent for a moment, remembering first the time when she stood naked on the crumbling balcony in Morgallis, and then the issuing of the challenge to the Daroth leader. She looked in the Duke's hooded eyes. 'You can rely on me, my lord. I know that what you say of me is true. I do, perhaps, love death, and I am at my most content when standing upon the edge of the abyss.' She laughed. 'Therefore, where else would I choose to be than Corduin? The abyss is coming – black and terrifying. In the spring it will be just outside the walls.'

*

When Karis had fled the city, Giriak had experienced two emotions. The first had been disappointment, for in his own way he had loved the warrior woman. Unlike any lover he had known Karis fired his blood, and his feelings for her were rooted deep. The second emotion, however, had been joy, for Sirano had given him command of her lancers. Giriak had always known he was as good a leader as she. Most of her victories, he believed, had been achieved due to his part in them. This was what made the current situation so galling, for since she had gone he had led two raids on the south, both of which had gone disastrously wrong. They would, he knew with absolute certainty, have failed even if Karis had been the commander. He was sure of that, even if his men were not.

The one quality, it seemed to Giriak, that Karis had enjoyed above all others was luck. That was the only difference; he told himself this time and again, as if the constant repetition would make it true. All his life he had been cursed by bad luck. At an early age he had discovered a talent for running and he had trained hard under the watchful eye of his father, the village blacksmith. But another boy had beaten him in the Shire Finals after Giriak had stepped into a rabbit hole and twisted his ankle. Dark and handsome he had even lost out in love. Gealla had been all that he had wanted; he had courted her, and won her heart. But one of his so-called friends

160

had told her of his illicit liaison with another village girl, and she had spurned him and married another. Even as a soldier Giriak had been overlooked – except by Karis. She had promoted him to be her second in command and here he had excelled, despite her occasional meddling in his decisions.

Giriak stepped down from the saddle and tethered the gelding. Then he climbed the rampart steps of the north wall, where the veteran Necklen was supervising repairs. The Lord Sirano – thank the Gods – had ceased using his magic on the Eldarin Pearl, and the minor earthquakes no longer struck the city. Not that it mattered much, thought Giriak. Morgallis was pretty much deserted anyway. Of the 85,000 people who had inhabited the city four months ago, now only around 5,000 remained. The rest had fled south to Prentuis where, according to rumour, they were housed outside the city in a huge camp of canvas tents.

All across Morgallis, taverns and shops were closed and boarded up.

'Almost there, Captain,' said Necklen, wiping sweat from his thin face and grey beard. 'The gap is filled, but the whole wall is riddled with cracks.'

'There is no force to assail the city,' said Giriak, gazing down at the work party, ferrying rubble and mortar to the wall. 'But Sirano wants the repairs done anyway.'

'We should be moving on,' said Necklen, keeping his voice low. 'This is like a city of ghosts. The men are getting anxious. Most of the whores have gone, and that takes all the fun out of a city.'

'We're still being paid,' Giriak pointed out.

'That's true, but it doesn't matter a damn if there's nothing to spend it on. Some of the lads are talking of desertion.'

'Which ones?'

Necklen gave a wry smile. 'Now, now, Captain, you know I'm no whisperer. I'm just alerting you to the prospect. They think Karis may have made it to Prentuis. They liked her, they want to serve her again.'

Giriak sat down on the battlements. 'I am as good as she. You know that, don't you?'

'You are a good man, Captain. Brave, loyal, steadfast.'

'Why does that sound like an insult?' asked Giriak, surprised at his own lack of anger. Of all the men who served under him, Necklen was the one he trusted most. Soft-spoken and loyal, he was an able lieutenant.

'It wasn't meant to be,' said Necklen. 'She is special, you know – got the mind for it. She could smell trouble when it was just a tiny seed. Put a halt to it before any knew there was a problem. That's why she made it all look so smooth. You and she were a wonderful team. But face it, Captain, it is not so wonderful without her.'

Giriak sighed. 'If any other man but you said those words, I would kill him.'

'The truth always has a bitter taste,' observed Necklen. 'I was there when she first learned to command. A group of us had been assigned to reinforce a garrison town. Soon after we arrived it was besieged. That was when Beckel was in command. He was all right, but he had one big problem; he was too intelligent.'

'How could that be a problem?' Giriak asked.

'Oh, it is a killer, Captain. Believe me. A man needs to know his limitations and that requires a certain humility. Beckel could multiply numbers in his head, recite ancient writings from memory, and knew every strategy ever used. But he couldn't lift them out of context. No imagination, you see. And that's what wins battles and wars. Imagination.'

'How did Karis come into the story?'

Necklen chuckled. 'She was his whore. When the siege started she came with him one day to the battlements. The enemy were cutting down trees. Beckel told her they were building siege towers. "The ground is too uneven," she told him, and she was right. No force on earth could have propelled towers over that landscape. "Catapults," she said. Then she shaded her eyes and scanned the walls and the land beyond. She pointed out where she thought they would raise the catapults, and the section of wall they would aim at. We'd been amused at first, but a little irritation came in then. Like, who does she think she is? You know what I mean, Captain?'

'Ay, I do,' said Giriak.

'Well, then she asks why we're not storing enough water. "'Cos there's a stream flowing through the garrison," says I, "and it has never been known to go dry." She just looked at me for a moment. You remember that look? Kind of still, as if she were studying you? Then she says: "It will dry up fast enough if the enemy block it behind those hills." Two days later that's just what happened. And they placed the catapult where she said they would. Beckel used her a lot after that, and when he was killed we just sort of turned to her for leadership.'

'Why are you telling me this, old friend?'

'I think maybe we should all go to Prentuis and seek her out. You'd be happier; you love the woman.'

Giriak pushed himself to his feet. 'You tell the lads that she won't be in Prentuis. She'd have cut west to Corduin. She knew Sirano would want her dead.'

'If you knew that, why did you send the riders south?'

Giriak shrugged. 'Love or stupidity – one or the other.'

'Both, maybe,' said Necklen, with a wry smile. 'By the way, the scouts you sent north have not returned. They are overdue by a day.'

'They probably found a village full of young women,' said Giriak.

'Perhaps. But Mell was leading them, and he's steady as they come; you can always rely on Mell. It could be that some enemy mercenaries have slipped by us.'

'Send out a rider,' ordered Giriak.

'Son of a whore!' hissed Necklen. 'Is that the Duke?' Giriak swung round to see Sirano striding down the road towards the rampart steps. His blond hair was lank and greasy, his face unshaven and his eyes fever-bright. He ran up the steps, his movements quick and jerky. Necklen saluted, but the Duke ignored him.

'The enemy is coming,' said Sirano. 'Gather your men.'

'What enemy, my lord?'

'We need archers: thousands of them, lining the walls.' Sirano stood stock-still, unblinking, his gaze fastened on the north. 'And cauldrons of oil. The best archers . . . with strong bows.'

'We don't have a thousand archers, my lord,' said Giriak. 'Who is the enemy?'

'This will be the spot; this is where they will attack. Tell your archers to wait until they are well within range. They have very tough skins. Strong bones. Send Karis to me. We must plan.'

Giriak and Necklen exchanged glances. Giriak stepped up to the Duke, taking him by the arm. 'How long since you slept, my lord?'

163

'Sleep? I have no time for sleep. They are coming, you see. I brought them back. It was never my intention, Giriak. Never!'

'Sit you down, sir,' said Necklen, taking the Duke's other arm and leading him to a bench seat. Sirano sat, but then swivelled and stared out over the ramparts. 'They will be here tomorrow, with the dawn,' he said. 'I have made a terrible mistake. And I cannot put it right. But the bowmen can. Fill the walls with them.'

'I'll do that, my lord,' said Giriak, soothingly. 'But let us first get you back to the palace. You need rest.'

He led the unresisting Duke back down to the lower level, then helped him to the saddle of his own gelding. With a wave to Necklen, he led the horse back along the deserted streets.

CHAPTER EIGHT

SIRANO LAY TREMBLING ON HIS BED, HIS BODY RACKED BY PAINFUL sobbing. He had not cried since he was a child, but now all his defences had been torn apart like paper. Clea, who had loved him, was dead, sacrificed by him in order to gain the power of the Pearl. The Eldarin, who had offered no harm to the human race, had vanished. And now had come the crowning glory of his achievements: the return of the Daroth. Sirano lay on the broad bed, hugging the Eldarin Pearl to him. 'Come back to me, old man,' he pleaded. 'For pity's sake, come back!'

Exhausted, he fell into a deep sleep full of bad, hurtful dreams. He saw his mother killed again and again, and watched his father die, the snake wriggling in his throat. Worse than both of these, though, was the vision of the overweeningly arrogant man he had become, plunging the world into war. And for what? To prove his father wrong? To show that he, Sirano, was a towering figure in human history?

He awoke, and found himself lying not on his bed but on a field of green grass, surrounded by the scent of spring flowers. The madness brought on by exhaustion and lack of sleep had passed, and he was himself again. Beside him sat the silver-furred Eldarin elder. The creature had huge, dark eyes, that radiated sorrow.

'Why am I here?' asked Sirano.

'Why indeed?' answered the spirit.

'I did not know the Daroth would come. You cannot blame me.'

'I do not apportion blame, human. You were warned, and you chose to ignore the warning. Who would you blame? You are a student of history. You know the Eldarin do not lie.'

'But I didn't know! If you had told me about the Daroth I would have desisted.'

'Would you?'

Sirano stayed silent. 'Where did you go?' he asked at last.

'Where do you think? The Eldarin exist within the Pearl, held frozen, awaiting the Day of Awakening. Just as we did with the Daroth. You loosed the chains that held the Daroth captive. But only one living man can free the Eldarin.'

'Tell me what to do, I beg of you! Advise me!'

The Eldarin shook his head. 'The situation is beyond my advice, Sirano. As of tomorrow, Morgallis will be destroyed. Nothing you can do can save it, nor save the thousands who still inhabit it. Death and destruction are upon you, and I pity you and all who serve you. Now go from here. And do not return.' The Eldarin waved his hand dismissively. Sirano felt a jolt, as if from a fall, and awoke again in his own bed. It was dark, and his body was cold. He crawled under the covers, shivering.

He lay there for half an hour, but as the sky lightened he pushed back the covers and moved to his study. From a large jar on the shelf above the window he took a dozen small glass balls, which he placed in a canvas bag. This he slung across his shoulder, and made his way down the stairs to the huge cellar beneath the great hall. There were hundreds of barrels here, scores containing lantern oil, others filled with brandy or fortified wine. One by one he placed ten of the glass globes among the lantern oil barrels. Lastly he turned on the taps. There were no drains here, nowhere for the liquid to go save to slowly cover the stone floor.

Moving upstairs and out into the night, Sirano ran through the deserted streets, heading for the north wall.

Giriak was there, with around forty bowmen and some 200 soldiers. Sirano ran up the steps. 'Are they here?' he asked.

'They will be soon,' said Giriak. 'According to our scout there are thousands of them. They are not human, Sirano.'

The Duke ignored the lack of formality. 'They are Daroth,' he said. The men gathered around him began to whisper amongst themselves. 'We cannot hold here,' Sirano told Giriak. 'The city is finished. Get your men back from the walls. Rouse as many of the citizens as you can, and try to reach Prentuis. Do it now!'

'What are you going to do?' Giriak asked.

'I'll stay and talk to them. Perhaps we can reach an agreement.'

'You hired me and my men. If you wish us to stay and fight, we will.'

Sirano smiled, and clapped the warrior on the shoulder. 'You are a good man, Giriak. You are all good men. Go now, and live!'

For a moment only Giriak stood his ground, then he swung away. 'You heard the Lord Sirano. Let's go!' Gratefully the warriors left the walls, leaving Sirano alone.

The sky was lightening now, the bright stars fading into the grey. The dawn sun crept over the eastern mountains, bathing the city in gold. Sirano sat on the ramparts and gazed back over Morgallis. Some of the buildings were ancient, built with love and care centuries before. This was his city. And he had destroyed it.

He hoped Giriak would rescue most of the city-dwellers, but knew that was unlikely. These last few thousand had endured earthquakes and war; they would not leave their homes. The lucky ones would die under the swords of the Daroth. The young and tender faced a different fate.

Sirano was alone. Not a human in sight. Suddenly he realized he had always been alone. This moment before the storm epitomized his life. The child ignored by the man he thought was his father, had grown into a man apart. Incomplete. Unfinished.

And self-pitying, he realized . . .

The sun rose higher, the land awakening. Sirano looked at the distant tree-line, waiting for the Daroth. As a child he had gone hawking in those woods, hunting rabbit and pigeon. He had swum in the streams, and climbed the tall trees. And in a glade, near the centre, he had played the mighty hero – fighting imaginary foes, defending his people.

167

Now the game was real and, unlike his childish fantasies, doomed to failure.

The first of the Daroth riders emerged from the woods. They came in a line, fifty abreast, and rode slowly towards the city gates. Sirano climbed to the ramparts and looked down on the riders. Creatures out of nightmare, colossal and unreal, they moved forward in silence. From the woods came thousands of foot-soldiers. There were no battle cries, only the slow drumbeat of their boots striking the ground in perfect harmony.

'What do you want here?' called out Sirano, as the first of the riders neared the wall.

The Daroth did not reply. Forty foot-soldiers dragged a bronze-headed battering-ram forward, lining it up against the gates. They swung it back, then thundered it forward. Sirano heard the splintering of the wood, and felt the impact on the parapet under his feet. Taking one of his remaining two glass globes, he hurled it down. It smashed against the ram. Fire exploded outward, engulfing the Daroth. Their armour glowing red, they staggered back, slapping at the flames which sprang from their clothing. Some fell, and not one of their comrades ran forward to help. The stricken Daroth blazed like torches, and died where they fell.

Forty more Daroth made their silent way to the smouldering ram. Four times it swung – and the gates gave. Sirano ran down the steps as the Daroth swarmed through, then sprinted along the street, heading for the palace. Daroth riders galloped after him.

He was breathing heavily when he reached the long, tree-lined avenue which led to the palace building, and could hear the pounding of hooves behind him. Swinging round, he threw the last of his globes. It struck a rider in the chest. Flames enveloped him. The huge horse reared, throwing the Daroth back from the saddle.

Sirano sprinted on, up the twelve steps to the main doors and on into the Great Hall. At the far end, beneath a huge stained-glass window, was the Ducal Chair, carved from mahogany and inlaid with ivory and silver. Upon it was the Eldarin Pearl.

Sirano ran to the chair and, taking the Pearl in his hands, sat down. Drawing in a deep breath he shouted out a single Word of Power. Below the Hall one of the globes scattered in the oil ignited, the flames spreading quickly across the cellar floor, licking at the wooden barrels.

Daroth warriors swarmed into the Hall. 'Welcome to Morgallis,' said Sirano, with a broad smile. 'Who is your leader?'

The Daroth approached him, spreading out in a wide circle. He stared at their bone-white features and their dark, soulless eyes. 'Afraid to speak?' he asked them.

A towering figure stepped from the ranks. 'I am the general,' it said. 'And tonight I shall feast on your heart.'

'I think not, you ugly whoreson! But let it not be said that Sirano did not give his guests a warm welcome.' Rising, Sirano shouted once more. All the remaining globes flared into life, the heat rising like a volcano. Beneath the feet of the Daroth the huge flagstones shifted. A wall of flame seared out. Then came a second explosion that tore the walls asunder, collapsing the roof.

Sirano, his clothing ablaze, was hurled up and back, his burning body smashing through the stained-glass window, where it crashed into the upper branches of a willow tree in the Ducal gardens. He fell through the branches into a deep pond.

His body a sea of pain, he dragged himself from the water and, still clutching the Eldarin Pearl, staggered out into the street beyond.

Behind him a tower of flame was roaring up a hundred feet, through the broken roof of the palace.

*

The Daroth army swept on towards the south, sacking villages and towns, until they reached the outskirts of Prentuis. There for the first time they came up against a human army, of 2,000 horse, 500 bowmen and 3,000 foot-soldiers. The humans were cut to pieces, the army scattered. The carnage inside the city was awful to behold, and the few survivors who made it to Loretheli on the coast told grisly stories of the massacre, and the terrible feasting that followed it.

In less than a month two of the great cities of the Four Duchies had fallen to an inhuman enemy. The Duke of The Marches had been killed on the battlefield outside Prentuis. Of the Duke of Romark there was no news.

The snows came early, and the Daroth withdrew. But no-one had any doubts that the spring would bring fresh terror.

CHAPTER NINE

BRUNE'S FEVER WAS HIGH, HIS BODY SWEAT-DRENCHED. THE elderly doctor leaned over him, closely examining the yellow-gold of his skin. 'It is not the plague,' he told Tarantio. 'But I do not like his colour; it suggests the blood is bad. However, I have bled him and leeched him, and there is little more that I can do.'

'Will he live?'

The doctor shrugged his thin shoulders. 'To be honest, young man, since I do not know what ails him I cannot say. I have seen yellow skin like this in patients before. Sometimes it indicates the kidneys are failing, at other times jaundice or yellow fever. In this case I do not know. You say the colour of his eyes was caused by the magicker, Ardlin. Were I you, I would seek out the magicker, and find out what he has done.'

'He left Corduin,' said Tarantio.

'As well he might. I have no time for magickers: a tricksy bunch, if you take my meaning. Now a man knows where he is with leeches. They suck out the vileness. Nothing magical there.'

Tarantio showed the man to the door, paid him, then returned to

170

the bedside. '*You should have made him eat his leeches*,' said Dace. '*The man was an idiot.*'

'*There was something in what he said. I think this illness is down to the magicker. You saw Brune's eyes. Both are golden now. There was no magic orb; it is just a spell of some kind. And it is spreading over him.*'

'Yes,' said Dace cheerfully, '*it is – and we should have killed Ardlin too.*'

'*Is that your answer to everything, brother? Kill it?*'

'*Each to his own*,' said Dace. Brune groaned, then spoke out in a language Tarantio had never heard. It was soft, lilting and musical. Tarantio sat beside the bed, laying his hand on Brune's fevered brow. He was burning up. Fetching a bowl of warm water, he drew back the covers and bathed Brune's naked body, allowing the evaporation to cool the skin. '*He is losing a lot of weight*,' said Dace. '*Maybe you should cook a broth, or something.*'

Brune's golden eyes opened. 'Oh, it hurts,' he said.

'Lie still, my friend. Rest if you can.'

'I am cold.'

Tarantio felt his brow again, then he covered him with blankets and walked out to the kitchen area. The young woman he had hired to cook for them had fled when Brune's fever began. There was no food in the house. Returning to the bedroom, Tarantio built up the fire then threw his cloak around his shoulders and walked out into the snow. It was a long walk to the Wise Owl tavern and he was frozen long before he reached it. Snow had begun to fall again, and his shoulders and hair were crowned with white.

He rapped on the door and Shira opened it. Stepping inside he brushed the snow from his shoulders. 'I am sorry to trouble you,' he said, 'but I have a friend who is sick, and there is no food. Could you prepare something for me to take back?'

'Of course,' she said brightly. As she turned away, he saw that she was pregnant.

'My congratulations to you,' he said.

She reddened. 'We are very pleased, Duvo and I.'

'Duvo?'

'The Singer. You remember?'

'Ah yes. I wish you both happiness.'

'Sit down by the fire and I will fetch you some mulled wine while

171

you wait.' She limped away towards the kitchens. Tarantio removed his cloak and squatted by the fire. He shivered as the heat touched him. Staring into the dancing flames he began to relax, and did not hear the soft footfalls behind him. But Dace did, and surged into control – rising and twisting, his sword flashing into his hand.

A lean, blond-haired man with green eyes stood there. 'I am Duvodas,' he said.

'You're lucky not to be a dead Duvodas,' said Dace. 'What are you doing sneaking up on people?'

'I was not sneaking, Tarantio. You were lost in thought. Shira tells me you have a sick friend and I was wondering if I could help.'

Dace was about to spit out a reply when Tarantio dragged him back. 'Are you skilled in medicine?' he asked. Duvodas said nothing for a moment, but his eyes narrowed. Tarantio wondered if, somehow, he had seen the transformation.

'I know a little of herbs and potions,' Duvodas said.

'Then you would be most welcome at my home. I have become rather fond of Brune. He is not the brightest of men, but he is honest and he doesn't talk much. And forgive me for my earlier rudeness. I have lived too long amid wars and battles. People appearing silently behind me usually wish me harm.'

'Think nothing of it, my friend.'

Shira returned with a canvas shoulder-bag, bulging with food. 'This should keep the wolf from the door for a day at least. Come by tomorrow, and I will have a hamper for you.' Tarantio offered to pay, but Shira refused. 'We still owe you a meal for the day you left, sir. Pay me for tomorrow's food.'

Tarantio bowed, then accepted the bag which he slung over his shoulder. Donning his cloak, he made for the door. Duvodas walked out into the snow with him. Tarantio looked hard at the man, who was wearing only a shirt of green cotton, thin leggings and boots. 'You will freeze to death,' said Tarantio.

'I like the cold,' said Duvodas, and the two men strolled out into the snow-covered street. An icy wind was blowing against them as they walked, the snow swirling round them. Tarantio glanced at Duvodas, wondering that the man seemed oblivious to the cold. Twenty minutes later Tarantio pushed open his front door and stepped inside. The living-room fire had burned low and he added fuel.

172

'You are a strange man,' he said. 'Were you raised in a cold climate?'

'No. Where is your friend?'

'In the first of the back bedrooms.'

The two men walked through the house and found Brune mumbling in his sleep. 'Do you recognize the language he is speaking?' asked Tarantio as Duvodas sat by the bed. Brune suddenly began to sing, and the room was filled with the scent of roses. Then he groaned and was silent.

'Where did that scent come from?' asked Tarantio. 'No rose blooms in the snow.'

'What magic was worked on this man?' asked Duvodas. Tarantio told him of the damaged eye and the visit to Ardlin.

'I did not see what he did. But Brune's eyesight is now phenomenal.'

'He is not dying,' said Duvodas. 'He is changing.'

'Into what?'

'I cannot say for sure. But the magic is powerful within him, and it is growing.' Brune's golden eyes opened and he stared at Duvodas. The Singer took his hand and spoke in the Eldarin tongue. Brune smiled and nodded; then he fell asleep once more.

'What did you say to him?'

'I thanked him for his song and the scent of roses.'

'Can you do anything to help him?'

'No. He needs no help from me. Let us leave him resting.' Duvodas returned to the living room and sat down by the fire. Tarantio offered him wine but Duvodas refused, requesting water instead. Tarantio brought him a goblet, then sat down opposite him.

'You are the man who killed the Daroth,' said the Singer. 'I have heard of you. The whole city has heard of you. You make the enemy seem mortal.'

'They *are* mortal.'

'They once destroyed an entire race,' said Duvodas. 'Wiped them out. Now they are lost to history. I was once in a temple that housed their bones. They were called the Oltor; they were Singers, Musicians and Poets. They believed the Universe was the Great Song, and all life within it merely echoes of the melody. Their music was magical, their magic was music. Their cities were said to be gardens of great beauty, at one with the land, harmonious and joyful. The Daroth

173

destroyed the cities utterly, dashed the statues to dust, burnt the paintings, tore up the songs. They are devourers, these Daroth. They live to destroy.'

'I am not a student of history,' said Tarantio, 'but I know how to fight. The Duke has commissioned new weapons, powerful crossbows that can put a bolt through six inches of teak. We will kill a lot of Daroth.'

'Sadly, that is probably true. There will be a lot more killing,' said Duvodas, 'but I shall not wait to see it. Shira and I will be leaving as soon as the snow melts. I will take her to the islands, far away from the war.'

'One day the Daroth might reach them,' said Tarantio. 'What will you do then?'

'I shall die,' replied Duvo. 'I am not a killer. I am a Singer.'

'Like the Oltor? A race that will not fight does not deserve to live. It is against nature.'

Duvodas rose. 'I was taught that evil always carries the seeds of its own downfall. One can only hope that it is true. When your friend awakes, feed him no meat and give him no wine. Give him bread, hot oats or dried fruit. And plenty of water.'

'Meat makes a man strong,' observed Tarantio.

'It will make him vomit,' said Duvodas.

'What is it that you are not telling me?' Tarantio asked.

'If I knew for certain, I would tell you. I will call again when he is awake.'

*

'Again!' shouted Karis, and began to count slowly. The fifty crossbow-men placed the heads of their black bows on the icy ground and began to turn the iron handles on both sides of the stock. By the time Karis had reached the count of twelve, they had notched the thick rope. Sliding bolts into place, they hefted the heavy weapons, rested them on the long support tripod, and took up their positions. The last man was ready as Karis reached fifteen. 'Shoot!' she called.

Fifty black bolts flashed through the air to hammer home into targets of solid oak set thirty paces from the bowmen. Karis loped across the target field. The bolts had all struck home, but not deeply.

Vint strolled across to where she stood. 'The accuracy is fine,' he said.

'The penetration is not,' she told him. 'At twenty paces the bolts smash through the wood. At thirty they barely scratch it.'

'Then we wait until the Daroth are within twenty paces.'

'Gods, man! Is your imagination dead? Yes, we will cut them down. Then, as the reloading takes fifteen seconds, they will be upon us before a second volley can be loosed. The Duke believes we can have five hundred crossbow-men ready by spring. We will need to kill more than five hundred Daroth.'

Vint shook his head. 'That presupposes we will be facing them on open ground. Surely the majority of our crossbow-men will be shooting from the walls?'

'The bows are too heavy for accurate use upon the battlements,' said Karis wearily. 'And shooting downwards lessens the target area. Two-thirds of the bolts would miss. We need something more. There must be another weakness we can exploit.'

Strolling back to the waiting bowmen, she signalled them to load again and to shoot without the tripod support. Half the bolts missed the target. She kept them hard at work for another hour, then dismissed them.

Back in the barracks building she studied the reports of the massacres at Morgallis and Prentuis. Sirano had destroyed his own palace, killing scores of Daroth in the process. The Duke of The Marches had been less successful. Reliable reports claimed that no more than fifty Daroth were killed in the battle. Several thousand trained men had been slain, and scores of thousands of civilians.

A servant brought her a meal of black bread and soft cheese. She ate swiftly then donned a sheepskin jerkin and made her way to the stables. Saddling Warain, she rode the grey out through the northern gates and across the open ground before the walls. Pausing a hundred paces from the walls, she looked back, picturing the line of crossbow-men. Heeling Warain into a run, she began to count once more. Three times she made the run at the wall, watched by perplexed soldiers on the ramparts. Then she turned away from the city and rode into the hills.

It was past dusk when she returned. Leading Warain to his stall, she rubbed him down with fresh straw, filled his feedbox with grain, and covered his grey back with a thick woollen blanket.

175

Returning to her rooms, she found Vint waiting for her. 'Did you clear your head, Karis?' he asked, offering her a goblet of mulled wine. She drained it in a single swallow.

There was a log fire blazing in the hearth. Karis moved to it and removed her wet, cold clothing. Vint crossed the room and began to massage her shoulders and neck. 'You are very cold,' he said, his voice husky.

'Then warm me,' she told him.

Later, as they lay naked beneath satin sheets and heavy blankets, Karis waited until Vint's breathing deepened, then slid silently from the bed and returned to the fire. It had died down and she placed two fresh logs upon it.

In order to use the crossbows to maximum effect, the Daroth charge would have to be slowed. Three volleys would cause carnage in their ranks, but that would involve holding up the Daroth for almost a minute within a twenty-pace range. Karis drank two goblets of wine, and still felt no drowsiness. She thought of waking Vint for another session of love-making, but decided against it. He was a caring and thoughtful lover, taking his time and making the moments last. At this moment Karis did not need such drawn-out intensity. Instead, she donned fresh leggings and a white woollen shirt, buckskin boots and her hooded jerkin, and walked from the palace into the night.

The streets were deserted and a bitter wind was blowing down from the north. Karis pulled her hood over her long dark hair, and turned down a side alley towards the Barracks tavern. Golden lantern light glowed from the windows and a rush of welcome heat enveloped her as she pushed open the door. There were two log fires burning, one at each end of the long room within, and the tavern was packed with soldiers. Karis scanned the room, spotting the red-bearded giant Forin sitting in a corner with a young whore perched upon his knee.

Karis eased her way through the crowd and removed her jerkin, draping it over the back of the chair opposite the giant. 'We need to talk,' she said.

'Will it take long?' he asked. 'I have plans for the evening.' He grinned up at the young whore, who forced a laugh and stared at Karis with open hostility.

'I want you to tell me everything you can remember of your father's stories concerning the Daroth. Everything!'

'Can this not wait until the morning?'

'No, it cannot,' said Karis. The young whore, sensing her payment receding, leaned forward, her face showing her anger. But before the girl could speak Karis drew her dagger and slammed it point first into the table. 'One wrong word from you and I shall cut your tongue out,' she said, her voice icy. The whore's painted mouth dropped open, fear replacing her anger. 'Now go away and find another client,' said Karis. 'There are plenty to choose from.'

The girl slid from Forin's lap and moved away into the crowd. Forin drained his tankard. 'You have lost me a night's pleasure,' he said.

'And saved you a dose of the pox, in all probability.'

Forin was about to reply when she saw him glance over her shoulder, his green eyes narrowing. Instantly alert to danger, Karis pushed back her chair and spun round. The young whore was approaching with two men. 'That's her! Pulled a knife on me, she did!'

'That was a mistake, bitch,' said the first of the two, a broad-shouldered young man with pockmarked features.

'Not as bad as the mistake you are about to make,' Karis told him, noting that the second man held a short iron club.

'Is that right?' he countered, lunging forward, his fist flashing towards Karis's face. She side-stepped suddenly and, thrown off-balance, the man stumbled forward – to be met with a head butt that smashed his nose to pulp. He dropped like a stone. The second man grabbed Karis by the arm, hauling her towards him, but she spun and rammed her elbow into his chin. He staggered to his right, dropping the club. Karis took a step back, then leapt high, her booted foot cannoning against his face to catapult him back into the crowd. He fell heavily and did not rise.

Forin moved alongside Karis. 'Perhaps we should continue our conversation somewhere private?' he offered.

'Why not?' she told him. Forin took a candle from the table and led her through to the rear of the tavern and up a flight of rickety steps. There was a narrow corridor leading to three doors. Forin opened the first and stepped aside for Karis to enter. The room was small, gloomy and cold. There were no chairs, only a roughly crafted double bed with a thin mattress. Using the flickering candle, Forin lit a lantern which hung on a hook above the bed, then moved to the small hearth where a fire had been laid; this he also lit. 'It will be warm soon enough,' he said.

She squatted down beside him, watching the firelight reflected in his green eyes. He was not a handsome man, she thought, but he had a quality that transcended good looks. Is it his strength, his size? she wondered. In the firelight he looked somehow larger, more impressive. Primal, perhaps? 'What are you thinking?' he asked her.

'I was wondering what you looked like naked.' she said.

'Wonder for a little longer,' he told her, with a broad smile. 'The room's not warm enough yet.'

'Then tell me of the Daroth, for I need to find a weakness.'

Forin sat back. 'There are none that I recall. You already know they do not like the cold, nor high places where the air is thin. They will not cross water if they can avoid it. But these things will not help us in Corduin. We are in low-lying land, the weather is clement in the spring, and there is no moat.'

'Even so, I believe there is something else.'

'Wishful thinking, perhaps?'

'I do not believe so. It is something I have seen, and yet not recognized. Something that is perhaps too obvious.'

'I am afraid you have lost me there.'

'Tell me a simple story of how they live.'

'You saw the city. They cluster together in domed dwellings. They cannot sit as we do, for their spines are thicker and less supple. They procreate without touching, the female laying an egg which the male fertilizes. There is no obvious difference between male and female. Both are equally strong, and – as we have observed – equally ugly. There are no children as such; the young emerge from their pods and grow within days to full-size adults, sharing the memories of whichever parent has died – if that is the term – beside the pod. They eat flesh, and require great amounts of salt.' He paused. 'Is this helping you?'

'I don't know,' she admitted. The heat in the small room was growing, and Forin peeled off his shirt; his upper body bore many scars. As he rose and stripped off his leggings, Karis pushed the thoughts of the Daroth from her mind.

His love-making was exactly what she needed – crude and powerful, animalistic and passionate – and Karis felt her body

178

echoing his need. His arms slid under her shoulders, pulling her hard against him; his body smelt of wood-smoke and sweat. It was not unpleasant, as she had feared. As her body tensed and moved in rhythm with the man upon her, her mind relaxed, as if she was floating free of the carnal. In this curiously detached state her body drew strength from the massive figure above her, while the problems that haunted her faded from her consciousness. She was free. Nothing else existed. The world had shrunk to a grimy, firelit room above a noisy tavern. There were no problems to solve, no logistics to calculate, no plans to study. And she did not even need to consider the pleasure of the man, for he, she knew, was oblivious to her as an individual. It was the only true freedom Karis ever knew.

Her legs locked about his hips, her nails raking his back, Karis found herself rising towards orgasm, which, when it came, sent her body into an almost painful series of spasms. Her head sank back onto the pillow and she closed her eyes, enjoying the small aftershocks that rippled through her system. Forin rolled from her and lay back with a sigh. For a long moment neither of them spoke, then Forin rose from the bed and moved to the fire. Karis watched him dress. 'I'll get us both a drink,' he said, and left the room.

After he had gone Karis also dressed. The room was warm now, the fire blazing. She moved to the small window and tried to open it, but the hinges were rusted and it would not budge.

Not waiting for him to return, Karis made her way down the stairs and out into the night.

Vint was still asleep when she returned, but she had no wish to climb in beside him.

Stretching out on a couch, she dreamt of a green-eyed giant with a forked red beard.

*

Tarantio rose with the dawn and moved through the silent house, as always enjoying the solitude, these brief moments without Dace. The kitchen was bitterly cold, the remains of yesterday's milk frozen in the jug. With a saw-edged knife he cut two thick slices of bread from a loaf, and carried them through to the living room. He had banked up the fire the night before, and the coals were still glowing. Tarantio toasted the bread and covered it with thick, creamy butter.

179

I ought to be making plans, he thought. Corduin will not resist the Daroth. But where to go? The islands? What would I do there? He ate the toast and, still hungry, went back to the kitchen to cut more bread. The loaf was gone.

Puzzled, Tarantio walked to the rear of the house, opening the door to Brune's bedroom. The bed was empty, and there was no sign of the young man. Retracing his steps he returned to the kitchen. The back door was still locked from the inside, the windows shuttered. Pulling back the bolts Tarantio opened the door. A blast of icy air struck him as he stepped out into the garden.

Brune was sitting, naked, on the wooden bench. All around him birds were fluttering, landing on his arms, and head and hands, pecking at the bread he offered them. A wide circle of grass was all around the bench, without a flake of snow upon it, though the rest of the garden still lay beneath a thick white blanket. Tarantio pulled on his boots and walked out across the garden. The birds ignored him, continuing to fly around Brune. As Tarantio sat down he felt suddenly warm, as if Brune was radiating heat in defiance of the elements.

The golden-skinned young man continued to feed the birds until all the bread was gone. Most of them flew away but several remained, sitting on his shoulders or on the back of the bench. They were, as was Tarantio, enjoying the warmth.

Reaching out, Tarantio laid his hand on Brune's shoulder. 'You should come in,' he said softly.

'I heard them call to me,' said Brune, his voice melodic and low.

'Who called you?'

'The birds. Up to two-thirds of their body weight can be lost on a cold night. They die in their thousands in the winter.'

Suddenly Brune shivered and the cold swept in, bitter and deadly. He cried out, and the birds around him panicked and flew away. Tarantio helped him back into the house, taking him to the fire. 'What is happening to me?' came the true voice of Brune. 'Why was I in the garden?'

'You were feeding the birds,' Tarantio told him.

'I am really frightened. I can't think. It's like there's someone else in me.' He was shivering, and Tarantio fetched a blanket which he wrapped around Brune's shoulders. 'I feel like I'm dying,' said Brune.

'You are not dying. It's the magic that cured your eye. It's spreading somehow.'

'I don't want this any more, Tarantio. I want to be what I was. Can't we get the magic taken out?'

'I don't know. Tell me what you remember about feeding the birds.'

'I don't remember nothing. I was asleep, and I had this dream. Can't remember much now. But I was in a forest, and there were lots of people – no, not people. They were all golden-skinned; they were . . . dying. Oh yes . . . there was Daroth there. Killing them. It was horrible. And then . . . there was nothing until I was sitting in the garden.'

'How are you feeling now? Is there any pain?' asked Tarantio.

'No. No pain. But . . .' Brune's voice tailed away.

'What? Tell me!'

'I'm not alone in here. I'm not alone.'

'Of course you are not alone. I am here,' said Tarantio soothingly.

'No, you don't understand. I'm not alone in my head.' Brune began to weep and Tarantio's anger flared, remembering the surprised look on the face of the magicker as he had entered the room.

The sudden anger woke Dace. '*What is happening?*' he asked.

Tarantio told him. '*Someone else in his head? Sounds familiar,*' said Dace. '*I knew Brune would be an entertaining companion. Perhaps what you and I have, brother, is contagious.*'

'*It is not funny,*' said Tarantio sternly. '*Brune is frightened. He thinks he is dying.*'

'*Everybody dies sometime,*' said Dace.

'*I think the Singer knows more than he is saying,*' said Tarantio. '*He is coming back today. I'll ask him.*'

'*Let me ask him,*' Dace urged.

'*Perhaps that will be necessary,*' Tarantio agreed. Taking Brune by the arm, he led him back to the bedroom. 'Get some rest, my friend. You will feel better for it, I promise you.' Brune climbed back into the bed, drawing the blanket over him and resting his head on the pillow.

'*Look at his ear,*' said Dace. Tarantio had seen it at the same time: the lobe was no longer smooth, but ridged like a seashell.

'*If I ever find that magicker I'll cut his heart out,*' hissed Dace.

*

The councillor Pooris stood shivering by the southern gate, counting the wagons as the oxen slowly hauled them into the city. The War of the Pearl had been a ruinous venture, disrupting trade, destroying farms, and taking young men from the fields and turning them into mercenaries.

Even without the threat of the Daroth, Corduin was slowly starving to death. Corn was five times last year's price, and the city treasury was emptying fast. A census ordered by the Duke showed that almost 70,000 people were now resident in Corduin. Many were now starving, and crimes against individuals and property was soaring.

As the last of the twenty-two wagons rumbled through the gate, Pooris ran alongside it and clambered up to sit alongside the driver. 'I expected forty wagons,' said Pooris. 'That is what was promised.'

The driver hawked and spat. 'This is all there is,' he said, brushing the ice from his beard. 'Be thankful for that.'

'We paid for forty.'

'That is not my problem, councillor. Take it up with the merchant, Lunder.'

Pooris hunkered down inside his hooded sheepskin coat and thought of the city's bakers, who later tonight would be queuing at the warehouses. Forty wagons would have been barely enough to supply the bakers with half what was needed. Twenty-two would mean riots in the streets tomorrow.

At Warehouse Street Pooris jumped down from the wagon and entered the small offices beside the guard gate. For several minutes he stood in front of a wood stove, warming his hands and thinking the problem through. The bakers were already rationed to 40 per cent of their needs. Now they would suffer a further 50 per cent cut.

A young cleric approached him, offering a mug of hot tisane, heavily sweetened with sugar. Pooris thanked him. The man returned to his desk and continued to fill in the ledger, noting down the wagons and the time of their arrival. Pooris glanced around the room. The ill-fitting windows had been sealed with paper, which was now sodden and dripping water to the walls below. 'Not the most comfortable of working-places,' remarked Pooris.

The young man looked up and smiled. 'I like it here,' he said. The cleric rose and donned a fur-lined cape. 'I must leave you, councillor. I need to check the unloading of the wagons.'

'Of course. My thanks to you.' Pooris held out his hand. The young man shook it, then opened the door and stepped out into the snow.

Pooris removed his coat and moved to the desk, scanning the ledger. The cleric's script was neat and easy to read. During the last two weeks some 320 wagons had been checked through, bringing corn, grain, salted meat, spices, dried fruit and wine from the islands. Almost all of the food had been shipped in through the port city of Loretheli, much of it arranged through the merchant Lunder. Flicking back through the pages, Pooris saw that the amount of food shipped had steadily decreased during the past three months, the prices rising in direct proportion. It was a simple economic law, Pooris knew, that when demand outstripped supply prices would take off like startled pigeons.

The young cleric returned, and looked surprised to see Pooris sitting at his desk. 'Is there anything I can help you with, councillor?' he asked. Pooris glanced up, and saw the nervousness in the man.

'I was just studying the shipments,' he said. 'We are fast approaching famine status.'

'I'm sure the Duke will think of something, sir,' said the young man, relaxing. 'May I offer you another mug of tisane?'

'No, I must be going.' Once more they shook hands. 'What is your name?'

'Cellis, sir.'

'Thank you for your hospitality, Cellis.'

Pooris wandered along Warehouse Street, cutting through the narrow alleyways to the central avenue and thence to the palace. Ensconced in his own small office, he called in Niro, a spider-thin cleric with close-cropped, spiky black hair. 'What do you know of the man, Cellis, who works at the warehouse guard gate?' he asked.

'Nothing, sir. But I shall find out,' Niro answered.

'Do it now, as a matter of urgency,' said Pooris, removing his coat and hanging it on a hook set in the wall. For just over an hour Pooris worked through the tasks he had set himself for the day, compiling a list of armourers, and the various orders for swords, spears, crossbow bolts and armour placed with them, along with the delivery dates promised. He was almost finished when Niro returned.

'I have some of the information you require, sir,' he said. 'Cellis has been working for us for two years. His father was a cobbler in the Southern Quarter, his mother a seamstress. He was educated by the Aver monks and passed his examinations with honours. He is not married, and lives in a hill house in Quarter Street. Was there more you wished to know, sir?'

'A cobbler, you say?'

'His father . . . yes.'

'Does he own the house?'

'I . . . I don't know, sir.'

'Find out.'

Once again Pooris returned to his work. He called in a cleric and dictated several letters, including one to Lunder asking why the number of flour wagons had been fewer than expected.

When Niro returned just before noon, he looked cold and his lips were blue. 'Sit you down, man,' said Pooris. Niro rubbed his thin hands together. Moving to the small stove, Pooris flicked open the door, allowing a rush of heat into the room.

'Thank you, sir,' said Niro. 'Yes, he does own the house. He bought it four months ago for two hundred gold. It is a fine house, with stables in the rear and an apple orchard.'

'How did a cobbler's son raise the capital necessary?'

'I thought you'd ask that, sir; that's why it took me so long. He borrowed the money from . . .'

'. . . the merchant Lunder,' finished Pooris.

'Yes, sir,' said Niro, surprised. 'How did you know?'

'Cellis wears a gold ring, set with an emerald the size of my thumbnail. No cleric could afford such a bauble. Go to the Hall of Records and find out how many warehouses Lunder owns or rents. Do it slyly, Niro. I want no-one to know.'

'Yes, sir.'

Pooris shut the stove door, put on coat and gloves and left the building, trudging through the snow towards the southern gate. A quarter-mile from the gate, he stopped at a row of terraced houses. They housed retired soldiers and their wives, and were a gift from the Duke – a reward for loyal service. Moving to the first he rapped on the door. There was no answer, and he walked to the second.

When he knocked, an elderly woman called out from within, 'Who is it? What do you want?'

'I am the councillor, Pooris,' he told her. 'I would appreciate a moment of your time, lady.'

He heard the bolts being drawn back, then the door groaned inward. Stepping inside he bowed to the frail, white-haired old woman. 'They said I could stay here till I was dead,' said the woman. 'Said it was my right. I won't live in no poorhouse. I'll kill myself first.'

'Be at ease,' he said softly. 'I have not come as a bailiff. Do you sleep well, my lady?'

'Ay,' she said cautiously. 'Though not as deep as I used to.'

'I was just wondering if the noise of the wagons disturbs you late at night.'

'No,' she said. 'I sit at my window sometimes and watch them go by. I don't get out much now. Too cold for me. It's nice to watch life below my window.'

'How often do they come through?' he asked.

'Maybe three times a week. Great convoys of them.'

'Did they come last night?'

'Ay, they did. Three hours before dawn.'

'How many?'

'Maybe fifty. Maybe a little less.'

'I thank you for your time.' He turned to leave. 'It is very cold in here. Do you have no fuel?'

'The Duke's pension don't extend to luxuries,' she said. 'My man fought for him for thirty years. He's dead now, and his pension is halved. I get food, though. As for the cold – well I'm used to it.'

'I shall see that coal is delivered to you before the day is out, my lady.'

Pooris bowed once more, then stepped out into the cold, fresh air.

CHAPTER TEN

THE CLERIC CELLIS WAS ARRESTED AT HIS HOME AND TAKEN TO THE palace dungeons, where he was offered the choice between confession and torture. An intelligent man, and not without bravery, Cellis knew that following confession they would torture him anyway, and he chose to remain silent.

Pooris, Niro, the Duke and Karis observed the beginning of Cellis's ordeal, then retired to the Duke's apartments. Niro was sent to man the small office at Warehouse Street.

Just after dawn, with the stove recently lit and the room still cold, Niro was studying Cellis' neat ledger when the door opened and a tall, burly man entered. Bald at the crown, his receding black hair cropped short, he removed a cloak lined with expensive fur and stood before the stove. 'Where is Cellis?' he asked.

'He has been taken ill, sir. I am Niro, and – temporarily one hopes – in charge here.'

'Ill? He seemed in good spirits yesterday.'

'Frightening, is it not, how swiftly the onset of illness can render a man incapable?' said Niro. 'How may I be of service, sir?'

'I have a convoy due today. But I fear it may be delayed until after dark.'

'I see, sir, and so you would like me to request written authorization for the guards to open the gates?'

'We could proceed that way,' agreed the man, pulling up a chair and sitting down opposite Niro. He was wearing a heavy silk shirt of blue, embroidered with gold thread, and a fur-lined waistcoat of soft grey leather. If Niro saved his meagre wages for half a year he could not afford to buy either garment. 'But it would be simpler,' the man continued, ' to find another solution.'

'Another solution, sir? How can that be? The Duke's orders are specific. The gates are closed at dusk and there can be no traffic thereafter, save with written authorization.'

'Indeed that is the case,' said the man. 'But, in my experience, such authorization takes time, and effort, and ...' he grinned '... a man's weight in paperwork. I am sure there is a good reason for the Duke to create such a rule, but poor merchants like myself need to earn an honest crust. Often that means conducting one's business swiftly – especially with perishable food.'

'I am sure that is true, sir,' said Niro, rising and adding two logs to the stove. 'However, my understanding is that there is no private trade in food at present. The Duke, through merchants like yourself, buys all available supplies to keep the city fed. Therefore, whatever food is contained in your convoy is already under the ownership of the Duke. Not so?'

'In theory, that is the case ... Niro, did you say?' The cleric nodded. 'Well, Niro, I can see that you are an honest man. Do you know how I can make such a judgement?'

'Indeed I do not, sir.'

'Your tunic cost around eight copper pennies. The cloak hanging from the peg was no more than three.' He glanced down. 'Your boots are worn thin, the leather poor quality. Only an honest man would wear them.'

'I take your point, sir. But surely to take that point a step further, I would have to say that you are a dishonest man, since your silk shirt must have cost ... ten in silver ... ?'

'Thirty.' The man gave a broad smile as he opened the pouch at his side. Removing two gold coins he laid them on the desk. 'Unless

187

I am mistaken,' he said, 'your wage for the year is less than the amount you see here.'

'You are quite correct, sir.'

'Take the coins in your hand. Feel the weight and the warmth. Gold has a special feel, Niro.'

The cleric's thin hand gathered the coins. 'So it does. So it does.'

'My convoy will be here by midnight. There will be no need to register its arrival.'

The man rose and swirled his cloak around his broad shoulders. 'Might I know your name, sir?' asked Niro.

'I am Lunder. Serve me well, Niro, and you will enjoy great fortune.'

'I thank you, sir. And you have saved me a journey.' Niro opened the desk drawer and produced a folded sheet of paper bearing the Duke's seal in red wax. 'I was asked to deliver this to you this morning.'

'What is it?' asked the merchant.

'I have no idea, sir. I am not privy to the Duke's thoughts.' Lunder took the paper and broke the seal. Then he smiled.

'I am invited to dine at the palace this evening,' he said.

'Congratulations, sir. I am informed that the Duke's chef is exceptional.'

*

The Duke's carriage – handsomely crafted from mahogany, and fitted with seats of luxurious padded leather – was drawn by six greys. Lunder sat back and enjoyed the ride. Velvet curtains kept out the winter wind and two copper warming-pans full of hot coals hung from hooks in the roof, filling the compartment with gentle heat.

Lunder was as happy as any man born in a crofter's hut could be to ride in such a carriage. He wondered what his father would think of him, if he could but see what a man he had become! A house with twenty-six servants, a mistress of great beauty, and a personal fortune greater even than the Duke's. All this, plus an estate in the islands should the Daroth prove to be the menace everyone feared. Lunder could hear the iron-shod wheels rattling over the cobbles, but inside the compartment there was little sense of movement. He gazed at the ornate panelling, wonderfully carved from red mahogany. I should have a carriage like this, he thought. And I will.

His thick fingers reached into the pocket of his velvet coat, drawing out a gold necklace and a tear-shaped amethyst set in filigree gold. An ancient piece, it had cost him 200 silver pieces. The amethyst was a present for Miriac, who loved such baubles. He would wake her when he got back, and watch her bright blue eyes go wide with joy. It was not a cause of irritation for Lunder that Miriac's ardour could only be awakened by such gems. Lunder himself found the acquisition of fresh wealth a continuing aphrodisiac. Added to which, all the presents he gave her were, in fact, registered in his name at the treasury, with bills of sale. If ever he tired of her, all the jewels would be his again.

He heard the driver call out to the horses and the carriage slowed to a stop. The journey had been much swifter than he had calculated. Surely they could not be at the palace already? He rapped at the small hatch. 'Why are we stopping?' he called. There was no answer. Pulling back the curtains, he gazed out onto a grisly sight. The carriage had stopped in Gallows Square. Torches were lit all around it, and in their flickering light he could see ten corpses hanging by their necks. 'Move on!' he shouted at the driver. This was no sight for a man about to dine.

A figure moved to the carriage door, wrenching it open. A soldier in a plumed helm pulled down the steps. 'Out you get, sir,' he said.

'What are you doing? I am a guest of the Duke; he is awaiting me.'

'Indeed he is, sir. Now step down.'

Lunder's mind raced, but he could think of no reason to refuse further. Taking hold of the door frame, he pulled himself upright and climbed down the steps. Duke Albreck was standing there, the councillor Pooris with him, and that fellow Niro from the warehouse offices.

'Good evening, my lord,' said Lunder. 'I am at a loss . . .'

'You recognize this man?' asked the Duke, pointing to the first of the corpses. It was Cellis the cleric. Lunder's mind reeled. 'You recognize him?' demanded the Duke again. The other corpses were sentries from the south gate.

'Yes, my lord, but I assure you . . .'

'Your assurances mean nothing, Lunder. You have defrauded me,

189

and caused unnecessary suffering in Corduin. Your goods are forfeit; your lands are forfeit. Your wealth is forfeit.'

Lunder was trembling now. 'My lord, I allow that I have been . . . lax in my dealings. But I never intended to defraud you. All the goods are waiting in my warehouses. I . . . I make a gift of them to you.'

'They are already mine,' said the Duke coldly. 'Hang him.'

Lunder heard the words – but could not believe them. 'Sir, I beg you . . .' he said, as two soldiers grabbed his arms and began to haul him towards the scaffold steps. As he reached them, he started to struggle, but a third man stepped forward and smote him hard in the face with a clenched fist. Lunder was half hauled up the steps. At the top his hands were tied behind him, a noose looped over his head and tightened around his neck. He began to sob, and scream for mercy. Then the floor gave way beneath him – and he dropped into darkness.

'I do not understand why he did it,' said the Duke. 'He was already rich. The prices he charged me were exorbitant, and his profits must have been huge.'

'For some men there is never enough wealth, my lord,' said Pooris. 'He knew that when the official warehouses were empty, people would pay anything for his goods. By smuggling them in, he would claim they were purchased before your decree was made.'

'I do not understand such greed,' said the Duke. 'But I understand the value of loyalty. You, Pooris, have done me a great service. You may have Lunder's house and his lands.'

'I thank you, my lord,' said Pooris, bowing deeply.

'And now my dinner awaits,' said the Duke, moving to his carriage and stepping inside. Niro approached Pooris. 'My congratulations, sir,' he said, with a bow.

The little politician chuckled. 'Seventeen warehouses packed with food – enough supplies to last most of the winter, and the treasury fuller than at any time since the war began. A satisfactory day, I think.'

'Indeed, sir.'

'Are those new boots I see, Niro?'

'Yes, sir. I bought them this afternoon.'

'They look expensive.'

'They were, sir. Compliments of the merchant Lunder.'

190

'What a benefactor he proved to be,' observed Pooris.

Early the next morning, Pooris rapped at the door of Lunder's house. Together with a troop of guardsmen, he entered the main hall and called for the Lady Miriac. She emerged from an upstairs room and, dressed in a gown of white, walked down the long staircase. Pooris marvelled at her beauty – the shining hair like spun gold, the porcelain loveliness of her skin. He took her into the main room and, as gently as he could, explained the circumstances of his visit. She sat demurely, saying little and showing nothing of her emotions.

'So,' she said, when he had finished, 'Lunder is dead, and the house is yours. How soon must I leave?'

'There is no need to leave, my lady,' said Pooris. 'In fact, I would very much like you to stay. I have brought with me a small gift for you.'

Reaching into his pocket he produced Lunder's necklace, with the shining amethyst shaped like a tear-drop. With delight he saw her eyes sparkle, and her hand reach out.

*

The walls of Karis's apartments were covered with sketches on paper. On the north wall were delicately drawn landscapes, showing the highlights of the land to the north of Corduin; the hills and valleys, the level ground close enough to the city walls for the Daroth to deploy catapults. On the west wall were sketches of the city's fortifications, the numbers of men needed to man the ramparts, the logistics of supplying them with food. On the south wall a huge map of Corduin itself, which Karis had marked with symbols denoting buildings to be used as hospitals or supply depots.

She was sitting on the couch studying the reports submitted by Pooris, concerning the manufacture of crossbows and bolts. With luck, they should have almost 800 weapons and more than 10,000 bolts by the first day of spring. A servant tapped on the door and entered, bowing. 'There is a man wishing to speak with you, my lady,' he said. 'He claims to be a friend.'

'He has a name, this friend?'

'Necklen, my lady.'

'Send him in.' Karis rose, and hid her sense of shock as the wiry soldier entered. Skeletally thin, his eyes sunken, Necklan looked twenty years older than when she had last seen him. A blood-soaked

191

bandage covered the stump where his left hand had been. 'Come in and sit down, my friend,' she said, then ordered the servant to bring food and wine.

Necklen slumped to a chair and closed his eyes. 'It has been a murderous ride,' he said, his voice slurred with weariness. His head sank back and his breathing deepened. When the servant returned with bread, butter, cheese and smoked meat, Karis told him to fetch the surgeon. Moving alongside the silver-bearded warrior, she touched his neck, feeling for a pulse. His blue eyes opened and he gave a weak smile. 'I am not dead, Karis. Though by rights I should be.' With a groan he sat up. Karis brought him a goblet of red wine, which he drained. He reached for the bread with his left arm, then stared bemused at the stump. 'Damn, but I can still feel my fingers. Strange, isn't it?' Karis cut him two thick slices, which she buttered. Then she sliced a thick chunk of cheese. Necklen ate slowly, then leaned back once more. 'I was at Prentuis. I tell you, no-one should have witnessed the slaughter I saw there. We rode out against the Daroth. Giriak led the charge, but our swords were like willow sticks against them. I slashed my sword across the neck of one: it bounced off! Didn't even gash the skin. He struck my shield with a return blow which clove the shield in two and tore off my hand. Within moments we were ruined, cut down in our hundreds. I saw a Daroth with maybe ten arrows jutting from him, but still fighting, unaffected. You want to know about Giriak?'

She did not, but she nodded anyway.

'He died bravely. Killed one of them, lanced him through the body at full gallop. Then he was cut down. You would not believe how short a battle it was, Karis. Within a few minutes we were cut to pieces and fleeing for the city. Thousands died on that plain. I was with the few hundred that made it through the gates; we thought we might be safe behind those walls.' Necklen shook his head. 'They brought up huge catapults which they used with stunning accuracy, hitting the same section of wall again and again. They smashed two broad holes in the north wall, then surged through. They know no weariness, Karis: they killed and killed from midday to midnight. Men, women, babes. Shemak's Balls, it was terrifying! I hid in a loft. Me and three women. You could hear the screams outside for hours. We escaped through the sewers. I was almost delirious with pain. The surgeons had covered the stump with hot pitch, and the

192

agony was indescribable. The women half-carried me. But we made it to the outskirts and fled south-west towards the coast.' His voice tailed away.

'You need to rest,' Karis said. 'We will talk more in the morning.' Helping him up, she led him to her bed, undressed him and covered him with thick blankets.

'Satin sheets,' he said, with a smile. 'How good . . . they feel.'

He was sleeping when the surgeon arrived. The man felt for Necklen's pulse and the warrior did not stir. 'Exhaustion,' said the surgeon, 'but his heart is strong.' Carefully he unwrapped the bandage and examined the blackened stump. 'No gangrene. The wound is clean,' he announced, applying a fresh bandage. 'He needs red meat and wine to fortify his blood and hot oats to clean his system. Honey is also good for strength.'

Karis thanked the man and offered payment. He shook his head. 'I am in the Duke's employ,' he said. 'He pays me well.'

After he had gone, Karis sat down once more with her notes. But she could not concentrate. Karis had never been a sentimental woman, but she was touched by the arrival of Necklen. The little man, maimed and hurting, had made a journey of almost 600 miles with no other purpose than to reach Karis. He would have been safe in the port city of Loretheli, screened as it was by high mountains. Instead he had come to her. Necklen had never been one of her lovers, but she had always considered him a friend she could trust – the kind of man she wished her father had been. Karis put aside her notes and walked to the window. The moon was high in the cloudless night sky, and the snow in the Ducal gardens shone with an eldritch light. The city beyond was silent and serene.

The door opened and a cool draught touched her back. Karis turned to see Vint striding across the room. 'I hear you have a man in your bed, my dove,' he said. His voice was light, but the smoke-grey eyes showed no humour.

'An old friend,' she told him. 'He was at the fall of Prentuis.'

Vint unhooked his black sable cloak and draped it over a chair. 'Was it as bad as we feared?' he asked.

'Every bit as bad. The Daroth breached the walls within a single day, and butchered the inhabitants.'

Rubbing his hand over his trident beard, he turned away and

poured himself a goblet of wine. 'I have seen those walls. Corduin's are no stronger, Karis.'

'There is less level ground here,' she said. 'But I will worry about catapults and siege-engines when the snow begins to thaw. Until then there are enough problems to consider. Have you rearranged your duel with Tarantio?'

He shook his head. 'I took your advice and went to the tavern. The story was as Tarantio told it. I have offered him my apology, which he accepted. Fairly gracefully, I might add.'

'I am glad. I need you both alive.'

Vint grinned. 'It touches my heart that you care so greatly for me.'

'Do not be too overcome,' she warned him. 'If you are to die, then I would prefer it to be in a useful manner.'

He stepped in close and made to stroke her hair. 'Not tonight, Vint,' she told him. 'Tonight I must make plans.'

He spread his hands. 'As you wish. Is there any way in which I can help?'

'I don't think so.'

Vint gathered up his cloak, then strolled through to the back bedroom. He returned within moments, looking embarrassed. 'I see what you mean by old friend,' he said.

'That he is. Good night, Vint.'

After he had gone she returned to the bedside, where Necklen was sleeping deeply. Tenderly she stroked his hair. 'I am glad you are here,' she whispered.

*

Ozhobar was a huge man with sandy hair and a chin beard that straggled like an old brush. He gazed at the sketch Karis offered him, then leaned forward, reaching into a pottery jar and drawing out a thick oatcake biscuit which he devoured swiftly.

'Can you make such a catapult?' Karis asked him.

'All things are possible,' he said.

'I did not ask what was possible. Can you *do* it?'

'There is no indication here as to what the arm is constructed from, nor the weight of the stones. You say the range is around two hundred paces?'

'That is what Necklen tells me, and he is reliable. And it

194

does not throw stones, Master Weapon Maker. It hurls balls of lead.'

'Hmmm,' said Ozhobar. 'That is how they maintain accuracy. The weight of each ball is identical.'

'Can you make it?' she repeated, her irritation growing as Ozhobar ate two more oatcakes, brushing the crumbs from his beard.

'I think we can do a little better than that. I take it the purpose will be to destroy the Daroth catapults?'

'That is my plan.'

'We do not have the means to make lead balls of the size your man describes. I would suggest a small refinement. Pottery.'

'Pottery?' she repeated. 'Glazed or unglazed?'

'Sarcasm does not become women,' he said. 'In order for the catapult to be accurately used, it will be necessary to place it where the men operating it can see the enemy. That leaves three choices. The first places the weapon outside the city. This is not – one would imagine – to be desired, for the Daroth could charge forward and capture or destroy it. The second is to place it on the walls. The parapets are around twelve feet wide, therefore the machine would have to be small, hence restricting the range. The third choice would be to strip the roof from the barracks building by the north gate, and set our catapult upon a platform there.'

Karis nodded. 'That sounds a good plan. But it does not explain your use of pottery.'

'We make hollow balls and fill them with flammable material – rags drenched in lantern oil, for example. Lighter than lead, our range would therefore be increased. What I need to design is a method of ignition that would allow the men loading the machine to be safe. One wouldn't want such a ball exploding on the barracks roof.'

'And you can do this?'

'I will think on it.' He reached into the jar and took another cake.

'They look good,' said Karis. 'May I try one?'

'No, you may not,' he told her sternly. 'They are mine.'

Swallowing her irritation, Karis thanked Ozhobar for his time and rose to leave. 'Come back and see me in three days,' he said. 'And send your man Necklen to me. I need to ask some more questions about the Daroth weapon. Oh yes ... and

195

we are running short of iron. I suggest you ask the Duke to requisition gates, old cooking pots, railings . . . you know the sort of thing.'

'I'll see to it,' promised Karis.

Outside it was snowing once more, but the temperature had lifted. Children were playing in the street, throwing snowballs at one another. Their squealing laughter lifted Karis's spirits as she strolled towards the practice field.

There were already forty men present, the largest and the strongest in Corduin. Forin and the officer Capel were putting them through a series of tests. Karis stood in the shadows and watched as they lifted rocks, or bent bars of iron. Forin was moving among them, issuing orders and directing events. She found herself strangely hesitant about seeing him again. He had been ever-present in her mind since the night in the tavern. But why? He was not an exceptional lover. Poor dead Giriak had been just as powerful. Yet something had moved within her at his touch, as if a rusted lock, long unused and almost forgotten, had given way, revealing . . . revealing what, she wondered.

This is nonsense, Karis, she admonished herself. The man means nothing to you. Put it down to the stress of the day. And, more importantly, cast it from your mind! She heard his laughter echoing across the field, the other men joining in. A donkey had strayed on to the field and taken a dislike to one of the contestants. It was chasing him, and nipping at his buttocks. Karis grinned – and regained her composure.

Stepping into view she strolled to a picket fence. Forin saw her and ambled across to where she stood. 'Good morning, lady,' he said. His voice was even, his manner guarded. Karis was pleased that there was no wink, or leer; no forced intimacy.

'How goes it, Forin?'

'There are some powerful men here. All are anxious to win the pouch of silver. I'd like to try for it myself.'

'Get me fifty strong men and I'll give you such a pouch.'

'What do you need them for?'

Karis climbed to the fence and sat back, looking down on the red-bearded giant. 'At some point the Daroth will storm the walls. Nothing will stop that. I need men who can stand against them; they will be armed with heavy double-headed axes, with hafts and

196

blades of steel. So it is not only strength I need. I want men with courage. You will lead them.'

'Is this a promotion or a punishment?' he asked. 'Hand to hand against the Daroth? Not a thrilling prospect.'

'It is a promotion. You will be paid well.'

He stood silently for a moment. 'Why did you leave the other night?'

'I had matters to attend to,' she said, keeping her voice cool.

'And I had served my purpose? Ah well, I have used many as you used me. I have no complaint. I will find you your fifty men.' He turned away and strolled back across the field.

Karis swore softly, then leapt from the fence and strode back towards the palace.

*

'How are you feeling today, Brune?' asked Tarantio.

'Better, thank you,' replied the golden-eyed young man. 'I slept well.' His voice too had changed, becoming more gentle, almost melodious.

Tarantio sat down beside the bed. 'I have been concerned about you, my friend.'

'You are a kind man, Tarantio, and I am in your debt.'

'*It is not him,*' said Dace.

'*I know.*'

The sun was high in a cold, clear sky, and the bedroom was bright and warm. The fire still burned in the hearth, and the pale golden figure lay back with his head on the pillow, his body relaxed. 'Where is Brune?' asked Tarantio.

'He is here with me. He is not frightened, Tarantio. Not any more. We are friends, he and I. I will take care of him.'

'Who are you?'

'Not an easy question to answer. I am the Oltor Prime, the last of my race. Does this mean anything to you?'

'The Oltor were destroyed by the Daroth,' said Tarantio. 'Perhaps a thousand years ago.'

'At least. Do not ask me how I came to be here, for I do not know. If I could leave I would. If I could surrender this body to Brune, I would. I have no purpose any longer.'

The figure rose from the bed and stood, naked, in the sunlight

197

streaming through the window. He was thin and tall, his six-fingered hands long and delicate. His eyes were larger than human and semi-protruding, his nose small with the nostrils widely flared. 'I stood in the forest on that last day,' he said sadly, 'and I watched my people die. I surrendered myself to the land. And I died too.'

'Did you have no magic to use against the Daroth? Could you not fight?' asked Tarantio.

'We were not death dealers, my friend. We killed nothing. We were not a violent people, we had no understanding of its nature. We tried to befriend the Daroth, helping them through the Curtain, giving them land that was rich and green and full of magic. They dug into it for iron, tore at it for food, and drowned the magic with their hatred. When we closed the Curtain on them, preventing more from joining them, they turned on us with fire and sword. They devoured our young ones, and slew the old. In despair we tried to run, to open the Curtain on another world. But the magic was gone, and before we could find new, virgin land they were upon us. I was not the Oltor Prime then. I was a young Singer, wed to a beautiful maiden.'

'What does this title mean? What is the Oltor Prime?'

'It is a difficult concept to verbalize in a tongue that is new to me. He – sometimes she – is the spiritual leader of the Oltor, possessing great power. When he died in the forest he turned and pointed at me. I felt his power course through my veins. But I surrendered it and died. Or so I thought. Somehow the magicker who tried to heal Brune brought me back. The "how" is a mystery.'

'You say you surrendered your life. Did the Daroth not kill you?'

'Yes, they pierced my hearts with harsh swords, pinning me to the ground. Then they struck off my head.'

'I believe I know the answer,' said the voice of Duvodas, and Tarantio turned to see the Singer standing in the doorway. Dressed now in a tunic of green silk, his blond hair held in place by a gold circlet, Duvodas entered the room and bowed to the Oltor Prime. 'Your blood soaked into the earth: the blood of the Oltor Prime. It lay in the stones. The Eldarin found them and took them back to Eldarisa, and they lay in the Oltor Temple for generations. Forty years ago one of the humans – allowed into the city for a special meeting – stole one red stone. It was for this reason that no human was ever allowed to enter again. I have spoken to some of the people cured by Ardlin, and they claim he held a block of red coral over their wounds. Used carefully, the magic would have no ill-effect on the patients. However, Tarantio told me of Brune's healing. It seems that Ardlin lied – he told them he had a magic orb to replace the injured eye, but there was no orb. What he cast was a spell of disguise – of changing! In his haste he made an error – and released the essence that had remained in the stone for generations. He released you, Lord of the Oltors.'

The Oltor Prime sighed. 'And here I stand – without purpose, or reason for being. Locked in my hearts are the histories of my people, each one of them. What am I to do?'

'You could help us fight the Daroth,' said Tarantio.

'I cannot fight.'

'Even after they destroyed all your people?'

'Even so. I am a Healer. It is not what I do, Tarantio; it is what I *am*. If I saw a wounded Daroth, I would heal it without a moment's hesitation. In that way I feed the land with magic. I create harmony.'

'I call that the coward's way,' said Dace aloud. 'Life is a struggle, from the agonies of birth to the railing against death. Devour or be devoured. The law of the wild.'

'This land was not wild until the Daroth came,' said the Oltor.

'Did the lion not hunt the deer, leaping upon it, tearing out its throat?'

'Yes, Dace, the lion did that, for that is the lion's nature. But at no time did the deer develop fangs and claws and rend the lion.'

Dace was stunned by the use of his name. 'You can see the difference in us? You can tell us apart?'

'I can. You were born in that terrible moment when a child, Tarantio, saw his father hanging from a beam. He could not face the sight, and in his terror he created a brother who could – a brother who could survive all the terrors the world could hurl at a child. You saved him, Dace. Saved him from madness and despair. Now he saves you.'

'I need no-one to save me. I am Dace. I am the best there is, the best there ever was. Hell's teeth, I am the best there ever will be! I am not weak. When an enemy comes for me I slay him – human or Daroth, lion or wolf.'

'And yet you wept when Sigellus was cut down. You tried to

199

stop him duelling; he was drunk, his powers fading. You almost begged him to let you fight in his place. But he was proud. When he died, you felt as though a hot knife was being dragged across your soul.'

Dace's hand flashed for the dagger at his belt. He staggered. 'I did not know that,' said Tarantio, his hand dropping to his side.

'He lies!' shouted Dace.

'There was never a need for lies in a culture that knew no violence, no anger, no despair,' said the Oltor. 'That is why the Daroth fooled us. They are telepaths, and they presented a mental wall through which we did not pass. It would have been discourteous to try.'

'We are now facing the Daroth,' said Tarantio. 'Your help would be appreciated.'

'I will heal your wounded, but more than that I cannot offer. I will rest now. Perhaps you would like to speak with Brune?' The Oltor closed his eyes. Brune opened them. 'He is very sad,' said Brune. 'He wants to die.'

Moving to his clothes, Brune dressed himself. His leggings were too short now, and his clothes hung upon his slender frame. He sat down by the window. 'Can't you do nothing for him?' he asked Tarantio.

'What can I do? He is the last of a dead race.'

'But he's so sad,' said Brune. 'And he's my friend.'

'Yesterday you were frightened,' said Tarantio, 'and rightly so. Can you not see that he is taking over your body?'

'I don't mind,' said Brune. 'All my life I've been frightened. Never knowing what to do, what to say. So many things I couldn't understand. People. Wars. I couldn't remember things. Places. I used to get lost. I'm not lost now. He teaches me things, he looks after me.'

Tarantio smiled, and patted Brune's shoulder. 'We all look after you, my friend. That is why we are concerned.'

'I'll be all right, honestly I will. You won't let no-one hurt him, will you? He's not like us. He won't fight.'

'I'll do what I can,' Tarantio promised.

'He has knowledge that could end disease and famine,' said Brune. 'The Oltor may be gone, but we humans could learn so much from him.'

'If we survive the Daroth,' said Tarantio.

CHAPTER ELEVEN

SHIRA WAS NERVOUS AS SHE LAY UPON THE BED, THE GOLDEN creature sitting beside her. 'Do not fear me, child,' he said.

'I have no fear of you, sir. It is just that it pains me to have anyone . . . view my deformity.'

'I do understand, Shira. If you do not wish me to continue, I will understand that also. It may be that I can do little, for I have never encountered humans before.'

She smiled at him, then looked to Duvo. 'Do you think I should?' she asked him. He nodded and Shira closed her eyes. 'Very well, then,' she said. Duvo moved to the bedside, his harp in hand.

'There will be no need of actual music,' said the Oltor. 'The song I sing cannot be heard by you.' The scent of roses filled the room. He laid his slender, golden hand on Shira's brow and her breathing deepened instantly. 'She sleeps,' he said, drawing back the sheet. Shira was dressed in a simple cotton shift, which the Oltor raised to her hips. The deformed leg was ugly and twisted, the muscles knotted and misshapen like rocks under the skin.

The Oltor Prime placed his hand on her thigh. Astonished, Duvo watched as the hand began to glow, becoming at first translucent and then transparent. Slowly it sank beneath the surface of Shira's skin. 'The bones of the thigh and shin were broken badly,' whispered the Oltor, 'and they have been set awkwardly and suffered severe calcification. The muscles around them are badly fibrotic, no longer wet tissue, and the tendons are now too short.'

Duvodas tried to mask his disappointment. 'It was kind of you to examine her,' he said.

'Be patient, my friend, we have just begun.' Shira's thigh was glowing now, and Duvo could see the Oltor's hand moving below the surface of the skin. There was a sudden crack, the noise like a whiplash in the quiet of the room. Duvo jerked at the sound.

'What are you doing?'

'Breaking the thigh-bone and re-setting it straight. It is difficult; it is taking longer than I had thought to heal and stretch the muscles.' Slowly the knots and lumps of Shira's thigh began to shrink. After an hour the Oltor removed his hand, and began again below the knee.

As dusk approached, the room grew gloomy and Duvodas lit a lantern. 'How long now?' he asked.

'Not long. Help me to turn her over.' Gently they rolled the sleeping woman to her stomach.

'The leg looks perfect,' said Duvo.

'It is, but the muscles of the lower back are also misshapen, as is the spine. This is natural after years of limping. I must be careful now, for your son must not be touched by the magic.' His hands moved over Shira's lower back, the long fingers gently kneading the flesh. At last he stood, and covered her with a sheet. 'You may wake her now,' he said.

Duvo sat on the bed and took Shira's hand, kissing it. 'Wake up, my love,' he told her. Shira moaned softly, and yawned. Her eyes opened. 'Time to get up,' said Duvo.

Sleepily Shira pulled back the sheet and allowed Duvo to help her to stand. There was no surprise as she straightened. 'This is a lovely dream,' she said.

'It is no dream. You are healed, Shira.' The girl stood for a moment, then took several tentative steps. Ignoring both men, she sat back down on the bed and drew up her cotton shift, staring down at the now perfectly formed leg. She stood once more, then spun on her heel in a graceful pirouette.

202

'She still believes it is a dream,' said the Oltor.

'Perhaps you should pinch yourself, Shira,' suggested Duvo.

'I don't want to wake up from this,' she said, tears in her eyes.

'I can promise you that you will not,' Duvo assured her. Shira hesitated, then dug her nails into the palm of her hand.

'It hurts,' she said. 'I am awake! Oh, Duvo!' She ran to him, throwing her arms around his neck.

He kissed her, and held her close. 'You are thanking the wrong person,' he said at last, and Shira turned to the Oltor Prime.

'I don't know what to say to you,' she said. 'I cannot believe it! How can I thank you?'

'Your joy is enough, Shira,' the Oltor replied. 'I think the journey to Loretheli will be a little easier now. How soon will you be leaving?'

'As soon as the weather begins to break,' Duvo told him. 'There are more than eight thousand people preparing for the journey. You should come with us.'

'I think not,' said the Oltor. Looking down at Shira, he smiled. 'Your baby is strong and healthy, lacking nothing. His development shows he will be a lusty infant.'

'A boy, then,' she said, taking Duvo by the hand. 'A son for you, my love!'

Duvo sat down upon the bed, holding her hand in both of his. 'A son for *us*,' he corrected her. Releasing her hand, he stroked her raven hair. 'I cannot tell you how happy you have made me. And I cannot believe how I could think that love would destroy my music. Every day with you makes the power swell within me.'

'I think you are embarrassing our guest,' chided Shira.

'Not so, Shira,' said the Oltor. 'But I think I will leave you. Tell me, Duvodas, is there a place within this city where land magic still flourishes?'

'Not with any strength,' said Duvo.

'I feared not. You humans are similar to the Daroth, in that you draw magic from the land without replacing it. You carpet the ground with dead stone. It is not healthy.'

'What is it that you need?' asked Duvo.

'I need to touch the stars. There are truths I must find, and riddles which must be answered.'

'There is a park close by,' said Duvo. 'Whenever I need to feel the magic, I go there. As I said, it is not strong, but then you are far more powerful than I.'

'Will you take me there?'

'I will. In summer it is a haunt of evil men – robbers and thieves. It is too cold for them now. We should be safe.'

Hooded and cloaked, the Oltor Prime walked through the winding streets alongside Duvodas, coming into Gallows Square just as the moon emerged from behind a screen of clouds. The Oltor paused and gazed at the line of corpses hanging there. 'You find it so easy to kill,' he said sadly.

'I have never killed,' Duvodas told him.

'I apologize to you, Duvodas. But you cannot know how much pain such sights cause me. Come, we must move on swiftly. This place is like a Daroth city. It is not just that the magic has gone, but there is force here, like a whirlpool that devours. I can feel the power being leached from me.' They hurried on, through the park gates and up the ice-covered slope to the small group of hills at the centre of the park. The Oltor Prime turned to look back at the glistening city. 'What will you humans do when you have drawn all magic from the land? What will you become?' he asked.

'Perhaps we will also find a way to put it back,' said Duvodas.

The Oltor Prime nodded. 'That is a good thought. Hold to it.'

'You say that without conviction,' Duvodas pointed out. 'Do you believe we are incapable of finding a way?'

The Oltor Prime shook his head. 'No, not incapable. Just different. If all the Oltor were struck blind, save for one man, then the rest would look to him for leadership. They would seek a way for all to see. You humans would not react in this way. The blind would be jealous of the man with sight, and seek to put out his eyes also. I learned much from Brune. There was a woman in his village when he was young. She had power; she was a Healer. But they burned her in a great fire, and rejoiced when they had done so. However, let us not dwell on such matters. Do not be concerned with what you are about to see,' he said. 'No human in the city below will observe it.' The Oltor walked to the highest point of the hill and knelt down in the snow. Within moments it had melted away and Duvo felt the warmth of a summer day radiating from the golden figure before him. The Oltor began to sing in a low, sweet voice, creating music more perfect than any Duvodas had heard. He sat down, lost in the wonder of the moment.

A shimmering blue light grew around the Oltor, and Duvo sat amazed as he saw the creature's spirit swell out from his body, shining and wondrous, growing, filling the sky – a colossal, towering figure, whose gigantic arms reached out to touch the stars, cradling them in his palms. Flowers sprang into life around the Oltor's body – small snowdrops, yellow daffodils, shining in the bright moonlight. Time ceased to have meaning for the human, and as the music faded he felt a wrench, and a sense of great loss. Tears fell from Duvo's eyes and he fought back a wave of sorrow threatening to engulf him. The Oltor Prime laid his hands on Duvo's shoulders. 'I am sorry, my friend. The magic was almost too powerful for you. Be at peace.' The sorrow faded, replaced by a sense of melancholy.

'I watched you touch the stars,' said Duvo. 'How I envy you that power!'

'There is more to see, if you have the desire,' the Oltor Prime told him.

Duvodas heard the sadness in his voice. 'What is it?' he asked.

'I have the answers, Duvo, but they are painful. When the Daroth had destroyed my people, they set themselves to obliterate the Eldarin. Like us the Eldarin would not fight, but they honed their magic and cast a mighty spell.' Reaching out to the edge of the snow, the Oltor swept his hand across it, scooping it, then rolling it into a ball. This he tossed into the air – where it instantly vanished. 'The Eldarin spell ripped out across the land, gathering power, swallowing the Daroth cities, and containing them in a black Pearl which the Eldarin hid within the topmost peak of the highest mountain. The threat was gone, yet not one Daroth was slain. When the human armies came against the Eldarin there were those who considered repeating the magic, trapping the humans. But the Council of Elders chose a different route. They cast the spell against themselves – leaving one elder to take charge of the new Pearl.

'The humans killed him. And the Pearl became a cause for yet another war. It was perceived as a magical artefact – which indeed it was. And now, as a result of the greed and lust for power of one man, the Daroth have returned and thc Eldarin Pearl is far from its home.' The Oltor Prime sighed, then he turned to Duvo and laid his hand on the young man's shoulder. 'Would you like to see the city of Eldarisa again?'

'More than anything.'

'Then stand close to me.' The Oltor rose and lifted his arms, and once more the bitter cold of winter enveloped the hillside, the circle of flowers dying within minutes. Clouds gathered, and fresh snow fell upon the parkland and the city. But it did not touch Duvodas or the Oltor. For now they stood on the barren rocks that had once been the land of the Eldarin.

And here there was no snow.

*

Karis was very drunk. She stared gloomily at the empty jug. Rolling to her knees, she forced herself upright, staggered, and fell heavily to a couch. It had seemed so easy when she had promised the Duke to control her rebellious, volatile nature. Day after exhausting day she had forced herself to behave like a general, coolly detached as she supervised training routines, discussed logistics and supplies with politicians and merchants, planned strategies with her captains. Today she had watched Forin take delivery of the new axes, double-headed and deadly, each weighing thirty pounds. Even the strongest of Forin's men had been surprised at the weight of the weapons. She had gone from there to the forge of Ozhobar, and viewed the construction of the catapult, and from there to the barracks building roof where carpenters and builders were arguing over the best way to strip it and lay a flat surface for the weapon. And that was only the morning.

An appealing thought struck her. She should run to the stables, saddle Warain and ride off into the mountains, heading south for Loretheli! There she could book passage to the southern islands, where winter had no hold. I could run naked on the sands, she thought, and swim in the warm sea.

Rising once more, she tugged off her shirt and leggings, throwing them across the room. Lifting the empty jug, she hurled it at the wall where it burst into scores of jagged fragments.

Hearing the noise, a servant entered, and stood staring open-mouthed at the naked woman. 'Get out!' she bellowed. The man turned and fled.

Karis staggered to the balcony window, pushing it open. The

cold struck her as she walked out and leaned over the rail, staring down at the snow-covered courtyard below. Brushing the snow from the rail, she hooked her leg over it. A strong hand grabbed her, dragging her back into the room. Swinging, she aimed a punch at Necklen's grey-bearded face, but he blocked her arm and threw her to the couch.

'What are you doing?' she cried. 'Get out of here!'

Necklen turned to a servant who stood cowering by the door. 'Fetch me a jug of water and some bread and cheese,' he ordered. Then he knelt by Karis. 'Let's get you to bed,' he said. Her fist snaked out, but sailed harmlessly over his shoulder. Ducking into her, he hauled her upright and half-carried her to the bedroom. She fell back on the bed, and noticed that the ceiling was gently revolving.

'I want to dance,' she said. 'I want another drink.' She struggled to sit up, but Necklen pushed her back.

'You just lie there, princess, until we can get some food into you.'

Karis swore at him, loud and long, using every gutter insult she knew. Necklen sat silently throughout the tirade. The ceiling was spinning faster now, and something horrible was happening to her stomach. Groaning, she rolled to the edge of the bed, where Necklen held an empty bowl beneath her and she retched violently. And passed out . . .

When she awoke the room was dark, a single candle flickering on the table beside her bed. She sat up. Her mouth tasted vile, and her head pounded. There was a jug of water on the bedside table and she filled a goblet and drank deeply.

'Are you feeling better?' asked Necklen. The old soldier was sitting in a chair in the shadows. He rose and moved to the bed.

'I feel like death,' she told him.

'The thaw has begun, Karis. Spring is almost here.'

'I know,' she said wearily.

'This is no time to be dancing naked on balconies. Giriak told me how you stood on the rail at Morgallis. He thought you were mad, but I told him you were merely eccentric. Eccentric and unique – and far too easily bored.' Tearing off a chunk of bread, he handed it to her. Karis chewed on it without enthusiasm. 'Everyone here is relying on you, princess.'

'You think I don't know that? And don't call me princess!'

Necklen chuckled. 'I've known many commanders during my life – steady ones, reckless ones, cowardly ones. But you are an original, princess. You can't be read. With you it is all instinct. I had a horse like you once: sweet as a berry one moment, vicious and deadly the next. Highly strung, he was. But a thoroughbred, faster than the wind, stronger than a bull. And fearless. Rode through fire for me, he did. I loved that horse, but I never understood him.'

'What are you prattling on about?' demanded Karis, swinging from the bed. She groaned as the pounding in her head increased.

'Drink some more water.'

'Shemak's Balls, but you sound like my mother!' Karis drank another goblet, then ate more bread. Glancing up, she grinned at him. 'But I love you, old man!'

'So I should hope.'

She saw that the bandage around the stump of his left wrist was seeping blood. 'Oh, Hell, did I do that?'

'You didn't mean to; you were thrashing around a little. It will heal. Now, to more important matters. I have sent scouts out to the north and south-east. And the Weapon Maker wants to know if you will be there when they set up the catapult.'

'Damn right I will! . . . How are you getting on with him?'

'At first he seems a pompous bastard, but his heart is in the right place. I like him. And he knows his craft, by heaven!'

'Don't try to steal his oatcakes,' warned Karis.

Necklen laughed aloud. 'He makes them himself, you know. They are damn good. He let me have one from a fresh batch. Just the one, mind!'

Karis lay back. 'How long before the dawn?'

'Another couple of hours.'

'I'll sleep,' she said. 'Will you wake me at dawn?'

'I'll be here.' Reaching out, she took his hand and squeezed it gently. He kissed her fingers, then covered her with a blanket. 'May your dreams be sweet,' he said. 'And don't forget to say your prayers.'

'Thank you, mother,' she said, with a smile.

He blew out the candle and walked back into the main room, shutting the bedroom door behind him.

*

Duke Albreck was tired, his eyes bloodshot and gritty. Pushing away the mass of papers before him he rose, opened the door to the gardens and stepped through into the moonlight. The fresh cold air revitalized him and he shivered with pleasure. A servant announced the arrival of the soldier, Necklen, and the Duke returned to the warmth of his rooms. The old soldier looked wary.

'How is she?' asked Albreck.

'Very well, sir. She is resting.'

Albreck had never known how to communicate with ordinary people. It was as if their minds worked at a different level; they were rarely at their ease with him, nor he with them. 'Sit you down, man,' he said. 'I see your wound is bleeding again. I shall send my surgeon to you.'

'It's stopped now, sir. Scar tissue broke, is all.'

'You are a brave man,' said Albreck. 'Karis tells me you have served her before, and know her well.'

'Can't say as I know her that well,' answered Necklen, guardedly. 'She's good, though. The best there is.'

'I think that is a fair estimate,' agreed the Duke. 'However, the pressures here are very great. The burdens are onerous. Sometimes even the best find such situations . . . intolerable. There are many stories about Karis. She has become something of a legend during these last few years. One man told me she once danced naked through a town, following a victory. Is it true?'

'There's always lots of stories about generals,' said Necklen. 'Might I ask where this is leading?'

'Oh, I think you know where it is leading,' said Albreck. 'This is my city, my responsibility. It is threatened with death and destruction, by an enemy more powerful and more evil than any it has faced in its long history. I have no right to ask you for honesty, Necklen. You are not sworn to me. But I would value it, nonetheless. Karis is a great fighter, and a fine tactician. She has courage, I don't doubt that. But is she steady? For that's what we need.'

Necklen sat silently for a moment, staring into the fire. 'I am not a skilled liar, my lord – never felt the need to acquire the skills – so I'll tell you plain. Karis isn't like anyone I've ever known. She's a mass of opposites, tough and tender, caring and callous. And she has a love of wine – ay, and men. She pushes herself too hard sometimes, and then she drinks. Too much, usually.' Necklen shrugged. 'Despite

209

that there is a greatness in her. That will carry her through, don't you worry none about that. When the Daroth are before the walls, you'll see that greatness shine. I promise you that.'

The Duke smiled thinly. 'I hope that you are right. I am a capable swordsman, but I was never a soldier. Nor did I wish to be one. My skill lies in judging men. Women, I am glad to say, remain a mystery to me.'

'A wondrous mystery,' said Necklen, with a grin.

'Quite so.' In that one, small moment, there was a flicker of camaraderie. The Duke felt it, and drew back.

Necklen sensed the change of mood and rose from his chair. 'If that is all, my lord?'

'Yes. Yes, thank you. Stay close to her. See that she doesn't . . . push herself too hard.'

'I'll do my best, sir.' As he left, the Duke leaned forward, lifting a sheaf of papers, and returned to his reading.

*

Duvodas and the Oltor moved across the desert of rocks which once had been the Enchanted Park of Eldarisa. Together they climbed to the first sandstone ridge of Bizha. Duvodas remembered the first time he had climbed the Twins, scaling Bizha and standing on the top of the natural stone tower, from there to leap across the narrow space to land – breathless with excitement and fear – atop Puzhac. All the Eldarin children made the jump. It was said to epitomize the journey from childhood to manhood.

Now, on this first ridge, Duvo shivered, more at the sadness of his memories than the cold winds howling around the rocks. 'Why are we here?' he asked the Oltor.

'Observe,' said the Oltor Prime. He began to sing, his voice melting into the wind, becoming part of it, dark as the night, icy as a winter peak; a song of starlight and death. The music filled Duvo's heart, and he unwrapped his harp and began to play the notes clear and clean in perfect harmony with the Singer. Duvo had no idea where the music came from. It was unlike anything he had ever played, weaving a mood that was dark and contemplative. Then it changed. The Oltor's sweet voice rose. Still matching the bitterness of a bleak winter, the Oltor introduced a light rippling chord, like the first shaft of sunlight after a storm. No, thought Duvo, like a birth on a battlefield, incongruous, out of place, and yet beautiful.

210

A gentle light began to glow some twelve feet above the rocky ground, spreading out like a mist across the land. Then it rose, fashioning itself into ghostly, translucent images. Duvo ceased his playing, and watched in silent awe as the city of Eldarisa was slowly sculpted in light. Not just the buildings, but the flowers of the park and the people of the Eldarin: frozen in place, transparent. Duvo felt he could step from the rock and become part of the light, for it glowed mere inches from the ridge on which he sat. He was about to do so when the Oltor ceased his song and laid his hand on Duvo's shoulder. 'You cannot walk there, my friend. Not yet,' said the Oltor Prime.

The golden figure raised his hands, palms pressed together as if in prayer, then drew a vertical line through the air. As his hands swept down Duvo felt a rush of warm air strike him. His eyes widened with shock as he saw sunlight stream through the line made by the Oltor's hands. The line opened further, and through it Duvo could see the City of Eldarisa, not fashioned in light but in stone and wood, solid and real, the grass of the park green and verdant.

'I have opened the Curtain,' said the Oltor Prime. 'Follow me.'

On trembling legs Duvodas stepped through. There were children, statue still, throwing a ball which hung in the air like a small moon. Older Eldarin were sitting on park benches. Not a movement could be seen. There was not a breath of wind. Duvo glanced up at the summer sky. Clouds stood motionless.

'How can this be?' he asked the Oltor.

'Time has no meaning here. Nor will it. Come, help me in what I must do.'

The Oltor Prime moved across the Great Square and up the broad flight of granite steps to the entrance of the Oltor Temple. There were some Eldarin inside. A father, statue-still, was pointing towards a section of bones laid upon a velvet-covered table. Beside him his children stood in silent, frozen wonder.

The Oltor Prime stood in the centre of the enormous hall, scanning the thousands of bones. Then he strode towards the high altar, and lifted a chunk of red coral. Duvodas followed him. 'This was once my lifeblood,' said the Oltor Prime. 'Now it will be the lifeblood of my people.' Lifting a section of blue velvet cloth, he tore a long strip loose. 'You will need to cover your eyes, my friend,' he said, 'for there will be blinding lights that would melt your sight away

211

for good.' Duvodas took the velvet strip and tied it around his head. The Oltor handed him his harp. 'You will not know the song I am to sing, but let your harp follow it as your heart dictates.'

Once more the Oltor's sweet voice broke out in song. Duvo waited for several moments, feeling the rhythm, charting the melody. Then he began to play. Even through the velvet blindfold he could see the brightness grow. It was sharp and painful, and he turned away from it. The music was similar to the Song of Morning which Ranaloth had taught him many years before. But it was infinitely more rich and multi-layered. And slowly the song swelled, other voices joining in, until it seemed that a great choir was filling the Temple with a magic so potent that Duvo's senses swam.

He sank to his knees and let fall his harp. The music washed over him like a warm wave, and he lay down upon the stones and dreamed. In his dream he saw the Oltor Prime, standing before a host of his people. The Curtain of Time was open once more, and the people filed slowly through it to a land of green fields and high mountains: a place of peace, harmony and tranquillity. Duvodas longed to go with them.

He awoke as the Oltor Prime touched his face, feeling more rested than at any time in his life. Pulling clear his blindfold, he saw that the Eldarin father was still pointing towards the high altar. But now there was nothing upon it. Swiftly Duvo scanned the great hall of the Temple. It was empty. Not one shard of bone remained – save the skull held in the hands of the Oltor Prime. 'You brought them back from the dead!' whispered Duvo.

'*We* brought them back, Duvodas. You and I.'

'Where are they?'

'In a new land. I must join them soon, but I need your help one last time.'

'What can I do?'

The Oltor lifted the skull. 'This is all that is left of me, my friend. I cannot join to it, for I cannot both sing and be born again. You must play the song you heard.'

'I cannot do it like you. I do not have the skill.'

The Oltor Prime smiled. 'You do not need the skill. You need the heart – and this you have.' The Oltor retied the blindfold. 'Join with me in the music. And when I fall silent, play on!'

Once more the song sounded. Duvo's fingers danced upon the

212

harp strings. There was no conscious creation of sound, no planned melody. The music he played was automatic and instantaneous. He failed to notice when the Oltor's voice faded away, and his fingers continued to dance effortlessly along the strings of his harp.

A hand touched his shoulder, and he let the music die away. 'We are here, Duvodas,' said the Oltor. Duvo untied the blindfold and rubbed his eyes. Lying on the floor was the sleeping figure of Brune. No longer golden-skinned, he was the sandy-haired young man Duvo had first seen in the Wise Owl tavern with the swordsman, Tarantio. Beside him stood the tall, naked figure of the Oltor Prime.

'I must leave now,' said the Oltor, 'and you must return to the world.' He handed Duvo a small piece of red coral. 'I have imbued this with a spell, which will open the Curtain twice only. It will take you to the land below a monastery on a high mountain some forty miles south-east of the ruined city of Morgallis. There you will find Sirano. He has the Pearl with him. Take Tarantio with you, if he will go.'

'Could you not stay and help us?'

'I wish to see no more wars. I have touched the stars, Duvodas, and seen many wonders. The Eldarin allowed the humans through the Curtain many centuries ago. Do you know why?'

'Ranaloth told me it was because our world was dying.'

'Yes, there was charity and kindness involved in the deed. But the underlying reason was that the Eldarin knew you were similar to the Daroth. They felt great guilt for imprisoning an entire race. You humans were not as grossly evil as the Daroth, but you had a capacity for vileness which the Eldarin were trying to understand. They believed that if they could master relations with the humans it would better help them when they restored freedom to the Daroth.'

'We are not like the Daroth! I cannot believe that.'

The Oltor sighed. 'But, deep down, you do, Duvodas. Yours is a race whose imagination is limited to its own small appetites. Greed, lust, envy – these are the motivating forces of humankind. What redeems you is that within every man and woman there is a seed that can grow to encompass love, joy and compassion. But this seed is never allowed to prosper in fertile ground. It struggles for life among the rocks of your human soul. The Eldarin came, at last,

213

to this realization. And here they are all around us, unmoving. Alive, and yet not living.'

'I thought this but a frozen moment in time,' said Duvodas. 'I thought you had opened a Curtain on a heartbeat from the past!'

'No, my friend, though it is a heartbeat frozen in time. This is the present. We are inside the Pearl.' For a moment only the words failed to register. Duvo looked around him at the silent buildings and the statue-still Eldarin. 'Rather than fight or kill,' continued the Oltor Prime, 'they chose to withdraw from the world. They left behind one elderly mystic to carry the Pearl to a place of safety. He did not survive.'

'How can I help them?' asked Duvo. 'How can I bring them back?'

'First you must find Sirano and the Pearl, then bring it to the highest mountain above Eldarisa. Lodge it there and climb the Twins. Then you must play the Creation Hymn. You know it – Ranaloth taught you.'

'I know it. But I was here once before. I cannot find the magic in these rocks.'

'And yet you must, if the Eldarin are to live again.'

Brune took a deep, shuddering breath and woke. He sat up and looked at the Oltor. 'You . . . are not with me any more,' he said, fear in his voice.

'A part of me will always be with you, Brune. And now it is time to say goodbye.'

*

Ozhobar was a large man, and distrustful of the spindly ladders giving access to the stripped barracks roof. Yet he climbed steadily, unwilling to allow his invention to be set in place by inferior hands. Coming to the roof, he stepped out and cast an expert eye over the work of the four carpenters, who stood by expectantly. They had constructed a large, flat surface of interlocking planks, set on four huge beams. Ozhobar strode on to it, stamping his foot here and there. It was solid, the joints neat, the pins planed down perfectly. Satisfied, he took a piece of string and summoned one of the workmen. 'Hold this in place with your thumb,' he said, laying one end of the string on the centre of the platform. Stretching the other end to its full length of five feet, he took a piece of chalk and traced a circle with a diameter of ten feet on the wood. The carpenter watched with curiosity as Ozhobar shortened the string by three inches, then traced a second circle within the first. Returning the string to his pocket, he called the carpenters to him. 'I want a series of holes drilled within the chalk lines, three inches deep and set four inches apart. No more, no less.'

'What are they for?' asked the team leader.

'Pegs,' said Ozhobar. 'I need the work completed by noon. The rails are being delivered then.' The Weapon Maker strode away from them to where a series of pulleys had been constructed, the ropes hanging down to the street far below. He had designed it himself to take three times the expected weight of the weapon and its ammunition. Even so his mind was full of calculations, possible problems and their likely solutions. Crossing the roof once more, he scanned the countryside beyond the northern wall. He already knew it was 400 yards to the first probable Daroth catapult site, 375 to the second, and 315 to the third. Prevailing winds in spring came from the south-east – but not always. In terms of maintaining optimum accuracy, the wind might still prove a problem.

He saw Karis on the wall some sixty feet to the north. She was talking to several officers and the veteran warrior, Necklen. Seeing him she waved and smiled. Ozhobar gave a cursory nod and turned away. Could he build a catapult? Could a blind man piss in the dark? Irritating woman.

His natural sense of fairness asserted itself and he felt guilty about his rudeness. It was hardly her fault that she, like all the others, failed to recognize his genius. People rarely did. The world was full, it seemed to Ozhobar, of men with small minds and little imagination. 'Why are there so many fools in the world?' he had once asked his father.

'Well, boy, the world is ruled by fools so that other fools might prosper. Men of imagination are not highly regarded, as I fear you will find.'

How true it had proved! At thirty-five Ozhobar had seen many of his inventions scorned by lesser minds, his written papers mocked by the wise men of the day. Only now, with Corduin about to be destroyed, had they come to him. And for what? His water-pumping machine? His designs for an inter-connected sewage system

215

to alleviate the spread of sickness and plague? His water-filtration device? No. For crossbows and armour and giant catapults. To call it galling would be an understatement.

'What diameter holes do you want, sir?' asked the team leader, moving up behind him.

'One inch should suffice.'

'I'll have to send down for new drill bits. It'll take time.'

'What size do you have?'

'Three-quarter, sir. And we've plenty of pegs that size to fit them.'

Ozhobar thought the problem through. The pegs would lock the wheels of the catapult into place, the rails allowing the weapon to be turned through 360 degrees. When the throwing-arm was released there would be a savage kick-back, driving the wheels into the pegs. Would three-quarters be thick enough? Should he design pegs of iron instead? That would be simple enough. But then iron pegs could damage the peg holes.

'Sir?'

'Yes, use three-quarters. But deepen the holes. If a peg snaps, it will need to be hammered through, so as to allow a fresh peg to be inserted.'

'Yes, sir.'

The man walked away. Ozhobar heard a distant voice call his name and he ambled across to the edge of the roof, gazing down to the street below. There was a cart drawn up there, carrying twelve of the huge pottery balls he had ordered; they were packed in straw. His irritation rose. They were not due until later this afternoon, and the canvas-roofed shelter had not yet been constructed for them.

His irritation flared into anger minutes later when the pulley crew, in their anxiety to finish the job swiftly, cracked one of the balls against the side of the building, smashing it to shards.

For the next hour the Weapon Maker moved back and forth between the pulley crew and the carpenters, checking the work. The pottery balls were stored against the western side of the roof, and covered with a canvas sheet. The circular iron rails arrived in the early afternoon, and Ozhobar himself fitted them over the chalk circles, hammering the iron spikes into place. It was almost dusk before the first sections of the catapult were hauled into the street below. Ozhobar oversaw the lifting of the cross-beamed base and the throwing-arm, then ordered lanterns to be lit so that the work could continue after dark.

It was midnight before the weapon was fully in place, its four wooden wheels set within the iron rails. The throwing-arm extended upwards more than ten feet, the bronze cup at the top gleaming in the lantern light. Ozhobar swung the machine to the right, and the wheels groaned as the catapult moved. He greased the axles. Now there was no sound as the catapult turned.

'I hope it works,' said the team leader, a thin-faced man with a seemingly permanent sneer.

Ozhobar ignored him, then smiled as he pictured the man sitting in the copper cup as the holding hook was hammered clear. In his mind's eye he could see the fellow sailing up and over the north wall.

It began to snow. Ozhobar ordered the catapult to be covered with a tarpaulin, then made the long perilous descent to the ground, four floors below.

Striding back through the city, he stopped at a tavern for a brief meal, then walked the mile and a half to his workshop. His burly assistant, Brek, was talking to Forin and the female general, Karis.

Ozhobar moved to the forge, holding out his hands to the heat. 'Are we ready?' he asked the black-bearded Brek.

'It is mostly assembled, Oz. A few minor additions will be needed to the helm.'

'Then let us go through,' he said. Aware of his earlier discourtesy, he bowed to Karis. 'After you, General.'

Karis moved through to the rear store-room. There, set on a wooden frame, was a curiously wrought breastplate of polished iron, with bulging shoulder-guards and a raised, semi-circular neck-plate. Brek walked to a nearby workbench and came back with a huge helmet which he fitted inside the neck-guard. 'It looks like a huge beetle,' said Forin, with a deep belly laugh.

'Put it on,' said Karis.

'You're joking!'

'I never joke. Put it on.'

Forin stepped up to the frame. Brek removed the helm, then lifted the breastplate clear, placing it over Forin's broad shoulders. The jutting shoulder-guards made him look even more enormous. The open sides were protected by chainmail, which Brek hooked into place. 'Now the helm,' said Karis.

The large, conical helmet was lowered into place, then hooked to the neck-guard. Forin's green eyes shone with humour as he gazed out of the slitted visor. 'I feel like an idiot,' came his muffled voice.

'How appropriate,' observed Ozhobar.

'What did he say? I can't hear a damned thing in here.'

Lifting a heavy broadsword from beside the black forge, Ozhobar swung it over his head and brought it down hard against the side of the helm. Forin staggered and almost fell; then he whirled on the Weapon Maker. Ozhobar struck him again. This time the sword snapped in two.

'Remove the helm,' ordered Ozhobar. Brek climbed on a bench and lifted the helmet clear.

'You whoreson!' stormed Forin. 'I'll break your . . .'

'You are alive, idiot!' snapped Ozhobar. 'Had you not been wearing the armour, I would have cut your head from your shoulders. I do not know how strong the Daroth will prove, but I am stronger than most men and I could not dent the metal!'

'He's right,' said Karis. 'How does the armour feel?'

'Damned heavy. But the helmet needs padding; it felt as if I was inside a town bell. I can still feel it ringing in my ears. Also we'll need eye-slits at the sides. The helmet isn't made to turn with the head; the head turns inside it. We need side vision.'

'That is already in the design,' said Ozhobar. 'As Brek said earlier, we still have to complete the helmet. That said, I am pleased with it. If it meets with your approval, General, I shall have the Armourer begin work on the others.'

'What about protection for the arms?' asked Forin.

'I am developing a complex design of interlocking arm plates,' Ozhobar told him. 'The first set should be ready by next week. The elbow section is the problem at present, but I will find a way around it. How are the axes?'

Forin shrugged. 'At first I thought they would prove impossible to wield, but we are getting used to them. The men improve day by day. Why did you design the blades to flare at the base and tip? They look like butterfly wings.'

'As indeed they were intended to,' said Ozhobar. 'The problem with the simple half-moon design is that when it smashes through the ribs it can catch within the body. The butterfly design will help to prevent such a possibility. I hope you have also noticed that the upward flare of the blades allows it to be used as a stabbing weapon.'

'An axe is not a stabbing weapon,' objected Forin.

Ozhobar moved to a bench at the rear of the room, lifting a black short-handled axe. Holding it like a spear, he suddenly threw it at a nearby door. The upper points of the head slammed deep into the wood. Ozhobar walked to the door, wrenching it open. Two shining points of steel had completely pierced the door, and were jutting like dagger blades from the wood. 'My axe is also a stabbing weapon,' he said. 'It just takes a little imagination to see it.'

'Your point is well made, Oz,' said Karis. 'And I am delighted with the armour.'

Only Ozhobar's closest colleagues were allowed to use the short form of his name, and inwardly he bridled at her casual use of it. But, almost in the same moment, he realized that he liked the sound of it from her lips. Reddening, he muttered something banal. She smiled then, thanked him and Brek for his time and, with Forin, walked from the room.

Brek was grinning. 'Don't say a word!' Ozhobar warned him.

'Perish the thought,' answered Brek.

*

Outside the snow had turned to sleet, the temperature just below freezing. 'Only a matter of weeks now,' said Karis.

'Ay,' agreed Forin. 'You look tired, Karis. You need some sleep.'

She chuckled. 'You were right. You did look like a giant beetle.' Then there was silence. Karis was loath to walk away from the green-eyed giant, and he too seemed ill at ease. 'I'll see you tomorrow,' she said at last.

'It is already tomorrow,' he pointed out. She shrugged and walked away. He called her name, his voice soft and low. Karis paused, then walked on. Damn the man, she thought. Why does he fill my mind?

As she strode on, a large black hound padded out from an alleyway and began walking alongside her. She stopped and glanced down. 'Where do you think you are going?' she asked. The hound cocked its huge head and looked at her. Squatting down, she stroked the squat muzzle, then patted its back; she felt the bones of its ribs

219

under her hand. A figure shuffled out of the darkness and Karis rose, one hand on her dagger.

'You won't need that,' said the elderly man. 'I'm harmless enough.' His back was arthritic and bent and he was struggling to carry a bundle of firewood.

'It is late to be out,' she said.

'The house was too damned cold, so I took the opportunity of ripping a few sticks from a rich man's fence.' He gave a gap-toothed grin, then looked down at the dog. 'He's called Stealer,' he said.

'Your dog?'

'No-one's dog. He lives by his wits – and by catching rats. Good judge of character, is Stealer. He has a nose for a soft heart.'

'His nose has betrayed him this time,' she said.

The old man was unconvinced. 'I don't think so. Anyway, the chill is getting to me, so I'll say good night to you.' He shuffled away into the moon shadows and Karis walked on, the dog padding alongside her.

At the gates of the palace she waved at the guards and made her way to her rooms. A servant had lit a fire some hours before, and the coals were glowing with a dying red. Stealer loped across the room and stretched himself out on a rug before the hearth. A covered platter had been left on the table. Karis lifted the lid and saw a plate of salted beef, a round of red cheese and a loaf. Suddenly hungry, she sat down. Stealer was immediately beside her, staring up at her with his large brown eyes. 'You are a beggar, sir,' she said. His head tilted. She fed him the meat, then tucked into the bread and cheese. Stealer watched until the last morsel was gone, then padded back to the fire. Karis added the last of the coal, then wandered into the bedroom.

Blowing out the lanterns, she took off her clothes and slipped under the blankets. Almost immediately a terrifying growl sounded from the main room. Throwing back the covers, she ran out to find Vint standing against the wall, knife in hand, the huge hound before him with teeth bared.

'Come here!' she called.

'Me or the beast?' enquired Vint. Karis chuckled. Stealer did not move. Karis strolled across to him and knelt down, stroking his muzzle.

'This man is, loosely, what one might call my friend. Therefore it would be best if you did not rip his throat out.' She patted the broad head, then stood and took Vint's hand, leading him into the bedroom. 'You are just what I need,' she told him.

Moments later they were both naked. As they were caressing Karis noted a swift change in Vint, a sudden softness. 'What is wrong?' she whispered.

'The damn thing is looking at me,' he said. Karis turned her head, to see that Stealer was standing with his front paws on the bed, his squat nose inches from Vint's face. It was too much for Karis, and her laughter pealed out.

Vint slumped down beside her. 'I don't think he likes me,' he said.

'Bring some meat next time you come. I have a feeling that Stealer's affections are easily bought.'

'He is the ugliest hound I've ever seen. How did you come by him?'

'He adopted me.'

'You do have an uncanny effect on males, Karis! I'll give you that.'

*

The winds were howling across the jagged rocks, whipping sleet against the cold walls of the cliffs. A violet light shimmered, then two men were standing where a moment before there had been only a long-dead tree and an empty trail.

Tarantio ran forward, ducking behind a rock as the icy needles of sleet slashed into him. Duvodas came alongside. 'This should be the mountain,' he said.

'I have to say, Singer, that I did not really believe your story. If I had, I would have thought twice about accompanying you.'

Duvo glanced up. The clouds were thick, the darkness almost absolute. Then there was a break in the clouds which lasted just long enough for both men to see the outline of the monastery, high up the mountainside. 'That's a long climb,' said Tarantio, 'and it will be a cold one.'

Duvo closed his eyes and warmth radiated from him, enveloping Tarantio. They stood and began the ascent. Despite the heat it was an uncomfortable climb, for the sleet melted into rain around them and both men were drenched within minutes.

The path grew narrow, and Duvodas slipped. Tarantio caught his arm. For a heartbeat only Duvodas found himself staring down over an awesome drop, his heart hammering in panic. 'Walk on the inside,' said Tarantio. Gratefully Duvodas exchanged places and they climbed on. The wind picked up, battering at them, the rocky path underfoot was icy and treacherous. Conversation was impossible, and they ducked their heads into the wind and slowly forced their way up the mountain.

The heat spell was useless against the power of the wind, and ice began to form inside their clothing. Duvo found his mind wandering; he sat down suddenly. Tarantio loomed over him. 'What in Hell's name do you think you are doing?' he shouted.

'I think I'll sleep for a little while.'

'Are you mad? You'll die.'

Duvo's eyes closed. Tarantio's cold hand slashed across his face in a stinging slap. 'Get up!' ordered the warrior. The sudden pain cut through his drowsiness and, taking Tarantio's hand, he hauled himself to his feet. As the two men struggled on, the wind grew into a storm which lashed at them, buffeting them against the rocks, making balance and movement a continuing nightmare. Arms linked, the climbers pressed on, finally rounding a bend and entering a cleft away from the wind. The relief was indescribable. Duvo pressed his back to the wall, and once more summoned the heat spell. Drawing Tarantio in close, the two men stood shivering as the warmth grew, easing through their icy clothing.

'We must be close,' said Duvo, his voice shaking.

'Let's hope they open the gate.'

'Why would they not?' Duvo asked.

'They might not hear us in the storm. I would guess they are all tucked up in their beds. Wait here. I'll find out.'

Tarantio moved away into the darkness and Duvo slumped down. Steam was rising from his clothes and the growing warmth was delicious. He lay down on the rock and fell asleep. Minutes later, when Tarantio shook him awake, Duvo was icy-cold. The heat spell could only be maintained while he was awake. Shivering uncontrollably, he fought to restore it. Tarantio sat down beside him. 'By the Gods, you are a fool!' hissed the warrior.

'I . . . am . . . sorry.'

'Not as sorry as I would have been, without a way back to Corduin.'

'Did you find the monastery?'

'Yes. It is around two hundred paces further on. There is a nasty section of rock, narrow and covered in ice. I think we should wait for the dawn before trying it.'

'I don't think I can stay awake that long.'

Tarantio's dagger pricked the skin under Duvo's chin. 'If you fall asleep, I think I know a way to wake you.'

The night wore on, seemingly endlessly to the exhausted Duvodas, and when at last the first rays of dawn could been seen illuminating the southern end of the cleft, he felt a surge of elation.

'What do we know about this monastery?' asked Tarantio – the first words he had spoken in hours.

'Very little. I looked for references to it in the library at Corduin. It was originally built by Priests of the Source hundreds of years ago. Now it is owned by a sect who call themselves the Letters of Revelation. Their cult believes the end of the world is upon us.'

'They may not be far wrong,' said Tarantio grimly. 'Let us hope they are early risers.'

The two men rose wearily to their feet and moved along the cleft. Duvodas stumbled to a halt before the narrow ledge leading to the gates of the monastery. It was around 100 paces long, ice-covered and slanted, in places no more than three or four feet wide. The drop to the left of the ledge was dizzyingly deep. 'How high do you think we are?' he asked Tarantio.

'A thousand feet. Maybe more,' answered the warrior. 'The height is immaterial. A drop of a hundred feet would see a man dead. All this means is that you will be in the air for longer.'

'I don't think I can walk across that,' said Duvo.

'Move ahead of me. I'll catch you if you stumble.'

'I can't.'

Dace grabbed Duvo's fur-lined cloak and slammed him back against the rock wall. 'You listen to me, you miserable whoreson! You've dragged me half-way across the land with your tale of woe, of rescuing the Eldarin and imprisoning the Daroth. And now a little danger has you pissing your breeches. You'll walk – or I swear I'll hurl you over the edge.'

'Not everyone is blessed with your courage,' said Duvodas, 'but

223

I will make the attempt. Not because you threaten me, but because you are right. It is more important to find the Pearl.'

Tarantio released him. 'Hold to the wall, and move slowly. If your foot slips, drop to your stomach. Do not try to maintain balance.'

Duvo took a deep breath and was about to step forward, when the sound of distant singing came from the monastery. A wall of warmth struck him. Ahead the ice began to melt on the ledge. The heat was now almost unbearable and both men turned their backs to it. As they did so, they saw the same effect flowing along the cleft. 'They understand the magic of the land,' said Duvo. 'They are clearing a path for us.'

The wall of heat moved on, flowing past them. Stepping out, Duvo ran along the ledge and up the small slope to the ancient gates. Tarantio came up behind him.

'They are not doing it for us,' said Tarantio. 'If they were, the heat would have stopped where we were. And they are still singing their magic.'

'I don't care,' said Duvo happily. 'We made it, Tarantio.' He thumped his fist on the gate. After several moments he heard a latch creak, and when the gate opened an elderly monk stood there in woollen robes of flowing white. He had kindly brown eyes and a gentle smile.

'Who are you?' he asked. 'What are you doing here?'

'Can we come in?' asked Tarantio. 'It has been a cold night and I would appreciate a warm meal.'

'Of course. Of course.' The old priest stepped aside. After they had entered he closed the gate and led them across a small courtyard and into the main building, up three flights of stairs and along a corridor. Here there was a long, narrow dining-room. Another white-robed priest was working in the kitchen area, cleaning dishes. The sound of singing was muted now, but the travellers could still hear it coming from far below.

'Good morning again, Brother Nemas,' said the old man to the dish-washing priest. 'We have two visitors. Is there any soup left?'

'Indeed there is, brother. Have they come to join us?'

'If they have, it is too late,' said the old monk. 'But at least we can give them a warm meal for their journey back to the damned.'

There was a bright fire burning in an iron stove by the far wall.

Tarantio walked to it and warmed his hands, then he moved to the window which overlooked the courtyard and the gates. The old priest set two bowls of steaming soup on the table. Duvodas thanked him. 'We are here looking for a man named . . .'

'Kario,' said Tarantio suddenly. 'A young man who was sent to join you. Have you seen him?'

'Kario? No, I don't believe we have any acolytes of that name. But then we may have turned him away. Now that the last days are upon us, there is no need of new acolytes. The evils of this world will be burned away and the Letters of Revelation will rule, as our prophet ordained. Have no fear, brothers, we will rule wisely and well, and the world will become a paradise of prayer and celebration. I am sorry that your journey here has been in vain.'

'We are grateful for your hospitality,' said Tarantio. 'And doubly grateful for the heat spell you sent down the path for us.'

'It was not for you, my friend, though I am glad you took benefit from it. The Servants of the Lord are coming, and we wished to show them courtesy.'

'The Servants of the Lord?' queried Duvodas.

'Those who are fulfilling His desires. The Cleansers. The Bringers of Fire and Destruction. As the Holy Word tells us: "Their swords will plough the cities, their spears will sunder armies. Fortress walls will shiver and fall at the sound of their hoof beats."'

'The Daroth,' said Tarantio.

'Indeed,' agreed the old man amiably. 'The Servants of the Lord. Your soup is getting cold. Eat. Rest.'

Tarantio sat down and ate, dipping bread into the soup. It was bland and tasteless. 'It is very good,' he said. 'Tell me, brother, why are the Servants of the Lord coming here?'

'We sent an emissary to them – to let them know that not all men are consumed by evil. We captured one of their enemies, the vile Sirano. He destroyed many of the Servants with devilish fire, then escaped into the wilderness. We have him here – awaiting their justice.'

The sound of singing faded away, to be followed by a booming noise coming from the gates. 'Ah, they are here,' said the old priest. 'Please excuse me. I must welcome them with my brothers.'

225

It was Dace who rose and moved to block the priest's path. 'Where is Sirano held?' he asked.

'Why would you wish to know that?'

'We are here to rescue him,' said Dace.

'You are Slaves of the Ungodly?' The old man took a backward step. 'I shall tell you nothing.' Dace drew a throwing-knife, then spun and hurled it into the throat of the priest in the kitchen. The man staggered back, then fell from sight. Dace drew a second blade and advanced on the old man.

'Oh, you will tell me, old fool. And you will tell me now!'

'He is in the upper turret,' wailed the old man. 'Please do not kill me!'

Dace sheathed the knife, and gestured to the priest to leave. 'Go,' he said coldly. 'Welcome your guests.' As the old man shuffled past the warrior, Dace slammed a blow to the priest's neck which snapped with a loud crack. 'Let's go,' he told Duvodas.

'There was no need to kill them,' stormed Duvo.

'Look out of the window,' ordered Dace, and Duvodas did so. In the courtyard below, some twenty Daroth warriors had marched through the gates. 'You think any of these priests will be alive come dusk? Now let's find Sirano.'

With a heavy heart Duvodas followed Dace. The two men left the room and ran along the corridor. Finding a set of stairs leading up, they took them two at a time. At the top was another corridor; moving along it they came to a spiral staircase. 'This place is like a rabbit warren,' said Dace. 'I can't tell where we are. Let us hope this is the way to the turret he spoke of.'

Running up the stairs they came to a bolted door. Dace opened it and stepped inside, but the room within was empty. He swore and moved to the window. There were three more turrets visible. 'Is there no magic you can use to find him?' he asked Duvodas.

The Singer shook his head. 'Not magic – but have you noticed only that turret windows has bars?' he said, pointing across the courtyard. 'The question is, how to reach it.'

'That, at least, is simple,' said Dace, opening the window and climbing out on to the narrow sill. The courtyard was some sixty feet down, but below the window, to the right, was a parapet that connected the turrets. Dace tensed, then leapt the gap. Duvodas took a deep breath and climbed out. Closing his eyes, he made the jump. Dace grabbed him, hauling him to safety, then together they ran along the parapet, entering a small door and emerging into a narrow corridor and a second circular stair.

At the top they unbolted the door and stepped inside, where a man was lying in a pallet bed. His face was hideously burned on the left hand side. Pus was seeping from the ruined eye-socket, and his hair had been burned away. He was unconscious.

'He looks close to death,' said Dace. 'You want me to carry him through?'

'You are right. He is on the verge of death.' Duvodas unwrapped his harp and sat beside the bed. His fingers rippled across the strings and the scent of roses filled the room. 'What in Hell's name are you doing?' hissed Dace. 'The Daroth could be on their way here now!'

'Then watch out for them,' said Duvodas calmly. His fingers danced upon the strings.

Dace ran from the room and down the stairs. Far below, someone screamed. Moving to a window, he gazed down to see a priest staggering out into the courtyard, blood streaming from a gaping wound in his back. The huge figure of a Daroth moved slowly after him. Other screams began. 'Well,' said Dace softly, 'you were right about the end of the world. Your world, anyway.' To Dace the screams were more musical than the hideous noise coming from Duvo's harp. How, he wondered, could people enjoy such sounds?

'*I do*,' said Tarantio.

'*Then you enjoy them, brother. Call me when killing is needed.*' Dace faded back and Tarantio rose and moved back up the stairs. The wounded man was awake now. His face was still badly scarred, but the wounds were clean.

Sirano sat up. 'Who are you?' he asked.

'I am Duvodas and this is the warrior, Tarantio. We have come to find the Pearl. We must return it to the lands of the Eldarin. We must bring them back.'

'What are the screams I hear?'

'The Daroth are killing the priests.'

Sirano gestured to a canvas pack by the far wall. When Duvodas moved to it and opened the flap, the Eldarin Pearl lay there. Reaching into the bag Duvo tenderly stroked the surface, which was warm to the touch. His hand trembled. The Eldarin were here, trapped within an orb of pure magic together with their homes, their lands, the rivers and streams that fed the earth, and the forests where Duvo had played as a child. All existed beneath his palm. Reverently he closed the canvas flap. 'Now we can go,' he said, looping the bag over his shoulder. 'Now there is hope.'

'We can talk about hope back in Corduin,' said Tarantio. 'Are you ready, Duvodas?'

'Ready for what?'

'To get us back with your Oltor magic?'

'We must make it back to level ground,' Duvo told him. 'Otherwise we might appear a thousand feet above Corduin.'

Tarantio swore. In the courtyard below three priests had tried to reach the mountain path. A long spear plunged through the back of the first, pinning him to the gates. The second was almost cut in half by a swinging broadsword. The third, a young man, fell to his knees and begged for his life. A Daroth warrior grabbed him by the hair and dragged him back into the building. Tarantio drew back from the window. 'There is only one way out,' he said, 'and the Daroth are there. Our only chance is to find a rope to climb over the battlements.'

Sirano rose and put on his clothes, which were scorched, blackened and bloodstained. The three men left the room and made their way back to the parapet door. Tarantio stepped through and peered down into the courtyard. Five bodies lay there, blood drenching the snow around them. There were no sounds of screaming now. Swiftly Tarantio led the others across to a second door and along a corridor, stopping to look into each room. Moving silently down another flight of stairs, they came to a store-room where there were barrels of wine and ale, casks of dried fruit, sacks of salt and flour.

In the corner lay two coils of rope. Sounds of booted feet on stone came from outside, and the three men ran to the rear of the store-room, ducking down behind the barrels.

The door opened and two Daroth entered. Duvodas heard the hissing sound of their breathing, and was sure they could hear the pounding of his heart. A clicking noise sounded, and Duvodas heard the scraping of a sack on the stone. Then there was silence. Cautiously he peered over the barrels: the Daroth had gone.

228

'They wanted the salt,' whispered Tarantio. 'I would guess they are about to feed.'

'Maybe we can slip by them,' suggested Duvodas.

'I doubt it. Any time now they will find Sirano gone; then they will search the monastery. Our best chance is to use the ropes and slip over the battlements.'

'They will be able to see us from the main building,' objected Sirano.

'You have any other suggestions?' Tarantio asked.

'Let them find me. Then you two can slip through the gate.'

Tarantio stared at the scarred young man. 'You want to die?' he asked.

'It holds no terrors for me. I brought the world to this. I destroyed the Eldarin and allowed the Daroth to live again. My city is destroyed, my people slain. Look at me. Disfigured and grotesque. Why should I fear to die?'

'*He has a point,*' said Dace. '*He is an ugly son of a bitch.*'

'It is true that you have been responsible for great evil,' said Duvodas, 'but no man should ignore the possibility of redemption.'

'I don't want redemption,' declared Sirano. 'I want revenge! That will best be achieved if you succeed with the Pearl. The Eldarin can destroy the Daroth. They have the power.'

'Even if we brought them back, they might not do it,' said Duvodas. 'They are not killers.'

'The more fool them,' said Sirano. 'But at the least they could cage them again. You have magic. You understand the heat spell?'

'I do.'

'Good.' Sirano moved to the shelves on the back wall. There were scores of empty bottles there; he took down several and laid them on the floor. 'Apply great heat to the necks and melt them, making a complete seal,' he said.

'For what purpose?' asked Duvodas.

'Because I ask it.'

Duvodas knelt on the floor and held his hands over the neck of the first bottle. Tarantio watched as the blue glass neck swelled, then sagged over, melting like candle wax. When six bottles had been heated, Duvo glanced up at Sirano. 'Now what?' he asked.

229

'Now you leave me. Get as close to the gate as you can. You will know when the moment to leave has arrived.'

Sirano knelt by the sealed bottles and began to chant.

'Sorcery!' whispered Duvodas.

'Yes, sorcery,' answered Sirano wearily. 'Black, evil sorcery.' Looking up at Tarantio, he smiled. 'I will give you a gift, warrior. Let me have your swords.' Tarantio pulled his short swords clear and laid them by Sirano. The Duke of Romark lifted the first and sliced the blade along his left palm. Blood welled and he smeared the blade with it. The chant began again. The blood on the sword hissed and bubbled, and the blade shimmered and shone like polished silver. Cutting his right palm, Sirano repeated the process with the second sword. 'Be careful as you sheath them,' he said.

'Why?' asked Tarantio.

Sirano lifted a sword and lightly swung it at a barrel filled with dried fruit. The blade sliced through the wood as easily as a wire through a round of cheese. Dried apricots spilled from the barrel. 'As I said, sheath them with care. Now leave me.'

Carefully Tarantio scabbarded the blades, then took Duvodas by the arm. 'It is his life,' he said. 'Let him live it – or lose it – as he will.'

As they reached the door Sirano's voice called out. 'Tell me, who is in charge of Corduin's defences?'

'Karis,' answered Tarantio.

Sirano smiled. 'Give her a message for me. The Daroth burn like wax. Naked fire is a terror to them.'

The two men stepped into the corridor and silently made their way to the ground floor. Ahead of them was the door to the courtyard. Bodies lay sprawled in the corridor; Tarantio noted that all of them were older men.

'What now?' whispered Duvodas.

'Now we wait,' said Tarantio.

CHAPTER TWELVE

IN ALL HIS YOUNG LIFE SIRANO HAD NEVER EXPERIENCED THE FOCUS he now applied to the Five Levels of Aveas. The bottles trembled with the power he transmitted, the glass warm to the touch. Lifting the last of them he unwittingly saw the horror of his reflection – the scarred bald head, the empty eye-socket, the side of his face melted away as if white candle-wax had been poured over the skin. 'What an evil countenance,' he said, aloud.

Evil. The word jolted him.

Are you evil, Sirano? he asked himself. Are the Daroth evil? It was an interesting thought. There were those who believed evil was an absolute – priests and holy men, mostly. In their view evil hung in the air, touching every man, woman and child, promoting the seeds of hatred, lust and greed, planting them in hearts and minds. Others, as Sirano himself had believed, considered it to be a movable feast. What appeared as evil to one man could be considered good by another. Much depended on the moral codes and laws that governed each society. What moral codes had the Daroth broken? Perhaps none, by their reasoning. Therefore were they evil?

Sirano chuckled. What a time, he thought, to be considering philosophical points. All that he knew for certain was that he himself had broken the codes of his society. He had killed a woman who loved him, had overseen the destruction of his people, and had brought horror and desolation to his lands. A great sadness touched him then, a sense of something lost which could never be recovered. Duvodas had spoken of redemption. For some crimes there could be no redemption . . .

Wearily Sirano rose and searched the store-room, finding a small pile of empty sacks. With his dagger he cut a four-foot length from a coil of thin rope. Making two slices in the neck of a sack, he tied the rope to it. Filling it with the six bottles, he looped the rope over his shoulder and stood, the bottles clinking against one another.

Tarantio had asked him if he wanted to die. Oh, yes, he thought. I can think of no greater relief than to fall into darkness.

Slowly he made his way out into the corridor, then along it and through a series of rooms until he came to a narrow staircase. He had last been here ten years ago, when he had endowed the monastery with a gift of gold. Then he had wandered the place and marvelled at the labyrinthine design. The large hall where now the Daroth would be feeding was on the lower level, but above and around it was a gallery. Sirano recalled his visit, trying to remember the routes through the monastery. Descending the stairs he cut left, then padded through a long library, checking his bearings by peering out of a window. Now he knew where he was. Down two more flights of stairs, and along another corridor he paused at the last door. Taking a deep breath, he eased it open and slipped through to the gallery. Smoke was swirling around the rafters and he could smell the sweet, sickly scent of roasting flesh. Glancing over the rail, he saw the Daroth below. They had torn up the slabs of the floor and broken them to form a low wall around a carefully fashioned cooking area. Red-hot charcoal burned within it and a body was spitted over it. There were bloody bones scattered around the floor, and most of the Daroth were sitting well back from the fire, eating in silence. Two others were standing by the open door, overlooking the gates.

Sirano dipped his hand into the bag he carried, pulling forth a bottle. Then he strode into view. 'I was asking myself,' he said in a loud voice, 'whether the Daroth could be considered to be evil. Do you see yourselves as evil?'

232

Heat and pain roared into his mind and he staggered. He thought he had been prepared for the mental onslaught, but it had come so swiftly he had no time to fight it. He did so now, summoning a masking spell which flowed through his mind like a cooling stream. 'Have none of you the wit to offer me an answer?' he called.

'We came for you, Sirano,' said a deep voice. He could not, at first, identify the speaker.

'And you have found me. Now answer the question. Are you evil?'

The two Daroth by the door had moved inside. Sirano scanned the group. Two were now missing. A towering Daroth warrior moved closer, carefully avoiding the fire. 'The word has little meaning for us, human. We are Daroth. We are one. There is nothing else of importance under the stars. Survival is the ultimate goal. What is good enables us to survive and to continue. What is evil threatens that survival.'

'How did the Oltor threaten you? I thought that they saved you.'

'They sought to deny us land. They closed the gateways to our own world.'

'And the Eldarin?'

'We will not coexist,' said the Daroth. 'Their magic was strong. They could have . . . troubled us.'

'So!' shouted Sirano. 'It was fear that prompted you.'

'We fear nothing!' declared the Daroth, his voice rising.

The gallery door swept open and a huge Daroth warrior surged inside. Sirano spun and let fly with the bottle, which burst on the warrior's chest. Flames spewed out to envelop the enormous white head, and a terrifying scream sounded. Fire consumed the towering figure, and the air was filled with black smoke. The Daroth crashed back into the door, then fell to his knees, his body flaring like a great torch. Blue flames hissed from him, and the heat was incredible. Pulling another bottle clear, Sirano swung towards the second door. As it opened he hurled the bottle – but it exploded harmlessly against the far wall. Climbing over the gallery rail, Sirano leapt to a ledge on one of the ten wooden pillars supporting the ceiling.

'You fear extinction!' he shouted. 'Your lives are ruled by terror! That is why you cannot coexist. You believe that every race is as vile and self-centred as your own. And this time you are right. We

233

will destroy you! We will hunt you down and wipe your grotesque species from the face of the earth!'

Three Daroth moved out onto the gallery. Sirano hurled another bottle, but they dived back and it too exploded without harm to the warriors. From his vantage point on the column, he saw the figures of Tarantio and Duvodas make the dash across open ground to the gates.

A hurled spear smashed through Sirano's belly, pinning him to the pillar. Pain engulfed him, blood spraying from his mouth as he sagged down against the spear.

'You pose no threat to us!' sneered the Daroth leader. 'Your pitiful race is weak and spineless. Your weapons are useless against us. We have crushed your armies, and destroyed two of your greatest cities. Nothing that lives can stand against us.'

Loosing the bag from his shoulder Sirano, with the last ounce of his strength, tossed it into the fire. It erupted with a tremendous explosion that hurled several Daroth from their feet, engulfing two of them in flames.

A second spear slammed into Sirano's chest. And with it came the gift he sought above all others.

Darkness.

*

As Duvodas entered the tavern Shira ran to meet him, throwing her arms around his neck. 'I was so frightened,' she said. 'I thought you had left me.' He hugged her close and kissed her cheek.

'Never! I will never leave you again.' His fingers stroked through her long dark hair, and her face tilted up towards him. Tenderly he kissed her lips, then eased free of her embrace and sat beside the fire. Her father, Ceofrin, ambled forward and patted Duvo's shoulder.

'You look exhausted, man. I'll get some food for you.' Ceofrin moved to the kitchen and returned with a bowl of porridge and a container filled with honey. It remained untouched.

'What happened? Did you find it?' asked Shira. Duvodas opened the canvas pouch and removed the Pearl, which shone brilliantly in the firelight. For a moment none of them spoke. The Pearl was warm in Duvo's hands, and the weight of responsibility was strong upon him. Shira's gaze moved from the orb to Duvo, and her love for him swelled. Ceofrin stood back. He did not understand the nature of the

234

Pearl's power, but he did know that armies had fought and died for seven years to possess it, and now it lay within his tavern.

'Oh,' said Shira at last, 'it is so beautiful. Like a moon fallen from the sky.'

'It contains the Eldarin, their cities and their lands. Everything.' Slowly he told them of the journey to the monastery and of the death of Sirano, Duke of Romark. 'What happened at the monastery was terrible,' he said. 'The monks were slain by the Daroth, the younger ones consumed by them.'

Ceofrin listened as Duvo repeated his tale. 'I can only imagine the anger you must feel,' he said.

Duvodas shook his head. 'The Eldarin taught me how to deal with anger: you must let it flow through you without pause. It was a hard lesson, but I believe I mastered it. Anger leads only to hate, and hate is the mother of evil. The Daroth are what they are. Like a storm, perhaps, destructive and violent. I will not hate them. I will not hate anything.'

'If you ask me,' said Ceofrin, 'you are walking a hard road. Man is born to love, and to hate. I do not believe that any teaching can alter that.'

'You are wrong,' said Duvodas. 'In my life I have seen evil in all its forms, great and small. They have not altered my perceptions.'

Ceofrin smiled. 'You are a good man, Duvo. May I touch it?' Duvo passed it to him. Hefting the Pearl in his huge hands, he stared hard into its milky depths. 'I cannot see cities here.'

'They are there, nonetheless. I must get the Pearl to the highest mountain of the Eldarin lands. Then they will return.'

'And help us destroy the Daroth?' asked Ceofrin.

'No. I do not believe they will.'

'Then why bring them back?'

'Father! How can you say that?' asked Shira. 'Do they not deserve to live?'

'I did not mean it in that way,' said Ceofrin, reddening. 'What I meant is that if they chose to hide from a human army because they do not like to fight, then why bring them back to face a Daroth one?'

'It is a good point,' conceded Duvodas. 'That said, the Eldarin are a wise people who may well offer alternatives to war. Their return alone will force the Daroth to reconsider their plans.'

'I hope that you are right, Duvo,' said Ceofrin, returning the Pearl.

'Now I must prepare the kitchens. There is food to be cooked, and ale to be brought up from the cellar.' He glanced once more at the Pearl and shook his head. 'It seems strange to think of such humdrum matters on a day such as this.'

'Life goes on, my friend,' said Duvodas, pushing himself to his feet.

Shira took his arm. 'You need some rest,' she said. 'Come. The bedroom is warm and there are fresh, clean sheets upon the bed.' Together they made their way to the upper rooms, where Duvodas laid his harp upon the table and stripped off his travel-stained clothes.

'Lie with me for a while,' he said, as he slipped under the covers.

'I have work to do,' she told him. 'And if I came in there with you, you would not rest!'

Duvodas rolled to one elbow and looked at her. The pregnancy was now well advanced. 'Are you still sick in the mornings?' he asked her.

'No, but I have the most incredible cravings for food. Honey-cakes dipped in gravy! Can you imagine?'

'Happily I cannot,' he said. Lying back on the pillow he closed his eyes. His body felt as if it were floating in a boat on a gentle current. He felt her kiss upon his cheek, then drifted away into a dreamless sleep.

When he awoke it was close to midnight and Shira lay fast asleep beside him. Reaching out he drew her to him, holding her close. In ten days they would join the first of the refugees, heading for Loretheli. Once he had settled Shira there, he would strike out south-west to the lands of the Eldarin. Shira awoke in his arms and snuggled closer. He could smell the sweet perfume of her hair and skin, and feel the warmth of her body.

Arousal grew in him and he made love to her, slowly and without passion, kissing her softly. Then he lay back, still holding her. 'I love you,' she whispered.

'And I you.' It seemed then that there was no world outside. The whole universe was contained in this one small, cosy room. Placing his hand on Shira's swollen belly, he felt the life there. His son. The thought brought a lump to his throat. His son! 'He will be born in the late spring in a city by the sea,' Shira had said. 'I will show him to the sunrise and the sunset. He will be handsome, like you, with fair hair and your eyes. Not at first, for all babies are born with blue eyes. But they will turn grey-green as he gets older.'

'Why should he not have beautiful brown eyes, like his mother?'

'Perhaps he will,' she had said.

*

Karis sat quietly as Tarantio told her of the journey, and the recovery of the Pearl. Forin, Necklen and Vint were sitting close by, while Brune was in the kitchen, preparing a supper for them all. 'You believe it? About the Pearl, I mean?' she asked.

'I do,' said Tarantio. 'Brune told me about the resurrection of the Oltor. And Brune does not have the imagination to lie.'

'I hope that you are right. What concerns me, however, is that the Daroth were at the monastery at all.'

'What do you mean?' Tarantio asked.

'All of our plans are predicated on the fact that the Daroth do not like the cold, and will not arrive before the full spring thaw. Now you tell me they climbed a mountain trail in sub-zero temperatures and murdered scores of priests. By that token they could be here within days. And we are not ready.'

Karis swung to Forin. 'What do you think?' she asked.

'There is a difference between a small group tackling the frozen wilderness and an army doing the same thing. In spring there will be sufficient water for their soldiers and their horses. In winter the streams and rivers are frozen. Likewise grass for their mounts, which at present is under the snow. I think we still have time – albeit less than we would like.'

'I agree with Forin,' said Necklen. 'And since there is nothing we can do about it, I suggest we move on as we have planned.'

Karis nodded. 'The new catapult is wonderfully efficient. Three more are being assembled now to protect the eastern wall.'

'What about west and south?' asked Tarantio.

'I am not too concerned about the western wall. The land falls away from it; there is no site for a catapult, and any charge from foot-soldiers would be slowed by the steep slope. In the south we could have a problem; but if we have weeks left before the siege then more catapults will be assembled and raised to protect it. I think the Daroth will strike first from the north, where they will

237

try to breach the walls and storm through. Our first – and main – task is to stop them there.'

'Ozhobar tells me you and he have other plans,' said Necklen. 'When will you share them with us?'

'I won't be sharing them, my friend,' replied Karis. 'The Daroth are telepaths. I do not believe they will seek to read our minds before the first charge, for they are arrogant and believe us to be pitifully weak. When we turn them back, however, that arrogance will begin to leach away. Then they will concentrate on learning what else we have in store. It is vital that our secondary plans remain secret. That is why neither Ozhobar nor myself will be on the walls – or in sight of the Daroth – at any time.'

'I take it,' said Vint, 'that is why the stonemasons have been gouging deep holes in the stonework behind the gates?'

'It is. You will see many such activities in the days to come. Try not to be curious.'

Vint laughed. 'Easier said than done, my lady.'

'I know. I remember the silly mind-games Giriak used to play. One of them involved not thinking about a donkey's ears for ten heart-beats. It was impossible. Even so, you must try. Also warn all the men along the north wall: any sudden headaches or feelings of warmth in the skull are to be reported and the men questioned. I tend to think the Daroth will concentrate on officers, but I could be wrong.'

'How many fighting men will we have, Karis?' asked Necklen. 'Already the numbers listed for the refugee columns have reached ten thousand, and they are still rising. Councillor Pooris says he and his department are weighed down by the requests.'

'The closest estimate is fifteen thousand fighting men,' said Karis. 'We should outnumber the Daroth by three to one. However, that statistic is meaningless, since our troops will need to be spread around the four walls. It is likely we will be evenly matched on the north wall.'

Brune brought in several trays of meat, bread and cake, and a large flagon of red wine.

'Prentuis fell within a day,' said Necklen. 'One blood-filled, terrible day!'

'This is not Prentuis,' said Karis. 'And they were not led by me.'

*

238

The logistics of the problem had initially excited Pooris. Several thousand refugees to be shepherded to the city of Hlobane, just under 300 miles south-west, and then a further 410 miles south and east to the port city of Loretheli. The problem was now much greater, and Pooris sat with Niro and a score of clerics in the hall above the Great Library, frantically trying to collate statistics.

Fourteen thousand people had now declared their wish to leave Corduin, almost 20 per cent of the adult population. The Duke's riders had made a score of hazardous journeys south with messages to and from Belliese, the Corsair Duke, who had demanded five silver pieces for every refugee, a further ten for any who wished to be transported on to the islands. The sum was not extortionate, but was now coming close to emptying the treasury.

Considering the fact that there were more than 10,000 mercenaries now in Corduin who demanded payment on the first day of every month, the problem was serious indeed. Without the windfall of the executed Lunder's fortune, the project would never have been begun. Even with it, Pooris now doubted whether the city's finances would stretch far enough.

The spidery figure of Niro loomed over his desk and Pooris glanced up. 'There are not enough wagons, sir,' said Niro. 'Not by half. The price of those there are has trebled already. It will rise higher.'

'How many have we purchased for movement of food and silver?'

'Thirty, sir. But the main holding yard was broken into last night, and five were stolen. I have placed extra guards there.'

'Were our wagons marked as ordered?'

'Yes, sir. A yellow strip hidden by the rear axle.'

'Order a full search. When the wagons are found the owners are to be hanged.'

Niro hesitated. 'You are aware, sir, that they will have been sold on in good faith? The people who now have them will not be the thieves.'

'I am aware of that. Before they are hanged they will be questioned as to those who sold them the vehicles. Anyone named will also be hunted down and hanged. We will leave no-

239

one in any doubt as to the severity of punishment should such thieving continue.'

'Yes, sir.' Niro moved away and Pooris leaned back and rubbed his chin. The bristle growing there surprised him. How long had he been in the building? Fourteen hours? Eighteen?

A young cleric approached him and bowed. Pooris was so tired he could not remember the man's name. 'What is it?'

'A small problem, sir. We have run out of red wax for the Duke's seal. There is none to be found anywhere.'

Every official refugee was to be given a note of authority stamped with the seal of Duke Albreck, and each, upon presentation of the seal, was entitled to remove from the treasury a sum not to exceed twenty gold pieces – assuming, of course, that they had money in excess of the sum banked there.

'Red wax,' mumbled Pooris. 'May the Gods spare me! What colours are there to be had?'

'Blue, sir. Or green.'

'Then stamp them with blue. It is the seal, not the colour, which gives authority.'

'Yes, sir.' The young man backed away. Pooris stood and moved to his private office, where the stove fire had died and the room was cold. There was a jug of water on the desk. Pooris filled a goblet and sipped it.

The convoy of refugees would probably spread out over two miles or more. They would have to be guarded from robbers, and fed, and housed in tents on the journey. It was like equipping an army for a campaign, thought Pooris. Gazing up at the map on the wall, he studied the terrain. A swallow would cover 512 miles to Loretheli, but on foot the refugees would have to skirt the mountains, adding almost 200 miles, much of it across rough, cold country with little game and less shelter.

The Council at Hlobane had been instructed to send out food wagons to meet the convoy. These would most certainly be needed. According to Karis, the refugees would average around eight miles a day. All told, the full journey might take three months.

And still 14,000 wanted to try it, to face the perils of cold and hunger, robbers and thieves. Many of the richer refugees would also be obliged to leave their fortunes behind, never to be recovered. All for the distant prospect of a safe haven. Some

240

would die on the journey; Karis estimated the number at around 2 per cent.

Three hundred people who would have lived longer had they remained in their own homes . . .

Pooris had been against the expedition from the start, despite his love of logistics. But both the Duke and Karis had been against him.

'You will not stop people deserting,' said Karis. 'If heroes came in great numbers we would not value them so highly. Most people have cowardly hearts.'

'And if we force them to stay,' put in Albreck, 'there will be panic when the Daroth arrive. We cannot afford panic. Let it be known that a refugee column will leave the city in the last month of winter; it will be escorted to Hlobane.'

'That will push up the numbers of those wishing to leave, my lord,' said Karis.

'I fear that is true, sir,' added Pooris.

'Let the faint-hearted fly where they will. I want only the strong. We will fight the Daroth – and we will beat him.' The Duke gave a rare smile. 'And if we do not, we will bloody him so badly that he will not have the strength to march on Hlobane. Is that not true, Karis?'

'It is true, my lord.'

True or not, it did not help Pooris as he struggled to make the arrangements for the civilian withdrawal.

A knock came at the door. He called out to enter and Niro stepped inside.

'Another problem?' he asked the man. Niro gave a shrug.

'Of course, sir. What else would you expect?'

Pooris gestured him to a seat. 'I was scanning the list of refugees. You asked for them to be compiled as to occupation.'

'Yes. And?'

'Twelve of the city's fifteen armourers have applied to leave. Not a good time, I would have thought, to run short of crossbow bolts and suchlike.'

'Indeed not.'

'Curiously, only two of Corduin's sixty-four bakers have applied to leave.' Niro grinned. 'Makers of bread are more courageous than makers of swords. Interesting, sir, don't you think?'

'I will raise the problem with the Duke. Well-spotted, Niro. You have a keen eye. How many merchants on the list?'

'None, sir. They all left soon after Lunder's execution.'

'Will you be leaving also?' asked Pooris. 'I understand that more than four-fifths of the city's clerics have applied.'

'No, sir. I am by nature an optimist. If we do survive and conquer, I should imagine the Duke would be most grateful to those who stood by his side.'

'Pin not your hopes on the goodwill of rulers, Niro. My father once told me – and I have seen it to be true – that nothing is as long-lived as a monarch's hatred, nor as short-lived as his gratitude.'

'Even so, I shall stay.'

'You have faith in our lady general?'

'Her men have faith. They have seen her in action,' said Niro.

'As have I. I watched her bring a mountain down on a group of Daroth riders. More importantly, to do so she crushed several of our own people. She is ruthless, Niro. And single-minded. I do believe that we are lucky to have her. Yet . . . the Daroth are not like any human enemy we have ever faced. Every one of their warriors is stronger than three of ours. And we have not yet seen what strategies they are capable of.'

'I shall observe them with interest,' said Niro, rising.

Pooris smiled. 'You are an optimist,' he said. 'And if we do survive I shall make sure you achieve what you hope for.' Niro bowed and Pooris gave a dry chuckle. 'Falling short, of course, of my own position.'

'Of course, sir.'

*

He was moving through the darkness of the tunnels, hearing the child's cry for help in the distance. He came to the coal face, and here there was – as he knew there would be – a jagged crack just wide enough for a body to squeeze through.

'Help me! Please!'

Tarantio eased himself through the crack and into the greenish glare of the tunnel beyond. Opal-eyed creatures shuffled forward, picks and shovels in their hands.

'Where is the boy?' he demanded.

The cries came again from far ahead and, drawing his sword,

Tarantio ran forward. The creatures scattered before him. At the far end of the enormous cavern stood a man, guarding a bolted door. Tarantio halted his run and advanced slowly on the swordsman facing him. His hair was white and stood out from his head in ragged spikes. But it was the eyes that caught Tarantio's attention: they were golden, and slitted like those of a great cat.

'Where is the boy?' demanded Tarantio.

'First you must pass me,' said the demonic warrior.

In his mind Tarantio sought out Dace, but he was not to be found. Fear rose in him, followed by a quaking certainty that he was looking into the face of death. His mouth was dry, his sword hand wet with sweat. 'Help me!' cried the boy. Tarantio took a deep breath and threw himself into the attack.

The demon lowered his sword and offered his neck to Tarantio's blade. At the last moment he swung the blow aside.

'Why do you want me to kill you?' he asked.

'Why do you want to kill me?' the demon responded.

'I just want to help the boy.'

'To do so you must kill me,' said the demon, sadly.

*

Tarantio awoke in a cold sweat. Rising from his bed, he wandered out to the kitchen and filled a long goblet with cool water. In the main room Forin was asleep on a couch; the others had gone. Tarantio entered the room, moving silently to the fire. It was dying down and he added a fresh log.

'You can't sleep?' enquired Forin, yawning and sitting up.

'No. Bad dreams.'

'The Daroth?'

'Worse than the Daroth. I've had the same dream for several years now.' He told Forin about it.

'Why didn't you kill it?' Forin asked.

'I don't know.'

'Silly things, dreams,' said the giant. 'I once dreamt I was standing naked in a marketplace, where all the stalls were selling honey-cakes riddled with maggots. Everyone was buying them and extolling their virtues. No sense at all.'

Tarantio shook his head. 'Not necessarily. You are a man of iron principles. Most are not. You know the values of loyalty

243

and friendship, where others see only the price to be paid for such comradeship. Merchants, town dwellers, farmers – all despise warriors. They see us as violent and deadly, and indeed we are. What we come to learn, however, is that life is often short and always unpredictable. We fight for gold, but we know that true friendship is worth more than gold, and that comradeship is above price.'

Forin sat silently for a moment, then he grinned. 'What has this to do with nakedness and maggoty cakes?'

'You do not value what they value. You would not buy what they buy. As to the nakedness, you have thrown off all that they are.'

'I like that,' said Forin. 'I like that a lot. What then does your dream mean?'

'It is a search for something that is lost to me.' Tarantio felt uncomfortable discussing it further, and changed the subject. 'I saw you and your men in that armour today. I see what you mean.'

'Ludicrous, isn't it?' agreed Forin, with a wide grin. 'But it works well. Especially the arm-plates; they are all individually hinged, allowing almost full movement. Incredible! I think I could take a Daroth wearing it.'

'You should be able to catch him unawares as he falls over laughing,' said Tarantio.

'Is there any wine left?' asked the giant, moving out to the kitchen without waiting for an answer. He came back with a jug and two goblets.

'Not for me,' said Tarantio. 'Drinking that will only give me more dreams.'

Forin filled a goblet and drained it in a single swallow. Wiping his beard with the back of his hand, he leaned back on the couch. 'What do you think of Vint?' he asked.

'In what way?'

'I was just wondering. He seems very . . . close with Karis.'

'They are lovers, I should imagine.'

'What makes you say that?'

'Common knowledge. Karis always has a lover somewhere; she's that sort of woman.'

'What sort . . . exactly?' said Forin coldly, his green eyes narrowing.

The swordsman saw the anger there. 'Is there something here that I don't understand?' he countered.

'Not at all,' answered Forin, forcing a smile. 'As I said, I was just wondering.'

'Karis is an unusual woman, that's what I meant. Whenever I've served with her, she's had a different lover. Sometimes more than one. But it does not affect her talents. She never seems to fall in love with any of them.'

'How many has she had?'

'Gods, man, how would I know? But Vint was one of them. Now he is again.'

Forin drained another goblet. 'I wish I'd never met her,' he said, with feeling.

Tarantio remained silent for a moment. 'When did you meet her?' he asked softly.

Forin glanced up. 'Is it that damned obvious?'

'What happened?'

This time Forin did not bother with the goblet but raised the jug to his lips, tilting it high until all the wine was gone. 'She came to me one night, asking questions about the Daroth. Then we . . . well, you know. Something happened to me; she got into my blood somehow. Can't stop thinking of her.'

'Have you talked to her about it?'

'To say what? She avoids me, Chio, unless she is already in company. Why would she do that?'

'I'm the wrong man to ask. I have never understood women.'

'Have you ever been in love?' asked Forin.

'Yes,' said Tarantio, surprising himself.

'Well, I haven't. I don't even know if this *is* love. Maybe if I slept with her again, it would all fall into place and I'd be able to smile and say goodbye, and she'd vanish from my mind.'

'*Ask him if she was good in bed,*' suggested Dace.

'Maybe that is her problem too,' said Tarantio. 'Maybe she feels something strongly for you. I don't think she wants to fall in love, and usually picks men merely to satisfy a need – a physical need.'

'I've never known a night like it. Maybe never will again,' said Forin. He gave a long sigh. 'If this is love, I don't think I like it.' He lay back on the couch, and within minutes was snoring softly.

'*What is wrong with you?*' asked Dace. '*You could have asked for details.*'

'*Do you dream, Dace?*'

245

'*I've told you before that I don't.*'

'*I know. I believe it to be a lie. Why would you lie to me?*'

'*That is a premise built on a foundation of feathers.*' Tarantio returned to his bed and lay down, drawing the blankets over him. As he drifted into sleep he heard Dace whisper, '*Thank you, brother.*'

'*For what?*' asked Tarantio sleepily.

'*For not killing us.*'

*

As the thaw continued, a sense of urgency surrounded all aspects of city life. Karis and Ozhobar met often, planning late into the night, testing new weapons in secret so that no knowledge of their purpose could leak out to the troops manning the walls. Vint led scouting missions to the north, watching for signs of the approach of the Daroth. Forin drilled his fifty soldiers constantly; always in full armour, until the heavy plate felt like a second skin. The Duke, Pooris and the other bureaucrats worked ceaselessly to prepare for the evacuation.

At last the day arrived – four days later than planned. Thousands of citizens assembled in the fields to the south of the city while the veteran officer, Capel, in charge of the exodus, tried to assemble the wagons into a convoy. There was a sense of joy about the proceedings, and safety beckoned for the refugees. Shira and Duvodas, having said farewell to the tearful Ceofrin, were in the last wagon to leave. They sat together on the driver's seat, waiting their turn. Duvo's hand absently strayed to the canvas pouch he wore, his fingers tracing the outline of the Pearl. I will bring you back, he promised silently, recalling the frozen figures in the silent city.

'It is a beautiful day,' said Shira.

'I don't think Capel would agree with you,' he answered, pointing to the grey-bearded officer as he rode up and down the line of wagons, seeking to instil some sense of order. The head of the convoy had set out almost three hours before, but the wagons in the rear were still waiting.

At last Duvodas received the signal to move, and he flicked the reins against the backs of the four oxen. The beasts leaned in to the traces and the wagon jerked forward. The land was hilly at the start of the journey, and before they had gone more than a mile from the city they came upon the first casualty. A wagon, taking a turn too fast, had tipped over and slid down the slope. Furniture was strewn over the snow-patched grass, and one of the oxen was dead. Soldiers were cutting away the traces as Duvo and Shira drove up.

Hitching ropes to their rear axle they hauled the other wagon upright. The soldiers repacked it, and the journey continued. On the last of the high ground, Shira swung round to see the distant city of Corduin, brilliantly lit by sunshine. 'Oh look, Duvo! What a wonderful sight!' He glanced at her and saw that her eyes were moist, her lips trembling. Putting his arm around her, he drew her to him.

'Your father will be fine.'

'I don't know. I just wish he had come with us.'

'So do I, my love. But, as he said, his life is in Corduin.' Cupping her face in his hands he kissed her. 'I will do everything in my power to make you happy for as long as we live. I will keep sickness from you and our son, and we will know great joy.'

'I already know great joy,' she said. 'From the moment you came into my life.'

The oxen had halted. Now Duvo rapped the reins and they moved on. For several hours they rode. As far as the eye could see, the line of wagons stretched out towards the south-west. Soldiers rode up and down the line, checking on the stragglers.

Towards mid-afternoon the rear of the line halted once more. To the right was a high cliff-face, to the left a wide-open section of gorse and heather. Duvo climbed down from the wagon. 'I'll see what's holding us up,' he said, loping off towards the south.

As he neared a bend in the trail he saw a wagon some fifteen paces ahead, its left rear wheel shattered. Men were unloading boxes and furniture, lightening the load so that a spare wheel could be lifted into place. There were enough bodies for the work, and Duvo turned back and strolled along the line. Suddenly a woman screamed.

Duvo's eyes sought her out. She was middle-aged and stout, and she was standing on the driver's seat, pointing to the east. He turned. Half a mile away, across the gorse, a long line of riders was moving slowly forward. They rode huge horses, and the faces of the riders were bone-white. Other people began to shout. Then to run.

He started to sprint back towards his own wagon. As it came into sight, he saw Shira standing up and waving to him – and behind her

247

two Daroth riders, galloping along the trail. Fear welled in him, and he continued to run towards her.

One of the Daroth levelled a long spear. 'No!' Duvo screamed. 'No!'

Shira turned. The spear took her in the belly, lifting her high in the air, the bloody point emerging from her back. Almost casually the Daroth flicked the spear and Shira was flung from it to the ground. All his life Duvodas had been taught to eliminate anger from his soul, allowing it to float through him, leaving him untouched. But it was not anger he felt in that dread moment.

It was a blind, bottomless rage.

Letting out an animal scream he pointed at the Daroth, sending out a heat spell which burst to life inside the creature's skull. With a hideous shriek, the Daroth dropped his spear and grabbed at his temples.

Then his head exploded.

The second Daroth bore down on Duvo. There was no fear now in the Singer, and a second heat spell exploded in the Daroth's chest, sending white blood and shards of bone spraying through the air. Duvo continued to run, coming alongside Shira and dropping to his knees. The wound was terrible, and he cried out in anguish to see it. Her body was almost torn in half, and Duvo saw the tiny arm and hand of his dead son protruding from the wound.

Something died in him then, and a terrible coldness settled on his soul. Trembling he touched his hand to Shira's blood, then smeared four bloody lines down his own face.

Duvodas rose and walked slowly towards the Daroth line. There were hundreds of riders, but they were not moving with speed. It was as if they wanted to delay the moment, so that every ounce of fear could be extracted from the helpless refugees.

'Fear,' hissed Duvodas. 'I will show you fear!' Raising his hands, he drew on the magic of the land. Never before had it felt so strongly within him, pulsing with a power he had not realized could be contained in a single human frame. Darkly exultant, Duvodas extended his arms, redirecting the magic, flowing it like a storm over the gorse and the heather. Every seed and root beneath the earth swelled with sudden, rushing life, writhing up from the ground, the growth of years erupting in seconds.

The ground below the Daroth writhed and trembled. At first it only slowed the huge horses, whose powerful legs broke the new roots and branches.

Stronger and faster grew the plants and bushes and trees. The horses were forced to a halt and the Daroth swung in their saddles, their dark eyes seeking out the sorcerer. Duvodas felt their power strike him, and he staggered. He sensed their hatred, and their arrogant belief that they had defeated him, and he allowed them a brief moment of exultation. Then he fed upon their hatred, and hurled it back at them with ten times the force. The nearest riders shrieked and pitched from their saddles. Sharp roots pricked at their skin, then burrowed through muscle and around bone. Horses reared and fell, toppling their riders. The Daroth tried to hack their way clear of the eldritch forest, but even their massive bodies were no match for the power of nature.

One Daroth tried to reach Duvodas, his huge sword cutting left and right to smash through the surging growth, but he stumbled and fell to his knees. A fast-growing oak sliced into his stomach, lifting him upright. One branch burst through his lungs and out through his back, another surged up his throat, slithering from his mouth like a grotesque tongue.

Roots clawed their way into flesh – ripping into bellies and chests, lancing through legs and arms and necks.

And still the forest grew. The struggling bodies of the Daroth and their mounts were lifted higher and higher, dangling like corpses on a colossal gibbet.

The refugees watched in awe-struck silence as hundreds of Daroth were destroyed.

At last Duvodas let fall his arms, and men ,women and children gazed upon the dangling corpses which moments before had been a terrible threat. There were no cheers from the saved. No one rushed forward to congratulate the blood-smeared young man who stood staring malevolently at the dead.

The officer Capel rode slowly towards him, dismounting by his side. 'I don't know how you did it, man, but I'm grateful. Come, let us bury your dead. We must move on.'

Duvodas said nothing. He stood stock-still, his body rigid. Capel placed his hand on Duvo's shoulder. 'Come now, lad. It is over.'

'It is not over,' said Duvo, turning his face towards the officer.

Capel blanched as he saw the blood red lines on the young man's face. Pulling a scarf from his belt, he gave it to Duvodas.

'Wipe your face now,' he said. 'You'll frighten the children.' Dumbly Duvo wiped the blood away. But it made no difference. The crimson lines remained, as if tattooed upon his skin.

'Dear Heaven,' whispered Capel. 'What is happening here?'

'Death,' said Duvodas coldly. 'And it is but the beginning.'

The Pearl at his side was forgotten now, as was his mission, as slowly he began to walk towards the new forest. Trees and roots shrank away from him, creating a path.

'Where are you going?' Capel called out.

'To destroy the Daroth,' said Duvodas, striding on faster now. And the forest closed in around him.

*

Leaving his lieutenant in charge of the convoy, Capel made the seven-mile ride to Corduin to report the bizarre events of the day. Despite the imminence of the Daroth threat, the Duke felt compelled to ride out to the scene of the slaughter. With Vint, Necklen and twenty lancers, the Duke arrived at the scene just before dusk.

The group drew rein at the edge of the forest. The bodies of the Daroth horses hung, skewered into the tree-tops. The Daroth corpses had withered away to dry skin, flapping in the evening breeze.

'I have never seen – or heard of – anything like it,' said the Duke. 'How could this happen?' No one answered him.

'I wish the sorcerer had come back to Corduin,' said Vint. 'We could certainly use him there.'

'Who was he?' asked the Duke.

'A harpist, sir. He sang at the Wise Owl tavern. I heard him once or twice; he was very good.'

'His name is Duvodas, my lord,' put in Capel.

The Duke turned his hooded eyes on Capel. 'My apologies, Captain, for doubting your story. It sounded incredible. But here is the evidence, and I do not know what it means. You had best rejoin the column, and I wish you good luck on your journey.'

Capel saluted. 'And may good fortune be with you, sir,' he said. Then he swung his horse and galloped off towards the south.

The riders reached Corduin just after dark and the Duke summoned Karis to his private chambers. The warrior woman looked drawn and tired, and there was about her a nervous energy that concerned Albreck. 'I hope you are getting enough rest, General,' he said, offering her a seat.

'Not a lot of time for rest, my lord. Apart from the attack on the convoy, our scouts report the main Daroth army is camped less than a day's march from the city.'

'So close? That is unfortunate.'

'They halted their march at the same time as the forest miracle,' said Karis. 'I would imagine the scale of the slaughter has given them a nasty shock. They would have had no reason to believe that any human would have such power.'

'I am rather shocked myself. How could this man have accomplished such a feat?'

'Vint is questioning the tavern-keeper, Ceofrin, and I have had a long conversation with Tarantio. It seems that Duvodas was raised among the Eldarin, who taught him many secrets of magic. Tarantio is stunned by the events; he maintains that Duvodas was a pacifist, wholly opposed to war and violence. He also told me a strange tale concerning Sirano.' Karis told the Duke of the attempted rescue of Sirano at the monastery, the coming of the Daroth and the recovery of the Eldarin Pearl.

'Sirano was right,' said the Duke, bitterness in his voice. 'The Pearl is a fearsome weapon. Why did this harpist not bring it to us? We could have destroyed the Daroth utterly!'

'Perhaps it is best that he did not,' answered Karis. 'Ever since Sirano unleashed his magic against the Pearl, nothing has been the same. And we cannot spend valuable time concerning ourselves with speculation. Perhaps within a day the enemy will be upon us. That must be our prime concern.'

Albreck offered Karis a goblet of wine, but she refused. 'I must leave you, my lord. I am meeting Ozhobar at his forge.'

'Of course,' said Albreck, rising with her. 'But first tell me how your plans are progressing.'

She shrugged. 'That is hard to say, sir. The weapons are untried against the Daroth, and much depends on the strategies they adopt.'

'And what of your strategies, Karis?'

She gave a weary smile. 'In war it is best to act, and therefore force your enemy to react. We do not have the luxury of such a strategy.

251

To attack the Daroth on open ground would be suicidal, therefore the first advantage is his. When you add to that the simple fact that our enemy is telepathic, and many times more powerful than any human warrior, our problems become mountainous. Because of their mental powers I cannot even explain my tactics to my commanders, for fear that the Daroth will discover them. All in all the prospects are bleak.'

'You sound defeatist,' he said.

Karis shook her head. 'Not at all, sir. If the Daroth act as I suspect they will, then we have a chance to hold them. If we can beat off their first attack, we will further sow the seeds of doubt in them. The miracle of the forest will have worried them. If we stop them without magic, it will worry them further. And doubt is a demon that can destroy an army.'

Duke Albreck smiled. 'Thank you, General. Please continue your duties.'

Karis bowed and left the room. Moving through to the rear of his apartments, the Duke lit two lanterns and stood staring at the armour hanging on the wooden frame. It had been his grandfather's, and had been worn by his father in several battles. Albreck himself had never worn it. The helm of iron, polished until it shone like silver, was embellished with the golden head of a roaring lion. The image of a lion had also been added in gold to the breastplate. It was altogether garish and hideously eye-catching. Albreck had always viewed it with distaste.

'A ruler has to be seen by his warriors,' his father had told him. 'And seen in battle as a colossal figure, a head and shoulders above other men. A leader must be inspirational. This armour you sneer at, boy, serves that purpose. For when I wear it, I am Corduin.'

Albreck remembered the day his father had led the army from the city. He had watched, with his mother and brother, from an upper balcony in the palace. And that night, when the victorious Duke had returned, he had understood his father's words. In the moonlight his father had looked like a god.

The memories brought a sigh from him, and he drew the longsword from its scabbard. It was blade-heavy, a knight's weapon, designed to be wielded from the saddle, striking down at enemy foot soldiers.

Albreck returned it to its scabbard.

A servant entered bearing a tray. 'Your supper, my lord,' he said.

'Set it upon the table.'

'Yes, my lord. Very fine armour, my lord.'

'Indeed it is. Tomorrow have it returned to the museum.'

'Yes, my lord.'

Albreck returned to the main room and sat down by the fire, leaving the meal untouched. He fell asleep in the chair. His night servant found him there, and covered him with a soft blanket.

*

Avil had never achieved any promotion. He had been a scout now for six years, and had done his job as well as any man. He had just been unlucky. Anyone could have missed a small raiding party coming through the Salian canyon; there were any number of branch passes along the route. It had been so unfair to be forced to carry the blame. Had they known he had been asleep during the raid he would have been hanged. But then a man had to sleep, and Avil felt no guilt about the incident.

But this new woman general, she knew his worth. She had spoken to him personally about this mission, and Avil intended to prove himself to her. She had summoned him to her private quarters, and given him a goblet of fine wine.

'I have been watching your progress,' she said, 'and it is my belief that you have been wrongly overlooked for promotion.' Even Avil had started to believe the stories of his carelessness. Now, however, someone in authority had seen his true worth. 'I need a good scout to give me an accurate estimate of enemy numbers,' she had said. 'I want you to observe them. See how they make camp, observe their actions.'

'Why is it important to see how they make camp?' he had asked.

'A good army is disciplined. Everything they do indicates how well they are led. A lazy general will be lax, the camp disorganized. You understand?'

'Yes, general. Of course. How stupid of me!'

'Not stupid at all,' she assured him. 'A sensible man asks questions – that is how he learns.' A huge hound padded over to him, resting his head in Avil's lap. 'He likes you,' said Karis.

'I know him. This is Stealer. He hangs around the barracks and steals scraps.'

253

Karis had laughed. She was not a great beauty, he thought, but there was about her an earthy quality that made a man think of nakedness and a warm bed. In that moment he understood one of her nicknames: some of the men called her 'The Whore of War.' Avil found his eyes wandering to her breasts; she was wearing a thin, woollen shirt and he could see their outline. 'You have heard, of course, about our magician?' she asked, dropping her voice.

'Everyone is talking about the slaughter of the Daroth,' he said, dragging his gaze from her body and trying to look into her eyes.

'We have three sorcerers,' she told him.

'Three?'

'Their powers are astonishing. One can bring fire from the sky. They were trained by the Eldarin. Naturally this must not be spoken of. You understand?'

'Yes, General . . . well, no. Would it not ease the fears of the people to know we have such power?'

'Indeed it would. But if the Daroth were to find out just how strong we are, then they might not come within the range of our spells.'

'Oh, I see. But surely they already know about the slaughter, and the magical forest?'

'I don't doubt that they do. That was unfortunate – but we had to protect our refugees. However, the Daroth know of only one sorcerer and one great spell. They probably believe they can overcome us despite his abilities. That is when the other two will wreak their terrible spells.'

She had offered him a second goblet of wine then. It was heady stuff. He told her of his plans and ambitions, and of his life back on the farm. She seemed fascinated by everything he said. No-one had ever been fascinated before. He told her this, and that his comrades called him dull. Karis assured him that he was far from dull. In fact, she had enjoyed his company immensely, and when he returned from his scouting mission they must meet again.

Avil was smitten. Her last words came back to haunt him now, as he sat at the feet of the Daroth general. 'Be very careful, Avil. If the mission goes wrong, do not allow yourself to be taken alive. They must not find out about our plans.'

'You can trust me, General. I will say nothing. I will cut my own throat before I betray you.'

Luck had deserted him yet again – for the last time. He had crept close to the Daroth camp, sure that he was unobserved; but then this terrible pain had struck his head and he had passed out. When he awoke he was in the centre of a circle of Daroth warriors. Their faces were blank, alien and unreadable, but Avil knew of their foul practices and his fear weakened his bladder. He felt the warm urine soaking his leggings and, for a moment at least, shame outweighed his terror.

'Give us your name.' said a deep voice. Avil jerked and gazed around, trying to identify the speaker.

'I am Avil,' he said, his voice trembling.

'You are frightened, Avil.'

'Yes. Yes, I am.'

'Would you like to be released to return to your city?'

'Yes. Very much.'

'Then tell me of the forces gathered there.'

'The forces? The Duke's army, you mean? I don't know how many there are. Thousands, I expect. Soldiers.'

A Daroth rose and, taking hold of Avil's hair, dragged him to his feet. The creature took hold of the young man's arm – and suddenly snapped it. Avil screamed. The Daroth released him and he fell to the ground, staring stupidly at the twisted arm. At first there was little pain, but it grew into a terrible burning that made Avil feel nauseous.

'Concentrate, Avil,' said the Daroth. Pain flared in his head again, then subsided. 'Tell me about the wizards.'

In all his life Avil had known no friends, and many nick-names – none of them a source of pride. But Karis had trusted him, and – merely with her conversation – had given him one of the finest evenings of his life. Frightened of pain, terrified of death, Avil was determined not to betray her. 'I know nothing of . . .'

'Beware, Avil,' warned the Daroth. 'I can inflict great pain on you. The broken wing will be as nothing to what you will face if you lie to me.'

Tears flowed from Avil's eyes and his lip trembled. He began to weep. Around him there sounded a strange clicking noise. He took a deep breath, and tried to control his fear as the Daroth spoke again. 'The wizards. Tell me of the wizards.'

'There are no wizards!' shouted Avil. I will die like a man, he thought, though I wish to all the gods that I could live to see the fire blast down on these devils!

'How will this happen?' asked the Daroth softly. 'How will the fire come?'

Avil blinked. Had he said it aloud? No, he wouldn't be that stupid. What was happening? 'Tell me of the wizard who makes fire from the sky,' the Daroth repeated.

Avil dropped his head, trying not to look at the Daroth. Then he saw his knife, still in its sheath; they had not bothered to disarm him! Grabbing the hilt, he dragged the weapon clear and plunged it deep into his chest. He fell back to the grass, and found himself staring up at the night sky and the bright stars.

I did not betray you, Karis. The bastards learned nothing from me. The clicking noise sounded again.

Hands pawed at the dying man, tearing away his clothes. Then he was lifted and carried towards a pit of burning charcoal.

CHAPTER THIRTEEN

'You realize the impossibility of what we are planning, don't you?' said Ozhobar, as he and Karis sat beside the forge, enjoying the last of its dying heat. 'You can't hide secrets from a telepathic race. Every weapon we have tested has been seen by our men. The Daroth will not be surprised.'

'That entirely depends on the manner in which their mental powers operate,' she said. 'Can they read all thoughts, or only those we are thinking as they view us?'

'We have no way of knowing,' said Ozhobar, stroking his sandy beard.

'Exactly. Therefore I will waste no energy in trying to second-guess their talents,' said Karis. 'Did you study Tarantio's swords?'

'Yes. Remarkable. It seems the spell has – among other things – significantly reduced the friction on the blades. But that is not what makes them so deadly.'

'Can you duplicate them?'

'Sadly, no. I am not a sorcerer, Karis. I am a scientist. The blades seem to shimmer in and out of existence. It is not possible, for

257

example, to hold the metal. I tried to put a clamp on one of the blades, but it just slid clear. They will cut clean through stone, wood, and leather. Even iron, though less cleanly.'

'I would give ten years of my life to have a hundred such blades,' said Karis. 'Why did Sirano have to allow himself to be killed?'

Ozhobar lifted a small linen sack and opened it, offering a biscuit to Karis. 'I do feel honoured,' she said. He chuckled.

'They were a gift from the Duke's chef. They are rather good – though not as fine as my own oatcakes.'

'This is why you are willing to share them?'

Ignoring the remark, Ozhobar reached down a second sack, considerably heavier than the first. From this he took a handful of what appeared to be small black pebbles. 'What do you think?' he asked, passing them to Karis.

'Better than stones,' she said. 'Iron?'

'Yes. Each ballista will loose around two hundred of these. The trick is to cause a spread that is not too wide. I think I have achieved it. Come and see.'

Together they walked to the rear of the building. In an enclosed area, hidden by high walls yet brilliantly lit by moonlight, there stood a giant crossbow with arms over ten feet wide, built on a criss-crossed timber frame. On each side of the frame were handles, which when turned drew back the giant arms. Striding past the machine, Ozhobar hauled an old door of thick oak to the far wall, resting it there. Then he returned to the machine and, together with Karis, wound the handles until the rope and its sling of leather dropped over a large bronze hook. Locking it into place, Ozhobar filled the leather cup with iron pellets. Having checked the alignments, he walked around to where Karis stood. 'The door is oak, almost two inches thick.' With a boyish grin he handed her a small hammer. 'Strike the release bolt hard. Do it from behind.'

Karis moved to the rear of the machine and struck the bolt. There was a sudden hiss, then a sharp clanging as the arms swept forward to strike the wooden restraints. Almost immediately came a series of small thunderclaps as the iron shot smashed into the door. Ozhobar ambled over to the ruined wood.

'Well?' he asked, as Karis joined him. The door was peppered with deep holes that in many places had completely pierced the wood; in the centre it was torn apart, ripped to tinder. Ozhobar grinned. 'You like it?'

'It is incredible! What kind of killing range?'

'Against the Daroth? Who can tell? Though I would guess at around fifty feet. After that the momentum will start to slacken. Fifty down to twenty-five would be the optimum.'

'Why not inside twenty-five feet?' she asked.

'Oh, it will still kill, but the spread will be small.' He pointed to the door. 'As you can see, at a range of only about fifteen feet the pellets struck in a rough circle of . . . what? . . . around four feet. That equates with one Daroth. But at fifty feet the circle of death will be much greater.'

'How many ballistae will we have?'

'That depends on how long the Daroth wait. If we can get five more days I can have three by the northern gate, two others ready for swift transportation across the city.'

'We will, I believe, have a few days,' she said. Something in her voice caught his attention, and he stared intently at her.

'You . . . instituted the plan?'

'Yes. The scout has not returned.'

'This troubles you,' he said softly.

'Would it not trouble you? I have no qualms about sending soldiers to their deaths, but this time I had to lie, to deceive. He was a dull man, but I don't doubt he deserved better than to be betrayed by his general.'

'You chose him because he was a careless man. Therefore it could be argued that his own carelessness killed him.'

'Yes, I could argue that – but it wouldn't be true. I think it will buy us time, though not much. It won't be long before they capture another scout, or get someone close enough to our walls to read another mind.'

'Five days. That is all we need.'

Ozhobar covered the ballista with a tarpaulin and led Karis back to the warmth of the forge. 'Did you overcome the recoil problem on the catapult?' she asked him.

'Of course. I weighted the cross timbers. It is a little less manoeuvrable now, but still accurate. Necklen has mastered the machine, and his crew operate well.'

'Let us hope so,' said Karis.

259

'Another biscuit?'

She smiled. 'No. I'd better be getting back. I still have work to do.'

A deep growl sounded from outside the main door and Karis strolled across to it. Outside, Stealer was baring his fangs at a huge figure.

'Call off the hound before I break its neck,' said Forin.

Karis bade Ozhobar good night, then stepped out into the night with Stealer padding alongside her, still keeping a wary eye on the man. 'What do you want?' she asked wearily.

'To talk,' said Forin.

'I have no time to talk.'

'No time or no desire?' he asked, pausing in his walk. She moved two paces ahead, then swung back to him.

'We shouldn't have made love,' she said. 'It was a mistake, and I cannot afford such mistakes. If it is any consolation to you, it was a wonderful night, and I will never forget it. But it will never be repeated. So stop following me around like a moonstruck idiot!'

She expected anger and his laughter surprised her. 'I am not moonstruck, Karis. I never was a great believer in love at first sight – or indeed at any sight. And, to be honest, I don't know what I feel for you. Had you stayed that night, and we had talked, there might have been no need for a meeting like this. But you didn't. You ran. Why? Why did you run?'

'It is late, and I am too tired for this,' she said, turning away.

'Not afraid to die, but terrified to live. Is that it?' he asked her.

She whirled on him then. 'What is it with you men?' she sneered. 'Why can your egos never cope with rejection? I don't want you, I don't need you. You helped me to relax. That was your role and you did it well.'

He laughed again, the sound rich and unforced. 'Of course no man likes rejection. And I have known my share. What I find hard to understand is not that you reject me, Karis; it is that you are frightened of me.'

'Frightened? You arrogant pig! Nothing on this earth will ever frighten me again. My father saw to that. Now get out of my sight!'

He gave a rueful smile and turned away. She heard his voice drift back across the moonlit street. 'I am not your father, Karis.'

260

Angrily she strode back to the palace and to her apartments, where Necklen was waiting. 'You have chosen the men?' she asked, stepping inside. Stealer had to leap aside as she slammed the door.

'Yes. A hundred stretcher-bearers, and sixty orderlies to assist with the wounded. You know there are only four surgeons left in the city?'

'I do now.'

'You want me to come back tomorrow, princess?'

'Don't call me that!' She slumped into a chair. 'Do you think I am frightened to live?' she asked the old man.

Necklen gave a wide grin. 'What do you want to hear?'

'The truth would be pleasant.'

'I never met a woman yet who wanted to hear the truth. Are we talking about Vint, or the dog-ugly brute in the dung beetle armour?'

'You think he is ugly?' she asked, surprised.

'You think he is not?' countered Necklen. 'He has a nose that looks as if it has been kicked by a bull, and a broad flat face and small eyes. Green, if I recall. Never trust men with green eyes.'

'How did you know it might be him? Has he been speaking of me?'

'No, princess. But, if you want the truth, I learned it from you. Whenever he is close you cannot keep your eyes from him. Did he accuse you of being too frightened to live?'

'Yes. You agree with him?'

'How would I know?' asked Necklen. 'But you do surprise me, girl. You obviously want him, and I've never known you to be coy.'

'I slept with him once. Now he wants to own me,' she said. 'I won't be owned. I won't be used in the name of love.'

'Did Giriak use you?' he asked, softly.

'Of course he didn't. But then I didn't love him.'

'And you love Forin?'

'I didn't say that!' she snapped.

'I'm not sure what you are saying.'

Relaxing into her chair, Karis let out a long sigh. Then she chuckled. 'Neither am I. Pass me the jug, my dear old fool. It is time to get drunk!'

*

261

Just before dawn on the morning of the fourth day, Vint left his quarters in the palace and strolled the half-mile to the northern wall. A cold wind was blowing down from the mountains and he held his sheepskin cloak tightly around his slim frame. Passing the old barracks building, he saw three men hauling a hand-cart on which was set a metal drum, and the smell of hot onion soup drifted to him.

As he neared the gates he saw scores of workmen laying stone walls across the entrances to the alleyways leading off from the main avenue. Karis and Ozhobar were moving among them, checking the work. Vint walked past them, trying to control his feeling of irritation. Karis had not invited him to her bed in days. His annoyance surprised him. He was not in love with her, nor had he any wish to build a lasting relationship. What then? he wondered, as he climbed the rampart steps. The answer was not hard to find. He smiled ruefully. She is not in love with you either. It was a blow to the morale to be so casually discarded.

At the top of the steps he saw the sentries squatting down below the ramparts, hiding from the bitter bite of the north wind. 'Soup is on its way, lads,' he said.

'Not onion again, sir, is it?' asked one veteran.

'I am afraid so!'

The dawn sun crept into view, its rays cutting through the wind. 'Are the scouts back?' he asked.

'Not yet, sir. They should be in sight any time now.'

Vint turned towards the north, scanning the hills. Nothing was moving there. Glancing back, he saw Karis striding across the avenue with the huge form of Ozhobar beside her. Her dark hair was drawn back into a tight ponytail, and she was wearing a rust-coloured tunic of wool, and green leggings; a wide leather belt emphasized the slimness of her waist. How many women have you discarded in a similar fashion? Vint asked himself, trying to ease his troubled mind.

'Why are they doing that, sir?' asked a young soldier, coming alongside him and pointing to the workmen building new walls to block the alleyways.

Vint swung on the man. 'The Daroth can read minds,' he said. 'Do you think that it is a good idea to voice such questions?'

262

'I don't see as it makes a lot of difference,' replied the soldier, with a shrug. 'We're not going to stop them with a few stones. Nor crossbows. Nor catapults. They butchered thirty thousand people at Prentuis. The entire city – and its army. They'll do the same here.'

'Then why do you stay?'

'It's what I'm paid for,' said the soldier grimly.

'Have you ever served with Karis?' asked Vint.

'No, but I know men who have and they say she's never lost. But then she's never faced a Daroth army either.'

'She will surprise them,' said Vint.

'Really? I don't think so. She told one of the scouts about a group of wizards who are going to destroy the Daroth. He was simple-minded and believed every word. Wizards! You think if we had anything that powerful we wouldn't have gone out after them? You think we'd be shut in here building pigging walls?' The soldier brought his hand up to his head, pinching the bridge of his nose.

'What's wrong?' asked Vint.

'Stinking headache,' said the man. 'It's this wind.'

Sudden pain struck Vint. Grabbing the man, he hauled him below the ramparts.

'What are you doing?' shouted the soldier, angrily.

'Where is your head pain now?' snapped Vint.

The man blinked. 'Well, it's gone,' he said.

Vint swore and then, keeping low, he moved to the steps and ran down to where Karis and Ozhobar were standing. 'Can we talk?' he asked her. Together they moved away from the group and Vint told her about the exchange with the soldier.

'I'm surprised it held them this long,' she said, turning away.

'You sent out a man knowing he would be taken by the Daroth? I hope you had the decency to bed him first.'

Her eyes were cold as she stepped closer to him. 'No, Vint, I *liked* him. It is a rule of mine never to bed a man I like.' Swinging away from him, she called out to Necklen. 'Find your crew, old man. The Daroth are coming!'

*

Twenty minutes later Necklen was climbing the rickety ladders to the roof of the old barracks building. Climbing with only one hand was difficult, and he was breathing heavily when he stepped out onto the roof. The four boys of his team were waiting for him. They were all young and beardless – just children, he thought. But they were nimble and quick, and they took his orders well.

'Are the wheels greased?' he asked.

'Yes, sir. And we brought the oil up last night,' answered Beris, a small lad with a shock of ginger hair and a freckled face.

'Good. Take to the handles!' Two boys on each side grabbed the iron handles and began to turn them. Slowly the great arm was winched down into place, then Necklen pushed the iron locking bolt through the metal hoops. Two boys ran back to where the pottery balls were covered by tarpaulin. Pulling back the sheet they rolled one of the balls to the catapult, then carefully lifted it to the bronze cup. 'Oil!' ordered Necklen. Then he swung around. 'Where is the brazier?'

'Sorry, sir, I forgot,' said Gelan, a thin, pockmarked boy.

'Fetch it. And do it now!' The boy ran to the ladders and swung down out of sight as Necklen strolled to the edge of the roof, staring out over the hills. Soon they would come. Walking back to the catapult, he checked the sighting wheel. The weapon was aimed at the first of the two probable sites for the Daroth catapults. So far Necklen and his team had loosed more than thirty practice missiles, and the accuracy rate was high, eight out of ten landing on the target.

Gelan came scrambling back into view with a small brazier strapped to his back, a lantern held in his right hand. Necklen set the brazier alongside the catapult, filled the lower half with oil-soaked rags, then kindling, and lastly added several handfuls of coal. Taking the lantern from Gelan, he lifted the lid and held the naked flame under the soaked rags. Flames seared up. Ginger-haired Beris brought five torches made from dried reeds and laid them alongside the brazier.

Satisfied the fire was going well, Necklen called again for the oil and watched as Beris poured it through one of six round holes in the pottery ball. Three more jugs of lantern-oil followed; the holes were then plugged with rags.

The sound of shouting came from the walls below, and Necklen saw the first line of Daroth horsemen breast the northern hills. Ahead of them rode ten warriors, each carrying a long spear.

Impaled upon the spears were the bodies of the ten Corduin scouts sent out the night before.

Necklen glanced at the boys, seeing the fear on their faces. 'You be steady now, my lads,' he said softly.

'Why did they do that to those men?' Beris asked.

'To frighten us, lad.'

'Are you frightened, Necklen?' asked Gelan.

'There's no shame in fear,' said the old man. 'But understand this – the coward is ruled by fear, while the hero rides it like a wild stallion. You boys are born to be heroes. Trust me. I am a fine judge of men. That's why I chose you.'

'I don't feel like a hero,' admitted Beris.

'You don't have to feel like one, boy. You live like one!'

*

As the full Daroth army crested the skyline and spread out along the slopes, Vint stood on the walls and tried to estimate their numbers. They were moving in columns of fours towards designated positions. They pitched no tents, but waited in five huge groups, each around 1,500 strong. Three of the groups were foot-soldiers, in black armour; they carried long spears with serrated heads. The other two groups were horse-soldiers.

The sound of running men could be heard behind the walls and some soldiers turned to look. 'Stare straight ahead!' bellowed Vint. The men swung back. Forty Daroth warriors put aside their spears and removed the packs from their backs, taking short-handled shovels and moving to two areas on the hillside, some 200 paces from the walls.

'What are they doing?' someone asked Vint. The swordsman shrugged. Swiftly the Daroth began to dig away at the hillside. They moved with great energy that did not slacken. Other Daroth moved in, removing their cloaks and filling them with earth, before carrying it away. The digging went on for almost an hour before Vint understood their plan: the Daroth were levelling two sections of ground.

Up on the barracks roof, Necklen realized what was happening. 'They are not going to use the ground we picked out, lads,' he said. 'They are building new bases for their catapults.'

Moving to the iron rails, Necklen pulled clear the retaining rods.

265

'Let's move her round,' he called. 'Beris, line her up with the first new site. Gelan, you and the others lift clear the ball. We'll need to loose her; the range is wrong now.'

The boys struggled to roll the ball clear. It was big and unwieldy, and oil was seeping from the rags. Necklen moved to help them. Once the ball was clear, he hammered the trigger bolt. The catapult snapped forward, the great arm thudding home against the sand-sacks roped to the frame. 'How far would you say to the site?' Necklen asked Beris.

'Around two hundred and . . . forty paces?'

'My eyes are not that good any more. I'll take your word for it. Heave her back into position.' The boys set to at the handles and, slowly, the arm was winched into place.

'We are in line,' said Beris. Necklen slid the retaining rods home behind the wheels and climbed onto the platform alongside Beris.

'Looks good,' said the older man. 'Replace the ball.' Gelan and the other two boys heaved the ball into the bronze cup.

Two Daroth catapults were pulled into view: huge machines, painted black. Necklen's throat was dry. He had seen these before, at the fall of Prentuis, the boulders of lead smashing the walls to fragments. Slowly the Daroth pulled the first of the catapults into position. 'Get back, lads, and we'll let her go!'

'Shall I light it, sir?' asked Gelan.

'Not this one, boy. This is a scout. We'll see where she lands.'

Taking up the small hammer, Necklen rapped it against the trigger bolt. The red pottery ball sailed high into the air, the wind whipping through the holes and creating an eerie scream. For a moment Necklen thought they were right on target, but then the ball dropped some twenty feet to the right and twelve paces short, smashing into hundreds of pieces. 'Haul her back, and bring the setting down one notch,' he ordered.

'Left one mark,' shouted Beris.

Necklen and the boys drew out the retaining rods, swinging the huge machine on its wheels. In their excitement they pushed it too far. 'Steady, lads!' he called. 'Take it slow!'

'They are arming their catapults!' shouted another boy.

Necklen did not pause. Applying the last rod he called for a second ball. It was rolled to the catapult, then lifted into place. Beris filled it with oil.

'It's coming!' yelled Gelan, and this time Necklen did look up. A huge ball of lead was sailing through the air. It passed over the wall, and only at the last second did the old soldier realize the Daroth were aiming at the catapult. The ball slammed into the edge of the roof, dislodging masonry and sending chips of stone screaming over their heads.

Necklen grabbed a torch, lit it from the brazier and applied it to the oil-soaked rags which Beris had rammed into the holes. 'Here comes another!' shouted Gelan.

'Well, let's send one back!' snarled Necklen, hammering the trigger bolt. The red ball, flames and smoke hissing from it, soared high – passing within yards of the Daroth shot. The black ball of lead struck the rooftop, hit a beam and crashed through to the empty second floor of the barracks building.

'Haul her back! Don't wait to look!' shouted Necklen, though he himself could not resist following the flight of their blazing shot. It struck the top of the first Daroth catapult – and shattered. Flames rippled down the black machine. The Daroth ran forward to hurl earth over the blaze.

A great cheer went up from the battlements.

'One more!' shouted Necklen, and second ball of flame flew into the sky. The Daroth scattered as it smashed down, fire exploding out in a huge circle. The wooden catapult was engulfed now.

But the second enemy machine loosed another shot which thundered against the side of the building, ripping away an entire corner which slid away to crash to the street below.

'Right three marks!' shouted Beris. 'Take her down two more notches.'

Slowly they swung the machine. 'One shot is all we'll have,' said Necklen, trying to keep his voice calm. 'Make it a good one, boy!'

'Yes, sir,' said Beris. Once they had loaded the ball and Gelan had filled it with oil, Necklen ordered the boys from the rooftop. Another huge lead ball soared by them, missing the catapult by inches and destroying the store of pottery ammunition. 'Get out now!' shouted Necklen.

The boys ran to the ladders as Necklen slammed the trigger bolt clear. He should have followed them, but he could not resist watching the flight of his last missile. Once again the Daroth loosed a shot. It left their catapult just as the pottery ball exploded over it, spraying burning oil over the machine. Two Daroth warriors were engulfed, and ran across the hillside like living torches.

'Yes!' shouted Necklen, punching the air. 'Did you enjoy that, you bastards?'

The last Daroth shot hammered into the platform, smashing the catapult. One of the retaining bars burst clear, striking Necklen in the shoulder and spinning him across the rooftop. As his legs slipped over the edge he threw out his hand, scrabbling at an edge of masonry, and clung to it with all his strength.

There was no way back. The old warrior did not possess enough strength in one arm to haul himself to safety. His strength was ebbing away when a face appeared above him and little Beris reached down and grabbed his arm.

'Let go, you fool! You can't take my weight. You'll be dragged over with me.' But the boy clung on.

'Gelan is getting . . . a . . . rope,' said Beris. 'I can hold you till he comes.'

'Please, boy! Just let go. I couldn't bear to take you with me.'

'No, sir,' said Beris, his freckled face crimson with the effort of holding on. Necklen gripped the ledge more tightly, fighting to stay calm. His fingers were tiring, and his arm began to tremble.

Just then Gelan appeared and threw a loop over Necklen's head. Pushing his useless left arm through it, he hooked himself to the rope. 'It is tied to a beam,' shouted Gelan.

'Good boy,' said Necklen. 'Now let go, Beris, there's a good lad.' When Beris did so, Necklen dropped around four feet; but the rope tightened and he dangled there, feeling sick with relief. Moments later three strong men dragged him back to safety.

Necklen grinned at the boys. 'I hope you never learn to take orders, lads,' he told them.

'Yes, sir!' they chorused, grinning.

But Necklen's smile faded as he saw the Daroth hauling another catapult over the hills.

*

As the first of the huge lead balls crashed into the wall beside the gate Vint ordered the troops back. The two blazing Daroth catapults were now oozing thick plumes of black smoke into the sky.

'What can you see?' yelled Karis. Vint eased himself up, and stared through the crenellated battlements.

'Two Daroth legions are massing,' he shouted. 'They are moving slowly forward.'

A second lead ball struck the gates, smashing two thick timbers and splitting the giant locking bar. 'They are coming at a run now,' yelled Vint. 'Maybe three thousand of them. The rest are just waiting.'

Another lead shot smashed home, tearing open the gates and rolling ponderously into the avenue beyond. Vint ran for the steps, taking them three at a time, then sprinted down towards a line of wagons stretching across the avenue. Karis, Ozhobar and Tarantio were already there.

Two hundred crossbow-men moved through a gap in the wagons and took up positions in front of them, one line kneeling and the other standing behind. They weren't going to stop the Daroth, thought Vint. Not 200.

The first of the enemy pushed their way past the ruined gates, saw the crossbow-men, and charged. They came in silence, save for the pounding of their boots on the cobbles. The silence itself chilled Vint. He drew his sabre, knowing that the weapon was useless against the leathery skins of the Daroth, yet feeling better for having it in his hand.

'Wait!' shouted Karis, her voice clear and calm. The twenty-wide mass of the Daroth attackers came closer. Seventy feet. Fifty. Forty. 'Now!' she cried. The kneeling line of crossbow-men loosed their shafts, which hammered home into the leading warriors. Scores went down while the rest charged on. 'Again!' yelled Karis. The standing line let fly, and a second black cloud of bolts plunged home. The charge scarcely faltered.

Suddenly crossbow bolts came shooting from every window on either side of the avenue. Bowmen rose up from behind the hastily erected walls across the alleys, sending volley after volley into the Daroth ranks.

Vint heard a whip crack. In an alley, hidden from sight, three oxen lunged into the traces and the wagons were hauled away, exposing three enormous steel-armed ballistae hidden behind them. The two lines of crossbow-men sprinted clear left and right, just as the Daroth charged again.

Ozhobar slammed his hammer against a release bolt and two

269

pounds of spreading iron shot screamed into the attackers, smashing the first line from their feet. Standing to one side, Vint saw a Daroth's face swept away in a milky blur, shards of bone spraying into the air. All around, mutilated Daroth warriors were hurled to the cobbles. A second ballista loosed its load, punching a great gap in the Daroth line. Vint stood back and watched three men smoothly drawing the deadly arms of the first ballista into position. Then the third sent its lethal missiles into the packed ranks of the enemy. Crossbow bolts continued to rain from the windows, and the carnage in the avenue continued. Now the first two lines of crossbow-men edged back along the walls, spreading out again behind the ballistae and loosing their bolts into the enemy.

One Daroth warrior, his left arm torn away, stumbled forward and then hurled his spear. It took a crossbow-man through the chest, hurling him back into a wall. Tarantio relaxed and allowed Dace to take control. He leapt forward and with one sweep of his blade disembowelled the creature, then beheaded him as he fell. 'That's one for Sirano and his spell swords,' said Dace.

As the enemy charged once more, the arms of one of the ballistae snapped off. Within seconds the Daroth had reached the weapons. Then the second ballista blasted lead shot into them at point-blank range, lifting three warriors from their feet and slamming them into their comrades.

From the alley alongside the ballista Forin and his fifty axemen charged into the fray. Dace was in with them, his eldritch swords cleaving a path through the enemy. Vint, his own sword useless, scrambled back from the action and joined Karis and Ozhobar. Taking up a crossbow, he cocked it and sent a bolt through the brain of a towering warrior.

A bugle blew.

Forin and his men ran left and right, opening a gap through which a ballista could send its murderous ammunition slashing into the Daroth ranks. Hundreds of the creatures were down now, more falling with every heartbeat as the merciless hail of death continued from the windows on either side.

There was nowhere for the Daroth to run. Ahead of them were the deadly ballistae, on either side the alleyways were blocked. And as the death toll continued to rise, they fought to make their way to the only haven: the north gate.

Forin took a blow to the head which sent him reeling, his helmet flying clear. As the Daroth ran in for the kill, the giant reared up to smash his axe into his enemy's face. The blade plunged home, then tore itself away. The spear of a second Daroth struck his breastplate, denting it deeply and bruising his ribs. Spinning, Forin lunged with his axe, stabbing both points through the Daroth's chest. The creature's fist crashed against Forin's brow. Stunned, the giant stumbled to his knees. Dace appeared beside him, his sword half decapitating the Daroth. Forin struggled to his feet, dragged his axe clear of the dead Daroth and charged back into the fray.

Her face expressionless, Karis watched the battle. Humans were dying now as the frantic Daroth warriors tore at the makeshift walls, hacking and stabbing at the crossbow-men on the ground level. At least fifteen of Forin's men were down.

Four Daroth warriors broke clear of Forin's line and made it to the ballistae. Dace ran up behind the last of them, cutting him down. Crossbow bolts slammed into the second and third men, but the fourth leapt straight at Karis.

Vint was the closest to her. He heard his name shouted and turned to see Tarantio throwing one of his swords. The shimmering blade spun through the air and Vint leapt to catch it, his hand curling round the hilt. Even as he caught it, he knew he would be too late. Spinning on his heel, he ran towards the Daroth. The creature's sword swept up, but Karis stood her ground, staring defiantly at him.

At that moment a hurtling black form crashed into the Daroth, Stealer's huge jaws clamping to his neck. Off balance, the Daroth fell back. Ozhobar lunged forward to send his hammer cracking against the side of the attacker's head. Vint sent Tarantio's sword slicing through his spine. As the creature fell dead, the hound continued to gnaw at his throat. 'Here!' called Karis. Stealer backed away, still growling.

A slow rumbling began, like distant thunder. Vint glanced round to see Necklen and ten men hauling a new catapult along the avenue. Behind it were several horse-drawn wagons, the first carrying fresh shot and a burning brazier. Ozhobar ran back to them.

The Daroth were streaming back for the gates as the bugle sounded. Forin, Dace and the surviving eleven armoured warriors turned and ran back towards the ballistae. A blazing pottery ball flew over their heads and exploded just below the gate tower.

Close-packed as they were, the flames engulfed twenty Daroth warriors. In panic the remaining Daroth trampled each other to escape, and the flames spread.

A second ball soared over the walls to scatter blazing oil over the warriors milling there.

The Daroth army fled back towards the hills.

'Clear the dead!' yelled Karis. 'Make way for the wagons.'

Dace ran among the Daroth corpses, checking them. Several of them were still alive, and these he despatched swiftly. Soldiers began to drag the giant bodies back to the walls on either side, and three wagons inched their way to the gates. Ozhobar rode the first wagon, and when it reached the gate tower he jumped down and called for help to unload. Each of the three wagons carried interlocking sections made up of long iron bars. Ropes and pulleys were assembled on the parapet above, hauling the sections into place, lodging them into the deep grooves which stonemasons had carved in the solid stone on both sides of the gate tower.

Behind the workmen the catapult was hauled into place. Necklen ran to the gate and gauged the distance to the Daroth weapon. No more than 200 paces. Moving back to the catapult, he passed the information to young Beris.

Moments later a blazing ball soared over the walls, exploding some thirty feet to the left of the Daroth machine. Soldiers on the walls cheered as Daroth soldiers hastily roped their catapult, dragging it back out of harm's way.

Slowly the iron portcullis was assembled, effectively re-blocking the gateway. Ozhobar stood back, hands on hips, admiring his handiwork. 'Not bad,' he said. 'Not bad at all.'

Across the avenue stretcher-bearers, Brune among them, were carrying away the Corduin wounded and dead. Vint moved amongst them, checking the numbers of injured and slain. He crossed to where Karis was standing with Tarantio.

'Forin lost thirty-nine men: thirty-seven dead, two badly wounded. Just under sixty other men died, or will not fight again. As far as I can tell we killed around two hundred and thirty Daroth.'

Karis nodded, but said nothing. 'You did it, General,' said Vint. 'You turned them back.'

'We've certainly made them think,' she agreed.

Vint offered Tarantio his sword. The dark-haired warrior grinned. 'Keep it! But be careful how you sheathe it.'

Vint nodded. 'If I had known how deadly it was, I'd have thought twice about catching it.' He glanced up. The sun was still climbing in the sky. 'Sweet Heaven,' he said. 'You would have thought it would be dusk by now, and yet it is not an hour since the charge began.'

Forin joined them. 'Will someone help me get this damned breastplate off?' he said. 'I can't breathe in it.' The armour was covered with deep dents, and there was a gash across the back where the metal had split. Once Tarantio and Vint eased the breastplate clear, Forin stripped off his shirt. His upper body was covered in bruises, and there was a shallow cut on his shoulder. 'I'm not looking forward to going through that again,' he grumbled, sitting down on a broken wall.

'You fought well, big man,' said Vint. 'I think you killed three of them.'

'Two. Tarantio took the last. But I marked a few too.' He looked up at Karis. 'You think they'll come back today?'

'Men wouldn't,' she said. 'The generals would get together and rethink their strategy. They are not men, however.'

'Do you have another fiendish plan for them?' asked the giant.

'No,' Karis admitted. 'Send for me if they charge again.' With that she turned and strode away, the dog Stealer padding alongside her.

'She's not much on celebration is she?' remarked Ozhobar.

*

As the day wore on, and the Daroth remained in their camp, an air of jubilation swept through the city. The invincible Daroth had been turned back by the strength and courage of the soldiers, and by the strategic brilliance of Karis. Crowds formed outside the palace, cheering her name.

Inside, Karis lay in a hot bath with Stealer lying at the edge, looking quizzically at his adopted mistress. Her thoughts were many and confused. Far from jubilation, she felt a sense of panic – almost of loss. It had begun when she had seen Necklen hanging from the rooftop; the old man meant more to her than she had realized. Then, when Forin charged in with his men, and she saw them cut down, one after another.

273

With each one that died, a part of herself faded. War and death.

She was suddenly tired of both. And yet this was just the beginning. The Daroth would be wary now; they would circle the city, looking for a weak spot, then launch another attack . . . and another. Even if Corduin held, what would be gained? There were seven cities of the Daroth, and their power was enormous.

Karis sighed, then ducked her head under the warm water, washing her dark hair. 'What is it for?' she asked Stealer. Cocking his head he gazed back at her. 'Is there a point to it all?'

'A drowning man doesn't stop to think about whether the sea has a reason for being,' said a voice. 'He just swims and fights for life.'

'What are you doing here, Forin?'

'I came to talk, but I'd just as soon have a bath.' Stripping off his bloodstained clothes, the red-bearded giant moved down the marble steps and sank down into the water. 'Ah, but that is good.'

'I don't want company,' she said, but there was no force of conviction in her voice.

'Yes, you do. You've lived and breathed the Daroth threat for weeks now – scheming, planning, worrying. And all for this day. Now it is over. And all the tension of those dark days is settling over you like a black mist.'

'I'm sick of it,' she said. 'Sick of seeing death and violence.'

'You are right to be sick of it, it is a sickening business. As to the point . . . ? Ask the living. There are crowds outside chanting your name . . . well, not exactly your name. "The Ice Queen", they are calling you now. They think you are a deliverer sent by the gods. Better than the "Whore of War", anyway.'

'I don't care what they think.'

'You should; they are what this is all about: the bakers and the carpenters, the dreamers and the poets. But you won't see that today, will you, Karis?'

'What is it you want from me?' she asked, rising from the water and climbing the steps. Servants had left thick towels by the bath side and Karis wrapped one around her torso, using a second to dry her hair. 'Well?' she persisted.

'I don't know. How did the hot water feel upon your skin?'

'What has that to do with anything?'

274

'It felt good, didn't it? Cleansing the skin, relaxing the muscles. Had the Daroth broken through, we would have all been dead. No more baths. No more wine. No more loving. They didn't break through, Karis. You stopped them. And here we are. And life is sweet! Tomorrow . . . ? Well, tomorrow can look after itself. What do I want? Pointless to say that I want you for eternity. We may only have a day. But if we don't use it then the Daroth might just as well have won.'

She sat down on a bench and smiled. 'That was a long-winded way of saying you want to take me to bed.'

He grinned at her. 'What I wanted most was to see you smile.'

She looked into his green eyes and was silent for a moment. 'Come and join me in a drink,' she said at last. He rose from the water and she threw him a towel.

Necklen, Vint and the Duke Albreck were waiting in her outer rooms. The Duke stood as she entered, then averted his eyes. 'My apologies, General,' he said. 'We will come back when you are attired for company.'

Karis bowed. 'With respect, my lord, please be seated. I am too tired to dress, and will soon be asleep. But for the moment I have enough wits about me to conduct a conversation.'

'As you wish,' he said, but he was clearly uncomfortable. Seating himself, he was about to speak when Forin walked in naked. Hastily the giant swept a towel around his hips, but as he bowed the towel fell away. Necklen roared with laughter and even the Duke smiled. Then Albreck turned to Karis. 'Firstly, let me congratulate you on today's victory. The people seem to believe it was a miracle. For myself I know it to be the result of careful planning and meticulous strategy. I am proud of you, Karis. Whatever happens from now on, nothing will change that.'

Karis reddened, seeming at a loss for words. The Duke rose and bowed to her, then swung to Forin. 'You lost a lot of men today, Captain. But you fought like a lion. Should Corduin survive this war, then there will be a place for you in my personal guard.'

'Thank you, my lord. I'll enjoy that.'

The Duke moved to the door. 'When you have rested, Karis, please come to my rooms. I would like to discuss tomorrow's plan of defence.' He paused before the door, which Necklen opened for him. Karis lay back on the couch, fatigue making her head swim.

'We'll let you get some rest, princess,' said Necklen, tapping Vint on the shoulder. Vint did not move; his face ashen, he was staring at Forin with undisguised hatred. Necklen leaned in to him. 'Time to go, my friend,' he whispered. Vint took a deep breath, pushed himself to his feet and stalked from the room. Necklen followed him.

'I think I've made an enemy of Vint,' said Forin. There was no reply from Karis, and the giant, moving alongside her, saw that she was asleep. Gently he lifted her into his arms and carried her into the bedroom. Pulling the sheets and blankets over her he kissed her brow, then dressed and wandered out of the palace.

*

Necklen caught Vint just as the swordsman was passing the side gates of the palace. 'Join me for a jug?' asked the older man.

'I don't think so.'

'It's what she is, Vint,' said Necklen. 'I love her like a daughter, but she's wilful.'

With great effort Vint held back the angry retort that swelled in his throat. Necklen was a good man, tough and loyal, and he meant well. The truth was simple: a man rarely understands the value of what he has – until he loses it. 'You mustn't blame Forin,' said Necklen.

'Blame? I don't blame anyone. I am angry, but that will pass. And now, if you'll excuse me, I'll return to the wall.'

Vint strode off. Everywhere there were crowds on the streets, laughing, singing, drinking. He moved through them like a wraith, oblivious to their joy. The black-clad figure of Tarantio was sitting on the battlements, staring out over the walls.

'Anything happening?' asked Vint.

'No. A whole group of them, maybe two hundred, have been sitting in a circle for the last couple of hours. Where's Karis?'

'Resting, apparently.' Tarantio caught the edge in Vint's tone and said nothing. 'Where next, do you think?' asked Vint. 'The east gate?'

'I have no idea. They are shocked, that's for sure.'

Vint glanced back to where the Daroth bodies had been dragged earlier. All that remained was what appeared to be a huge pile of white sacks and oddments of armour and weapons. 'What happened to the Daroth dead?' he asked.

'That's them,' said Tarantio. 'The bodies just shrivelled away. The stench was dreadful for a while. I saw a snake shed its skin one time; it was something like that.'

'It was the same at the miracle forest,' Vint told him. 'They really decompose fast, don't they?'

'If that is what is happening,' said Tarantio. 'That farmer who was taken by them . . . Barin. He said they were immortal – reborn every ten years. Maybe there's a new body for them back in their city.'

'What a loathsome thought.'

The bearded soldier who had spoken to Vint just before the attack walked up the rampart steps. He was weaving slightly, and holding a jug in his hands. 'What a day!' he said, slumping down beside the two men. 'What an incredible day! Did you know the whores are not accepting money today? Everything's free: women, drink, food. What a day!' The man lay down on the stone and, using the empty jug for a pillow, fell asleep.

'Let's hope he has the same sentiments tomorrow,' said Tarantio. 'People are treating this as a great victory, when in fact it is only the starting skirmish.'

Brune ran up the steps, tripped at the top, recovered his balance and then moved alongside Tarantio, handing him a package wrapped in muslin. Tarantio opened it to find fresh bread, salted beef and a pottery jar containing butter. 'It's amazing back there,' said Brune. 'Everyone's so happy. A woman kissed me!'

'She must have been drunk,' teased Tarantio.

'Yes, she was,' admitted Brune. 'It was still nice, though.'

'How is the eye?' asked Vint.

The sandy-haired youngster gave a shrug. 'It's not as good as it was when it went gold. But it's all right.'

'You can shoot straight now?'

'I don't know. Haven't tried.'

'Brune has decided that war is evil, and he will have no part in killing,' put in Tarantio. 'Isn't that right, Brune?'

'Yes. I don't want to kill nobody.'

'Putting aside the double negative for a moment,' said Vint, ' I think that is a laudable point of view. But what do you do when a Daroth warrior is about to behead you with a large sword? Do you just die – or do you fight?'

'I'll die, I reckon,' said Brune.

'Could you offer some validation for this philosophy?'

'What did he say?' Brune asked Tarantio.

'I think he wants to know why you have decided not to fight.'

'Oh. It was the Oltor. I can't explain it, but when he was . . . you know, part of me, I could feel what he was thinking. What he was feeling. And it was good, you know? It was . . .' he paused '. . . right. Yes, that's it. It was right. You understand?'

'Not a word,' admitted Vint. 'You think it would be better to be dead than to fight for your life?'

'Yes, I think so. That's what the Oltor done.'

'And they were wiped out.'

'Yes, but they're back now.'

'What is he talking about?' Vint asked Tarantio.

'It is a long story.'

Vint was about to question him further when movement began in the Daroth camp. Hundreds of Daroth warriors moved to the lower hillside and began to dig while others could be seen returning from the woods carrying the trunks of felled trees. Within minutes the area was the scene of frenzied activity. The diggers soon disappeared from sight, but the watching men could see earth being thrown up from the pit. The Daroth brought up empty wagons, which they filled with earth; these were then trundled away, returning empty minutes later. Ropes and pulleys were assembled above the pit, drawing up dirt, while planks and timbers were lowered down.

Realization dawned on Vint and he felt a chilling fear spread through him. 'They're building a tunnel,' he said. 'They are going to burrow underneath us!'

CHAPTER FOURTEEN

THE HOUSE WAS COLD AND TARANTIO LIT A FIRE. BRUNE WAS staying in the new barracks building with the other stretcher- bearers, and the house seemed lonely without him. '*I miss him too,*' said Dace. Tarantio smiled. '*You remember that first day? "He hit me with a lump of wood*",' he mimicked.

'*He is a good man. I hope he survives.*'

Tarantio sat before the fire, enjoying the new warmth. '*We don't make many friends, do we, Dace? Why is that?*'

'*We don't need them, brother.*'

'*So why Brune? Why do we miss him?*' Dace remained silent and Tarantio wandered out to the kitchen. There was a stale loaf there and he cut several slices from it, bringing them back to the fire and toasting them. He ate only one, then lay down on the goatskin rug, weariness washing over him. The Daroth were still digging, the mouth of the tunnel illuminated by lanterns. Soon they would erupt out of the ground somewhere within the city.

'*We won't die, brother,*' said Dace. '*I'll kill them all.*'

'*I've always loved your sense of humour.*'

'*Don't go to sleep yet. I feel the need to talk awhile.*' Dace sat up and added a log to the fire. 'Chio? Chio!' he said, aloud. He swore softly, and tried to summon Tarantio. He could now feel the weakness in their body, the muscle fatigue and the bone-numbing weariness. It was not a sensation Dace enjoyed. Pushing himself to his feet he walked to the kitchen and drank several cups of cold water, then scraped the last of some honey from a pottery jar. It was sweet and good.

His keen hearing picked up the sound of someone walking along the path to the door, and he opened it. There, framed in the moonlight, the hood of a dark cloak hiding her golden hair, was the Lady Miriac.

'Are you not going to invite me in?' she asked. Dace stepped aside.

Her blue silk skirts swished against the floor as she moved through to the fire and sat down. Dace could hardly believe this was happening. It seemed so long ago when Tarantio had bedded her and Dace had fought for control, determined to draw his knife across her slender throat. In terror Tarantio had run from the room of mirrors. Now she was here. And Tarantio was asleep.

'Why did you not tell me you were back in Corduin?' she asked.

'I did not know you were still here,' said Dace, his fingers idly stroking the hilt of his dagger.

'Did I do something wrong?' she asked. 'We . . . blended so well. I felt . . . I don't know what I felt. But I have thought about you constantly.' She rose and stepped in close to him, putting her arms around his shoulders. He felt the warmth of her body, and pictured the blood gushing from her. Smoothly he drew the dagger, bringing it up behind her back. Her lips brushed against his cheek, then touched his mouth, and he felt her soft tongue upon his. All weariness fled from him, and he was suddenly filled with an aching need. Stepping back she loosed the cloak, letting it fall, then undid the ties at the front of her silk dress. Dace watched in silent amazement as the garment fell to the floor. 'Why are you holding a dagger?' she whispered. He hurled it aside.

They made love before the fire, their passion fierce and uncontrolled, and when it was over Dace – for the first time in his life – began to weep. She held him close, stroking his back and

280

whispering gentle endearments to him. It seemed to Dace that walls were collapsing in his mind, and emotions long hidden were washing out like the swollen waters of a flood. He saw his father hanging from the beam, and instead of being filled with a bitter hatred of the man's weakness he remembered his father's kindness and the love they had lost. He felt he was drowning in a sea of emotions he never knew he possessed. And he clung to Miriac, whose soft caresses and gentle words aroused him again.

He took her to the bedroom where they made love slowly and with great tenderness. Later, as she slept, Dace sat up and stared down at her as she lay with her golden hair spread out on the pillow, her slender left arm draped across the bed. She was the most beautiful woman he had ever seen.

'*And you wanted to kill her,*' said Tarantio.

'*I have wanted many things,*' Dace told him. '*But mostly I wanted us to stay together.*'

'*We are together.*'

'*You don't understand, Chio. We are not real, you and I; we are both creations of the child trapped in the mine. He created me to deal with his terrors, and in doing so gave birth to you. For only you could control me. Don't you see? And the pull is getting stronger. One day he will draw us both to him, and we will cease to be.*'

'*You cannot be sure of this,*' argued Tarantio.

'*Oh, I am sure. I can hear him calling me even now. And I can no longer resist.*'

'*Why?*' Tarantio asked.

'*Because I have known love – and that is not what I was created for. Goodbye, brother,*' said Dace aloud, an infinite sadness in his voice.

Tarantio jerked back into awareness. 'Dace!' he called, but there was nothing.

Miriac stirred. 'Did you call me?' she whispered.

Tarantio sat very still, a yawning sense of emptiness sweeping through him.

Dace had gone . . .

*

The mood in the Meeting Hall was sombre as Vint gave his report. The Daroth had moved mountains of earth from their tunnel, and by morning would be close to the walls. By late tomorrow they would be under the city. Duke Albreck listened in silence, but cast a searching gaze around the room and its occupants. The little councillor, Pooris, looked glum and uncertain. Karis sat with eyes downcast, contributing nothing. The giant Forin was only half-listening to Vint; he was casting furtive glances towards Karis, and his look was one of concern. The dark-haired, skeletal cleric, Niro, sat forward attentively with his eyes fixed on the speaker. Neither Tarantio nor Ozhobar had so far arrived. 'I cannot see,' concluded Vint, 'how we can combat this new initiative. If it was men we were facing, I would suggest digging down to intercept them. But Daroth? They would cut us to pieces in moments.' He sat down, and the silence that followed his words was ominous.

Duke Albreck waited for a moment, then took a deep breath. 'Our thanks to you, Vint. Your report was clear and concise. Any comments?' The silence grew again. 'General, do you have anything to add?' Karis shook her head, but did not look up. The Duke chose his words carefully, speaking without any hint of criticism. 'My friends we have worked hard and long to plan our defences, and to secure a future for the thousands of Corduin citizens who remain. It would be less than courageous to give in now, before the enemy has breached our walls. There must be something we can do.' He glanced at Pooris. The little man wiped the sweat from his bald head.

'I am not a warrior, my lord, as well you know. But I fail to see how we can combat these tactics. The Daroth could come up anywhere, and the only real weapons we have against them are too cumbersome to haul around the city. The way to the south is still open; the Daroth have not surrounded us. It seems to me that we should order a mass evacuation.'

'How far would we get?' asked Forin. 'At best such a column could make eight miles in a day. The Daroth riders would be upon us within the hour.'

The door opened and Ozhobar strolled in, carrying a bundle of scrolls under his arm. He gave a cursory bow to the Duke, then pulled up a chair. 'Have I missed anything?' he asked.

'You appear to have missed out your apology for lateness, sir,' chided the Duke.

'What? Ah, I see we are still observing the niceties. That's rather good. We dangle from the crumbling lip of the precipice, but we retain our manners.'

'We do, sir,' said the Duke curtly.

'My apologies for my late arrival, my lord,' said Ozhobar, rising and bowing once more, 'but I needed to obtain these items from the Great Library. Some fool of a cleric told me that it was closed, but would re-open at its usual time tomorrow. He too was observing the niceties.' His pale eyes gleamed with anger. 'This of course meant that I had to waste time fetching a large hammer from my forge and beating down the door. However, that is largely of no consequence now. I have, I believe, found a way to fight the Daroth.'

Duke Albreck swallowed his irritation. 'Would you enlighten us, my dear Ozhobar?'

'Certainly, my lord.' He passed one of the scrolls to the Duke, who opened it. He recognized it instantly.

'These are your plans for a city sewerage system. I recall you brought them to me last year.'

'Indeed I did. After examining them you passed them on to the City Council for perusal. From there, it seems they were sent to a treasury team, then to the councillors responsible for public works. Lastly they were lodged in a small room at the rear of the Library, perhaps waiting for future generations to study them. It took me a long time to locate them, but here they are.'

'I see the plan,' said Vint dryly. 'We swiftly build a sewer system, and when the Daroth break through they are washed away. I think it is brilliant.'

'Dolt!' said Ozhobar, passing the other scrolls around the table. 'I am talking about the reason why such a sewerage system was feasible in the first place.'

'The catacombs,' said the Duke, unable to keep the excitement from his voice.

'Precisely, my lord. They spread under the city in all directions. I believe the Daroth will break through into one of the natural tunnels below the old barracks building. Now, if they have any sense at all they will not dig any further, but follow the tunnels to any one of seventeen exits within the city itself.'

'And that is a help?' sneered Vint, his face pale and angry.

'Perhaps if I speak more slowly your simple mind might be able to keep up,' said Ozhobar.

Vint fought for control. 'Be careful, fat man. Your life hangs on a thread.'

'Somewhat similar to your brain, then,' observed Ozhobar. Vint lurched to his feet at the insult.

'That is enough! Both of you!' said the Duke, without raising his voice. 'What is your plan, Ozhobar?'

'I don't make war plans. I leave that to Karis. But there are many chambers in the catacombs. I have walked them, and I know.'

Karis looked up. ' Before I speak it is vital for Vint and Forin to leave the room.'

'Why?' asked Forin.

'Because both of you will be fighting the Daroth, face to face. Ask no more questions. The answers should be obvious.'

'Indeed they are, Karis,' said Vint. The warrior swung to Ozhobar, and when he spoke his voice was flat and cold. 'You have nerve, fat man; I'll give you that. And because of your discovery, I will not kill you for your insolence.'

'Decent of you, I'm sure,' retorted Ozhobar.

The two warriors left the room. Karis rose, and Duke Albreck was delighted to see the glint in her eyes. 'We can lead the Daroth to the exit we prefer,' she said. 'We need a fighting force below ground. They will attack the Daroth, then retreat before them. The Daroth will follow. If we can maintain a fighting retreat, we can ensure that we have ballistae, crossbow-men and catapults waiting for them above ground. The difficulty will be in preventing the Daroth from recognizing the plan; if our men are retreating towards a set exit, they may well suspect a trap.'

'I see the problem,' said the Duke. 'If our men are told of the plan, the enemy will read their minds. Yet if we don't tell the men which way to retreat, the scheme is doomed anyway.'

'Then what do you propose, Karis?' asked Pooris.

'I don't know yet. But I will, councillor. Be assured of that.'

*

Necklen poured himself a goblet of wine and sipped it. It was a fine vintage, yet its flavour was lost on the veteran. The stump of his left arm was throbbing, and he felt every inch his fifty-seven years. Normally he avoided mirrors but, fortified by the wine, he sat before the oval mirror set above the dresser and stared gloomily at his reflection. There was not much dark hair left in his almost silver beard, and his leathery skin was criss-crossed with wrinkles. Only the eyes remained alive and alert.

No-one knew exactly how old he was. He had always lied about his age, for few captains would have knowingly hired a mercenary over fifty. I hate being old, he thought. I hate the aches and the pains that come with the winter winds and snow. But most of all he hated the chasm it created between himself and Karis. He could still remember the day four years ago when he discovered – to his utter amazement – that he was in love with her. It was after the victory at the Boriane Pass, when she had wandered away to sit alone by a small waterfall. She was by the waterside, surrounded by daffodils, when he had taken her some food the camp cook had prepared, and was surprised to find her weeping.

'One usually weeps when one has lost a battle,' he said softly, sitting down beside her. Her dark hair had been tightly drawn back into a ponytail. Karis loosed the tie and shook her head. It was in that moment, her hair hanging free, tears in her eyes, that Necklen fell in love for the second time in his life.

Karis wiped her eyes. 'Stupid woman,' she said. 'I thought they would have surrendered. Outnumbered, outflanked, what else could they do? But no, they had to fight to the death. And for what? A little village that will still be there when we have all gone to dust.'

'They were brave men,' he conceded.

'They were fools. We are fools. But then war is a game made for fools.'

'And you play it so well, princess.'

She looked at him sharply. 'I don't think I like that term.'

'I'm sorry,' he had said, reddening. 'I haven't used it in years. It was what I used to call my daughter.' That was a lie; it was the pet name he had called Sofain, his wife.

'Where is she now?' asked Karis.

'Dead. She and my wife were visiting their family in the islands when the boat was caught in a storm. They were washed overboard.'

'I am truly sorry, Necklen. Did you love them very much?'

'It is curious, but I loved them more when they had died. You don't know how valuable love is, until something takes it from you.'

'How old was your daughter?'

285

'Five. Dark-haired like you. She would have been about your age now – young, and full of life. Married, probably, to some farmer.'

'And you would have been a doting grandfather with babies on your knee.' He chuckled at the thought. 'I need to swim,' she said. Rising, she had stripped off her boots, leggings and tunic and dived into the pool below the falls. Necklen had rarely felt as old as he did at that moment.

He was dragged from his reverie by the sound of the door opening. Karis moved across the room and sat down opposite the old warrior. He forced a cheerfulness he did not feel. 'You are looking brighter, princess,' he said. 'What can have changed your mood?'

'One more tactic against the Daroth,' she said. 'The last one.' She told him about the catacombs, and her plans for a rolling retreat to draw the enemy to a desired location.

'But if there are seventeen exits, the Daroth might split their force and not follow our men. Or they might read their minds and realize the trap.'

'Exactly! That is what we must work out. How do we misdirect the Daroth?'

'Well, firstly, is there a need? In the darkness of the catacombs, amidst the chaos of a rolling retreat, the Daroth may not be able to read minds.'

She shook her head. 'We cannot rely on that.' Moving to the table she spread out a map of the catacombs. 'Six of the exits emerge into the Great Park. Only one of these is surrounded by flat land where we could assemble all our ballistae, spreading them in a half circle around the exit. Then, when the Daroth emerge we can cut them to pieces.'

'There is a second problem there, princess: they will not emerge all at once. Let's say twenty scramble out, then charge the ballistae. We shoot, they fall, then fifty more emerge while we are reloading. We will also need a plan that allows the greatest number of Daroth to rise from the darkness – before we shoot.'

'One problem at a time, old one.' They talked on for more than an hour, discussing possible strategies, then Karis called a halt. 'I will sleep on it,' she said. Necklen rose to go, but she lifted her hand. 'Wait for a few moments, my friend,' she said.

'What else is troubling you?' he asked.

She gave a wistful smile. 'Nothing of great importance – not to the city anyway,' she told him. 'You once told me about your wife. Did you love her?'

'Ay, I did. She was a fine woman.'

'How did you know you loved her?'

The question took Necklen by surprise. 'I can't say I know what you mean, princess,' he said. 'How does anyone know? It just happens.' She looked disappointed, but said nothing and Necklen felt he had failed her. 'How do you feel when you are in love?' he asked.

She shrugged. 'I never have been.'

'But you've . . .' he faltered.

'Had a hundred lovers,' she finished for him. 'I know. I've always been careful. Never rutted with a man who touched my soul.'

'In Heaven's name, why?'

Karis half-filled a goblet with wine, then added water. But she did not drink; she merely stared into the wine's crimson depths. Necklen was about to ask her again when she looked up. 'I don't remember how old I was when I first saw my father punch my mother. But I was very small. I saw her thrown across a table, and lying upon the floor with blood seeping from her smashed lips. He kicked her then, and I began screaming. Then he struck me.'

'What has this to do with your falling in love? I don't see the connection.'

'You don't? She married for love. It destroyed her.'

'And you feel it would happen to you? Why should it?' he asked. 'You think all men are like your father?'

'Yes,' she answered, simply. 'They all want control. They see women as possessions, and I will not be possessed.'

'Forin,' he said. 'You are in love with Forin. He is the last person you think of before going to sleep, and the first person you see in your mind's eye when you wake. Yes?' She nodded. 'Ah, princess, you are a fine, intelligent lass, and yet dumb as a jackass. Of course love is dangerous and wild and irresponsible. By Heaven, that's what makes it so wonderful!'

'You think me stupid?' she asked him, her voice soft, barely above a whisper.

'I adore you, princess, but you should not be looking at love through the eyes of the frightened child you once were. Let me go

287

and find him. I'll send him to you.' As Necklen pushed himself to his feet, Karis rose and stepped close to kiss his bearded cheek.

'I love you, old man,' she said. 'I wish you had been my father.'

'I love you too,' he said.

And, with despair in his heart, strode off to find Forin.

*

The sun was high in the sky as Ozhobar and Vint stood on the parapet of the north wall watching the Daroth toil. 'They have hit rock,' said Ozhobar. 'It has slowed them considerably.'

'Maybe they will not be able to pass it,' suggested the swordsman hopefully.

'They will pass it,' said Ozhobar grimly. 'Before long we will be able to hear them below us, like termites.' He switched his gaze to the soldiers on the wall; they were stern of face, and there was little conversation. The celebrations in the city had died away as the news spread of the new Daroth initiative. Already citizens had begun to report sounds underground, which they became convinced were Daroth engineers. It was hard to allay the fears, and fresh columns of refugees had already started to stream towards the south.

The smell of onion soup drifted up to them. 'I cannot stand another day of that,' said Vint. 'Join me for breakfast?'

'I thought you wanted to kill me,' Ozhobar observed.

'I also want to eat,' said Vint coldly. The two men left the ramparts and walked to a nearby tavern, where they breakfasted on eggs, bacon and beef, washed down with cider. 'Where are you from?' Vint asked the Weapon Maker.

'The islands. My father was a blacksmith and an inventor.'

'What brought you to the mainland?'

Ozhobar shrugged. 'I thought I'd travel and see the world. Thought there'd be more scope for my talents.'

'Well, you were right about that.'

'I didn't mean with weapons,' said Ozhobar sadly. 'Prentuis had a sewerage system – not a very good one, mind, but they survived the plague better than any other city. Less filth on the streets. Less disease.'

'The city doesn't exist any more,' said Vint.

'That's not the point I am trying to make. Life could be so

much better for people if we weren't always fighting, using all our resources for weapons and armies. I suppose, however, that life would be exceedingly dull for you if peace ever came?'

'No, I would paint and write,' said Vint, draining the last of his cider.

'You are a painter?'

'Ah, I have surprised you,' said Vint. 'Yes, I paint. Landscapes mostly, but I have tackled portraits. I would offer to paint you, Oz, but I fear I wouldn't have a canvas large enough.'

Ozhobar laughed. 'Vint the painter and Ozhobar the sewer designer. What a pretty pair!'

'Indeed we are,' agreed Vint. 'And now, I fear, it is time for the return of the Swordsman and the Weapon Maker! Shall we tour the catacombs?'

*

Servants were rushing about the house packing valuables into chests and carrying them down to the two wagons drawn up outside. Miriac walked past them into the main room to find Pooris pushing papers into a leather shoulder-bag.

'What is happening?' asked Miriac.

'My dear, it is time to leave. The city is about to fall. I have had most of your clothes packed and loaded in the wagon. We set off for Hlobane within the hour.'

'I thought you had decided to stay,' she said.

'That was then,' he told her. 'Now events have overtaken my plans. The Daroth are tunnelling beneath the city as we speak.'

'And the Duke has allowed you this leave of absence?'

'I am not a bondsman,' he said curtly. 'I can go where I will. Now please look to your personal possessions and make yourself ready.'

Miriac left the little man and moved back into the hall. Stopping a servant, she told him to unload her chests and return them to the master bedroom. Pooris heard her and rushed out. 'Do not be stupid,' he said. 'The Daroth will have no need of courtesans, my dear – save to cook you over a charcoal pit.'

Leaning forward, she kissed the crown of his bald head. 'You go, Pooris,' she said. 'I will stay and look after your house.'

'You don't understand . . .'

289

'I understand well enough. The Daroth are tunnelling beneath us and you believe the city is about to fall. You wish to save yourself – that is entirely natural. Do as you think fit, Pooris. But I will remain.'

'But . . . I need you.'

'No. You want me. There is a difference.' He stood very still, and she could see the confusion on his face. Even more, she could understand the warring emotions within him. Pooris was not a coward but, like all politicians, he was a pragmatist. If the Daroth had won – which he believed they had – then it was only sensible to retreat before them. Now Miriac had presented him with a fresh dilemma. He loved her, and, as a man, wanted to protect her. He could not do this from Hlobane or Loretheli. Realistically, however, he could not do it here in Corduin either; the tiny councillor would be no match for a Daroth. 'I want you to be safe,' she told him. 'You are very dear to me. I think you have made the right decision.' She saw him relax then, as she had known he would.

Without further conversation, she went upstairs to her rooms and began to unpack the chests. She had promised Tarantio to return at dusk, and had been wondering how to break the news to Pooris. Now there was no need.

The councillor came to her an hour later, and stood in the doorway of her bedroom. 'Please come with me,' he said. 'I beg you.'

'No, dear heart.'

'I have great wealth, much of it invested in Loretheli and the islands. You would be like a queen there.'

'Go, Pooris. The Daroth may even now be riding to intercept the convoys.'

Moving forward, he kissed her cheek, then turned and ran from the room.

Miriac heard him on the stairs, then returned her gaze to the long mirror on her dressing table. 'You are a fool,' she told herself. Then she remembered the time with Tarantio, the warmth of his body upon hers.

She had thought of him every day since the curious events two years before, after the duel with Carlyn. The Duke had asked her to entertain his new champion, and she had done so to the best of her considerable abilities. It had been a wondrous night, and she had been surprised by the intensity of his virgin love-making.

Then he had fled. No other word could describe it. The following morning she had tried to dismiss it from her mind, yet she could not. Investigations revealed that Tarantio had spurned the Duke's offer to become champion and instead had enlisted as a mercenary. There was no sense to it. Why would any man turn down the promise of riches and comfort for a life of hardship and premature death?

For some time she continued to ask about him. Then she met the merchant Lunder, whom Tarantio paid to invest his hard-earned silver. Through Lunder she knew where Tarantio was, and what battles he had fought in. It was a tenuous link, but a link nonetheless.

When she had gone to him last night she had hoped to find him less fabulous than in her memories, so that she could finally be rid of the torment of thinking of him. Instead she found the experience enriching, and she still felt an inner glow as she recalled his tender touch.

'I will not lose you again,' she said.

*

In the three days that followed, the Daroth made one half-hearted attack on the eastern gate, but were driven back by the fireballs of two catapults. Meanwhile the endless tunnelling continued. Minute by minute, Daroth engineers could be seen leaving the mouth of the tunnel bearing sacks of rock which were loaded to wagons, then ferried away out of sight. They worked ceaselessly, and always at the same pace. 'They are like machines,' said a soldier to Forin, as he and Karis observed the work. 'Do they never rest or sleep?'

'Apparently not,' replied Forin. 'But they die, boy. And more of them will die when they break through.'

'It is said they don't die,' put in the soldier. 'They go back to eggs or some such, and are born again.'

Forin did not reply. When Karis walked away, he followed her. 'You are pensive today,' he said, as they strolled along the avenue towards the palace.

'I have much to think about.'

'We will survive, Karis. I'm sure of that.'

'It would be nice to be so sure.'

'I don't intend to fall before some whey-faced giant termite – not now I've found you.'

'I hope that you don't!'

'You have a plan yet?'

'If I tell you, then you will not be able to lead the fighting in the catacombs. Do you want me to tell you?'

He paused. 'I would dearly like to say yes to that, but I cannot. Tarantio and Vint have their magical swords. I have my strength. It will be needed in the catacombs. Speaking of Tarantio, I haven't seen him for days. Where is he?'

'I don't know,' replied Karis. 'He has failed to attend two meetings. I want him there tonight.'

'I'll fetch him myself,' promised Forin. She made to walk on, but he gently took her arm. 'When this is over, would you consider marrying me?' he asked her.

'You are certainly an optimist, Redbeard.'

'Always. But especially now. You think I will allow the Daroth to steal my joy?'

Karis looked up into his broad, flat face and met the intensity of his green gaze. 'You are the strongest man I've known. Perhaps you can survive. Ask me again when the Daroth are defeated.'

He moved to kiss her but she stepped back, her eyes cold. 'Not in the open, Forin.'

'Are you ashamed of me?' he asked, bewildered.

'Have you not heard what they call me? "The Ice Queen". Let them keep their illusions. Now is not the time for them to see Karis the woman.'

She swung away from him and strode on. Forin cut off to the left and made his way to the small house Tarantio had rented. He hammered on the door, but at first there was no reply. Four times more he thumped his fist against the wood, then finally the door swung open and Tarantio stood there, bare-chested. 'Sleeping in the middle of the day? You are getting old, man.' Without waiting to be invited, Forin stepped inside, walking through to the main room. His nostrils flared; the smell of strong perfume lingered in the air.

'I am sorry, my friend, I did not know you had company.'

'Well, I have,' said Tarantio. 'What brings you here?'

'Karis wanted to make sure you would attend tonight's meeting.'

'Tell her I will not be there.'

'You must be – that is where we will plan the fight in the catacombs.' Swiftly he told Tarantio of the caverns under the city. 'Ozhobar thinks the Daroth will break through sometime tomorrow.'

'I am no longer willing to fight,' said Tarantio.

'Is this a joke? You think you have a choice?'

'A man always has a choice. I am leaving tomorrow.'

'I don't believe it,' declared Forin, stunned. 'You of all people! How can you consider leaving us to fight alone? You are the best swordsman I ever saw, and you have a magical blade. We need you, man.'

'The sword is by the door. Take it when you go.'

Forin looked at him quizzically. 'What has happened to you, Chio? You are not the man I knew. You are certainly not the man who said he could swallow me whole if someone buttered my head and pinned my ears back. Gods, man, has the heart gone out of you?'

'Yes,' said Tarantio. 'The heart has gone out of me.'

Disgusted, Forin swung away from him and headed for the door. The sword belt was hanging on a hook and the giant lifted it clear.

'I am sorry,' he heard Tarantio call out.

'Rot and die,' replied Forin.

*

Dressed in a loose-fitting white gown, the ties undone, Miriac came out of the bedroom as the front door closed behind Forin. For a moment she said nothing, but stood looking at Tarantio. He smiled at her. 'Would you like some wine?'

'He was your friend,' she said.

'Yes. Would you like some wine?'

'No. I don't understand why you told him that.'

'What is there to understand? I'm not going to fight any more. I want to get you somewhere safe.' He reached for her, but she drew back. 'What is wrong?' he asked her.

'I don't know – but he was right, Chio. Something has gone out of you; I've sensed it for days.'

'Is it that obvious?'

'It is to me. I love you, but you have changed. Have I done this to you? Have I robbed you of your courage?'

293

'My courage has not gone!' he said, but the words came out defensively and he could hear his own fear echoing in his denial. 'It has not gone,' he said. 'He wasn't my courage.'

'He?'

'I don't want to talk about it.'

'Not even to me?'

Tarantio turned away from her and stared around the room. Miriac remained quiet and still, allowing the silence to grow. He moved over to the fire and added coal to the embers, then sat down on the rug and looked into the flames. In a low voice he told her of his life, and the birth of Dace, and how they had lived together ever since. 'I am not insane,' he assured her. 'Dace was as real to me as you are. You asked me why I fled that night. Dace wanted to kill you; he felt my love for you, and saw it as a threat. When you came to the house two nights ago, it was Dace who met you.' He fell silent, and did not look at her.

She moved alongside him and sat down beside the fire. 'I don't understand,' she said gently. 'I have never heard of anything like this. But I do know that the man who met me was not you. And when I kissed him he was holding a dagger.' Taking his face in her hands, she looked into his deep blue eyes. 'And his eyes were grey,' she said, ' and fierce.' Her hands fell away, and she leaned in and kissed his cheek.

'I am not insane,' he repeated, 'but the next morning Dace said goodbye to me – and I can no longer find him. I call, but he is not there.'

'And that frightens you?'

He nodded. 'Dace could fight his way clear of any danger. He feared nothing in combat. But I do. And I do not want to die – not now I have found you again.'

'We are going to die,' she said. 'Perhaps not today or tomorrow – but sometime in the future we will cease to be. It cannot be avoided, no matter how far or how fast we run. I do love you, Chio, but I do not know you very well. So I may be wrong in what I am about to say, but I will say it nonetheless: you will come to hate yourself if you run now. I believe this to be true.'

'You want to stay here? And face the Daroth?'

'No, I want to run too. Yet I will stay. I will stare my fears in the face, as I have always done – not over my shoulder as I flee.'

'I don't know what to do,' he said miserably.

'Look into your heart, Chio. How did it feel to have your friend look at you with contempt? How do you feel about yourself?'

'Lessened,' he said simply.

'Then go to the meeting. Take back your sword. No-one can take away your pride; you have to willingly surrender it. Once you do so, you will never be the same man again.'

'I don't know if I'll be much use to them without Dace.'

'Perhaps you are Dace. Perhaps he is merely another manifestation of you. Even if he is not, you are still a man of courage. I know this, for I could never love a coward.'

He smiled then, and she saw his expression lighten. 'You are a wonder,' he said.

'Indeed I am,' she told him. 'And if Dace returns, tell him I love him too.'

*

The Meeting Hall was filled with officers and men. The Duke, dressed in a tunic and leggings of black silk, sat at the head of the table, with Karis to his right. The white wall behind him had been stripped of paintings, and Ozhobar had sketched out a map of the catacombs on the bare plaster.

The Duke rose. 'This will be the final battle,' he told his grim-faced audience. 'Below the ground, underneath the city, you will face a terrible enemy. Karis will explain the strategy to you. It will not be easy to carry out the orders – which is why every man here has been hand-picked. You are the most courageous fighters we have, and I am proud to stand in this room with you.'

With that he sat down, and Karis pushed back her chair and moved to the wall. Using a slender rapier, she pointed to the map. 'This area is where we expect the Daroth to break through. Already we can hear them. Lanterns have been placed around the catacombs, so that you will be able to see your targets. The object is to hit the enemy hard, then fall back to our second line of defence, which will be here,' she said, pointing to an area where the tunnels branched and narrowed.

'Excuse me, General,' said an older officer, a tall man sporting a curling moustache but no beard, 'but I know the catacombs. Wouldn't it be wiser to fortify the main tunnel? You have us retreating along a branch section.'

295

'That is a good point,' she admitted, 'but the main tunnel branches further back, then splits into a honeycomb of passages. We could lose a great many men there.' He made to speak again, but Karis raised her hand. 'Do not question me further, sir; you are overlooking the menace of the Daroth talent for reading minds. I don't know how strongly they will be able to penetrate our plans once the killing begins. But I do not want us – here and now – to examine all the possibilities for defence or counter-attacks. What is vital is that you all listen, and obey your orders to the best of your abilities. The fate of the city will depend on you.'

In the silence that followed she mapped out the line of the rolling retreat, the numbers of crossbow-men and the positions they should occupy. 'As each group retreats they should keep close to the walls, so that the next line of bowmen can rake the enemy. When you pass through the lines, take up positions to the rear and prepare to cover your comrades as they in turn retreat.' Slowly and methodically she covered the plan again, then asked questions of the officers until she was sure they knew what was required.

The man with the curling moustache spoke again. 'And what if the line breaks, General? What do we do?'

'You get out as best you can,' Karis told him. Seeing that, he was about to speak again, she raised her hand to halt him. 'No more questions,' she said. 'Go and gather your men, give out your orders, then assemble at the park entrance to the catacombs. Vint and Forin will be there waiting for you.'

'As will I,' said Tarantio, from the rear of the room. Forin swung in his seat and gave a broad grin. As the officers filed out Tarantio moved over to Forin. 'I think you have something that belongs to me,' he said.

'Indeed I do, man. It is good to see you.' Unbuckling his sword belt he passed the weapon to Tarantio.

'What changed your mind?' asked Karis.

'The love of a good woman,' Tarantio answered.

'You and Vint will cover the withdrawals. You will rove freely, making use of the available cover – and there is a great deal of that. The catacombs are a maze of stalactites and stalagmites.'

'I never could remember the difference between the two,' muttered Forin.

296

'Neither could I,' said the Duke. 'Think of the "c" and the "g" as standing for ceiling and ground. Stalactites grow from the ceiling downwards, stalagmites from the ground up.'

'Thank you, my lord,' said Forin. The Duke gave a short bow.

'When I say free roving,' said Karis, 'I mean exactly that. But do not allow yourself to be drawn away from the retreating lines. There are a number of blind tunnels that lead nowhere, and a great many more that have hidden pits, some of which are very deep. The main areas we are defending have been marked by white paint. Keep to those.'

Vint spoke up. 'I know this is a difficult area, Karis, but all the men who were here heard you talk about a rolling retreat. Retreats do not win battles. They *know* you will have a secondary plan of action; we all know it. Therefore so will the Daroth. It has to involve the exits; you will be planning to ambush them as they come out. Therefore they will probably not follow us.'

'Forgive me, General,' said the Duke, 'but I was thinking the same thing. Once the battle begins, the Daroth can take any number of exits.'

'That is true,' said Karis, 'but firstly the Daroth may not yet know about the catacombs. Secondly, even if they do, they will not be familiar with the layout.'

'Every man here will have seen the map,' said Forin.

'Yes,' agreed Karis, 'but we cannot cover all the eventualities. As you can see, if the Daroth are drawn into the first series of tunnels the number of exits available to them drops to eight. The further we pull them, the fewer their options.'

'At the risk of labouring the point,' said Vint, 'everything you are telling us can be learned by the enemy.'

'That is why I am not telling you everything. Trust me, Vint. We will surprise them. You see, they also will face a difficult dilemma. They know I have misdirected them once before, by planting false information in the mind of one of our scouts. Therefore, in the chaos of battle within the tunnels, they will not be able to trust completely in the thoughts of the men facing them. That will lead to confusion, believe me.'

'I believe you, Karis,' said Vint. 'I just don't want to be used like that poor scout.'

'You are being used in exactly that way,' she told him coldly.

297

The smell of lantern oil hung heavily in the still air of the catacombs, and the warriors crouched in nervous silence, listening to the steady thudding sound of Daroth hammers and pick-axes coming ever closer. Forin wiped sweat from his face and glanced at Vint, who was standing beside the column of a towering stalagmite. The swordsman's face seemed strained and tense in the yellow, flickering light of the lanterns. Some way to his left Tarantio was sitting on a jut of rock, head down and arms on his knees. Forin took a deep, calming breath and walked back among the kneeling crossbow-men. No-one spoke, and the sheen of fear-sweat was bright on every face.

For the second time in an hour Forin strode forward, crossing the cavern floor all the way to the far wall. Once there, heart pounding, he placed his hand on the rock. This time he could feel the vibration of the Daroth hammers tingling against his palm.

Tarantio looked up as the giant returned, lantern light gleaming on the polished iron breastplate. 'Soon,' whispered Forin.

Where are you, Dace?

There was no response. Tarantio was trembling and terror was growing within him. A splintering thud, louder than before, caused him to jerk as if stung. Rising to his feet, he found his legs unsteady and was filled with an urge to run from this dark, shadow-haunted place. Even as the thought came to him, a young crossbow-man to the rear dropped his weapon and scrambled back along the paint-marked tunnel. Other men stirred and Forin moved amongst them, patting a shoulder here, pausing to whisper encouragement there, his colossal presence calming them. He gave the signal to cock the weapons.

Tarantio's mouth was dry, and he thought of Miriac waiting for him back at the house, the bright sunshine streaming through the open windows. If the Daroth were to break through here . . . The thought was too awful to entertain.

The edge of a pick-axe smashed through the black rock. The crossbow-men set up their tripods, resting their heavy weapons upon them, aiming at the wall. Vint and Tarantio moved back away from the killing area. Tarantio drew his sword, which shimmered in the lantern light.

A large section of rock fell away – then another, crashing to the cavern floor. A huge Daroth engineer stepped into sight. Three crossbow bolts smashed through his skull and he pitched to the ground. Frenzied activity began in the tunnel, picks and hammers crashing at the last barriers. The hole widened and the Daroth swarmed through, their faces ghostly white, their massive forms throwing giant shadows on the walls.

Crossbow bolts tore into them, and they charged. Tarantio darted from behind a stalagmite and sent a slashing cut through the ribs of the first Daroth warrior. Ducking under a thrusting sword-blade, he speared his own weapon through the belly of a second. On the other side of the cavern Vint lanced his sword into the chest of a Daroth warrior, then spun on his heel to send a reverse cut across the throat of a second. Behind them the crossbow-men were retreating to the second line of defence.

Vint leapt back, then turned on his heel and ran for cover, keeping close to the right-hand wall. A hurled spear smashed into a stalagmite, sending shards of stone into his face and neck. Ahead was a line of sandbags, with crossbow-men kneeling behind them. As Vint leapt over them, then spun to face the enemy, he saw Tarantio running along the far side of the cavern, scrambling to safety.

The mass of Daroth surged forward. The crossbows sang, and fifty bolts slammed into the leading warriors. The Corduin soldiers struggled in vain to reload – a few succeeded – but the Daroth were upon them, serrated swords smashing through armour, flesh and bone. Vint leaped forward, cutting and killing. 'Back!' he shouted. The defenceless crossbow-men needed no instructions; they fled along the tunnel. Vint followed them, Tarantio to his right.

There was no sound of pursuit. Spinning, the two men looked back. The Daroth were standing by the sandbag wall, then they filed away to the right. Vint swore.

Karis's plan was not working.

*

Alone in the dark Ozhobar listened to the distant sounds of battle, the screams of wounded men, the clash of steel, the hissing song of crossbow strings. Appalling sounds, he thought.

Evil.

Ozhobar was not a religious man. He had prayed only once in

his life. It had not been answered, and he had buried the ones he loved, the plague continuing to sweep through the islands causing misery and desolation to those left behind. But one did not need to be religious to understand the nature of evil. The plague had an evil effect, but was merely a perversion of nature; it was not sentient. The Daroth, on the other hand, Ozhobar believed to be evil incarnate. They knew what they were doing, the pain they caused and the despair they created. Worse, they had fostered hatred in their enemies that would last for generations. And hatred was the mother of all evil.

'You will not make me hate you,' thought Ozhobar. 'But I will kill you!'

The sounds of fighting died away. Ozhobar lifted the glass from his lantern, exposing the naked flame, then rose and glanced down the sloping tunnel. He could see no movement, so he closed his eyes and listened. At first there was nothing, then he heard the sound of boots upon stone. The mouth of the tunnel was over 100 feet from where he now stood. Lifting the lantern, he moved behind the huge pottery ball and lit the oil-soaked rags wedged into the holes.

Ahead he could see flickering shadows as the Daroth moved up the slope.

Ozhobar sat down with his back to the wall, placed his boots against the burning ball and thrust hard. It began to roll, slowly at first on the gentle slope; then it gathered pace. The Daroth came into sight. Ozhobar took up his crossbow and aimed it, sending an iron bolt into the ball, shattering a section of the pottery. Blazing oil spilled out, and flames erupted through the Daroth ranks.

Not waiting to see the result Ozhobar scrambled back, replaced the glass on the lantern and then climbed further up the slope, traversing a ledge that brought him out high above the cavern floor. He could clearly see the stream of burning oil flowing out of the tunnel. A flash of bright light came from the far side, and he saw Daroth warriors fleeing from the mouth of a second tunnel. Two of them were engulfed in flames, their comrades staying well back.

Ozhobar's assistant, Brek, came into sight, emerging from a cleft in the tunnel. The Daroth saw him and surged forward. Brek ran towards a tunnel mouth, but a jagged spear smashed through his back and he fell.

High on the ledge, Ozhobar felt the sting of grief. Brek had been a good man, solid and trustworthy. With a sigh, Ozhobar watched the Daroth milling in the centre of the cavern. Then they broke into a run and surged forward.

Towards the waiting crossbow-men.

*

Three volleys of bolts plunged into the advancing Daroth, but there was no slowing them now. Tarantio killed two, then dashed to his left as a spear smashed into the rock by his head. Three huge warriors ran at him. Cut off from the main body of defenders, he ran into a narrow tunnel, then turned swiftly and drove his blade through the white skull of the first pursuer. A spear slammed into his left shoulder, the serrated blade tearing up through his collar-bone. Blood sprayed from the wound. Tarantio swept his sword across the Daroth's belly, then backhanded a cut that half-severed his head.

The pain from his wound was intense, blood was flowing freely inside his shirt and pooling above his belt. Movement was agony, but he scrambled further back into the tunnel, searching for an exit. Another spear flashed past him.

Spinning once more, he swayed away from a wild, slashing cut. His riposte passed through the Daroth's forearm, to send the limb spinning through the air. Still the Daroth rushed him, his great fist clubbing into Tarantio's chest and hurling him from his feet. Tarantio rolled as the creature leapt for him feet-first. Pushing himself upright, the swordsman plunged his weapon into the Daroth's chest. 'Now die, you whoreson!' he hissed.

As the sound of pounding boots came from the tunnel mouth, Tarantio swore and stumbled further back into the darkness. There were no lanterns here, and only the shimmering glow from his sword offered any light. He felt a touch of cool air brush his cheek. It came from above, but his left arm was useless and there was no way he could climb to the opening. The tunnel itself petered out into a black wall of rock. Two Daroth spear-men came into sight. The first lunged at Tarantio, whose sword swept across his body – slicing through the shaft – then reversed and tore open the Daroth's throat. The second spear slammed through his side and deep into the rock behind. Cutting through the shaft he flung the blade like a knife. It slammed point first into the Daroth's ridged brow, sinking in all the way up to the hilt. Tarantio tried to move forward to

301

retrieve the blade, then cried out in agony, for he was pinned to the wall.

He could hear the stealthy footfalls of more Daroth approaching. His heart sank and he ceased to struggle. If that was death, so be it, he thought.

'A pox on you, brother! I'm not ready to die yet!'

Dace hurled himself forward, his wounded body sliding clear of the broken spear-shaft. He hit the ground hard, the impact jarring his broken collar-bone. Reaching out, he grasped the hilt of his sword and then struggled to his feet.

Four Daroth swordsmen rounded the bend in the tunnel and, with a bloodcurdling scream, Dace charged them – his sword slicing through the chest of the first, the skull of the second and the ribs of the third. The fourth stumbled; Dace leapt upon him, using his sword like a dagger which he drove down through the neck and into the lungs.

Dace fell with him, then staggered upright. 'Where are you, you bastards?' he screamed. 'I'll kill you all!'

'Dace, for the sake of Heaven, let's find a way out of here!' cried Tarantio.

But Dace ignored him. He took three running steps, then pitched sideways into the wall and half-fell. Blood-drenched and swaying, he made it back to the main tunnel and saw the bodies of a score of Daroth and as many Corduin men. Picking his way through them he heard the sounds of battle up ahead.

'I'm coming for you!' shouted Dace, his voice echoing through the tunnels. He stumbled on, then fell to his knees.

'Stop, Dace,' Tarantio urged him. *'Stop now. We are dying.'*

Dace sat with his back to the wall and gazed down at his blood-drenched clothes. There was no feeling in his right leg now, and his vision was swimming. 'I am not going to die in the dark,' he said.

With a great effort he rolled to his knees, then got his good leg under him, forcing himself upright. As two Daroth warriors came into sight, Dace blinked sweat from his eyes. 'Come on!' he called. 'Come and die, you ugly whoresons!'

They rushed forward, but the first suddenly swayed to his left with a crossbow bolt through his skull. The second lunged at Dace. The swordsman's blade flashed up with impossible speed, blocking the thrust. Off-balance, the Daroth fell forward and Dace's blade swept through his thick throat. 'Where are the rest of you?' shouted Dace. Then he fell unconscious into the arms of Ozhobar.

*

Dressed in black leather leggings and a silver satin tunic shirt, the Duke stood silently in the park. Though surrounded by men he was alone, as he always had been. His eyes scanned the hillsides, remembering far-off days when he had played here with his brother. Bright and adventurous, Jorain had been the only person to reach the shy, introverted child the Duke had once been. When he had died he had taken a part of Albreck with him. A loveless marriage, and twenty years of ruling a people he neither liked nor understood, had been the life of Albreck following the death of Jorain. You would have been so much better than I, thought Albreck. The people loved you.

Albreck switched his gaze to the catacomb entrance. Reinforced by two elaborate stone pillars and a white lintel stone, there were steps within that led down to the crystal cavern. Jorain had told him it was an entrance to Hell, and the six-year-old Albreck had been afraid to enter.

Now the childish game had become a reality. It *was* an entrance to Hell.

And I have come here to die, thought Albreck. The thought made him smile, he didn't know why. Are you waiting for me, Jorain? he wondered. The Duke had brought no sword or dagger and he stood now, arms folded, waiting patiently for whatever would follow. He glanced at Karis. The warrior woman was now wearing a dress of white silk she had borrowed from the wardrobe of the Duke's wife; around her slim waist was a blue sash. She looked so incongruous now, surrounded by warriors, like a virgin bride waiting for her groom.

'Why do you need the dress?' he had asked her.

'Don't ask, my lord,' she said.

Under torchlight, Karis was organizing the placements of the five ballistae, forming a wide semi-circle some hundred paces from the entrance to the catacombs. Four hundred crossbow-men, in three ranks, were positioned between the weapons: the front line kneeling, the second standing, the third, higher still, positioned on the backs of a circle of wagons.

The Duke saw the veteran warrior Necklen approach Karis and take her by the arm. He could not hear their conversation, but he could see anxiety in the warrior's face.

*

'There is no need for you to die,' said Necklen, moving alongside Karis. 'I could do it!'

'I am not planning to die,' she told him, 'but it is a risk I cannot avoid. You said it yourself – how can we get them to mass in the centre of the killing circle? This is the only way I could think of.'

'All right. But why you? Why not me?'

'You have no rank, old man. They would believe in an instant that it was a ploy.'

'And it isn't?'

'No, it is not. Now go to your position. And do as I bid.'

'I couldn't kill you, Karis. Not if my life depended on it.'

She put her slender hands on his shoulders. 'Thousands of lives may depend upon it. And if it comes to it, promise me you will obey my order. Promise me, Necklen, in the name of friendship.'

'Let someone else do it. I'll stand beside you.'

'No! If you cannot do your duty, then get you gone and I'll find a man who can.' The sharpness in her tone stung him, and he swung away from her. She called to him instantly, her tone contrite. 'I love you, old man. Don't let me down.' He couldn't speak, but he nodded and walked back to his ballista, checking the load and the release pin. Then he took up his hammer.

The Duke approached Necklen. 'What is she doing?' he asked.

'Getting ready to die,' whispered the old man.

'What do you mean?'

'She is going to talk to them, forcing them to mill around her. She'll ask for peace. If they say no – which they will – she will raise her hand. When she drops it, the killing begins.'

The Duke said nothing, staring at the woman in the white dress standing in the moonlight. She looked so frail now, ghostlike and serene. He shivered.

A soldier at the catacomb entrance called out: 'I can hear them. I can hear the screams.'

Karis strode forward. 'Get back to your position,' she told the soldier. Gratefully the young man ran back to the wagons, climbing

304

to the back of one and retrieving his crossbow. Karis stood some thirty feet from the white stone of the entrance and waited, longing to see Forin emerge unscathed. A few crossbow-men made it into the torchlight, and stood blinking; their friends called to them and they sprinted for cover. Then Vint appeared, blood on his face and arms. He ran to Karis, but she ordered him back. 'The Daroth are right behind. You must take cover,' he said.

'Get back. Now!'

He hesitated, then ran to where Necklen stood, his face pale, his eyes haunted.

Forin came last, his armour once more dented and split, a deep gash upon his brow masking his face with blood. He stumbled towards Karis and grabbed her arm, dragging her back. Her hand lashed across his face, the sound like a whiplash. 'Let go of me, you stupid ox!' His hand fell away and he stood staring at her. 'Get back now!'

'They are upon us.' He reached for her again.

Spinning on her heel she pointed to a crossbow-man. 'You! Aim at this man's heart, and if he isn't moving when I drop my arm – kill him!' She raised her hand. 'Now move, goat-brain!' she thundered. Furious, Forin stalked back towards the wagons.

Karis let out her breath. She wanted to call out to Forin, to explain. But there was no time. The first of the Daroth moved out into the torchlight, which glistened on his ghost-white face and beaked mouth. 'No one shoot!' yelled Karis. 'Where is your leader, Daroth?' she asked. Heat began to grow inside her head.

'It is time to end this war. It is time to end this war! It is time to end this war!' She repeated the thought over and over, like a prayer. 'I wish to speak to your leader,' she said, aloud. More and more Daroth were moving out of the entrance now, spreading out, staring at the ballistae and the crossbow-men, their jet-black eyes unreadable. A warrior taller than the others stepped through the mass. 'I am the Daroth Duke,' he said. 'I remember you, woman. Say what you have to say, and then I shall kill you.'

'And what purpose will that serve?' she asked him. 'In the few months since we have learned of your threat, we have already designed weapons that can destroy you in great numbers. We are an inventive people, and we outnumber you vastly. Look around

305

you now. How many more of your people must die in this insane manner?'

'We do not die, woman. You cannot kill us. We are Daroth. We are immortal. And I tire of this conversation. You have gained time, and you will now destroy more of our bodies. Then we will sack the city and kill everyone in it. So give your order – and let it begin.'

'That is not what I wish, my lord,' she told him.

'Your wishes are of no consequence.' His sword came up and Karis raised her arm.

*

Duvodas had not eaten or slept for five days, yet there was no sensation of hunger or weariness. Nor did he feel the biting wind from the north, nor the heat of the midday sun as he crossed the mountains and descended into the verdant valleys below.

There was no sensation for him, and his mind was empty of all emotion – save one: the burning need to wreak revenge upon the Daroth. His clothes were filthy and mud-spattered, his blond hair greasy and lank as he moved through the darkness towards the domed city. No Daroth riders were in sight as he walked in the moonlight, and he made no attempt to move stealthily.

For two days now he had been aware that the land below his feet was devoid of magic. It did not matter, for sorcery, dark and terrible, coursed through his veins – feeding him, driving him on. The power within did not lessen; instead it seemed to grow with every step he took towards the city.

There were no walls. The Daroth, in their arrogance, did not believe that an enemy would come this close. Had there been walls, Duvodas would have broken them. Had there been gates, he would have torn them asunder. He paused for the first time in five days and stood, staring at the moonlit city. An owl swooped above him, and a small fox scuttled away into the undergrowth to his right.

Sitting down on the ground, he let fall the two shoulder-bags he carried. The canvas sack slid several feet down the gentle slope and the Eldarin Pearl rolled clear, moonlight shimmering on its surface. Duvodas blinked, and a tiny needle of regret pricked his soul. He remembered Ranaloth warning him of the perils of love, and he knew now what the old Eldarin had meant. Like light and shadow, love and hate were inseparable. One could not exist without the other. Rising he gathered the sack and reached for the Pearl. But as his hand touched the milky surface, he recoiled in pain and stared at his palm. Blisters had formed there, the skin burnt by the contact. Carefully covering the orb with the sack, he eased it back into place.

'What have you become that you cannot touch it?' he asked himself.

The answer was all too obvious. Duvodas returned his stare to the city, and thought again of his plan. It seemed awesome now in its evil. Shira's beautiful face swam before his eyes, and he saw her once more lifted on the Daroth spear, the life torn from her. His resolution hardened.

'You who bring death and despair to the world deserve no mercy,' he told the distant city. 'You who live for destruction and pain deserve no life.'

By what right do you judge them?

The thought sprang unbidden, as if whispered on the wind.

'By the right of power, and the needs of vengeance,' he answered.

Does that not make you as evil as the Daroth?

'Indeed it does.'

Looping his bags over his shoulder, he walked on. There were no sentries, and he passed the first buildings without incident.

Then a Daroth moved into sight, carrying two buckets on a yoke across his shoulders. His black eyes fastened on the human. Duvodas pointed a finger and the Daroth died, his body crumbling to the ground with steam erupting from his eyes, ears and mouth. Duvodas did not even see him fall. On he walked through the night-shrouded city, searching for signs of his intended destination. Three times more he slew unsuspecting Daroth who stumbled across him. He had expected more of them to be on the streets, but the night was cold and the vast majority of the city-dwellers remained snug in their domed homes.

Duvodas saw twin towers in the distance, smoke drifting from them, and steadily he made his way towards them. Closer now, and he could feel the pulsing of life from the caverns deep in the ground. Ahead was a huge dome, where two sentries stood before the doors. Levelling their spears, they approached him.

He felt their feeble attempts to read his thoughts. This he allowed. 'I have come to destroy you and all your people.'

307

'Impossible, human. We are immortal!'

'You are doomed!' They rushed him then, but twin blasts of fire speared from his fingers, piercing their bodies and burning huge holes in the wall of the building behind them. Duvodas walked to the great doors and pushed them open. Within was a circular hall, and a vast empty table. Pulling shut the door he searched for a stairwell, finding it at the rear of the chamber. Behind him he could hear the city-dwellers running from their homes, a huge mob racing to stop him.

He did not increase his speed. Opening his thoughts, he reached out, feeling the panic in the minds of the Daroth. 'I am vengeance,' he told them. 'I am death.' The steps were shallow, and wound down deep below the city; there were no lanterns here, and the darkness was total. But Duvodas raised his hand, and his palm began to glow with a fierce white light. Down and down he moved, descending to a wide corridor and a second stairwell. The heat here was intense. Pausing, he knelt and touched the floor. The stone was warm, and he could feel hot air blowing against his skin. His glowing hand illuminated an air vent close to the wall.

Ahead was a wide entrance in the rock, blocked by a huge steel portcullis. Duvodas reached out and touched it and it began to glow – faintly red at first, then brighter and brighter. The centre sagged and melted away, smoke and steam hissing up from the floor as rivulets of molten metal swirled around his feet. He was about to enter the cavern beyond when he heard the sounds of booted feet upon the stairs behind him. Spinning, he threw out his hand. The first two Daroth warriors ran into sight; both burst into flames.

The pulsing of new life was almost overpowering now as Duvodas strode into the massive chamber. More than 600 paces long, and at least 200 wide, it was filled with thousands of yellow and black pods – huge cocoons, many of them throbbing and writhing.

The Daroth were indeed immortal. Twice in every generation they were reborn through these pods. And that, as Sirano had known, was their greatest weakness. That is why they feared coexistence – for should an enemy ever reach where he had reached, their immortality would be lost. A human had but one life to lose, and that was hard enough. But to lose eternity . . . ? The fear was colossal.

He could feel it now in the panic of the Daroth as they surged down the stairwell behind him.

Several of the pods burst open and small, naked Daroth wriggled free. He felt the pulsing of their thoughts; two were the sentries he had despatched earlier. '*Tell me again of your immortality*,' he pulsed at them.

Drawing in a deep breath, Duvodas spread out his arms. The temperature around him plummeted, ice forming intricate patterns on the walls – spreading, flowing, bright and white against the black rock. The heat from the vents caused sleet to swirl, settling on the pods and frosting them with death.

The ice cold power of Duvo's hatred swelled out, and the nearest pods shrivelled and cracked. The three Daroth young who had emerged began to scream and writhe upon the ice-covered floor.

Duvodas began to walk the length of the immense cavern, radiating the bleakness of a savage winter with every step. Yellow-black pods cracked and burst all around him, disgorging their infant contents. The cavern echoed to their high-pitched, dying screams.

Hundreds of full-grown Daroth warriors ran into the chamber behind him. One charged at Duvodas but, as he neared, ice forming all around him, he began to slow. Desperate to save the pods, the warrior pushed on until his blood froze and he fell dead to the floor. Others hurled spears, but upon striking the walking man they shattered as if made of glass.

Within the chamber and throughout the city, thousands of Daroth adults began to scream and die, their bodies shrivelling as the symbiotic link between them and their pods was severed.

And Duvodas walked on.

A glistening column of white light opened out before him, and he saw the golden figure of the Oltor Prime, his hand outstretched.

*

The Daroth Duke dropped his sword and a strange high-pitched scream was torn from his throat. Karis stood stunned as the huge warrior suddenly crumpled. All around her Daroth warriors were dying, their inhuman wailing filling the air. Others merely stood, swords and spears dropping from their hands as they knelt beside the shrivelling corpses.

Forgotten, Karis moved back to the ballistae. 'Do we shoot now?' asked Necklen.

'No,' said Karis. 'We wait.'

The old man cast her a quizzical look. 'We can finish them, Karis.'

'I'm sick of killing,' she told him. 'Sickened to the depths of my soul. If they pick up their swords we will attack them, but something is happening here and we may yet end the slaughter.'

The bodies began to putrefy at an alarming rate, and the stench was overpowering. Duke Albreck moved through to stand beside Karis. 'Did you do this?' he asked.

She shook her head. 'They talk of immortality – but I think they have just experienced genuine death. I don't know how.'

The kneeling Daroth suddenly rose. Not one of them reached for a weapon, but one of the ballistae engineers panicked and struck his release bolt. Iron shot tore into the enemy ranks, smashing a score of warriors from their feet. Thinking an order had been given, three of the other ballistae were loosed, and the crossbow-men added to the carnage.

The Daroth did nothing. They merely stood and they died. Horrified, Karis shouted for the killing to stop, but blood-lust and hatred were high now and the crossbow-men continued to shoot. She saw the ballistae arms being drawn back once more.

Running out across the killing ground with her arms held high, Karis continued to shout: 'It is over! Stop shooting!'

Black bolts slashed the air around her, and Necklen scrambled from behind the ballistae, running towards her. Forin too dashed across the open ground, trying to reach her. Panic welled in him. 'Karis!' he yelled. 'Get down!' He even saw the bolt flying towards her. For a moment only he thought he could hurl his body across its deadly line, but it flashed by him to plunge into her back.

Karis staggered, but did not fall at first. Slowly she sank to her knees, blood soaking through the white dress. The crossbow-man dropped his weapon and put his face in his hands. Only then did the killing stop, as the Corduin army gazed in stunned disbelief at the kneeling figure of the dying Ice Queen.

Forin reached her side, dropping to his knees where she lay only yards from the surviving Daroth. He put his arms around her, holding her close. 'Sweet Heaven, don't die on me, Karis! Don't die!'

The Duke, Vint, and Necklen joined them. Karis felt no pain as her head sagged against Forin's shoulder. He kissed her brow. 'Where is the surgeon?' he shouted.

'Calm yourself,' she whispered. There was no tension in her now, no fear. The killing was over, and she felt strangely at peace. Looking up, she saw that fewer than fifty Daroth were still standing. 'Who is the leader now?' she asked, directing her question at the nearest warrior.

The Daroth's white face turned towards her. 'You will now destroy us,' he said. 'The Daroth will be no more.'

'We do not . . . want to destroy you,' Karis told him. Gentle heat grew inside her head, and she sensed that all the Daroth were now mind-linked to her. 'What we desire . . . is an end to war.'

'There can be no end,' said the Daroth. It seemed to Karis that a wealth of sorrow was hidden in those words and then, as if a door had been opened, she was allowed to share the emotions of the Daroth, their anguish at the death of their kindred and their fears for the future.

She could scarcely feel Forin's arms around her now, and she was almost overcome by a need to let go, to fly free. Struggling to hold on she whispered to the Daroth: 'Come closer.' Clumsily the Daroth knelt before her. 'Take my hand,' she said, and his thick fingers reached out to curl around Karis's slender palm. 'There can be no . . . end without . . . a beginning. You understand?'

'We have great hatred for you,' said the Daroth, 'and we cannot coexist. For one to prosper, the other must die.'

Karis said nothing, and the silence grew. 'Oh, no,' said Forin. 'Oh, no!' He hugged the dead woman close to him, cradling her head. Tears streamed to his cheeks as he rocked her to and fro.

'We cannot say whether this be true,' said the Daroth, still holding to the limp hand. 'We have no experience of it. But we shall do as you say.'

'Who are you talking to?' asked the Duke.

'The woman. She speaks still. You cannot hear her?'

The Duke shook his head. Releasing Karis's hand, the Daroth stood. 'Your wizard with the face of blood has destroyed our Life Chamber. Half of all our people are dead now, never to come again. Karis says we should return to our city. We will do so.'

'To prepare for war – or peace?' the Duke asked.

'We cannot say . . . not at this time.' The Daroth gazed down at the dead warrior woman. 'There is much to consider. You are not immortal – and yet Karis gave her one life to save ours. We do not understand it. It was foolish, and yet . . . it speaks to us without words.'

'Is she with you still?' asked the Duke. Forin glanced up.

'No. But her words remain.'

The Daroth swung away and walked to the catacomb entrance. One by one the surviving warriors followed, vanishing down into the dark.

*

Tarantio remained unconscious for eight days, and missed the state funeral the Duke gave for Karis, the Ice Queen. All of the citizens of Corduin lined the route, and Karis's body was borne in the Duke's carriage, drawn by six white horses. Karis's war-horse, Warain – led by Forin – walked behind, followed by the Duke and the army she had led. Spring flowers of yellow, red and blue were cast into the street ahead of the procession, and the carriage rolled slowly on over a carpet of blooms.

Vint did not attend. He sat in his apartments at the palace and watched the procession from his balcony. Then he got drunk, and let his grief flow where none could see it.

Karis was laid to rest in a tomb built on a high hill, facing north. A bronze plaque, cast by Ozhobar, was set into the mortar. It said simply:

Karis – the Ice Queen

The Duke made a speech at the tomb. It was simple, dignified and, to Forin, deeply moving. Then the crowds were allowed to file through, past the open coffin, to pay their respects. It remained open for two days, then was sealed. In the months to come a statue would be raised upon it of a warrior woman, her sword sheathed, her hand extended towards the north.

Tarantio opened his eyes on the morning of the ninth day to see Miriac sleeping in a chair beside the bed. His mouth was dry and his body ached; he tried to move, and groaned. Miriac awoke immediately and leaned over him. 'They told me you would die,' she said. 'I knew they were wrong.'

'Too much to live for,' he whispered.

'*That's true*,' said Dace.

Tarantio felt a surge of emotion that brought a lump to his throat.
'*Thank you for coming back, brother!*'

'*Don't go maudlin on me, Chio. Where else could I go?*'

Tarantio closed his eyes.

'*What about the child in the mine?*'

'*He can wait for a while longer. One day, maybe, we'll find him together.*'

Tarantio felt the warm touch of Miriac's hand on his own. '*Don't go back to sleep,*' said Dace. '*Tell her we love her, you fool!*'

*

Forin stood alone before the newly sealed doors, remembering what had been and mourning what could have been.

'I can't stay in Corduin, Karis,' he said. 'There is nothing for me here without you.'

He strode away in the gathering dusk, only pausing at the foot of the hill to look back. Seeing that a dark shape had moved out of the trees and hunkered down by the door, Forin retraced his steps. Stealer looked up as he approached, bared his teeth and growled.

'I don't much like you, either,' said Forin, reaching out his hand. For a moment it seemed that the hound would snap at him, then Stealer sniffed his fingers, and he ran his hand over the broad, ugly head. 'How do you feel about travelling south?' he asked. 'We'll see the ocean and live like lords.' Rising, he took several paces down the hill. 'You coming or not, you ugly son of a bitch?'

The hound cast a lingering look at the tomb, then rose and padded after him.

EPILOGUE

THE OLTOR PRIME BROUGHT DUVO TO THE CENTRE OF THE DESERT which had once housed the city of Eldarisa. There were no buildings now, sculpted in light, merely a great emptiness and an ocean of barren rock.

'Why did you come for me?' asked Duvo. 'I would have killed them all.'

'That would be reason enough, Duvodas.'

'They deserve to die.'

The golden figure stepped back from Duvo and the human refused to meet his eyes. 'I have brought you here so that you might learn a terrible truth. I wish it were not so.'

'What truth? I have no need of truth! There is a war being waged, Oltor, and I am a part of it.'

'There is no war, Duvodas. It is over.'

The young man surged to his feet, his clenched fist raised. 'Then I did it! I ruined them!'

'I cannot say that your actions did not affect the outcome,' said the Oltor. 'For they did. But what made the difference was not,

314

ultimately, your slaying of the Daroth, but the death of a single human. Though that is a riddle you are no longer equipped to fathom. I wish you well, human.'

The Oltor Prime's hands swept down and a curtain of bright sunlight opened on to the darkness. Without another word he stepped through, and then Duvodas was alone. He felt suddenly weary, and he slept until the dawn. Then, with renewed energy, he climbed the tallest peak and – careful not to touch the surface of the orb – removed the Pearl from its sack and wedged it deep into the rocks.

It took most of a day to climb down to the lowlands, but Duvodas felt a longing to see the return of Eldarisa, and to be with the Eldarin again. Pushing on without rest, he reached the Twins by late evening and carefully climbed to the ledge where he had stood once before with the Oltor Prime. Taking his harp in his hands, Duvodas prepared for the Creation Hymn. It did not concern him that there was no land magic here, for never before had he experienced such power as had flowed in his body since the Daroth slew Shira.

His fingers lightly stroked the strings, and a jangle of discordant notes jarred the night air. At first he was untroubled and tried to re-tune the instrument; then his fingers touched the strings again. The noise that came was a screeching travesty of music. With increasing panic he sought the notes of the Hymn, but there was nothing there. No music at all moved within him.

All night he struggled, but with the coming of the dawn not one pure note had sung from his harp. It was as if he had never known how to play. He thought of the simple melodies he had learned as a child, lullabies and dancing songs. Not one could he remember.

Through the long day he sat upon the ledge, and at the last he remembered the words of Ranaloth so many years before. 'Many among the Eldarin did not want to see a child of your race among us. But you were lost and alone, an abandoned babe on a winter hillside. I had always wondered if a human could learn to be civilized – if you could put aside the violence of your nature, and the evils of your heart. You have proved it possible and made me happy and proud. The triumph of will over the pull of the flesh – this is what the Eldarin achieved many aeons ago. We learned the value of harmony. Now you understand it also, and perhaps you can carry this gift back to your race.'

'What must I beware of, sir?' he had asked.

'Anger and hatred – these are the weapons of evil. And love, Duvo. Love is both wondrous and yet full of peril. Love is a gateway through which hatred – disguised and unrecognized – can pass.'

'How can that be so? Is not love the greatest of the emotions?'

'Indeed it is. But it breaches all defences, and lays us open to feelings of great depth. You humans suffer this more than most races I have known. Love among your people can lead to jealousy, envy, lust and greed, revenge and murder. The purest emotion carries with it the seeds of corruption; they are hard to detect.'

'You think I should avoid love?'

Ranaloth gave a dry chuckle. 'No-one can avoid love, Duvo. But when it happens, you may find that your music is changed. Perhaps even lost.'

'Then I will never love,' Duvo had promised.

But he had loved, and the Daroth had stolen it away, torn it from him on the point of a spear.

In despair now, Duvo returned his harp to the bag and slung it over his shoulder. Then he climbed from the ledge and, leaving the Pearl where he had placed it upon the mountain-top, began the long walk from the desert.

For weeks he wandered, coming at last to a high mountain valley. There, on top of a hill a mile above a lake, he came upon an old man sitting in the captain's chair of a fishing boat. The old man waved to him as he approached and Duvo climbed to the deck.

'Why are you staring at me so?' asked Duvo.

'You have flames around your soul, young man. You must be in great pain.'

'You see a great deal, sir. Tell me, why have you built a boat upon a mountain?'

'First you tell me why you have scarred your face with blood.'

As they sat quietly in the sunshine Duvo told him of the death of Shira, and the war against the Daroth, and lastly of the Pearl and his failure to bring back the Eldarin. The old man, Browyn, listened, and at dusk led Duvo back to his cabin, where they ate a simple meal of hot oats and milk sweetened with fruit syrup.

'I think you should stay here for a while, my boy. Rest. Let the mountain air clear your mind.'

Duvodas had nowhere else to go, and was grateful for the invitation. He stayed throughout the summer, and on into the autumn. Then, as the weather grew colder, Browyn caught a chill which became pneumonia. Duvodas could not help him, for he had lost the power to heal.

'It does not matter,' Browyn told him, lying back on his pillow with eyes closed. 'I am ready to die.'

'I think that I am too,' said Duvodas.

'Nonsense. You have not yet brought back the Eldarin.'

'I cannot. I have told you – the magic is lost to me.'

'Then find it, boy! Don't you understand? Nothing in terms of the soul is irrevocable. Once you were pure, and the magic flowed in you. It will do so again. Already, in your time here, I see the chains of fire have died down. You know what you must do. Begin the journey back to what you were.'

'It is not possible.'

'Pah! Nothing is impossible – especially not in terms of the human soul. If that were true, every soldier would become evil and every priest would have healing hands. You know what talent makes us great?'

'No.'

'The best of us just never know when to give up.'

True to his own description Browyn survived the pneumonia, much to his surprise, and lived throughout the winter and the spring of the following year. But in the summer he developed a hacking cough and began to lose weight. By the first day of autumn he was barely skin and bone, and Duvodas knew that he was dying. Towards the end Browyn became delirious. Duvodas took to carrying him up into the mountains, where the old man could sit and look out over the vistas and the distant lake.

On the last morning of Browyn's life, as he sat on the mountainside, he became suddenly lucid. 'I have always wondered,' he said, 'if my boat could sail.'

'We shall see,' said Duvo. Taking a large hammer, he knocked away the restraining planks and focused his energies on the earth below the boat, drawing up water from deep in the ground. It bubbled through the grass and pooled around the hull, slowly lifting the vessel,

317

which began to move down the hill on a cushion of water. The slender craft sped down into the valley, spearing into the lake before bobbing up gently on the surface, its momentum carrying it forward towards a pine-crested island.

'Ah, what a beautiful sight,' murmured Browyn. He died soon after, and Duvodas buried him in the shade of a spreading oak.

'Farewell, my dear friend,' he said, when the grave was completed. Then he sighed as he realized, with a touch of regret, that Browyn had never told him why he had built a boat on a mountain.

Duvodas stayed on in the cabin. There was nowhere else he wished to be. On the last day of autumn he tried to play the harp again but, as ever, the music was a travesty. Laying the instrument on the floor, he walked out into the meadow beyond the cabin.

And froze.

Twenty Daroth horsemen were riding slowly up the hill. Gazing at them, he knew he could kill them all without effort. The thought was not a good one, and a great sadness fell upon him. I will kill no more, he told himself, and he strode out to meet them.

The leader climbed down from his horse and approached. He was carrying a small, sleeping child wrapped in a blanket. 'You are the harpist Duvodas?' he asked, his voice deep and resonant.

'I am.'

'I am the ambassador to Loretheli. We came upon an old human dying on the road; he told us his name was Ceofrin. He was trying to reach you, to bring you this child, but his heart was not strong.'

'Why should he send a child to me?' asked Duvo.

'He is your son,' said the Daroth.

'My son died,' declared Duvo, feeling the anger rise in him. 'Torn from life by a Daroth spear.'

'Not so, human. As Ceofrin lay dying we touched his mind. We know how Shira died, but when they came to bury her a female saw the child move. Nursed to health and taken to Loretheli, he was returned to his blood kin Ceofrin when the war ended. The old man tried to find you, but no-one knew where you had gone. Then word reached him of a man with the face of blood, living in the mountains. Ceofrin knew he was dying and wanted the child raised by blood kin, so he tried to reach you. You understand this?'

As Duvo stepped back, his mind reeling, the Daroth spoke again. 'You are the sorcerer who destroyed our Life Chamber.'

He nodded dumbly, unable to think clearly. For a moment there was silence and he looked up into the face of the Daroth, then ran his gaze along the line of riders. No-one spoke. Then the Daroth leader stepped forward. 'Here is your son,' he said, offering the child.

Duvodas reached out and took him. His hair was dark, like Shira's, and he could see her beauty in the lines of his face. The boy yawned and his eyes opened. In that instant Duvo heard Shira's voice echoing in the halls of his mind. 'I will show him to the sunrise and the sunset. He will be handsome, like you, with fair hair and green eyes. Not at first, for all babies are born with blue eyes. But they will turn grey-green as he gets older.'

'Why should he not have beautiful brown eyes, like his mother?' he had asked.

'Perhaps he will,' she had said.

The boy's eyes were brown, and shining with the innocence only the young can ever know.

Duvodas looked up at the Daroth towering above him. 'I thank you,' he said.

'The war between us is ended,' said the Daroth.

'Yes, it is,' agreed Duvodas.

Without another word, the Daroth strode to his horse and mounted. The troop rode away down the hillside. Duvodas carried the child into the cabin and sat him on the floor. Rolling to his hands and knees, the boy saw the harp and crawled towards it, his chubby hand reaching out and dragging at the strings. A jangle of discordant sounds rang out.

But within the sounds was one clear, pure note.

And, for a moment only, the scent of roses filled the room.